THE DARK FANTASTIC

BOOKS BY

MARGARET ECHARD

The Dark Fantastic

If This Be Treason

Before I Wake

A Man without Friends

Stand-in for Death

MARGARET ECHARD

THE DARK FANTASTIC

DOUBLEDAY & COMPANY, INC.

GARDEN CITY, N. Y. 1947

TO YOU, DAD

AUTHOR'S NOTE

In my great-grandmother's house in Indiana, shortly after the close of the Civil War, a series of extraordinary events transpired which were never satisfactorily explained. The house was renowned for its hospitality and witnesses were not lacking to testify to the strange disturbances which in time became a legend.

Those disturbances are recorded in this novel as the subjective experience of one of the characters, and to that extent the work is founded on fact; but the story is fictitious and the people in no sense represent real persons living or dead.

THE DARK FANTASTIC

"... I' the name of truth,
Are ye fantastical, or that indeed
Which outwardly ye show?"

Macbeth, ACT I, SCENE 3

CHAPTER 1

Candles were still used to light one to bed; kerosene lamps still exploded. Stagecoaches made six miles an hour, and one traveled by rail at the risk of one's neck. Gentlemen wore greatcoats instead of overcoats, and male quartets sang "The Drummer Boy of Shiloh." Hoops were going out, bustles were not yet in, but ladies achieved quite as telling effect with tight lacing and layers of petticoats. The war referred to in conversation was *not* World War II.

Conversation, however, held a not unfamiliar ring. Returned veterans complained that civilians had all the jobs. The older generation complained that the younger generation was going to the devil. The younger generation retorted that they had inherited a world which their elders had treated like H. Dumpty's egg and now expected them to put together again. Barring a few of Mr. Edison's inventions and the fact that the Republican party was in power, times were not so very different then from now.

There was the usual postwar wave of spiritualism; the usual postwar depression. Eggs were selling at ten cents a dozen; butter at eight and a third cents a pound. Quack medicine, paper money, and Grant campaign buttons flooded the country. And Edwin Booth was making his first midland tour since the tragedy of Ford's Theatre in Washington.

It was the decade following the Civil War.

On a certain evening in November, Miss Judith Amory stood before her mirror in an Indiana boardinghouse and dressed to go to the theater. Her chin was tilted at a belligerent angle and for good reason. She was going alone. Without male escort, without even a female companion, she was going to an evening performance of *Macbeth*. It would have been a daring thing to do even in her home city of Chicago. In provincial Terre Haute it was unheard of. Sheltered young ladies who had no one to take them to the theater remained at home and embroidered chaste mottoes on sofa pillows or played sentimental ballads on the piano. But Miss Judith Amory was not a sheltered young lady. She was an extremely competent young woman who had been taking care of herself for more years than she cared to admit and was perfectly capable of going anywhere alone. Besides, she had never seen Cushman and Booth together.

Any one of the widows or spinsters in Mrs. Prewitt's Genteel Boarding Establishment for Ladies would have been pleased to accompany Miss Amory as her guest. But none of them would have considered the excursion worth the price of a theater ticket. By the same token, neither did Judith consider their company worth the price. Autumn was well advanced and she had not yet secured a position for the winter. It was really the height of extravagance for an unemployed teacher of English literature to squander two dollars on a balcony seat.

But that only lent zest to the indulgence.

She dressed with care, prolonging the pleasures of anticipation. First the cotton chemise, then the corsets laced to exactly nineteen inches, then the short muslin petticoat, then the long plain petticoat, then the full ruffled petticoat, then the ruffled petticoat with tucks and embroidery, then the petticoat with lace-edged ruffles, and finally the sheer cambric petticoat flounced to the waist with ruffles on each flounce. Last of all the full gathered skirt of blue poplin with the tight buttoned bodice and the black velvet ribbon at the waist. There was also a black velvet ribbon around her bare white throat. Velvet neck ribbons were the fashion, and

Judith was fortunate. On her long slender neck they were becoming.

She looked very well when dressed. She had a slim graceful figure and a thin eager face to which excitement lent a glow which gave an illusion of beauty. Yet she was not beautiful. Her eyes were too close together, her nose too long, her mouth too wide. But sparkling animation, a provocative manner, and a low pleasing voice made her attractive, particularly to the opposite sex. Given wealth and family background, she might have made a very good marriage. But without a tie in the world, without a dollar she had not earned, she had small chance of even meeting an eligible man, much less marrying one. She faced this fact and accepted it. Since she could not bring herself to marry any of the men whom it was possible to meet and could not manage to meet any of the men she would choose to marry, this charming young woman was, at the age of twenty-five, still Miss Judith Amory.

Mrs. Prewitt's ladies were in the back parlor when Judith came downstairs. The opening strains of "I Dreamt That I Dwelt in Marble Halls" warned that someone was at the piano and about to burst into song. At sight of Judith in jacket and toque and carrying her small velvet muff, the music stopped and the ladies turned with flattering interest to the stairs.

"Miss Judith! You are going out?"

"I'm going to the theater."

"The theater!" This from the widow of a Methodist bishop.

"I'm going to see *Macbeth*."

"Oh." A sigh of doubtful relief granted partial absolution. After all, Shakespeare was sometimes mistaken for the Bible.

Mrs. Prewitt, a motherly Mrs. Grundy, smiled on Judith and brought another lamp.

"I'll put a light for you in the front parlor, my dear. You won't want me bringing your gentleman friend back here."

3

Judith braced herself. "I'm not expecting a gentleman, Mrs. Prewitt. I'm going alone." And then, with the sound of a concerted gasp behind her and the vision of Mrs. Prewitt's plump face settling like a shocked cheese, she went swiftly out the street door before the word "Alone!" could explode behind her.

"Well!" said the bishop's widow. "That's what comes of being born and brought up in Chicago."

According to Terre Haute standards, Chicago was what had risen from the ashes when Sodom and Gomorrah were destroyed.

Judith, meantime, had caught the horse trolley on the next street and was rolling away to town without being in any way molested.

"It's ridiculous," she fumed inwardly, "for women to be unable to go where they please by themselves. Someday they will. Someday women will do everything men do and nothing will be thought of it. But it will probably take another war to do it. Women are greater slaves than the Negroes ever were."

But she could not let her irritation annoy her now. She possessed one of those fortunate dispositions (fortunate to the owner, at least) which enables one to concentrate on his immediate purpose to the exclusion of all else. Her immediate purpose was to enjoy her evening's excursion. No annoyance was sufficient to distract her interest.

The horsecar dropped her two blocks from the theater. She hurried briskly through the November darkness. City streets at night did not alarm her. Descending from Chicago cabs and trolleys with her father was among her earliest recollections. She thrilled to lighted street lamps and busy pavements. But advance notices had warned that the performance started punctually at eight o'clock. She did not want to miss the thrill of that first curtain.

The theater lobby milled with the cream of Midwest society. Calmly, determinedly, Judith pushed her way through bouffant petticoats and satin-lined opera capes, her head high, her assurance so impeccable that people making way for her failed to notice that no escort hovered at her elbow. But when she had gained the sanctuary of the dimly lit theater it took all her *savoir-faire* to present her ticket to the brisk young usher and murmur in reply to his astonished eyebrows, "There is no one with me."

She had chosen her balcony seat for two reasons. It was cheaper; also, it rendered her solitary state less conspicuous. But as she felt the eyes following her lone progress down the shallow steps to first-row center, second seat from the aisle, she wished for a moment that she had not been at such pains to get the best possible reservation. She would have been less noticeable farther back.

But seated, and sufficiently rallied to look down on the proscenium directly opposite and only a little below her, she congratulated herself that she had one of the choice seats in the house and she didn't give a continental how many people were looking at her.

The aisle seat on her right was vacant. On her left a family party composed of father, mother, and two half-grown daughters gave her a half-guilty feeling of protection. For all her brave insouciance, she was keenly conscious of being alone. When the mother in the family changed places with her husband, thus taking the seat next Judith, that independent young woman was shamelessly relieved. She even smiled at the woman, making some small remark, in the hope that people behind her might take her for a late-arriving member of the party. She began to speculate on the chance of the aisle seat remaining unoccupied.

The house filled rapidly. A trap door in the orchestra pit yawned and disgorged musicians and instruments. In a

5 ❧

short while the house lights would dim. Meantime, there was the fascinating distraction of the program.

PRESENTING
MR. EDWIN BOOTH &
MISS CHARLOTTE CUSHMAN

IN

MACBETH
A Play
by
WILLIAM SHAKESPEARE

She had no need to read the cast. The supporting players were unfamiliar, unimportant, many of them recruited locally. Booth was notorious for his carelessness in minor casting. But who cared? What difference did it make who read the lines of ghosts and porters when Cushman and Booth read the immortal dialogues.

ACT I, SCENE I .... *An Open Place.*

It was not a theater with a drop curtain and an orchestra tuning its instruments. It was a caldron where witches brewed enchantment.

This moment of expectancy. This moment of burning cheeks and icy hands, while music played and chattering voices gradually hushed and lamps dimmed slowly to dusk before the glowing footlights of a stage. This moment before the rising of the curtain was worth all the adventure had cost her.

A large and substantial presence sank into the seat on the aisle and made quite a commotion shedding a bulky coat. She neither saw nor felt the intrusion. She was conscious of nothing but Act I, Scene I—An Open Place.

Not till the lights came up at the end of the act did she move. Through the scene changes she sat tense, leaning slightly forward, oblivious of her surroundings. When the final words came in the great tragedian's matchless voice, " 'False face must hide what the false heart doth know,' " and the curtain slowly descended, she roused like a sleeper from a drugged slumber and sat limply back in her seat.

It was then that she became aware of her new neighbor.

He, too, was relaxing as though from the grip of tension. Remembering just in time that she was a lady, she did not look at him but assiduously studied her program. The family on her left were having open discussion on the merits of the production. The youngest daughter, in pigtails and hair bows, was disappointed in the Witches. They had not been gruesome enough.

The man on Judith's right was having trouble with his greatcoat. There was no place to put it that was not in someone's way. He murmured apologies which Judith quite properly ignored. He was a tall man, and his long legs took up more than his share of room without a heavy cloak piled on his knees. She wondered why he didn't check it.

And then the lights began dimming again and she forgot the man and his troublesome coat.

At the next intermission a number of people went down to the lobby to stretch their legs. The family on her left departed. Judith was left in her seat beside the stranger.

Why didn't he go out too? It was the gentlemen mostly who were leaving.

But instead he arranged his coat over the back of his seat and settled himself to study his program. Judith likewise kept her eyes glued to the folder which she now knew by heart. But every nerve was tingling. The women beside her had left the balcony, the women behind her were waiting for their escorts; but, worst of all, the man beside her knew that she was unattended. If she had had presence of mind she would have followed the family party out and no one would have been the wiser.

And then her modern scorn for conventions reasserted

7 ੴ

itself. Rules of conduct were for timid people, not for Miss Judith Amory. Defiantly she turned her head—and found herself looking straight into the eyes of the man beside her. Whether he had been watching her, or whether their eyes met by accident, they both looked swiftly away.

But she was no longer uneasy, nor even embarrassed. The man whose eyes she had just encountered would never annoy a woman.

She began to steal surreptitious glances at him from under lowered lids, at first lifting her eyes no higher than his hands. Long, well-shaped hands, but with nails pared close and skin redly clean as from much scrubbing. The sleeves of his coat were worn at the wrist, as though the fabric were not new, yet it was a broadcloth sleeve and the wristband beneath it was linen. Judith's eyes moved upward and caught the gleam of a heavy gold chain across a broad expanse of smoke-gray vest and the flowing ends of a carelessly knotted silk tie. His dress was that of a gentleman, yet his hands did not look like her father's. She wondered who and what he might be.

Then her eyes moved higher and she forgot about his hands.

His head, she decided, should have belonged on George Rogers Clark. It was beautifully molded, covered with thick, curling brown hair, and he carried it like a man accustomed to looking over the heads of lesser men. His face was bronzed as though from long exposure to sun and wind, and the blue of his eyes was in such startling contrast that they seemed to smolder with blue flames. This was no man about town. This was no townsman at all. Hands, face, physique set him apart from the pallid city folk who filled the theater.

He turned his head and found her watching him. If he had been an urbanite she would have frozen and looked right through him. But because she was sure he was a country man she was no more disconcerted than if she had been caught admiring a fine horse in a pasture.

She smiled a little, and he responded with the eagerness of a lonely stranger.

"Magnificent, isn't it?" he was referring, naturally, to the performance of *Macbeth*.

She nodded. "My little friend didn't care for the Witches."

It wasn't exactly a falsehood, but it implied a connection with the family party.

"Now that's strange," he said. "Children as a rule are quite taken with the Witches."

"I'm afraid she takes her supernatural too literally. In Shakespeare it's always subjective." Judith thought, "There I go, talking as though I were in a classroom."

He was taking vigorous issue with her. "Do you really think the Weird Sisters were a figment of Macbeth's imagination?"

She quoted: " 'Spirits that tend on mortal thoughts . . .' What are the Witches except the incarnate evil that is already in Macbeth? If he had not already thought of removing Duncan from the throne he would never have met three witches who would foretell his doing it."

"Then you think his crime was motivated purely from within?"

"Assuredly."

"That makes him a monster."

"How do you see him?"

"As a tragic study of fiend-inspired criminality. I think he was inherently a heroic character, impelled toward crime by a demoniacal power."

"You wouldn't be alluding to his wife?"

But Judith could not distract him with humor. He was very earnest in his conception of the play. Any other interpretation, he maintained, made Macbeth a mere ruffian, a sort of medieval Bill Sikes.

Judith thought, "He knows his Shakespeare," and wondered more than ever who he was.

9

"Mr. Booth seems to have the same idea of the part," she said. "Have you ever seen his Hamlet?"

"No." He spoke regretfully. "I saw his Othello once in Indianapolis and his Lear. I preferred McCullough's Lear. But Booth's Hamlet is something I've yet to enjoy."

"You're quite a lover of Shakespeare, aren't you?"

"Isn't everyone who comes to a Shakespeare play?" he asked naïvely.

"Goodness no. Those people down there"—she indicated the fashionable crowd in the orchestra rows and boxes—"came to show off their clothes. And the people up here came for any number of reasons; principally to see the brother of the man who killed Lincoln. It's the people in the gallery who really came to see Shakespeare."

The aphorism was not original. She was quoting her father, who in turn had quoted Mr. William Winter.

"Then I should be sitting in the gallery. So should you."

"I beg your pardon?" The conversation was beginning to get slightly out of hand.

"When a young lady comes alone to see *Macbeth* it must be from love of Shakespeare."

Both tone and manner were respectful, but the blue eyes held a twinkle that made Judith blush furiously and fix her own with marked attention on the curtain. She had learned her lesson. This was what came of talking to strange men.

But when the third-act curtain had descended they turned to each other spontaneously, like companions of long standing impatient to resume an argument.

"Did you notice?" demanded Judith triumphantly.

"The ghost of Banquo did not appear."

"Only the empty chair."

"Yet the way Booth gazed upon that empty chair made the ghost more real than if it had been visible."

"Henry Irving uses a visible ghost all daubed with phosphorus. It's very bad. Because the whole idea is subjective. Like the Witches."

But he refused to go with her that far. "The ghost is subjective," he admitted. "The ghost is Macbeth's conscience. But the Witches are preternatural, occult power which impels him against his better nature. Macbeth is the embodied conflict between good and evil. That's what makes it poetic tragedy. Otherwise it's just a murder story."

"Where did you study Shakespeare?" asked Judith respectfully.

"At Asbury College," he replied.

When the curtain fell for the fourth time he remarked, exactly as though she would know to whom he was referring, "I must try and remember every detail. So I can tell the children."

She had a sensation of being suddenly dropped from an elevation.

"Children?"

He nodded, smiling, and glanced at the two little girls in pigtails.

"Next time I shall bring all three of them with me."

Suddenly, illogically, Judith's evening went flat. How silly she had been to fall into conversation with a stranger.

"Doesn't your wife care for Shakespeare?"

He had not mentioned bringing his wife to see a play; only his children. Maybe he was a widower.

There was a noticeable silence. She glanced at him and was startled at the change which had come over his face. It was as though a mask had dropped over his features, conforming to their outline but extinguishing their light.

He said, "My wife is an invalid."

Suddenly Judith felt impelled to explain herself to this stranger; to make it clear to him that she was a teacher of literature who attended Shakespearean performances solely for educational purposes and that she had no interest in life outside her work. She drew a self-portrait of intelligent female independence that would have disarmed any man. It disarmed

11 ॐ

the man who had spoken with such warmth of his children and over whose countenance a mask had dropped when he mentioned his wife.

"I should never have taken you for a schoolteacher." He looked at Judith with interest. "Where have you taught?"

She mentioned the day school for young ladies in Chicago where she had taught before coming to Indiana.

"I thought it must be something like that. You're not big enough to handle boys. I'm looking right now for a man who can whip the Pettigrew kids."

"You're looking for——" Judith's surprise was genuine.

"I'm a township trustee," he explained. "The teacher in our district met with a serious accident. He'll be out for the rest of the winter."

Judith drew a long breath. "Where is your school?" she inquired casually.

"About twenty-five miles from here."

"On a railroad?"

"On the Logansport line. Not far from Woodridge."

"I see. To whom would one apply for the school?"

"You know of a man?"

"I—might."

"Tell him to see Richard Tomlinson, Timberley farm. Anyone in Woodridge can direct him to Timberley."

He whispered the last words hurriedly, for the lights were dimming. But Judith's mind made careful memorandum.

She slept late the morning after *Macbeth*. There was no need for early rising. She had no classes to meet.

"We don't feel, Miss Amory, that you are quite the person needed here at Oaklawn. Or perhaps we should say, a female seminary is not the place for some of your ideas."

"If you're referring to my statement in class that English divorce laws were responsible for George Eliot's——"

"Please, Miss Amory! You have been told repeatedly that

neither the books nor the life of George Eliot are fit matters for discussion with young female pupils. You have willfully ignored the express ruling of your superiors. Your services will not be required further."

Which explains why Judith was able to sleep late the morning after *Macbeth*.

There was nothing to be gained by going down to breakfast and facing a roomful of disapproving widows and curious spinsters who had learned by this time that she had not come in till nearly midnight. For that matter, there was nothing to be gained by facing Mrs. Prewitt and being reminded that she was in arrears with her board. It was pleasanter to lie in bed and relive last night's enjoyment.

> *If it were done when 'tis done, then 'twere well*
> *It were done quickly: if the assassination*
> *Could trammel up the consequence, and catch,*
> *With his surcease, success . . .*

What an unforgettable voice Booth had! What agony of soul could be borne on a single cadence. How manifest had been the haunted condition of Macbeth's mind. He had indeed seemed driven by some external power of evil.

"But I still don't believe he actually met the Witches."

Of the Lady Macbeth of Charlotte Cushman she was inclined to be critical. True, the great actress had been superb in her embodiment of a character almost savage. But she had been too masculine, too lacking in the feminine charm by which woman captivates and dominates her man. There had been too much magnificent elocution; too little soft subtlety.

"She never could have handled Macbeth that way. He never would have stood for browbeating. She should have been wily, clever—ruthless, yes—but it all should have been more mental. If I had her voice I could have done a better job."

She lay for a while toying with the picture of herself coming

13 ఆ

down a stairway in a white robe, a flickering taper in her hand. She watched herself set the candle down and rub her hands, one over the other, as though washing them.

Out, damnèd spot! out, I say!

Under the bedclothes her hands were dripping wet. She turned on her side, laughing all by herself at her own histri·onics.

"I should have been an actress. That's the best possible life for a woman with no money and no chance of a good marriage. At least it's better than teaching horrid little girls who 'yes' you to your face and make mouths behind your back. Smirky little hypocrites! I hate girls—all girls—big, little, old, and young."

She buried her face in the trough between the hard boardinghouse pillows and shed a few tears for poor Judith Amory who had been so shabbily treated by the lady principal of Oaklawn Female Seminary. Then suddenly she flopped on her back, eyes dry as shale on which rain leaves no trace. Her thoughts had leaped to the point toward which they had been veering from the moment of waking, the man who sat beside her the night before.

His name was Richard Tomlinson and he lived near Woodridge. He was a farmer, but well to do; note the gold watch chain, the linen wristbands, the broadcloth coat. He had been to college; he spoke with the cultured accent of the educated man. He was township trustee for a school that was without a teacher. He had three children and an invalid wife.

Here Judith's racing thoughts stopped as at a sudden hurdle.

What a damnable irony was that invalid wife!

For the first time in her life she had met a man whom, had there been no obstacle, she would have chosen to marry. And, she confidently believed, might have accomplished her purpose. She recalled their shared enjoyment of the night before. It had been like a mutual discovery.

Had his wife disapproved of his going to the theater? Or had he deceived her about the purpose of his trip to the city? He did not look like a man who would bother to deceive. Besides, he had said he must remember the play so that he could tell the children about it. She remembered the set of his mouth when he said that. As though he might have defied someone's displeasure in coming and would further defy it by talking about a forbidden subject on his return. He was probably stubborn as a mule, in a good-natured sort of way.

Of course she was imagining his whole background. All that she knew for a fact was that his wife was an invalid. All that she knew which in any way concerned Miss Judith Amory was that he was trustee for a school that was without a teacher.

He had stated that male teachers only need apply.

But Judith guessed, with sly intuition, that if an attractive young woman appeared in the neighborhood of Woodridge inquiring for Mr. Richard Tomlinson he would be at a loss to explain where and how he had made her acquaintance except on the grounds of school business.

She smiled to herself and stretched luxuriously, like a cat who knows of a promising mousehole.

CHAPTER 2

Woodridge, the county seat of Woods County, was a flourishing town of some three thousand souls. Situated not only on a railroad but on the equally prized hard-surfaced turnpike, it was the cultural center of one of the richest farming districts in the state.

Four churches reared their spires within a stone's throw of the square—Methodist, Baptist, Presbyterian, and Catholic—and a small society of Quakers met in the Odd Fellows' hall over the Farmers and Merchants Bank. But the institution which gave the litt. ? town its prestige was the academy.

Housed in a one-room frame building, its faculty consisting of one professor, there was nothing about the Woodridge Academy (outwardly) to justify the pride it evoked in the breasts of the citizenry. But whereas a pupil in the district school could go no further than McGuffey's reader and Milne's complete arithmetic, from the academy he could enter college with full credits. The teacher of the academy was, of necessity, a man of many talents.

The present incumbent, John Barclay by name, was such a man. He taught in winter and farmed in summer, and rumor had it that he could have been a professional musician had he desired. Certain it was, he had given up the violin—as some men give up liquor—upon joining the church, and subscribed (outwardly, at least) to the local opinion that the instrument was a tool of the devil. He refrained from playing it openly; but many a loiterer, passing the academy late at night, could testify that the schoolmaster indulged his vice in secret.

Those same loiterers, when they lingered to listen, sometimes encountered the big blacksmith, Doc Baird, heading in that direction; and sometimes when the station hack pulled up they would see dapper Lucius Goff, who worked on a Terre Haute paper, leap out and swing jauntily through the gate; and sometimes they would find tall, handsome Richard Tomlinson tying his black horse to the hitching rail. When this happened they would know that the four greatest friends in the county had gathered to spend an evening together.

There was much talk about the oddly assorted friendship of these four. It was rumored that all sorts of unorthodox subjects were discussed among them: mesmerism, some queer new cult called telepathy, and—most devilish of all—spiritualism. It was claimed on good authority (Lawyer Otis Huse, no less) that Doc Baird and Lucius Goff indulged in table tipping. But then Otis Huse was known to have no love for the Tomlinsons and was ready to cast suspicion on anything with which Richard was connected.

But there were other people to testify that Doc Baird possessed magnetic power of some kind. He had been known to cure headaches, pains in legs and backs, and various nervous ailments by the simple laying on of hands. Jed Weatherell, an epileptic, asserted that when he felt a fit coming on Doc Baird could put it back, if he could get to him in time.

Old Dr. Caxton, a bona fide physician known far and wide as Rockgut Caxton, snorted derisively at such gullibility and denounced the blacksmith as a quack. But as the smith accepted no fees and solicited no patients—he was kept busy six days a week at his trade—he could hardly be accused of charlatanism.

Yet there was some point to the skeptics' demand that if Doc Baird possessed the skill with which he was credited why had he never been able to cure Richard Tomlinson's wife? Surely, if he had any power at all, he would have used it for his friend.

One evening, about a week after Richard Tomlinson's trip to the city, John Barclay sat before the hard-coal burner in his schoolroom and waited for his friends to gather. He thought, as he cuddled his violin, how good was male companionship—not that he didn't love his wife and family of daughters, but—how satisfying was the good hearty man talk that presently would fly back and forth across this glowing stove. What would they be arguing about tonight? Lucius would have the latest news. It was he who usually set the evening's discussion. Last time he had been full of this greenbacker talk.

"It's the only thing that will prevent a panic. There's no currency in the country. How long has it been since you've

17 &

seen a silver piece, John Barclay? Or you, Doc; how are you paid these days? In produce, I'll be bound. This whole community's living by a system of barter. Isn't that a fact, Richard?"

"We haven't seen any silver at Timberley since the war."

They had had a rousing discussion that night over the greenbackers.

What Lucius would have on the griddle tonight there was no telling. But you could count on its being fresh and full of interest. Lucius was the spice of the quartet, just as Doc was the leaven and Barclay himself the flavor. It was Richard who was the substance.

"If his wife does die," thought the schoolmaster, "I hope he never marries again. After all he's been through he deserves a rest."

A heavy step on the wooden porch made him lay aside his fiddle. That would be Doc Baird, usually first to arrive. He was unmarried and had no womenfolk to cajole into good humor before leaving the house. He lived in a two-room cottage back of his shop and "did for himself." Many a harassed family man envied the big blacksmith.

He came in now, with step surprisingly light for so huge a frame, and said as he took the schoolmaster's stoutest chair, "Richard won't be in tonight. His wife's worse."

John Barclay nodded, as though this was to be expected following Richard's trip to the city.

"Been out there, Doc?"

"No. Richard was in town today. The black horse cast a shoe. He asked me to tell you. He didn't like to call you out of school."

The schoolmaster rose and got a jar of tobacco from a cupboard where also reposed a box of chalk and a couple of blackboard erasers. He set the tobacco jar in the center of a small table, and both men filled their pipes.

"She's heading for another spell," said Barclay dryly.

Doc nodded. "I look for it to break tonight."

"Do you suppose you could do anything for her, Doc?"

"I don't know. I've never had a chance to try."

"Richard won't let you?"

"*She* won't let me. Goes in her room and slams the door when Richard takes me out there."

"You needn't take it personally. She orders Dr. Caxton out of the house too."

"It's nothing to me. It just embarrasses Richard."

"Yes, it would." The schoolmaster sighed. Then to his own surprise he heard himself saying for the second time, and aloud:

"If she ever does die, I hope Richard has sense enough not to marry again."

The blacksmith shook his head. "Not a chance."

"He doesn't need a wife," persisted Barclay. "His mother runs the house and she's certainly raising his children."

"A man needs a woman," said Doc solemnly.

"You're a great one to talk."

"I don't mean me—or you—or even our friend Lucius. I mean Richard. He's only twenty-five. If Abigail dies he'll marry in six months, mark my words."

"I don't believe it. He's had enough. I can tell. Besides, there'd be the same thing to go through again."

"You mean the little girl?"

John Barclay nodded. The blacksmith cleared his throat.

"I still say Richard'll never stay single. The women won't let him. Man alive, he'll be the best catch this side of Indianapolis."

"If he's ever a widower," said the schoolmaster dryly. They had both been talking as though Abigail Tomlinson's death were an assured fact.

The train was late that evening, as usual. Due at six-fifteen, it was after seven when the brisk tattoo of a light walking stick announced Lucius Goff. Lucius had become quite a dandy since going to work on the Terre Haute paper and he always carried a malacca cane. As he came in now, his cloak draped over his shoulders, his hat rakishly tilted, he gave the impression of a devil-may-care fellow who didn't give a damn what people thought. Which was exactly the impression he intended to give.

He was pricking with excitement for some reason. He looked about the room, his nostrils quivering like an expectant whippet's, and demanded, "Where's Richard?"

"He's not coming," said John Barclay. "His wife's sick." Then, thinking to himself, "Lucius has news," he added, "Take off your coat and sit down. We're here, if Richard's not."

But Lucius stepped to the window and peered up the quiet little street. It was dark, except where street lights glimmered, and the square was practically deserted. There was no light visible in any window except the drugstore, before which the station hack had halted. Tom Stickney, the druggist, stood in his door as if watching to see whether the passenger alighting from the hack was coming in.

The passenger was.

Lucius, from the window of the academy, could see straight into the lighted drugstore. He stood motionless, watching.

Doc Baird and the schoolmaster exchanged glances. Then John Barclay stepped behind Lucius and looked over his shoulder. Through the lighted drugstore window could be seen the trim silhouette of a modish young woman. She was talking to Tom Stickney.

Barclay said, "Humph!"

Doc, who without moving was looking over the heads of the other two men, said, "Who is she?"

Lucius spoke without turning his head. "I don't know. She was on the train as I came out. From Terre Haute. We rode up from the station together. I tried to speak to her—

and got the icy stare." He grinned. "Then—after putting me in my place—she calmly asked the hack driver how she could get in touch with Richard Tomlinson."

The consternation of his listeners was like applause to the drama-loving reporter.

"Tomlinson! A woman from Terre Haute asking for Richard?" said Doc Baird.

"I don't believe it," said Barclay flatly. Then, to appease the black flash of Lucius's eyes, "You misunderstood, surely. Richard knows no one in Terre Haute. No women, I mean."

"How do you know?" retorted Lucius. "He went up there about a week ago, didn't he?"

"On business."

Lucius laughed, not in malice, but in sheer appreciation of his news. "I'll tell you what his business was. He went to see *Macbeth*. I know because I covered the play and I saw Richard in the first row of the balcony. Furthermore, he wasn't alone. He was in the company of a young lady. And if I'm not mistaken that same young lady is talking to Tom Stickney at this moment."

Three pairs of eyes focused on the drugstore window. No one spoke for seconds. Something was happening that boded no good for their friend.

Then the schoolmaster said, "This thing can be explained. Richard Tomlinson is a good man."

"Too damned good," snapped Lucius. "Ye gods, after all he's put up with, he's certainly entitled to——"

Doc Baird spoke. "She mustn't be allowed to go out there. Abigail's in a bad way."

John Barclay sucked a swift breath. "Surely she wouldn't try——"

"Stickney seems to be giving her some sort of directions. See—he's pointing her down the street."

Lucius muttered excitedly, "By Jove, she's coming this way."

They watched, the three of them, as the trim figure stepped

off the porch of the drugstore, lifted her skirts daintily, and crossed the street. They held their concerted breaths as she came briskly down the boardwalk to the academy. And then as they saw her set down a small traveling bag to unlatch the gate they backed away from the window like three bewildered hounds who had caught a cross scent and didn't know what to do with it.

Doc whispered, "She's coming here!" and looked at Lucius, who, for reasons of his own, became suddenly self-effacing. Giving the nod to the schoolmaster, he retired behind the stove while Barclay went to the door.

A pleasing feminine voice said, "Good evening. Is Mr. Richard Tomlinson here?"

The three men had never seen anyone quite like the young person who stepped across the threshold in response to the schoolmaster's invitation. Poised and self-assured; smartly, though somewhat shabbily attired; not a man among them— not even the urban reporter—could have told offhand whether or not she was a lady.

She looked about the square low-ceilinged room with its double row of unvarnished desks. She had never been in such a schoolroom before. If its crudity dismayed her, she gave no sign. She merely repeated the object of her visit.

"I was told that I might find Mr. Tomlinson here."

She addressed herself to the schoolmaster, but her glance included the blacksmith and the individual behind the stove. She recognized Lucius as the man who had tried to talk to her in the hack. It amused her to find him among those present and absurdly trying to conceal the fact.

"Mr. Tomlinson isn't here this evening," said John Barclay.

"He will be later, I understand."

The druggist had evidently explained to this stranger the custom of the four friends to congregate.

"I'm afraid not. His wife is ill."

"But she's always ill, isn't she? I mean—she's an invalid."

This was indeed ominous. It could not have been Tom Stickney, surely, who had discussed Abigail Tomlinson's health with this stranger.

The schoolmaster and the blacksmith exchanged glances. Lucius, in his corner, grew uncomfortably warm and wished himself elsewhere as the young woman set her bag on one of the desks and moved over to the stove. She ignored him as though he were invisible, stretching her gloved hands to the rosy isinglass windows in perfect composure.

Suddenly she inquired how far it was to Timberley.

John Barclay gasped, "Timberley!"

"That's Mr. Tomlinson's home, isn't it?"

"Y-y-y-yes—but——"

"He told me anyone in Woodridge could direct me to his place."

"You mean"—the schoolmaster eyed her keenly—"Richard Tomlinson invited you to his house?"

"Invited is scarcely the word for a business appointment, is it?"

Suddenly the schoolmaster saw a light. But before he could speak the young lady was explaining:

"I met Mr. Tomlinson in Terre Haute—quite by accident— and he mentioned that the Timberley school was without a teacher. He said if I was interested in applying to come to see him. I told him I had never taught rural school and was not sure it would appeal to me. But I had just completed the half term at Oaklawn Seminary and wasn't altogether happy in my associations there. So last week I handed in my resignation and decided to accept Mr. Tomlinson's offer."

Thus, with only a slight variation of the truth, Judith expunged her humiliation at being fired from Oaklawn and put Richard Tomlinson on record as having offered her employment. She sat down in the chair which was now pushed forward for her and drew a deep breath of satisfaction.

The reactions of the three men were characteristic. Doc Baird and the schoolmaster accepted the glib explanation with relief, Lucius Goff with suspicion. That the young woman was telling only part of the truth, he was convinced. Richard had doubtless met her in Terre Haute, but why had he offered her the school? She was not the type of person needed at Timberley. Either Richard had been drunk (which was unlikely) or he had acted under pressure. Remembering his friend's domestic situation, Lucius's mind clutched at the darkest and most interesting possibility.

No such thought troubled the schoolmaster.

"Well, well, so you are a teacher. Richard never told us that he had engaged anyone for the Timberley school. As a matter of fact, the business is not solely in his hands. The district votes at a school meeting. But they usually take whomever the trustees recommend. So you can probably settle everything when you talk to Mr. Tomlinson tomorrow."

"Tomorrow? I thought I might drive out there this evening. It's early, you know. Not yet eight o'clock."

At the coolness of this proposal there was another uneasy exchange of glances.

"I wouldn't advise going out there tonight," said Doc Baird flatly. "Not with Richard's wife the way she is."

John Barclay explained: "I'm afraid you'd find it an unfortunate time to see Mr. Tomlinson. On your own account, I mean. Better wait till morning. One of Moss Henderson's boys—he has the livery stable—will drive you out."

"But where am I to spend the night? I couldn't go alone to a hotel."

The town's sole hostelry on the north side of the square was distinctly no place for a lady. It had a bar.

A sardonic voice replied, "Were you thinking of spending the night at Timberley?" And Lucius Goff stepped dramatically from behind the stove.

The young woman was not one whit disconcerted.

"Certainly I expected to stay at Timberley. I'm to board there if I take the school."

This was pure bluff and fabrication, but Judith knew that no one present was in a position to call her hand. So she acknowledged with cool bravado the reporter's smile and bow.

"My apologies," he said. "Permit me to introduce myself. Lucius Goff of the Terre Haute *Express*. I had the pleasure of seeing you on the train, Miss——"

It was the moment he had been waiting for. Judith was forced to give her name.

General introductions followed, Lucius taking charge with a *savoir-faire* designed to show his less sophisticated friends how a man of the world handled these situations.

"Now if I may make a suggestion, Miss Amory. I'm on my way out to my father's place, four miles west on the corduroy road. I keep a rig at Henderson's. If you'll wait here a few minutes I'll be only too pleased to take you out home with me. I'm sure my sister can make you comfortable. Then tomorrow I'll drive you over to Timberley and you can settle your—ahem!—business with Mr. Tomlinson."

Nothing could have exceeded the courtesy with which the invitation was extended. But that little cough before the word "business" made Judith turn with relief at the first halting word from the schoolmaster.

"There doesn't seem much point in going four miles the other side of town when Timberley's east of here. Our house isn't large—we've no spare room—but if the young lady's not afraid of a folding bed—there's one in the parlor——"

The young lady was not at all afraid of folding beds. Before John Barclay could wipe his spectacles, wondering belatedly what his wife would say, his reckless gesture of hospitality was being accepted.

"Thank you so much, Professor Barclay. And you too, Mr. Goff. I'm sure you understand that it will be more convenient for everyone if I stay in Woodridge tonight."

So, without further ado, John Barclay escorted the young woman to his house, which was only a block from the academy. His two friends watched from the window.

Doc Baird said, "Wonder what Ellie Barclay's going to say when that young lady walks in."

Lucius Goff snapped his fingers, disposing of Ellie Barclay.

"Wait till the lady walks into Tomlinson's. That's when all hell will break loose."

CHAPTER 3

Very early in the morning did Judith, the erstwhile sluggard, rise and begin making preparations for her drive to Timberley. Accompanied by one of the Barclay girls, she walked across the square to Henderson's livery stable and engaged an elderly bay mare and a light wheeled buggy for the day.

She considered the advisability of taking Jennie Barclay with her—the twelve-year-old girl was plainly hoping to be invited—but she decided against it. Dropping Jennie off at her own front gate, she thanked her so graciously for her assistance that Jennie glowed with admiration and forgot that her hints had been ignored.

"Tell Thorne hello for me!" she called after the phaeton.

And Judith nodded, without bothering to inquire who Thorne might be.

It was a bright crisp morning, ideal weather for a drive. Indian summer was gone, but winter had not yet mired the road. The gravel was hard and smooth and the old mare's hoofs rang sharp in the bracing air. Trees were naked, except where leaves still fluttered like red-winged birds from the boughs of maples. Dry leaves heaped the fence corners and lay

26

thick and rotting in the furrows between shocks of corn. Fields were brown and dotted with fat gold pumpkins and goose-necked squash. Roadside grass and bushes were rimed with last night's frost. In barn lots idle mules and horses huddled together in the chill of morning, and from fattening pens came the squeals of hogs stampeding for their breakfast. It was a morning when it was good to be alive and rolling smoothly toward one's objective.

At the tollgate the fragrance of coffee and fried mush suggested that the gatekeeper's family was still at breakfast, a fact corroborated by the appearance of the man himself with a trickle of molasses on his chin. With true Hoosier sociability he commented favorably on the weather and inquired whether the lady wasn't a stranger in these parts.

Judith responded by asking how far it was to Timberley.

"School, farm, or store?"

"I want the Tomlinsons'."

"Then keep right on this road till you pass the covered bridge over Little Raccoon. There's a finger post pointing to the stage stop. You can see the house from there. Sits on top of a knoll. Highest point between Indianapolis and Springfield, Illinois. The stage stops at the foot of the hill."

"And the school?"

"The school ain't on the pike. It's about half a mile south on Little Raccoon. There's a lane leads through the woods to the schoolhouse. And about a mile farther on the pike is the next tollgate and five or six houses and the crossroads store."

Less than a mile beyond the covered bridge Judith came to the thick woods through which ran the lane to the schoolhouse. At this point the long hill which the old mare had been steadily climbing all the way from Woodridge took a perceptible rise so that when she had cleared the woods she saw the pike falling away in front of her and when she looked back it dropped behind her in the same manner. She was at the summit of the road.

But she was not yet at the summit of the land. That point

lay off to the south, rising smoothly in one of those strange knolls with which the ancient mound builders had adorned this level territory centuries before. At the foot of the mound timber encircled it like a girdle, and rising clean above the timber stood a large white pillared house.

Anyone viewing the Southern colonial dwelling, with its kitchen of whitewashed logs attached to the main structure by an enclosed passage, would have guessed that the Tomlinsons came from Virginia. The first Tomlinson in Indiana had been born in Rockbridge County, Virginia, near neighbor to the McCormick who later had invented a machine for reaping grain.

Tall poplars guarded the white gate in front of the stage stop and lined the drive that led up to the house. As Judith drew rein she felt her brash young assurance suddenly desert her. This was the home of a simple country gentleman. He had a wife who was ill. It was too early in the morning to be paying a call.

Turning the mare, she drove back down the hill to the lane. She would look over the schoolhouse first.

In the whitewashed log kitchen of Timberley black Millie moved sluggishly from table to stove. The only Negro this side of Woodridge, Millie was further proof of the Tomlinsons' Virginia origin. Technically on free soil ever since she and her husband had come out with the young Roger Tomlinsons forty years ago, Millie scorned all ideas of emancipation as bloodily achieved in the recent war. Of that original young quartet, half white, half black, there were only Ann Tomlinson and Millie left. And they belonged to each other. Hadn't they both buried their husbands right on this same ground? All the proclamations ever proclaimed could not free Millie from Miss Ann, nor Miss Ann from Millie.

She was alone in the kitchen this morning, which marked it as a morning extraordinary, for usually Miss Ann's cheerful presence pervaded the place. Without it, slow-moving Millie never could have achieved the preparation of breakfast. And breakfast at Timberley was an important meal. It was not served at daybreak, according to the custom of other farmers in the district. The Tomlinson men had been out and about their work for some time before the big bell rang, and when they came in it was to sit down to a table at which all members of the family gathered, not only for food but for morning prayers. There were never fewer than ten about that well-spread table, and seldom was the number that small. For rare was the day that some relative or neighbor or stranger waiting for the stagecoach did not sit down to table with the Tomlinsons. Richard's wife said they might as well be running a tavern. But neither Richard nor his mother would have it any other way. It had been like that in Roger Tomlinson's time; like that it should continue.

As Millie wrestled with the breakfast this morning she could see through the window young Will Tomlinson and Jesse Moffat, who had finished feeding long ago and were washing at the bench outside. Heads together, they talked earnestly as they bent over the washbasin, and Millie knew what they were talking about. Her black face puckered with anxiety.

Through this same window she had a view of the small courtyard formed by the jointure of the kitchen and the west wing of the house. Just beyond this was a well, and beyond the well a white picket fence which separated the back yard from the vegetable garden. There was a gate in this fence and two paths diverged from it. One led to the big barn set high on an adjacent knoll; the other led through a grape arbor to the orchards beyond. Between was a good clear view of open pasture and a glimpse of a small frame house. This cottage, built years ago by a Kentucky neighbor and abandoned when his wife died of malaria, had been bought in by the Tomlinsons and christened by Millie "the weanin' pen" because first one, then another of the Tomlinson daughters had set up housekeeping there when first married. At the present time it was occupied by the youngest daughter, Jane, and her husband, Alec Mitchell.

Someone was coming from the cottage now. A small form, moving in swift leaps and canters like a frolicsome colt, was crossing the open field. Millie recognized the runner even at a distance and called to young Will.

"Thorne's comin'! Keep a lookout, Mistah Will, and don' let her go into the house."

Will lifted his head and looked toward the gate. Already a flash of pink was moving swiftly through the autumn naked-ness of the grape arbor.

"Where's she been?" asked Jesse Moffat.

"Mother sent her over to Jane's last night and told her to stay there," frowned Will.

"Here, you!" He flung the water from his hands and dashed after the pink flash, which had darted through the gate and was streaking toward the side door of the house. He seized it at the very edge of the porch and dragged it back to the kitchen doorstep.

"You were told to stay down at Jane's till you were sent for. Why are you back here this morning?"

That the small person addressed was an alien in this sober, respectable household was evidenced in the bright mobility of her face and a certain delicate impudence of manner. Small-boned and fragile, she was none the less intrepid.

"I've got to see Richard," she said coolly.

"Richard's not here. And even if he were you couldn't see him."

"Where is he?"

"Gone to Woodridge. For Dr. Caxton."

The pink-sleeved arm gave a sudden twist and slipped from Will's grasp.

"No, you don't. Come back here." He recaptured his quarry and gave her a brisk shake.

"I'm just going down to the lane and wait for Richard."

"You're not going anywhere except back to Jane's like Mother told you. She's got enough on her hands without having you around. And *keep away from Richard*—if you don't want to get hurt."

She said carelessly, "I'm not afraid."

"Maybe not," retorted Will. "And maybe nobody cares whether you are or not. But it would be embarrassing for Richard if anything happened to you." And satisfied that he had given her sufficient jolt to hold her for the time, Will turned to the black woman standing in the kitchen doorway. "Keep Thorne with you, Millie, till Mother comes out."

Millie said, "Git in dat kitchen foah I paddles de bottom offen you," and Thorne obeyed, not because she feared the threat but because Millie shrewdly followed it with one more potent. "I'se goin' tell Mistah Richard how you disobeyed his ordahs."

Thorne said quickly, "Did Richard say I was to stay at Jane's?"

"He not only say you to stay there, he say he don' wanta see hair nor hide of you aroun' heah fo' de nex' six months."

"I don't believe it," said Thorne calmly. Then, before Millie's swelling wrath could discharge itself, she asked in a lowered voice, "How is she, Millie? Is she any better this morning?"

"I don' know. I ain' seen nobody to ask. All I know is nobody in this house got any sleep las' night. And all on account of you."

"I didn't do anything," protested Thorne.

"You don' have to do nothin'. Jus' bein' heah is enough."

A footfall sounded in the covered passage, and a small woman came briskly down the shallow steps that bridged the space between the two floor levels. Ann Tomlinson had borne nine children and buried four of them, but she still had at sixty the energy of her younger son Will. She looked like Will.

In fact, she and Will were exactly alike. But it was her older son Richard whom she idolized.

She spoke to Millie, paying no attention to Thorne, whom her keen eyes spotted immediately.

"Take a tray in to Miss Abigail and stay with her while the rest of us have our breakfast."

"Is she by herself?" asked Millie uneasily.

"No. Kate's with her. When you go in, send Kate out here to help me." Miss Ann was already spooning fermity into a bowl from the iron pot on the back of the stove. She dropped two eggs into a boiling kettle and forked three crisp pieces of side meat out of a sizzling skillet.

Millie muttered, "She won't eat all that."

Miss Ann said firmly, "You must see that she does."

Millie's eyes rolled heavenward.

"She needs food," Miss Ann went on. "She's half starved. If she could be got to eat like other people she would get well." Opening the oven, she added a couple of delicately browned soda biscuits to the tray Millie was holding and gave her a slight shove. "There, go on. Get cream and butter from the table in the dining room. And hurry!"

Millie ambled up the steps, and Miss Ann turned to the small figure hunched beside the window, eyes watchfully focused on the lane. She regarded the child thoughtfully, as a problem to be solved.

"I told you to stay at Jane's house today, Thorne."

"I had to come back. I've something to tell Richard."

"Richard is not to be bothered today. Anything you have to tell him can wait."

Kate came down the steps, her youngest son in her arms. She at least seemed glad to see Thorne.

"Thank goodness somebody's here to mind Hughie. Take him, Thorne. And don't go giving him sugar to keep him quiet."

Kate, the second daughter, was married to Hugh Turner and lived three miles away on the Turner farm. Kate was the one whom Ann Tomlinson now called in family emergencies, her oldest daughter Annie having moved with her husband to Kentucky the year before.

The family was at the breakfast table when Richard returned with the doctor. They were sitting with bowed heads while Miss Ann (in her son's absence) said grace, rather sternly, as though reminding the Lord that she had her hands pretty full and could do with a little assistance. The two men, entering from the side porch, waited respectfully until the petition was concluded, then with a nod to those at the table crossed the room to the hall which led to the downstairs bedroom.

Kate looked at her mother and said, "Do you think one of us should go in there?"

Her brother Will said sharply, "No. It's Rick's affair. Let him handle it."

Her mother said, "If Richard wants one of us, he'll call us."

Young Will scowled. "It's time Rick understood there's a limit to what the rest of this family can put up with. If she's sick and has to be humored, then for heaven's sake humor her and give the rest of us peace. And if she's *not* sick, then by George, it's time somebody took strong measures. If she were my wife, you'd see how I'd handle her."

Miss Ann said warningly, "Sssh! The children."

Four pairs of young eyes were fixed with varying degrees of interest and anxiety on Will's face. Kate's oldest boy, Richard's two little sons, and Thorne were listening attentively.

Will rose from the table and called to Jesse Moffat to come out to the barn when he had finished eating. Jesse, who enjoyed his meals and the accompanying family conversation, took another helping of fried apples and lingered, hoping to hear Dr. Caxton's verdict on Abigail.

He was not disappointed. In a short time the doctor returned to the dining room, took a seat at the table, and immediately began upon the hearty breakfast set before him. In reply to inquiries he reported that Abigail was coming out to breakfast. Richard was helping her dress.

"You mean—she's—reasonable?" asked Miss Ann.

"Perfectly reasonable. My advice is for the rest of you to take no notice. As I've told Richard all along, there's not a thing the matter with her that a new baby wouldn't take care of."

The old doctor was speaking to Richard's mother and married sister. But Ann Tomlinson, conscious of the hired man's unabashed interest and the round-eyed curiosity of the children, said, "You young folks are through eating. You can go with Jesse up to the barn."

The children needed no urging. They were mortally afraid of the tall black-browed doctor and the vile-tasting medicine he carried.

There was no one left at the table except Dr. Caxton and the two women when Richard led his wife into the dining room. The invalid's eyes quickly searched the room, and Miss Ann knew that she had done well to send at least one of the children away before Abigail came in.

To the casual stranger Abigail Tomlinson was a pitiable object. But to the people who had to live with her she was a devil—or a cross laid on them by the Lord—according to individual viewpoint. Even in the full bloom of health she had been a difficult person. Now ravished by all the torments which beset neurotic invalidism, she was indeed a trial. She had been pretty at twenty, when Richard married her. But there was little trace of beauty in her now. Thin to the point of emaciation, her features sharpened by the ravages of insomnia, she looked like a woman of forty instead of twenty-seven.

But she was the woman Richard had married, she was the mother of his children, and for their sake and the sake of his vows he would deal gently and patiently with Abigail as long as the two of them lived.

He drew out a chair for her now and seated himself beside her. Then, as though it were familiar routine, he began feeding her as he would have fed a child.

The others tactfully ignored this procedure. It had happened so often before. Except for its unusual violence Abigail's "spell" was following its ordinary course. Her attacks always ended with collapse and total dependence upon the ministrations of Richard.

As she sat now, her eyes on his face as he fed her, there was something of triumph in her look. There was also something of pathos. Dr. Caxton, missing no move of his patient, thought, "Damn it! The woman's unhappy. She may be driving everybody crazy, but she's not suffering from hallucination. She's got some real grievance, and damned if I don't believe Richard knows what it is. Wonder what she's saying to him?"

The sick woman's lips were moving, but her words were inaudible except to the one for whom they were intended.

"You won't leave me today, will you, Richard?"

"I won't go far."

"You won't go over to Jane's to fetch that girl home?"

"She can't stay at Jane's all winter."

"Promise you won't bring her back yet."

"Eat your breakfast, Abigail, they're watching us."

"I won't eat another bite till you promise." Clawlike fingers gripped his wrist and stayed the hand that was feeding her.

"Very well. I promise." Beads of perspiration stood on the man's forehead.

The thin tight fingers slackened their hold. The doctor, watching, saw a look of satisfaction steal over the woman's face.

They were sitting thus when a horse-drawn vehicle turned into the lane and stopped outside the picket fence. Kate, who was facing the window, saw a woman approaching the house

35 &

and rose hurriedly to go to the door. There was a bell on the front door, and Abigail had been known to scream when suddenly startled by its jangle.

A few minutes later Kate returned with an announcement more jarring to her sister-in-law's nerves than the peal of any doorbell. A lady from Terre Haute to see Mr. Richard Tomlinson.

Richard rose, but not before his wife's thin clutch had clamped upon his wrist.

"What woman do you know in Terre Haute?"

"None. Who is it, Kate?"

"She said you wouldn't know her name."

"What does she want?"

"She wouldn't say. You'll have to go see for yourself."

But Richard could go nowhere with Abigail's fingers binding his wrist.

"If some woman wants to see Richard, let her come in here."

He looked at his sister and said, "Ask the lady in here, Kate. There's no heat in the front room," quite as though that were his only reason for not going himself like a free man and finding out what was wanted.

Judith, waiting in the front room, looked about her with lively interest. It was an unusual room, to say the least; long, low-ceilinged, with a huge fireplace in the center in which hung a crane and copper kettle. Yet shelves of books flanked the fireplace, a square rosewood piano filled the space between the windows, and on the marble-topped table beside the family Bible and wax nosegay under glass lay a copy of *David Copperfield*—face down to mark the place.

Facing the chair in which Judith sat was a tall grandfather's clock. Its pendulum was still, and no reassuring tick noted the passing moments. Though the morning was still young, the hands of the clock pointed to half-past one. So like a ghostly presence was the silent timepiece that she turned her chair to escape it—and saw the quaintest feature in the room.

In an alcove stood a great four-poster bed. Canopied and neatly spread with a handsome patchwork coverlid, it added rather than detracted from the charm of the room. Yet it was undeniably a bed, with a trundle bed beneath it. Judith wondered if it was used regularly or kept for unexpected guests.

And then her speculations were cut short by a pleasant voice inviting her into the dining room where there was a fire.

What Richard Tomlinson's real reaction was to the unexpected appearance of his chance companion at *Macbeth* would have been hard to guess from the immobility of his countenance.

"I don't know if you remember me, Mr. Tomlinson——"

"Oh yes. I remember you quite well, Miss——"

"Judith Amory."

"I didn't get your name in Terre Haute." Certainly none of the interested onlookers could have accused him of trying to hide anything.

"I must apologize, Mr. Tomlinson, for intruding——"

"No apology is needed. You've come about the school, of course."

Judith almost gasped, so precipitately had her ruse worked. In the presence of his family Richard Tomlinson lost no time in establishing the basis of their acquaintance. Timberley school was as good as hers.

He introduced her to the others, and his mother insisted on her taking a place at the table. Hungry after her drive in the crisp morning air, Judith did not demur, and when a huge black woman lumbered in with fresh hot biscuits she helped herself copiously. Sweet country butter, strawberry preserves, and whole spiced peaches, delectable in their own tangy juice, were pressed upon her. Now that the nature of her call was established, the Tomlinson women accepted her with the hospitality for which they were noted.

Meantime, the hawk-nosed doctor was enlarging upon the subject of the school. He, too, was a trustee, though he hadn't a child to his name, being a bachelor well past sixty. But he had ideas about education, and one of them was that no woman—particularly a young and delicate one (no compliment intended)—had any business teaching a country school.

"We've got boys at Timberley bigger than Richard himself. It takes a man to lick those fellows."

Judith was too shrewd to let herself be drawn into an argument with the old misogynist. She let him hold forth upon his favorite theme—woman's total inadequacy in any sphere outside the home—while she studied the women of Richard Tomlinson's household. His mother and sister she dismissed for what they appeared to be: two healthy, wholesome women, secure in their own small world.

But his wife was not so easily appraised. This was the invalid, who had been reported critically ill. Yet here she was sitting at the table in a rather handsome challis wrapper and apparently nothing the matter with her. She was frightfully thin and her color was bad, but to Judith, who had never seen Abigail Tomlinson in health, she did not look at all sick. She looked merely hungry.

The discovery came with something of a shock.

Then, while she answered questions put to her by the doctor, Judith became aware that Abigail was listening with keen interest to this talk about hiring a new teacher.

"You see, miss," Dr. Caxton was explaining, "nothing can be done until the school meeting. Mr. Tomlinson and I are only trustees, which means we handle funds and pay the teacher's salary after the district has selected him. We can call a meeting at the schoolhouse and place your application before it, but personally I think it's just a waste of time. Timberley district has never had but one woman teacher—Rosie MacGrath, who stood six feet and weighed a hundred and ninety—and even Rosie wasn't a success. It's my opinion that the teaching profession is a strong man's job, barring female seminaries, which is where you've been teaching, you say."

Unfortunately Judith had already admitted that her experience had been confined to girls.

"But I can't agree with you, Doctor, that boys present the only disciplinary problem to the teacher. I've taught girls who were quite as difficult to control as any boy. Boys may be noisier, but girls are more sly. The more innocent they appear, the more likely they are to set the school in uproar, without ever being caught in mischief themselves."

Abigail Tomlinson opened her mouth as though to speak, then closed it.

Judith went on: "I don't believe any school can be controlled by force. If a teacher can't gain the respect of her pupils there will be no discipline, even though there are whippings every day. But if corporal punishment is needed at Timberley, I can administer it. To girls and boys alike."

An unexpected voice said harshly, "I think it's time Timberley had a woman teacher."

The effect was startling. The last person in the group from whom Judith had expected support was the wife of Richard Tomlinson.

"We've had men teachers for the last three years and all they've done is whip the boys ever so often to make the trustees think they're earning their salaries." Abigail looked at her husband accusingly.

He said to Judith, "The last teacher spanked our six-year-old and I'm afraid my wife has never forgiven him." It was the first word Richard had spoken since his visitor sat down at the table.

"I never heard of a girl getting whipped," retorted Abigail, "though I could name one that needs it."

Her husband made no reply. She went on in the same harsh tone:

"You should call a school meeting at once. Then you and

39 ❧

Dr. Caxton should tell the district that Miss Amory is exactly the person we need at Timberley. Tell them how smart she is. They'll vote her in. They do pretty much what the trustees advise."

Thus coerced, Richard Tomlinson had no alternative but to promise to call the meeting.

Judith asked practically, "How soon can that be?"

"Let's see. This is Friday. I'll post a meeting for Monday night."

That was three days hence. Judith was not sure she could remain that long at the Barclays'.

Abigail said, "You can stay here if you like."

If Ann Tomlinson had extended the invitation Judith would have accepted. But Ann and Kate had excused themselves some time ago.

Judith said, "Thanks, but I don't like to impose on anyone. Isn't there a boardinghouse in this vicinity?"

"This is as near a boardinghouse as anything you'll find," said Abigail tartly, and Judith wondered what gnawing grudge gave an edge to every word this woman uttered.

"Perhaps I can arrange with Mrs. Barclay to board me until Monday," said Judith. "And if I secure the school"—she just glanced at Richard Tomlinson—"I suppose other teachers have found board this side of Woodridge."

He answered, "The teachers of Timberley school have always boarded at Timberley."

He held the door for her as she went out, then followed her to the picket fence where her horse was tied. Four children who had been playing in the yard left off their game of hopscotch to watch in silence while Richard helped the stranger into the livery-stable buggy and untied the mare. Judith was too annoyed to notice whether the children were boys or girls, because their presence prevented her saying anything to Richard Tomlinson beyond a perfunctory good-by. But as she drove away she got the impression of children immediately

swarming over him, and she was quite sure that the one clinging tightly to his arm was a girl.

CHAPTER 4

Late Friday afternoon small printed handbills appeared in Woodridge announcing the meeting to be held
Monday evening at Timberley school. Dr. Caxton had placed
the order with the *Sentinel* upon his return to town and the
bills were run off and distributed in time to catch the Saturday market crowd. John Barclay reported Saturday night that
interest was running high and Miss Amory could expect a full
turnout.

Judith was spending the intervening time at the Barclays'.
Grateful as she was for their makeshift hospitality, she still
smarted with resentment that she had not been urged to stay
at Timberley. But Richard Tomlinson had not seconded his
wife's somewhat ungracious invitation. It was evident that he
did not want Miss Amory at Timberley school. She wondered
why. Her curiosity was stronger than her resentment, particularly when she remembered his wife's attitude. If his wife had
opposed her she would have understood his aloofness. But
Abigail had proved her ally, and the man on whom she had
counted had maintained a cold neutrality.

She had plenty of time during the interim for shrewdly
directed conversation with Mrs. Barclay.

"Abigail Tomlinson is spoiled and always has been," said
Ellie Barclay with a sniff. "She was a Huse, and the Huses
always thought they were blood relations to the Almighty.
She got religion when she was a girl and it went kinda sour on
her. No man ever born was good enough to be her husband.

She came mighty near being an old maid through her sanctifiedness. The Tomlinsons didn't know what they were taking on when they let Richard marry her. Richard's a good man, but he's the kind of man women can't seem to let alone. These spells Abigail has are nothing but jealous fits. She doesn't want him out of her sight, so she takes to her bed and won't eat unless he feeds her. Invalid, nothing! She's just a jealous fool."

"Jealous!" thought Judith, remembering the sick woman's open partisanship toward herself.

"Mrs. Tomlinson was very nice to me," she said.

"Oh, she wouldn't be jealous of you," was the prompt though unflattering assurance.

On Sunday, as a matter of policy, Judith went to church with the Barclays. She was quite sure that church attendance in this community would be a definite asset. She had another object, more personal, which was doomed to disappointment. Not until she was tightly squeezed into the Barclays' Baptist pew did she learn that the Tomlinsons were Methodists.

On Monday the question of her own presence at the school meeting became an issue. John Barclay assured her it was not required. She would be notified of the outcome of the voting.

"Don't you think an applicant has a better chance if she meets personally the people who are to decide on her merits?"

"In case of a man, yes. But where the applicant is a lady—if you'll pardon my saying it, Miss Amory—I believe you'll do yourself more harm than good by attending."

Judith thought otherwise.

Late that afternoon she walked across town to the Henderson livery stable for the purpose of again securing the bay mare and phaeton. She would take Ellie Barclay with her for propriety's sake, but nothing was going to prevent her attendance at Timberley schoolhouse that night.

A voice accosted her as she crossed the courthouse square. If she had not heard her name spoken she would have ignored the flourish of the lifted hat, for she was holding her head very high to show these country bumpkins that she was a lady. But she was forced to pause when a masculine voice spoke her name.

"Miss Amory! May I speak to you a moment?"

It was Lucius Goff of the Terre Haute *Express*.

At Judith's chill greeting he fell into step beside her, because it was not good manners to stand talking on the street.

"John Barclay tells me you won't be at the schoolhouse tonight. If you'll pardon me, Miss Amory, I think you're making a mistake. In a district solidly prejudiced against female instructors, your only chance is to meet with the voters personally. If they could see you and talk to you they would change their minds."

This was Judith's opinion exactly, but she was too wise to respond to Lucius's flattering smile. When it was followed by an offer to drive her out to the schoolhouse that evening she declined with thanks. Shrewd judgment warned that her appearance at the school meeting thus squired might create the wrong impression.

"I've already arranged to attend the meeting, Mr. Goff."

"Really? Then I shall hope to see you there. And may I wish you the best of luck?" He stood courteously, hat in hand, as she bowed and went on her way. But she was conscious of the sly amusement in his smile.

The rig at Henderson's was available. She invited Mrs. Barclay and Jennie to accompany her. They accepted with enthusiasm.

By seven o'clock Timberley schoolhouse was crowded; not solely through interest in things educational, but because a gathering of any kind was a social event. Bachelors, spinsters, and childless widows drove five and six miles to vote for a teacher they might never meet. Parents of school-age children were only slightly in the majority. The most belligerent member of the district was old Alf Butterick, none of whose ten daughters had ever darkened a schoolhouse door. Butterick was fanatically opposed to female education, and it was a foregone conclusion that he would block any attempt to hire a woman teacher at Timberley.

All this Mrs. Barclay explained to Judith as they sat at a double desk in a rear corner, from which vantage point Judith had a good view of the room in which she hoped to teach.

It was a square enclosure of four log walls, chinked and calcimined against the weather and perforated along the sides with small deep windows. A rusted stove, a teacher's desk on which reposed a globe slightly bashed at the equator, a blackboard, a wall map, a shelf of miscellaneous debris, and five rows of rough pine desks and benches completed the furnishings. Never had Judith Amory taught in such crude surroundings. Yet never had she so coveted a position.

"That's Jane Mitchell and her husband over there." Mrs. Barclay pointed to a young woman in a scarlet hood with a grinning young man in tow. "Now I believe Alec Mitchell might vote for you. He's a good-natured fellow. He hasn't been married very long. Suppose I take you over and introduce you."

Judith declined. She would rather no one knew of her presence yet. Not even to herself did she admit that she was waiting for Richard Tomlinson.

When he came in he did not even see her.

He shouldered his way through the crowded room and mounted a little platform. He wore the same dark blue greatcoat which had been so much in his way that night at the theater, and his handsome head towered above the heads about him as it had towered that night. He was again the man Judith had met under adventurous circumstances, and she thrilled at sight of him until her own tingling cheeks warned her that Mrs. Barclay's sharp eyes missed nothing.

She glanced swiftly around to see if anyone else was watching and encountered Lucius Goff's amused recognition. He and Dr. Caxton had followed Richard in. The doctor had gone forward, but Lucius remained near the door. He had missed nothing of Judith's reaction to Richard Tomlinson's entrance.

She acknowledged his bow with a frosty little nod.

The meeting was called to order and proceeded at once to the business of considering the application of Miss Judith Amory for the balance of the school year at Timberley.

Three men were on their feet immediately.

"Mr. Chairman, we don't want any women——"

"We need a man at Timberley big enough to whip those Pettigrew young ones——"

"Mr. Chairman, I move——"

Richard Tomlinson rapped for order.

"You will please wait until the Chair calls for discussion."

There was a lull. Timberley district was the home of the monthly debating society. *Robert's Rules of Order* was revered like the Decalogue.

Richard continued: "In presenting this application I would like to state that it has been carefully considered by the trustees. Dr. Caxton and myself have met the applicant and examined her. It is true that the applicant is a woman. But we believe she is sufficiently intelligent to handle the school without recourse to corporal punishment."

A voice from the back of the room called, "You got a point there, Richard. Good hickory switches are gettin' scarce around here."

The laugh that followed eased the hostile atmosphere. Judith looked round to see the rustic wit who had come to her aid. Mrs. Barclay whispered, "Henry Schook. He's a great cutup." Richard Tomlinson talked on to a roomful of people who were suddenly amenable to persuasion.

And he could persuade them, if anyone could.

Mrs. Barclay whispered, "Don't you love his voice? He studied for the ministry, you know."

This information came as a surprise to Judith, who had been

remembering a man who slipped away to see a Shakespeare play.

As he talked on, earnestly building up the case for a female instructor at Timberley, she wondered at his reversed attitude. Had he changed his mind or had his wife changed it for him? Did he really want Miss Amory teaching the school, or was his first cool response his true feeling?

Suddenly, from trying to hide behind Mrs. Barclay, Judith sat up as tall as possible to attract the speaker's attention. She wanted him to see her and be caught off guard. She wanted to surprise his honest reaction to her presence when his wife was not beside him.

The man in front shifted his position, Judith moved a little, and Richard looked straight into her eyes.

His whole face kindled with surprised pleasure. He interrupted his own remarks:

"I find that the applicant is here this evening. You can see and hear her for yourselves. Miss Amory, would you please come to the platform?"

Judith responded. She spoke briefly, stressing the need for mental, not physical, superiority in the matter of discipline. She was willing to take the school with the understanding that she would resign if found incompetent. Her cool assurance made a stronger impression than any record of accomplishment. Hostility and skepticism gave place to conviction that here was a smart young woman.

Elated, she looked over the crowded room. Her eyes encountered Lucius Goff's. He nodded with a congratulatory grin. She looked swiftly away and met another pair of eyes. A little girl, leaning on the desk in front of her, was watching the two people on the platform. Her eyes moved from Judith to Richard, then back to Judith again. They were large dark eyes and so arresting in their gaze that Judith began to feel uncertain and confused. She hastily concluded her remarks and sat down.

When the vote was taken and her application accepted, she had a cowardly impulse to run and hide. So acute was her discomfort by this time that she began to wish she had never applied for this school. And all because a mere child had looked with strange intentness upon two people as they stood together on a platform.

Strangers were crowding around to meet the new schoolma'am, and over their heads Judith saw Mrs. Barclay's hand waving triumphantly and Lucius Goff's hat held high in a flourish. Even gruff old Dr. Caxton was shaking her hand and pledging his support. Everyone seemed bent on wishing her well. Everyone but the man for whom her eyes were searching.

She saw him standing a little apart, talking to the young Mitchells. Jane Mitchell had removed her scarlet hood, and her resemblance to Richard was so strong that Judith guessed her to be another of his sisters. The little girl with the disturbing eyes was hanging on his arm, and suddenly Judith recalled the girl who had clung to him that day as she drove away from Timberley. It was the same child.

Straining a listening ear, Judith heard her plead:

"Let me go home with you, Richard. Please!"

He put an affectionate arm around her, but his answer was inaudible.

"But why, Richard? I don't do anything. I'll keep out of her sight. If you'll just let me come back with you."

The three adults talked on. Suddenly the young husband's voice rose above the others.

"Understand, Richard, we don't mind having her. But there's only one bedroom, you know—and Thorne's getting to be a big girl—and with Jane the way she is——"

For the first time Judith noticed that the young wife was pregnant.

Richard said, "You and Jane go on, Alec. I've this business here to finish up, then I'll stop on my way home and talk things over." He looked down at the child. "Don't worry,

47 ॐ

Cricket. We'll have you home before long." And playfully rumpling her hair, he told her to run along with the Mitchells.

Judith's eyes followed the trio as they made their way out. Then she turned to discover, with a start, that Richard was standing at her elbow.

"There are some details which we might as well settle to-night, Miss Amory. How soon will you be ready to start? . . . Next week? . . . Good. We've lost time enough already."

His manner was crisp and businesslike. She replied in the same tone:

"I'll have to go back to Terre Haute first. But I can be ready a week from today."

"I'll have the building cleaned and we'll see if something can't be done about that stove. By the way—you'll board at Timberley. If that's satisfactory to you."

"Perfectly satisfactory," said Judith.

"Dr. Caxton will settle the remaining details. Don't hesitate to call on me for anything needed. And now, if you'll excuse me, I'll say good night."

"Good night, Mr. Tomlinson."

He was gone without even a handshake.

Dr. Caxton was saying, "The only thing left to be settled is the salary, and there's nothing to settle about it because it's forty dollars a month, take it or leave it."

At the moment Judith felt like leaving it.

Instead, she found the salary quite satisfactory and herself engaged to teach the Timberley school.

CHAPTER 5

Five weeks from the night Judith faced her reflection in Mrs. Prewitt's cracked looking glass while dressing to go to the theater she sat before the mirror in what the Tomlinsons called the bird's-eye-maple room. The face that looked back at her seemed to belong to a different person. Gone was the taut anxiety of the mouth, the pin-point sharpness of eyes worn with contriving. For the first time since her father's death Judith Amory knew the luxury of a home.

She thrilled to the knowledge that the whole family welcomed her presence. Richard's mother, his married sisters, even his young brother Will seemed pleased to have the schoolmistress in the house. Their cordiality had in it something of relief from strain. A far less discerning person than Judith would have sensed that her presence had much the effect of a cup of oil poured on bubbling waters. For the simple reason that Richard's wife had taken a fancy to her.

To Judith this paradox was exquisitely humorous.

She was too smart, however, to misinterpret the invalid's good will. For some purpose of her own the wife of Richard Tomlinson wanted Miss Amory to have the Timberley school. Judith was not long discovering what that purpose was.

Abigail wanted a teacher who would promise to whip Thorne Tomlinson.

She did not put the matter in plain words. The new teacher might go to Richard and ask questions. But she let Judith know that she favored her because of her stand on the subject of discipline for girls. Abigail had fallen into the habit of calling the schoolmistress into her room when she came from school in the afternoon and asking how the Tomlinson young people were doing. Judith soon learned that there was only one with whom she was really concerned, and that was the girl with the starry eyes. She inquired perfunctorily about her own little boys in the primer class, likewise the Turner nephews and nieces. But when she asked about Thorne her eyes glittered and she licked her lips eagerly when Judith confessed the child was something of a problem.

"She's like what you said, isn't she?" said Abigail. "One of those sly sneaking things that throw a whole school in a turmoil."

Honesty compelled Judith to deny that she had found anything sly or sneaking in Thorne.

"On the contrary, she's quite open in her mischief. She's forever playing tricks to amuse the other children. Sometimes I think she lacks concentration. Yet she seems remarkably bright, if only she would pay attention. I've about made up my mind to speak to Mr. Tomlinson about her."

And this was true. Judith had been puzzled by the puckish behavior of the half-grown girl who went by the name of Tomlinson yet who called Richard by his first name while the other children called him either Father or Uncle. She had asked no questions, and no one had offered an explanation. But whatever Thorne's status, she was hated by Abigail Tomlinson with a jealous hatred that was hard to reconcile with the difference in their ages.

"Don't talk to Richard about her," said Abigail sharply. "Anything that concerns Thorne you're to take up with me. Understand?"

When Judith had acquiesced Abigail went on:

"She needs discipline. You have my permission, Miss Amory, to use any means you like to bring about results. Mr. Tomlinson is too easy. He doesn't realize that girls have to be whipped sometimes—whipped hard—harder than boys. I've a very good whip if you need it." The sick woman raised herself on her elbow and pointed to a peg in the corner. "There it is, an old riding whip that I once used on a bad-tempered horse. Perhaps you'd better take it with you."

There was something fantastically ugly in this sick, frail woman half rising from bed to point out a cruel whip with which she wanted a little girl flogged. But to please the invalid Judith took the whip and promised to use it at her own discretion.

A few days later, when she was again summoned to Abigail's room, she gave her a conspiratorial smile and reported that Thorne was behaving much better.

"You whipped her?"

"Sssh!" Judith put her finger to her lips and saved the necessity of direct falsehood. "We don't want anyone else to know, do we?"

"You mean Richard?" Abigail's eyes gleamed jealously. "She'll tell him."

"I don't think she will," said Judith smoothly.

To the Tomlinsons she never could have explained her method of appeasing the invalid. If she had said, "All you have to do is lie to her," they would have been shocked. In this stanch Methodist household a lie was an abomination and no extremity of circumstance justified its use. To the young woman who had lived all her life by her wits, deception was one's first expedient. She could pretend to anything that served her purpose, and her purpose just now was to cement the friendship of Richard Tomlinson's wife.

She had arrived a bit wistfully at this compromise with certain groundless hopes. For the memory of a night at the theater still lingered like the scent of a rose. A single incident had pressed it imperishably.

It was the custom of the Tomlinson household to gather about the fire of an evening, and while knitting needles clacked and jackknives plied, Richard would read aloud. Many a sock was knitted, many a whip mended, amid wholesome chuckles at the antics of Mr. Pickwick and Sam Weller. Dickens was the best-selling author of the day, and the family reading circle was about halfway through *David Copperfield* at the time of Judith's advent.

There had been no evening readings for some time previously because of Abigail's illness and Thorne's enforced absence. But on the first evening that the new boarder took her place among them they were all present, Abigail sitting up for the first time in days, and Thorne back among the other youngsters clustered about the fire.

The fat red volume of Dickens still lay face open on the table where Richard had last laid it. But instead of resuming the novel he went to the bookcase and took from it a small black book well worn with much reading.

"Aren't we going to hear some more about Uriah Heep?" demanded his son Ricky.

"Suppose we let Uriah rest for tonight. Here's something more exciting."

"What?"

"A play called *Macbeth*."

"How does it begin?"

"Oh, it begins with a bang. Listen." He began to read: " 'Act I, Scene 1—An Open Place. Thunder and lightning. Enter three Witches.' "

And then he lifted his eyes from the book and looked straight at Judith.

That was all. Just a twinkle of the eye. But it brought again the shared thrill of waiting for a curtain to rise and it sent her spirits soaring. That had been her welcome from Richard Tomlinson.

So far, it was the only welcome he had given her. She had not talked alone with him once. They met at mealtimes, but he was usually engrossed in some talk about the farm with his brother or Jesse Moffat. During the day their paths seldom crossed, and at other times he was generally to be found with his invalid wife. Abigail seemed jealous of every moment that he was out of her sight.

It was a strange marriage, Judith decided. From what Ellie Barclay had told her and what her own sharp eyes had seen, she was able to conjecture pretty accurately how it had come about.

Richard Tomlinson had been in his second year of college when he came to the conclusion that he was not fitted for the ministry. His decision had been a crushing blow to family and friends. So marked were his talents that it seemed even to the materialistic that he was throwing away a brilliant career, for it was a day of pulpit oratory. But Richard considered the pulpit something more than a rostrum for rhetorical eloquence. Far from being irreligious, as of course he was branded, he was deeply conscious of the sacredness of the high calling to which so many ambitious men aspired. To his mother he explained that he did not consider himself good enough to be a preacher. And that was the only defense he ever offered.

His father, even then in his last illness, never recovered from the blow. He had hoped to see his son ordained before his death. Now that hope was blasted. But a stubborn belief that Richard might yet be brought to see the error of his ways led the dying man to arrange a marriage which was to prove a calamity to the entire family.

Abigail Huse, at twenty one of the zealots of the Methodist Church, was chosen by Roger Tomlinson as a fitting wife for his son. She was a couple of years his senior and her religious zeal, so his father hoped, would inspire Richard to resume the work for which he had been preparing.

Richard, eager to appease his disappointed father, had entered into the marriage without protest. Abigail was pretty, angelically "sweet," and he was barely eighteen years old. He was prepared to be a loving husband.

But scarcely were they joined in wedlock when he realized that he was yoked to a woman who was "good" in every negative connotation of the word. Abigail's was a nature in which religion's only property was to curdle what milk of human kindness it exuded. All that was harsh and repressive in the doctrines of the church she adhered to. All that was gracious and loving she distrusted. Her outward sweetness was a mask which she did not bother to wear in private. She had married Richard to save him from the devil, and this she would do if she had to take him personally to hell in order to negotiate.

Their marriage was a nightmare from the beginning. On their first night together he had found himself clasping a snow maiden who would not melt or even thaw in his arms.

"Richard! I thought you were a gentleman."

"I'm your husband, Abigail."

"That's no excuse for behaving like a brute."

If it had been left to the bewildered, apologetic boy, the marriage would have terminated right there. For he had married a fanatical prude whose frigidity was matched only by her arrogance.

But Abigail had intelligence of a sort, and much reading of the Old Testament enlightened and finally convinced her of the nature of the curse laid upon Eve. With an air of martyrdom she informed her husband that she was ready to obey the biblical injunction. In due course of time their son Richard was born.

A year later—again by Abigail's decree—there was a second son. But when, after the usual interval, she stonily signified her willingness to assume again the burden of reproduction, Richard told her they would have no more children. He was kind enough to imply that consideration for her health was the reason.

But Abigail knew better. For perversely, with the birth

of her son Roger, some belated seeds of passion stirred in her frozen nature and with her husband's announcement sent forth shoots, seeking a sun which no longer shone. From that moment her life was like a creeping vine.

They continued to occupy the conjugal bedchamber, for separate quarters would have meant a community-wide scandal, and Richard had enough talk to live down as it was. But though he preserved the outward semblance of his marriage, his private conduct toward his wife was as chaste as hers had been on their wedding night.

Abigail's desires, thus frustrated in their inception, found vent in the pursuit of her original purpose. Night and day she exhorted and berated her husband for his refusal to enter the ministry. When he turned a deaf ear she denounced him as no Christian.

Perhaps he was too much a Christian to be a theologian. Though Abigail never could have understood a thing like that. Even he did not understand it. What he did know and could not explain was the riotous joy of living which throbbed in his veins and which his strict upbringing made him distrust. Perhaps, as he feared, his Puritan soul was housed in a pagan body. Perhaps he had merely a love for things of the earth. Every opening bud, every note of mockingbird and cardinal, was a delight to him. In spring, when redbuds blossomed and honey locusts made him half drunk with their sweetness, he felt quite sure he was not called to tell other people about their sins.

So he had settled down to the business of managing the farm (an occupation for which his younger brother was better fitted), and for enjoyment he turned to books and for escape there was the occasional trip to the city and perhaps the theater. This last indulgence was frowned upon by Abigail, but he did not let it deter him. He no longer tried to explain himself to Abigail, nor to his family, nor to anyone.

Not until a vagabond child came to Timberley did Richard find it possible to explain himself. And to her, it was unnecessary.

There was no one in the front room when Judith came downstairs. She had changed from her school dress to her dark red merino and she had tied a velvet ribbon around her throat. It was a Friday evening, which meant that young Will would go to see the girl whom he was currently "sparking," and there would be no one in the fireside reading circle except the children and their grandmother and Richard and Judith.

Abigail had taken to her bed again.

But the fire, which was never lighted in this room till after supper, was already brightly ablaze. The piano was open, the chairs grouped around it as though in expectation of a gathering. No open book, laid face down to mark a place. Judith had a premonition of disappointment.

When she went out to the dining room Miss Ann confirmed her fears. Richard was having company this evening.

"Lucius Goff, John Barclay, and Doc Baird. The four of them get together about once a month—at the academy, as a rule—but since Abigail's been sick she doesn't like having Richard out at night, so the men are coming here. I told Richard they could have the front room to themselves. You and I and the children will sit out here till bedtime. We can have our apples as usual and maybe you can read to us instead of Richard. We're all on pins and needles to see if anything's turned up yet for Mr. Micawber." Ann Tomlinson laughed merrily and tucked a curly gray lock under her neat little cap. It was impossible to resist her good humor. Judith agreed to carry on with the misfortunes of the Micawbers.

Abigail registered disapproval of the evening's program by refusing to appear at the supper table. She kept to her bed the greater part of the day, but she usually got up for the evening meal. Richard's habit was to enter the house through her room, which had an outside door, assist her to dress, and bring her out to the dining room. But tonight she was not with him.

He came alone from his wife's room, carefully shaved and brushed and wearing his broadcloth suit in honor of the expected company. But his lips were tight and there was color in his cheeks as he explained that Abigail did not feel like coming to the table. Could Millie fix a tray?

"Do you suppose she'll eat it?" said Miss Ann doubtfully.

"I'll have to feed her," he said.

Impulsively Judith spoke. "No. You must stay with your friends. Let me take the tray in. I can get her to eat."

He looked at Judith with a curious mingling of gratitude and desperation.

"Do you suppose you could?"

"I can try. She seems to like me."

"Yes, I've noticed that." He spoke in an odd tone, as though the fact puzzled him.

"But Miss Judith shouldn't be allowed to spoil her own supper waiting on Abigail," said his mother.

"No, of course not," he said quickly. "Though I appreciate your kindness, Miss Judith."

It was not her supper which Judith was loath to miss, but the enjoyment of dining with Richard and his friends. Nevertheless, she insisted:

"Your place is in here. Please let me take the tray to Miss Abigail. We can eat our suppers together."

In the end he acquiesced.

She found the invalid lying flat on her back, hands crossed on her breast, looking as much like a corpse as possible. When she set the tray on a table by the bed Abigail demanded:

"Where's Richard?"

"He's taking care of his friends. Don't you hear them?"

Already the sound of masculine voices and laughter floated down the hall. Judith drew a chair to the bedside and spread a napkin over Abigail's nightgown.

"Would you like to hold your own plate, or shall I feed you? I know it's hard to feed oneself in bed," said Judith tactfully.

But Abigail would neither eat nor be fed.

"I told him I wouldn't eat any supper. I'll show him."

For a second Judith contemplated the exquisite pleasure it would afford her to strangle the woman on the bed.

She set the plate back on the table and picked up her own knife and fork.

"I hope you don't mind if I go on with my own supper. I've had a busy day. I'm hungry."

Judith began eating with as keen an appetite as though the sick woman were not lying there watching her like the death's-head at the feast.

When she had finished her meal she tried once more.

"Shall I have your supper warmed up for you? I'm afraid it's getting cold."

Abigail said, "I don't want anything. Take it away."

Judith pushed the table back against the wall.

Abigail's hands still lay folded upon her shrunken breast. Her eyes stared at the ceiling. She said in a hollow tone, "I'm dying. He'll see. When I'm dead he'll believe I knew what I was talking about."

Her face in the lamplight was bloodless. For a moment Judith felt a thrill of alarm.

Then Abigail flopped on her side and with reassuring spitefulness demanded, "Where's that girl?"

"What girl?"

"You know what girl. The one you whipped."

"Oh, you mean Thorne? She's at the Mitchells' this week."

"She hasn't been around here?"

"I haven't seen her."

A look of satisfaction stole over the sick woman's face.

"Have you whipped her any more?"

A feeling of revulsion swept Judith. She felt something akin to abhorrence for the woman on the bed.

"No, Mrs. Tomlinson, I have not whipped Thorne. She hasn't needed it. She's not a bad girl. She's just—a little different."

"That's because she's a witch!"

Judith remained silent, too exasperated to argue.

"You don't believe in witches, do you?" said Abigail.

"Certainly not."

"That's because you don't read your Bible." Abigail rose on her elbow and reached for the well-worn Testament on the stand. "Here, read Luke 8:2 if you think I'm crazy."

Judith took the book and turned the silky pages till she came to the passage:

"'And certain women, which had been healed of evil spirits and infirmities, Mary called Magdalene, out of whom went seven devils . . .'"

"There!" Abigail interrupted triumphantly. "Do you believe the Bible, or don't you?"

Judith laid the book back on the table.

"Devils, as referred to in the Orient," she said, "mean nothing more nor less than epilepsy. Is Thorne an epileptic?"

"She's a witch. Like those witches in the play Richard read to us." Abigail, who frowned upon all profane literature, had been avidly interested in the reading of *Macbeth*. "They weren't epileptics, were they? Neither were the witches in the Bible epileptics. I haven't got an Old Testament here"—she was sitting up in bed now in her excitement—"but just you read the story of Saul and the witch of Endor. First Book of Samuel 28:7."

Judith had read the story. She inquired, "Is Thorne mediumistic?"

This was a strange word in Abigail's vocabulary. "What do you mean?"

"The witch of Endor was a medium. She called up the spirit of Samuel and let Saul talk to him. Does Thorne claim to get messages from people who are dead?"

Abigail lay back on her pillow with a disgruntled sniff.

"I don't know. I wouldn't be surprised. She's full of tricks."

"What kind of tricks?" asked Judith curiously. She had often wondered what went on behind Thorne's big geography in school to cause such distraction among the pupils.

"Devilish tricks," said Abigail. "I've seen her make a rose bloom right out of thin air. And once she took a live baby chick out of Jesse Moffat's cap when he had just taken it off his head."

Judith was suddenly enlightened. "But that's not witch-craft! That's sleight of hand. I saw a man in Chicago do that sort of thing. Where did Thorne learn such tricks?"

"That's what I want to know. Nobody could do things like that unless they were in league with the devil."

But Judith was thinking rapidly.

"How did Thorne come to live here?" she asked.

"There was a terrible storm one night and the bridge over Little Raccoon went out. A covered wagon went with it. Richard was coming home from the Debating Society and saw the accident. Everybody in the wagon was drowned except this girl. At least, that's the story he told. Though it always seemed funny to me that no trace of wagon, horses, or drowned bodies was ever found."

"And he brought the child home with him?"

"Yes," said Abigail shortly. "I was sitting in the front room with Miss Ann—my own two babies asleep in the trundle—when he came in. He had this girl in his arms, wrapped up in his coat like a drowned puppy. All she could tell about herself was that her folks had been moving to Kansas."

"How long ago was that?" asked Judith.

"More than a year ago."

Thorne must have been about twelve then. She couldn't be much over thirteen now.

Abigail went on bitterly: "He promised that he would find a home for her. Right away. But she's still here."

"It isn't always easy to find a home for an orphan."

"He won't try. He refused to give her to a family in Woodridge who wanted a girl to work for her board and keep."

No, thought Judith, it would have taken a harder man than Richard Tomlinson to have given that elfin child into servitude.

Abigail continued bitterly: "She's bewitched him. He won't let her be treated as one of the help. He gives her his name and sends her to school and treats her like his own child—except that she's much too old to be his child. He thinks more of her than of his sons. He thinks more of her than he does of me."

Aye, there was the rub!

Judith said discreetly, "I can see how you might have found it inconvenient to take another child to raise when you already had two of your own. But of course she's not a witch."

But Abigail's gloom did not lighten. "I've been ill ever since she came here. How do you explain that?"

Judith might have explained that jealousy was slow poison, but she only smiled.

"That's just a coincidence. You're not really ill. Only nervous. You'd be well in no time if you'd start eating again. Come, let's begin now. I'm going to take your supper out to the kitchen and warm it up. Then I'm coming back and sit with you while you eat."

Abigail made no protest as Judith carried out the tray.

CHAPTER 6

The dining room was deserted except for the children. Male voices mingled with the sound of the piano indicated that Richard and his friends had adjourned to the front room. The supper table was cleared, but at one end of it three heads were bent over some toy or game. As Judith passed through with Abigail's tray she said pleasantly, "Hello, Thorne. I didn't know you were here," and the dark head came up in startled alarm.

"She's staying with us while Aunt Jane and Uncle Alec go to choir practice," explained Ricky.

"I just came," said Thorne quickly.

She had worn Jane's scarlet hood, and it still hung by its strings about her shoulders. Her eyes were bright and her cheeks rosy from her run through the crisp night air—the Mitchells had dropped her at the lane—and she seemed alert with some happy expectancy.

Judith, fresh from her talk with Abigail, wondered if Richard knew the child had come.

"Does anyone know you are here, Thorne?"

"Gran'ma knows," said Ricky. "It's all right."

"You won't tell Miss Abigail?" said Thorne anxiously.

Judith shook her head. "Don't make any noise though, or she'll hear you."

"We won't," was the solemn promise, and the three heads bent once more over some object in Thorne's lap.

Judith, curious, paused behind Thorne's chair. The object on her lap was a remarkably homely rag doll. A scrap of flowered challis was pinned to its cotton body, and on its blank muslin face unspeakably leering features had been worked in darning cotton. Thorne was stitching a wad of auburn hair combings to its shapeless head.

"My goodness, Thorne, can't you make something prettier than that?"

"It isn't finished, Miss Judith. The dress is only pinned on."

It wasn't the dress that made it hideous. It was the grotesque face and the homemade wig.

"Where did you get the hair?" asked Judith.

"From the little china box in Mama's room," five-year-old Rodgie piped up. "Millie was going to empty it in the trash, but I saved it for my dolly. It is my dolly, isn't it, Thorne?"

"It is not, it's mine," said his older brother. "I got the dress, didn't I, from Mama's piece bag?"

They were still arguing ownership of the doll as Judith went down the covered passage to the kitchen.

Miss Ann was setting yeast for Saturday's baking, while Millie washed the vast array of supper dishes piled on the zinc-topped table. Judith explained her errand, which Miss Ann immediately vetoed.

"My dear, you're not going to spend your entire evening with Abigail. Just set the tray down on the oilcloth table and as soon as I get my hands out of this yeast I'll warm some soup and take it in to her. You've done enough by sitting with her while the rest of us ate supper."

Judith made but a halfhearted protest. She had had enough of Abigail for one evening.

"Isn't there something else that I can do? You seem to have your hands pretty full."

"You can take some cider in to the front room if you like. It's already been brought up from the cellar. In that jug there, under the pump, keeping cool. Just pour some in that blue pitcher. And you'll find glasses on the shelf in the cupboard. There's another tray, too, on top of the safe—reach it down for her, Millie—and that plate of gingerbread goes with it. Jesse Moffat hasn't brought the apples up yet. When he does we'll take a bowl of them in too. Now, have you got everything?" asked Miss Ann briskly as Judith hesitated, tray in hand.

"Do you suppose it's all right for me to go in there?" She felt a sudden reluctance to crash the all-male gathering.

"To be sure it's all right." Ann Tomlinson's blue eyes twinkled. "Lucius Goff was disappointed when he didn't see you at supper."

It was not Lucius Goff whom Judith feared to offend, but she could not explain that to Richard Tomlinson's mother.

She went back through the covered passage to the dining room, where she paused to rest her heavy tray and compose herself before entering the front room. She felt unaccountably warm and flushed.

Giggles from the foot of the table were quickly smothered at her reappearance. She wondered irritably why children always reacted to a schoolma'am as though she were an ogre. She wanted Richard's children to like her, not fear her. So she asked brightly how the doll was coming on.

Ricky cried eagerly, "Oh, I've got something better'n a doll. I've got a cow and she——" and then choked and sputtered as Thorne's hand clapped over his mouth, extinguishing his enthusiasm.

"What about the cow?" asked Judith.

"Nothing," said Thorne. "I just made him a cow so he wouldn't want Rodgie's doll."

Judith went closer to look at the cow. It stood on toothpick legs in a flat saucer, looking exactly what it was, a ripe cucumber with a small potato stuck on one end. But the eyes of the potato gave it a ludicrously lifelike appearance, just as there had been something queerly expressive about the features of the doll.

"Her name's Flossie," said Ricky, " 'cause she's got a face just like Mr. Schook's Flossie that stays in our pasture."

Henry Schook had been pasturing his cows at Timberley until he got rid of the wild turnip that was infesting his own land.

Judith laughed at the cow and asked Thorne where she had found a cucumber so late in the season. She had brought it with her, she explained, from the Mitchells'. It was the last cucumber on the vine.

Stealthy quiet settled behind Judith's back as she went out of the dining room. She wondered what the little imps were up to now; then forgot all about the children as she paused outside the door to the front room.

Here, too, all was quiet. Where a short time before there had been laughter and music, there was now not even the murmur of conversation. The children back in the dining room were no more ominously hushed than were the men in the front of the house.

There was no answer to Judith's knock. After a second knock she quietly opened the door. The light from the hall lamp fell upon a room that was in darkness except for the glow of the fire.

Richard Tomlinson stood with his back to the hearth. John Barclay sat on the piano stool. Both were intently watching a small table at which sat Lucius Goff and Doc Baird. The hands of these two were lightly resting on the table.

Judith's apologetic "Please don't let me disturb you" brought an explosive "Damn!" from Lucius and a discordant crash from the piano as John Barclay's arm hit the keyboard. Doc Baird pushed the table aside, and Richard touched a paper spill to the fire and lighted the candles. Then he came forward to relieve Judith of her tray.

"Thank you so much." His smile was reassuring, but she was conscious of nothing but a desire to be elsewhere. She turned quickly to leave, but he stopped her. "Please don't go yet. I'd like to present my friends."

Gathering together what shreds of dignity remained, Judith acknowledged the introductions. It seemed unnecessary to mention that she had met the gentlemen before. Nor did John Barclay or Doc Baird allude to any previous meeting. But Lucius Goff, who seemed still irritated at the interruption, drawled, "Charmed, Miss Amory! I'm *always* charmed to meet you," then, coolly turning, spoke to the other men as though there were no lady present.

"I tell you it can be done under the proper circumstances. Doc and I had great success when we tried it alone. We've never succeeded with other people around, but that's because something always occurs to break the concentration—like to-night."

He did not glance at Judith, but his rebuke was no less pointed.

"I don't say it can't be done," said John Barclay. "I merely say it's no proof of supernatural manifestation. We all know Doc Baird has some sort of magnetic power in his body. We've seen him cure too many headaches to doubt it. If he can stop a pain by laying his hands on the spot, there's no reason why he can't cause a table to move the same way. But that doesn't prove that spirits of the dead can communicate with us. I still say the Fox sisters were frauds."

Lucius retorted: "You're dodging the issue. Doc's power to cure aches and pains has nothing to do with psychic phenomena. I don't claim that table tipping is supernatural manifestation. But I do assert it is the power of mind over matter."

The schoolmaster smiled, but he shook his head.

"I've yet to see a piece of furniture move by someone's will power. You admit the table does nothing until *Doc* lays his hands on it. You and I tried it. You and Richard tried it. But only when Doc's hands touch it does it so much as quiver. Maybe it's just as well Miss Amory opened the door when she did. This is a good Methodist table, and I'm sure it would have been scandalized if Doc had raised it clear off the floor."

There was a laugh at that. Richard said hastily, before

Lucius's quick tongue could reply, "How about some more music? Perhaps Miss Judith will play for us and we can have a little harmony."

Judith had been listening with interest. She could have held her own in this argument. Her father had been a keen student of the occult. He had gone in for mysticism as some men go in for stamp collecting. Judith had a small trunkful of his books upstairs.

But it seemed there was to be no further discussion. The schoolmaster was relinquishing the piano stool to her; Richard was thumbing through a song book for some of his favorites. The room soon rang with "Captain Jinks" and "Nellie Gray" and "Camptown Races." Miss Ann and Millie, in the kitchen, hummed together over their work. The children in the dining room sang at their play. And Abigail, lying wakeful in her bedroom, sat up suddenly and reached for her wrapper. Through two closed doors, and under cover of a male quartet, she had caught the sound of a voice for which she had been listening.

After the last verse of "Annie Laurie" Judith excused herself. Much as she wanted to stay, she had the good sense to leave her audience clamoring for more.

"I'm sorry, but I really must go. I promised the children I'd read to them."

But when she had closed the door behind her she leaned against it for a moment, smiling in elation. Richard Tomlinson's obvious disappointment at her withdrawal was something to sleep on. She decided to go on up to her own room and not bother with the children tonight.

And then she heard a door open and close somewhere. Shuffling footsteps sounded along the passage. She knew those steps. Abigail was up and moving around in her clumsy bedroom slippers.

Judith thought, "She'll go into the dining room and find Thorne, and then there'll be the devil to pay." She had a swift vision of Richard humiliated before his guests. She had better take Thorne upstairs with her before Abigail made any discoveries.

The children still sat at the lower end of the dining table, so quiet that for a moment Judith thought they were asleep. But no, their eyes were wide open, fixed spellbound on the cucumber cow which Thorne had made. It still stood in the china saucer, and Thorne was pretending to milk it. She talked softly to it, the way a milkmaid talks when coaxing an animal to give down milk.

Judith went close and leaned across the table—if she called to Thorne, Abigail might hear—and then she stood stock-still with astonishment.

Thorne was actually milking the cucumber cow.

Incredible as it seemed, with each pressure of the small brown fingers on the toothpick udders, a tiny stream of milk squirted into the saucer.

How long Judith stood there, she was never sure. She never heard the opening of a door or the shuffling of bedroom slippers across a carpet. She heard nothing, saw nothing, except a slowly widening pool of milk in the bottom of a saucer.

Suddenly Thorne sat back in her chair and made a graceful little gesture of finale. "There, that's all!" She relaxed, as though her performance had been something of a strain.

But her juvenile audience was not satisfied. "Do it again, Thorne. Make Flossie give more milk."

"Flossie can't give any more milk."

"Why?"

"She's sick. See? She can't hold up her head."

And in truth the weight of the potato on the quill toothpick had caused it to sag in the overripe cucumber.

"Is Flossie going to die?" asked Ricky anxiously. After all, the cow was his property.

Suddenly Thorne saw a dramatic finish for her act and a way to avoid an encore.

"Flossie'll never give milk any more. She's dead."

She gave the wobbly head the slightest prod and it fell off. The legs crumpled beneath the cucumber, for all the world like the legs of an animal succumbing to sickness. There was nothing left of Flossie but a couple of vegetables and a few toothpicks.

And a small puddle of milk.

The little boys said solemnly, "Flossie's dead."

Judith came out of the grip of a spell incredibly potent. She opened her mouth to say, "A great performance, Thorne. Now tell us how you did it." But the words were never spoken. For another voice, harsh with triumph, came from across the room.

"Now do you believe she's a witch?"

Abigail stood there, clutching her challis wrapper around her emaciated body.

Judith thought swiftly, "She shouldn't have seen this," and wondered how she could prevent a scene.

"It's a trick, Mrs. Tomlinson. A sleight-of-hand trick. Thorne's very clever that way."

"It's witchcraft! I saw what she did. *I saw her milk that* cucumber. Roger, go tell your father to come here."

Rodgie, always fearful of his mother's wrath, moved promptly. But Judith's hand stayed him.

"Wait, Roger. Please, Miss Abigail, don't call Mr. Tomlinson. It's nothing to bother him about. I've been watching the children's play. It's only innocent make-believe."

"You saw her get milk from that cucumber after telling the children it was a cow."

"I saw her *pretend* to get milk from the cucumber."

Abigail thrust a finger into the saucer, then licked her finger.

"It's milk! Taste it, if you don't believe me."

"I don't have to taste it. I know it's milk. But it didn't come out of the cucumber."

"Then where did it come from?"

Judith was baffled. For a moment she could neither credit nor deny what her eyes had seen. Again Abigail ordered her son to fetch his father, and Judith watched the child depart, powerless to forestall the thing she had tried so hard to prevent.

All this time Thorne had said not a word. She stood a little apart from the others, her hands behind her back.

Judith turned on her with crisp schoolroom authority.

"Come, Thorne, show us how you played that trick."

She retrieved the toothpicks from the china saucer and stuck the legs back on the cucumber. But it was soft with much handling and immediately collapsed.

"Flossie can't stand up," said Ricky. "She's dead."

"Nonsense!" Judith spoke sharply to Thorne. "Make the cow stand up."

"I can't," whispered Thorne. It was plain she was frightened half out of her senses.

"Of course you can," said Judith. "You made the cow perform once. You can do it again. We all know it's just a trick. We want you to show us how it's done."

But Thorne's fear of Abigail had frozen her. She seemed unable to move or speak.

Abigail said, "She won't do it again because Richard's coming. She doesn't want him to know what devil's games she's been playing with his children. But Richard will know. Because she can't lie out of it this time. It won't be her word against mine. Nobody can say I was having hysterics this time. Because you saw it too, Miss Judith."

As her voice rose shrilly the hall door opened and Richard stood there. His glance swept the circle of frightened faces and came back to his wife.

"What's the matter, Abigail?"

"Maybe you'll believe me now, Richard. Maybe you'll believe this girl is a witch." Abigail pointed vindictively to Thorne.

"What are you talking about?"

"She made a cow out of a cucumber and *milked it* right in front of our eyes. If you think I'm crazy, ask Miss Judith. *She's* not your wife. *She* has no grudge against your little pet. Ask Miss Judith whether or not I'm telling the truth."

It was ghastly, indecent, the way the woman's voice rose higher and higher, screaming her senseless jealousy to all the house. Judith burned with vicarious humiliation for the man who stood so quietly under his wife's tongue.

He asked Thorne gravely, "Have you been playing tricks again, Cricket?"

His own youngsters clamored to testify. The six-year-old said, "She milked the cow, Father. We saw it." And the five-year-old, who had followed close on his father's heels, added, "When the cow died, no more milk would come."

Still Thorne would not speak. She looked at Richard silently, desperate appeal in her eyes.

He sat down at the table and drew her to him.

"Now, Thorne, I want you to make me a cow just as you did for the children. See, here's the cucumber and the potato. We'll put them together with these toothpicks. And then you'll show me how to milk her. Don't be afraid. No one's going to scold you. I just want to see how it's done."

What might have happened if a door had not opened: whether Thorne, in the protecting circle of Richard's arm, might have demonstrated the simple legerdemain, will never be known. For Jesse Moffat, coming in from the barn with the nightly basket of apples, made the announcement that he had just come across Henry Schook's cow lying dead in the pasture.

"Hadn't been dead long, either. Musta had poisonweed in her stomach when she come here. Why—what's the matter?" He stared blankly at the shocked faces about him.

Richard was on his feet as if bracing himself for an expected blow.

71 ৪�

Abigail was screaming, "Now will you believe me? Now will you send that little witch away before she kills us all?"

"Abigail, will you be quiet?"

But the hysterical woman could not be quieted.

She turned on the startled farm hand. "Henry Schook's cow never died from poisonweed. She died from witchcraft, and there's the witch who killed her!" She pointed to the white-faced girl.

"No, no! I didn't kill the cow." Thorne looked at Richard frantically. "You don't believe I killed the cow, do you?"

"Certainly not. How could you kill anything by sticking toothpicks in a cucumber? Come, Abigail, you know you don't believe any such nonsense. You're just working yourself into a nervous spell."

Richard put his arm about his wife to lead her back to her room, but she pushed him away.

"You think I'm crazy! But ask Miss Judith. She saw that girl get milk from that thing she made. How did she do it, if poor Flossie wasn't bewitched?"

It seemed to Judith that the room was suddenly filled with people. Through the open hall door she saw the faces of Lucius Goff and Doc Baird and the schoolmaster. And in the doorway of the covered passage peered the round black face of Millie over the shoulder of Ann Tomlinson. Abigail's screams had penetrated the far corners of the house.

Judith said to Richard, "I saw Thorne milk the cucumber cow. But I've seen similar tricks before. It was just a piece of parlor magic. Of course it had nothing to do with the death of anyone's cow. But if Thorne would perform the trick again and show us how it was done, I think Mrs. Tomlinson would feel better."

Thorne was unable to perform the trick again. Even with Richard putting the cow together and making it stand, she could not draw milk. She was too nervous. Her hands shook so that she could only fumble and murmur frantically, "I can't, I can't."

"You see?" cried Abigail. "She drew the life from Flossie when she milked that toy. Now her victim's dead, she can't do anything with her witch doll."

At the word "doll" Thorne's eyes turned fearfully to the chair behind Abigail. Judith's eyes followed their glance. On the chair lay the rag doll Thorne had brought to Rodgie. All she had ever read on the subject of witchcraft warned Judith that Abigail in her present state must not see that doll.

"That's the way witches work," Abigail was saying. "They make dolls to represent their victims. Then they work their evil charms on the doll until their victim dies. Ask Millie. She knows."

But Millie had vanished. Doubtless she had been the source of much of the invalid's information.

Other eyes than Judith's had followed Thorne's glance. Other minds had telegraphed alarm. Lucius Goff signaled Richard, and Richard tried to draw his wife toward the door. But Abigail, faint now from long standing, pushed him away and sank down upon the very chair that held the doll. She felt the lump beneath her and pulled it forth. When she saw what it was her face turned the color of death.

For seconds it seemed that no one breathed while the sick woman examined the doll.

"My clothes," she muttered.

The scrap of challis was a piece of the material from the wrapper Abigail was wearing.

"My hair."

No one else in the Tomlinson household had auburn hair.

"She has made a doll to look like me. And she has stuck pins straight into its body."

The unfinished dress was indeed pinned fast to the cotton torso.

"She's killing me, Richard, as she killed the cow."

Abigail looked up at her husband, and whether lucid or insane, there was no doubt she believed her own words.

"Abigail, you are beside yourself."

"Oh no, I have witnesses." Her voice was faint now from exhaustion. "All these people see this doll with the pins stuck in its body. They have seen this girl kill a cow by sticking toothpicks in a cucumber. Unless you send her away, Richard, I shall die. Just as surely as Henry Schook's cow died."

Long afterward that thin voice came back like an eerie echo to every ear on which it fell that night. *I shall die, Richard, unless you send her away.* But at the moment no one attached any significance to the words except the obvious one; Abigail had worked herself into a dangerous state.

"We must get her to bed," said Ann Tomlinson, and Richard lifted his wife in his arms. But she fought and struggled, screaming, "I won't go to bed till you send that girl away," till in the end Doc Baird had to help him carry a woman who weighed less than a hundred pounds.

It was a frightening, humiliating scene. The people left in the dining room avoided each other's eyes.

Lucius Goff offered to go for the doctor and on receiving a nod from Miss Ann departed with John Barclay. Miss Ann started to the bedroom, then paused to regard the frightened huddle of children, as though wondering what to do with them.

"I'll put them to bed," said Judith, and Ann Tomlinson hurried away.

But left alone with the children, Judith faced a delicate problem. Against one of these children a distraught woman was screaming two doors away. Was it wise to put Thorne to bed in this house?

"Are the Mitchells coming for you, Thorne?"

The girl shook her head. "They're spending the night with Mr. Alec's folks."

"She's sleeping here tonight," said Ricky. And Rodgie added, "Gran'ma said so." That settled it.

Ordinarily Thorne slept in the trundle bed when the spare

room was occupied, but under the circumstances it seemed wiser to remove her as far as possible from Abigail's proximity. So Judith led all three children upstairs and told Thorne to go into her room while she put the little boys to bed in their grandmother's room.

But when she returned a little later she found Thorne standing at the top of the stairs, listening for some sound from below. When Judith spoke to her she started nervously.

"Is Richard going to send me away?" she whispered.

Judith led the little girl into her own room and closed the door.

"I don't know what Mr. Tomlinson plans to do," she said gravely, "but his wife is very sick, and those tricks you play frighten her. It is wrong to frighten people, Thorne."

Into Thorne's young face, still pale with alarm, crept a gleam of wisdom older than time.

"She's not afraid—really. She just doesn't like me. She wants Richard to send me away. If he doesn't do it she'll probably die just to prove I'm a witch."

Judith struggled between a desire to laugh and a tingling sense of foreboding. There was a fey quality about this child.

"People don't die just to prove a point," she said dryly. "Come, let me unbutton your dress. It's too cold to stand around without a fire. You must get to bed."

As the close-fitting sleeves of her dress were pulled down over Thorne's arms something dropped from one tight-clenched hand. Swift as a hummingbird, she swooped to retrieve it. But Judith's hand was quicker.

"Thorne! You foolish child."

The object picked up from the carpet was a tiny squirt gun.

"Why didn't you show this to us down in the dining room?"

Thorne went on undressing. Judith began to get rather cross with her.

"A very clever trick, I'll admit. But it was wrong not to explain when you saw that people were frightened. Who taught you the art of legerdemain?"

But Thorne had nothing to say. She undressed in stubborn silence and climbed into bed.

Judith looked at her thoughtfully before blowing out the candle. She lay in a little huddle, her face buried in the pillow. Perhaps she was crying.

"Don't worry, Thorne. Go on to sleep. I'll explain everything to Mr. Tomlinson."

There was no sound from the little heap under the bedclothes. She was a strange child.

Judith blew out the light and went quietly back downstairs.

CHAPTER 7

A strange hat on the hall table indicated that the doctor had arrived. Hushed stillness behind the closed door of the sickroom warned that the patient had been given a sedative and was not to be disturbed. Judith went back to the dining room.

The rag doll, cause of so much disturbance, lay on the floor where Abigail had dropped it. Judith's immediate impulse was to get rid of it. She would put it in the kitchen stove and burn it up.

As she entered the covered passage she heard voices in the kitchen. Will Tomlinson, returned from his evening's courting, was listening to Jesse Moffat's account of the recent excitement.

"Me—I don't believe in witches—leastways not since I joined the church. But Henry Schook's cow is dead, no two ways about it. You can't blame Miss Abby for throwing a fit.

She and the schoolma'am both saw Thorne get milk from that thing she made out of a cucumber. Millie saw it, too, didn't you, Millie?"

"Yassuh, Mistah Will, I seen it with my own eyes."

Will Tomlinson's answer was a laugh.

"Don't let nobody tell you there ain't no such thing as witches, Mistah Will. They's witches in the Bible."

"I'm sure there are witches, Millie. And I think one of them has bewitched my worthy brother."

Judith slipped quietly away. This did not seem a propitious time for burning the doll in the kitchen fire.

She went back upstairs to her own unlighted bedroom. Thorne's regular breathing told that she slept. Groping in the dark, Judith opened the drawer of her bureau and stuffed the doll far back beneath a pile of underclothing.

When she came downstairs again the doctor's hat was gone and from the front room came the sound of voices.

"I'll not send her to Belcher's, Mother. All they want her for is a servant. Before I'll see Thorne turned into a kitchen slavey——"

"You'd let your wife die, Richard?"

"Abigail won't die."

"You heard what Dr. Caxton said."

"He said there was nothing the matter with her physically."

"He said if there was anything to be done to ease her mind he advised doing it without delay."

There was silence, while Judith waited, breathless, for the man's voice again.

When it came it sounded hopeless.

"If only Thorne could stay with Jane and Alec this winter. By spring Abigail will surely be better."

"Jane's baby comes in February," said his mother. "Ollie Tucker is going to stay with her and look after things. There'll be no room in the cottage for Thorne when Ollie comes."

"No, I suppose not." There was a heavy sigh.

"And you know how it is with Kate. Living with Hugh's people, she hasn't much to say about things. So it seems to me, Richard, that if these Belchers will give Thorne a home you'd better think twice before turning their offer down."

There was a light footfall: the sound of a door closing. Ann Tomlinson had gone back into the sickroom.

Judith waited a moment before opening the door.

Richard sat by the fire, his tall body slumped in utter dejection. He started to rise, but Judith stopped him.

"Please sit still, Mr. Tomlinson. I know you're tired."

"Not particularly." He smiled, but it was a forlorn effort. "Won't you sit down, Miss Judith?"

She took the chair his mother had vacated. "I came down to show you something. I thought you might be interested in knowing how Thorne performed the trick of milking the cow." And she laid the tiny squirt gun in his hand.

She had expected an immediate lightening of his gloom. But he only said, "I knew it was something like this. I brought the children one of those prize packages from Terre Haute. This toy was in it, probably," and dropped the trinket into his pocket.

But Judith pursued the subject.

"I can't understand why Thorne didn't reveal her trick down in the dining room."

"I can understand," said Richard, but he did not explain himself.

"Of course, she was badly frightened," Judith went on.

He flushed darkly. "She has lived in fear ever since she came here. This is not a pleasant thing to say, Miss Judith, but I honestly believe that if my wife were allowed to whip Thorne she would half kill her."

Judith shared his belief. But she said tactfully, "Your wife is ill, Mr. Tomlinson."

"The doctor can find nothing wrong with her."

"Not with her body, perhaps. But in her state of mind it is

impossible to reason with her. She has fixed on Thorne as the source of her distress because the girl, unluckily, came into the family about the time her nerves began to give way. Of course, getting rid of Thorne would be a temporary expedient. But if she were removed your wife's imagination would soon go to work on someone else."

"You really think so?" Richard was listening with keen attention.

"Certainly. It might be your mother—or one of your sisters —anyone for whom you have affection. Because she wants you all to herself. I overheard your mother talking just now. She seems to think there'll be no peace until Thorne is sent away. In my opinion there'll be no peace until you call your wife's bluff."

Judith stopped, a little startled at her own temerity. But she was not sorry she had spoken. Richard Tomlinson had risen to his feet like a man renewed.

"By calling her bluff, do you mean that I should keep Thorne here?"

"That's exactly what I mean," said Judith. "Your wife doesn't really believe that child a witch. She's an intelligent woman, but she's also hysterical. She saw a chance tonight to take advantage of you before your friends. I think you'd be very unwise to yield to her. She'll never get well as long as she can coerce you."

Richard drew a long breath of release.

"Miss Judith, you don't know—I can't tell you—I was at the end of my tether—family, friends, doctor—everyone seemed to think my wife's condition demanded that I take the step that——" He stopped in his stammering speech and looked straight into Judith's eyes. "I'd rather cut off my arm than send that child to Belcher's. They're a bad lot."

Judith was strangely moved. Not by any compassion for a homeless girl, but by the depth of a man's nature unconsciously revealed.

"I think you are the kindest-hearted person I ever knew," she said.

He seemed surprised. "Oh no. It's not kindness. It's just that—no one seems to understand how I feel about Thorne."

He leaned on the mantel, staring moodily down into the fire. And Judith waited curiously, hoping to hear how these two had come together. She was quite sure he had not fished Thorne out of a flooded creek.

When he began to talk it was to tell her what she had already half guessed. He had brought the child home from the Bridgeton fair.

He had gone to the fair that morning still smarting from a scene with Abigail. She had learned from some source (her cousin, Otis Huse, no doubt) that Richard had sat in on a game of cards one night at Stickney's drugstore. Abigail had walked the floor half the night in consequence. For now Richard would surely go to hell.

Instead he went to the fair.

It was about noon when he found himself standing in the crowd about Cheap John's wagon, listening to the familiar harangue which had fascinated him since boyhood.

> "Wade and Butcher on the blade,
> Wade and Butcher it was made,
> Wade and Butcher on the case,
> But it will not butcher on your face."

The spieler was a little red-haired Jew who had been hawking his merchandise at county fairs so long that he knew his customers by name.

"What am I offered for this fine new razor? Ten cents? Shame on you, Willie Hicks. What do you want with a razor anyway? You've got nothing to shave. Who'll give me a dollar for this Wade and Butcher razor? If I never see the back of my neck, I won't take a penny less. You, Pap, you with the beard! Tell you what I'll do. I'll put in this bright shiny new saucepan for Ma. Now then, who'll give me a dollar for the razor and the pan? The gentleman in the felt hat, did you raise your hand, sir? If I never see the back of my neck, I'm losing money! But here's what I'll do. See this paper of pins? Hard to get these days. Now watch! I take the razor, the pins, and two sticks of horehound candy—and I put them in the pan. Now who'll give me a dollar for the lot?"

Richard raised his hand to brush away a fly, and Cheap John shouted:

"Sold! To Mr. Richard Tomlinson. And if I never see the back of my neck, sir, you've got a bargain."

Richard good-naturedly paid for the merchandise he had not wanted and then wondered what to do with it. It would never do to take his purchases home with him. They were incriminating evidence that he had been to the fair.

In the next wagon, under a weather-stained marquee flaunting the talents of Thorndyke, the Magician, a small girl dressed as a page boy was assisting a shabby prestidigitator. She stood at the edge of the platform made by dropping the end of the wagon, and during lulls in her own performance watched with childish interest the antics of Cheap John. She was thin, starved-looking, and dirty in spite of her tawdry finery, but there was a saucy gallantry in her small figure and a pixie quality in her smile that caused Richard impulsively to thrust his purchases into her hands.

Sometime later he was eating his dinner at one of the bare pine tables in the fry tent, when someone touched his arm. It was the magician's youthful assistant. She had removed the tights and page boy's doublet, but she was even less conventional-looking in a brief and very soiled calico apron. Her hair was an uncombed tangle. Her fingernails were in mourning. But she had the poise of a princess in disguise.

"I thought you might need this more than I do," she said,

and handed him the razor. Her pixie smile twinkled mischievously and they both laughed.

"I want to thank you for the presents," she said politely.

"Oh, you're quite welcome," said Richard, charmed by her quaint manner.

"People often throw things on the stage when they like the act," she explained, "but not candy. It was very good candy." She said this earnestly, her eyes fixed upon his well-filled plate.

Suddenly he realized that she was hungry.

"Won't you join me for dinner?" he asked, as courteously as though she were twice his age instead of half.

"Thank you. I don't care if I do." And slipping into the chair beside him with a nonchalance that was both humorous and pathetic, she dropped her adult manner and fell upon the plate of food set before her as voraciously as a hound puppy.

He watched her as she ate. It was impossible to guess her age. She might have been older or younger than she looked. In spite of a coltish thinness, she was exquisitely molded. Her dirty little face was lovely in its structure. A dimple at the corner of her mouth gave that pixie quality to her smile; but the line of her chin, the tilt of her nose, and the curve of brow and temple held promise of beauty to come.

But Richard saw nothing of that. He saw only a scrap of a girl bolting her food like a starved animal, and the sight made him indignant.

"How old are you?"

"I don't know."

"Don't know?"

"I've been ten years old on the handbills now for two seasons. And I seem to remember being nine for quite a while. It's my private belief I'm past twelve." She winked at him merrily over the rim of her mug as she drained the last drop of milk.

Then she pushed back her plate with a sigh of repletion.

"I hope my appetite didn't shock you. This is the first time I've eaten today."

"What!"

"I'm being disciplined, you know."

"For what?"

"Cutting a show yesterday. It was so hot I went swimming in the pond. I didn't get back in time."

Richard's indignation boiled. Any man who would force a growing child to stand for hours without food in her stomach should be tarred and feathered.

"It's a wonder you didn't faint."

"I did. But it didn't do any good. Pete saw I was faking."

"Is Pete your father?"

She gave him a withering glance. "Do I look like I belonged to that tramp? My father was an artist. And my mother was a lady."

It might have been idle boasting, but Richard preferred to believe it. There was breeding in every line of her fragile body.

"Where are your parents?"

"Dead. My father had a beautiful act. Played nothing but theaters. Pete worked for him and after he died stole his props, his act, even his name."

"Pete is the magician, Thorndyke?"

She nodded scornfully. "But his name isn't Thorndyke. It's McGraw."

"And what's your name?"

"My father called me Thorne, just to round out the act. But his name wasn't Thorndyke really. I don't know what it was."

A nameless waif, that was all. With an intrepid spirit and a dangerous promise of beauty to come. He wondered with queer anxiety what would become of her.

"Is Pete good to you?"

"He is when he's not drunk. But he gets drunk every night."

83 ৡঌ

"Why do you stay with such a man? Why don't you run away?"

She demanded practically, "Where to?"

"Surely there are kind people who would give a little girl like you a home."

"Name one," was the shrewd rejoinder.

Richard was silent.

When they came out of the fry tent he asked if there was anything else she would like and she promptly replied, "Yes. I want to ride on the merry-go-round." She had been at the fair a week and watched other children ride the fascinating ring, but not once had she set foot in one of the gilded chariots.

Richard bought a sheaf of tickets, and the two of them climbed aboard. For the first trip she kept her eyes fixed on the man in the center who rode round and round the central pole on a big white horse, propelling the carrousel. But after that her dizziness subsided and she was able to watch the revolving landscape about her. She did not talk; the music of the calliope drowned conversation. But she smiled at Richard from time to time and gave him moist, friendly pressures of the hand.

When their tickets were all used up she confessed she had had enough.

"If I go again I'll lose my dinner, and I can't afford to do that."

They played chuck-a-luck. They lost fifty cents on the shell game. They watched half a dozen men and boys try to catch the greased pig. They consumed quantities of molasses taffy and popcorn and pink lemonade. They finished off the afternoon at the races.

"I hope you won't be late again for your show," Richard said dubiously when this last jaunt was proposed.

"I might as well be killed for a sheep as a lamb," was the philosophical retort.

It was late afternoon when they parted in front of the hokey-pokey stand. He told her simply and honestly that he had never had such a good time in his life.

"Me too, I've had a swell time," she mumbled, her mouth too full for articulation. "Good-by." And she was gone, leaving him suddenly conscious of being alone.

It was late when he turned homeward. The various shows and concessions were being dismantled, for it was the last day of the fair and a storm was brewing. He mounted his horse and rode slowly around the edge of the crowd milling toward the gates.

As he passed the magician's wagon he caught the sound of blows and sobbing. He spurred his horse around behind the wagon and in another moment he was on the ground, grappling with a total stranger. Never had Pete McGraw received such a thrashing as the one that descended on him from the fists of a man he had never seen before in his life.

"If you lay a hand on her again I'll break every bone in your body!"

The luckless prestidigitator struggled to his feet and spat out teeth.

"I'll learn her to cut shows," he muttered, and then demanded not unreasonably, "What the hell's it your business?"

"If you lost money by her absence this afternoon I'll settle it. How much does she owe you?"

A crafty gleam lighted Pete's unclosed eye. "You mean for cutting *this* show?"

Suddenly Richard knew the child could never go back to this man.

"For cutting all your shows for the rest of her life. I'm taking her home with me."

There was a slight business transaction then, consisting of the transfer of all Richard's available cash to Pete's pocket. Truth to tell, the man was glad to be rid of the girl. He had always feared that when she grew older she would claim her father's properties and oust him from the act, for she was far cleverer than he. Now he was sole proprietor of Thorndyke, the Magician.

As Richard rode home with the child behind him, his mind struggled with the problem of how best to report his rash act to Abigail. He explained to Thorne that his wife did not approve of shows and play acting and it might be better not to mention her connection with them. The threatened storm caught them before they reached home. When they came to Little Raccoon they found the bridge out and were compelled to ford the swollen stream. This gave Thorne an idea. The story of the wreck of a covered wagon and rescue of its sole survivor was a product of her creative genius. And its recital was proof of Richard Tomlinson's histrionic ability.

To their joint relief the story was accepted, and from that day to this neither Richard nor Thorne had divulged the truth about her background.

When he had finished the story Judith said, "You'd never forgive yourself, Mr. Tomlinson, if you sent that child away."

The look he gave her was eloquent assurance that she had said what he wanted to hear.

"I think, though, your wife should be told the truth," Judith went on. "If she knew Thorne's early history it might put an end to talk about witches. I wish you'd let me tell this to her. Maybe I could convince her she has nothing to fear."

He said eagerly, "Do you think you could?"

"I could try," said Judith, and rose to say good night.

Impulsively he put out his hand and clasped hers.

"I don't know how to thank you, Judith."

They stood for a moment in silence, hand clasping hand.

Then very gently she withdrew her hand and said good night and went out and closed the door. But her heart beat fast as she climbed the stairs. For he had held her hand. And he had called her Judith, without the "Miss."

CHAPTER 8

Jesse Moffat's tongue could not be bridled. Before sundown of the next day every man, woman, and child from Timberley to Woodridge had heard of the mysterious death of Henry Schook's cow and how Thorne Tomlinson had drawn milk from a cucumber named Flossie. They had learned about a doll she had made and dressed in a scrap of Abigail Tomlinson's wrapper. They heard how the sick woman had been seized with a violent illness when she discovered pins stuck into the doll's body.

By nightfall Saturday, it was being openly talked in the public square at Woodridge that Richard Tomlinson's wife was dying of witchcraft practiced by the elfin foundling whom he had brought into his home.

Mitch Rucker, a distant cousin of the Tomlinsons, stood on the very steps of the academy and related to all who would listen how he had told his cousin Richard time and again that there was something queer about that child and he'd better get rid of her. Mitch Rucker's words carried weight because he was a war veteran and had been at Appomattox. To be sure, he had done little since except stand around and talk (he found it uncomfortable to sit down), telling over and over how he had driven an ammunition wagon for four years and never got a scratch until the very last day of the fighting. But he was a hero for all that, and when he declared his belief that the girl at Timberley was a witch his words carried the ring of authority.

They also carried to the ears of the schoolmaster. John Barclay, usually the mildest of men, exploded when he heard Mitch Rucker's talk.

87 ॐ

"I forbid you to repeat such malicious gossip."

"You forbid? Since when does a schoolmaster decide what fighting men shall think?"

"I'm not deciding. I'm merely asking that you *do* think and stop spreading fantastic lies. I was at Timberley last night. I happen to know there's not a word of truth in this wild tale that's going about."

"Henry Schook's cow died, didn't she?"

"Yes, but——"

"And that girl got milk from a cucumber."

"She played a trick—a sleight-of-hand trick. It had nothing to do with Schook's cow. Use your head, Mitch. You're not superstitious, I hope."

Mitch Rucker's retort became a classic: "I went through four years of fighting without getting a scratch, without eating anything stronger than mule meat. And then, by golly, on the last day I got a bullet in my behind. And you ask me if I'm superstitious!"

The talk reached Lucius Goff as he was boarding the evening train for Terre Haute. Bombarded with queries about alleged table tipping, he airily equivocated:

"Nothing to it. We played and sang and pulled a few tricks of parlor magic which frightened Mrs. Tomlinson. I know nothing about anybody's cow."

Dr. Caxton, assailed by direct questioning, bluntly told people to mind their own business. He admitted having been called to treat Abigail Tomlinson. She had had a nervous spell but otherwise was in sound health. He disclaimed any knowledge of dead cows or childish pranks. He professed total ignorance on the subject of cucumbers stuck with toothpicks, or dolls stuck with pins. At mention of witchcraft he snorted, blew his nose, and said, "Damnation!"

When the story came to the blacksmith shop it was greeted with stolid silence. Not until late afternoon, when a red-whiskered man strode into the shop, did Doc Baird lay down his tools and give heed to a questioner. For the man was Otis Huse, a lawyer and near relative of Abigail Tomlinson. He could cause Richard trouble if he had a mind. So for his friend's sake Doc Baird gave a brief account of the occurrences at Timberley the night before.

"All this talk can be laid to Jesse Moffat. Jesse is a stupid fellow and likes to feel important. Children's pranks and a cow dropping dead made a good yarn. So he lost no time in spreading it."

"What about my cousin's strange seizure?"

"Your cousin, Mr. Huse, has been having strange seizures ever since I've known her," said Doc calmly. "If there's any persecution going on at Timberley, it's Richard, not his wife, who's the victim."

He regretted afterward that he had let his feeling get the better of him. For Huse's sandy face flushed ominously, and he left the shop without another word. Doc watched from his doorway and saw him turn into the parsonage of the Methodist Church.

The minister, an easygoing, kindly gentleman (admittedly not much of a preacher), listened while his visitor talked. He had heard about the gossip that was sweeping the town but had decided to ignore it. Upon Otis Huse's sharp insistence that there was more to it than gossip, he said mildly:

"Surely, Mr. Huse, a man of your mental caliber puts no credence in witchcraft."

"I'm not talking about witchcraft. I'm talking about the situation at Tomlinson's. I think you, Brother Jameson, as pastor of the church, ought to do something about it."

Mr. Jameson sighed. People were always asking him to meddle in other people's business.

"What can I do, Mr. Huse?"

"You can find a home for that girl Tomlinson insisted on taking into his family."

"That's easier said than done."

"Doesn't the church help support an orphanage near Green-castle? I seem to recall being asked to contribute to it."

There was such a place. The minister had once talked to Mr. Tomlinson about the orphanage. He had been opposed to sending the little girl there.

"It's your duty to talk to him again," said the lawyer harshly. "I'm convinced my cousin will never be well as long as that girl is in the house."

Mr. Jameson made no promises, but the next morning at the preaching service he looked expectantly toward the Tomlinson pew. Neither Richard, his wife, nor his mother was present. There were only young Will Tomlinson and the three children, besides the schoolteacher who was their boarder.

Mr. Jameson purposed to speak to Will Tomlinson after church, but before he could reach him the young man was out of the building. When the minister finally made his hand-shaking way to the door, only the schoolteacher was in sight. She had come back for a reticule left in the pew.

"Miss Amory—if you please—just a moment——"

"Oh, good morning, Mr. Jameson. You'll pardon my haste. The others are waiting for me in the surrey."

"I wanted to inquire about Miss Abigail. How is she?"

"Too ill to come out this morning, Mr. Jameson."

"Is it anything serious?"

For a moment the minister saw—or fancied he saw—a look of guilt in the young woman's eyes. And then it was gone and her gaze was clear and candid.

"We hope not, Mr. Jameson, though we're all worried about her."

He expressed his sympathy and concern and said that he would be out to see her. Miss Amory thanked him and said that she was sure a visit from her pastor would do Mrs. Tomlinson good.

The minister watched with curious interest the trim figure of the schoolmistress as she crossed the church lawn and climbed into the Tomlinson buggy. There was an odd exuberance in her walk, a touch of proprietorship in the way she took her place on the back seat with Richard's children. The little girl who was the subject of all this controversy was on the front seat with young Will.

And then Mr. Jameson realized that other people were waiting to shake his hand. He was forced to put the Tomlinsons out of his mind.

CHAPTER 9

The Christmas season was upon them. Under ordinary circumstances the house would have been filled with company and much time and thought devoted to the festivities for which Timberley was noted. But this year there were neither guests nor merrymakings.

Judith, with the help of young Will, arranged a tree at the schoolhouse to which all the neighborhood flocked, bringing gifts for each other to hang upon its branches. There was also a larger tree at the church in Woodridge on Christmas night. Again it was Judith and Will Tomlinson, in company with the Turners and Mitchells, who took the children to see Santa Claus. He came in through the basement (on account of the stovepipe) and bore a remarkable resemblance to Jesse Moffat.

But at Timberley there was neither tree nor Santa Claus. There was only the abundant feast-day dinner, for which the weary, sorely tried family had little appetite and of which Abigail refused to partake.

From the moment of her alarm on that fateful Friday evening she had failed rapidly. For Richard still refused to send

Thorne away. And Judith continued to support him in the stand he was taking.

"If you give in to her now you will be a slave for the rest of your life. There is no tyranny like that of the chronic invalid. When your wife realizes you can't be coerced she'll begin eating again and get well."

"You don't think she's in any real danger?" He asked this question repeatedly. Judith always reassured him.

Once he told her, "I feel as if you were the only friend I had left."

His entire family—mother, brother, sisters, and brothers-in-law—were beginning to urge him to get rid of the child who seemed, by some strange alchemy, to be responsible for his wife's condition. Judith alone upheld him in his determination.

"I don't know what I'd do without you," he said.

These were precious days to Judith. In a house where gloom and anxiety darkened every face, where laughter was hushed because a woman lay wasting away, the lonely schoolteacher lived in a world of secret happiness. Heretofore Richard Tomlinson had turned, in all the trials of his life, to his mother. Now he turned to a woman he barely knew.

If Ann Tomlinson felt any resentment, she did not show it. She was too generous to feel jealousy, too honestly concerned for her son to add to his distress by any word of her own. She did not understand her daughter-in-law's condition. She accepted the doctor's diagnosis that there was nothing physically wrong with Abigail. But Miss Ann had seen too many people die not to recognize the face of death afar off.

She appealed, in her usual direct manner, to Judith.

"I know you're doing what you think is right, Miss Judith, in befriending a homeless child."

Judith had taken Thorne into her own room since the night she had talked with Richard.

"None of us has any feeling against the girl," Miss Ann

went on, "nor do we begrudge her a home. But under the circumstances, she ought not to be here. You're making it difficult for the rest of us."

"I'm only doing what Mr. Richard asked me to," said Judith.

His mother replied, "But *he* doesn't understand that his wife is dying. You and I do."

The two women looked at each other in silence. Then the eyes of the younger woman fell.

All this time Abigail lay upon her bed, refusing to eat, growing thinner day by day, until it seemed that nothing but the clawlike hands and burning eyes and dark red braids of hair remained of the wasted body under the bed quilts. She was proud of her quilts, some of which were made entirely of silk and satin pieces hoarded for years. They were usually kept in a big oak chest with some of her family heirlooms. But now she had them all brought out and piled upon her bed because she complained of being cold. There was a fire in the room day and night, but the snows of January were now piled thick upon the window ledges, and her starved body was always cold.

The January snows thawed under the first pale suns of February. The false spring froze in the icy blasts of March. But Abigail never rose from her bed after the night Thorne made the cucumber cow.

Some of the family sat in her room all the time. They took turns sitting with Abigail. All except Thorne. Great care was taken that Thorne's face was never glimpsed by the woman lying in the tall oak bed. Thorne was forbidden to pass by the windows on that side of the house. She was made to go round by the road when returning from school, instead of taking the short cut through the lane. Her name was never mentioned. Her presence in the house was tacitly ignored.

But Abigail knew she was there.

Day after day, to each member of the family, she put the question: "She's still here, isn't she?"

Being Tomlinsons, they did not lie. "The child is not bothering you, Abigail. She keeps out of your way."

"She doesn't have to see me to kill me. All she needs do is torture that doll. If she isn't doing things to that doll, why won't she tell you where it is?"

The disappearance of the doll was a mystery. Thorne insisted that she had never seen it since the evening she brought it to Rodgie. The little boys were questioned. A thorough search of the house failed to produce it. But Abigail's imagination licked ceaselessly at the doll as a dog's tongue licks at a sore.

She had other company besides the family: neighbors from the countryside, members of the church where she had once been an active leader, and the minister, Mr. Jameson. As time went on she took a morbid pleasure in having visitors, for to all who came she talked about the doll and how she was dying from witchcraft as Henry Schook's cow had died. It was very embarrassing to the family.

Henry Schook himself came one afternoon, a tall gaunt scarecrow of a man, clean-brushed as though for Sunday, and with him his lean work-worn wife, wearing her best bonnet. The Schooks had had nothing but ill luck since coming into the state, and the loss of their cow was a serious calamity. Privately they were ready to believe that not only Flossie but their whole enterprise was bewitched. But they had heard of Abigail's strange obsession and they had come out of the kindness of their hearts to explain that their cow had undoubtedly eaten poisonweed before coming to the Timberley pasture.

"We lost three cows from it before putting Flossie on your land, Miss Abigail," said Henry Schook. "I said to Marthy then, 'Maybe we can save Flossie.' And she said, 'Provided she ain't already got the weed in her belly.' Those were her very words. Weren't they, Marthy?"

"I said stomach," corrected his spouse. "But the cow had weed sickness on her. That I am sure."

Abigail fixed her hollow eyes on the well-meaning pair and demanded, "How much did my husband pay you for coming over here and telling me this tale?"

The Schooks were hurt and embarrassed. They took their departure soon after.

The minister happened to be calling that same afternoon. He had been a witness of the Schooks' kindly effort and dismal failure to relieve Abigail's fear. He appeared to be unmoved by either. He sat silent throughout, watching the school-teacher, who had brought her work downstairs and was grading papers at a small table near the window.

When the other visitors had gone Mr. Jameson said, "I wonder whatever became of that doll Mrs. Tomlinson seems so distressed about?"

The schoolmistress, apparently absorbed in her task, started nervously and dropped a sheaf of papers.

Then she answered coolly enough, "I'm sure I don't know, Mr. Jameson," and went on with her work.

But the minister had surprised a look in her eyes he had seen there once before.

Abigail had days when her flickering strength revived and she would ask to be propped up in bed and given her piece-work. This was her favorite employment and consisted in cutting out quilt pieces with a pair of very sharp scissors. She found the same enjoyment in slicing odd shapes from a scrap of cloth that a child finds in cutting out paper dolls. She liked to display her skill in this handiwork to Judith.

The schoolteacher was still her choice of companions. She no longer looked upon her as an ally against Thorne, for nothing escaped her eyes and ears, and she knew that Judith was upholding Richard in his stand. But she derived a perverse satisfaction from discussing with the schoolmistress the inevitability of her own death.

"I'm dying. You know I'm dying," she would say, grimly

triumphant, almost as though she were willing to die to prove her point. "I'm worse than I was yesterday. You can't deny it."

Judith would answer dogmatically, "If you persist in thinking you are worse you create conditions for it. Have you forgotten what I read to you yesterday?"

With Richard's permission she was reading to Abigail from the books in her father's trunk, in the hope that the invalid might be made to understand the power of mental suggestion.

"You read me the book on black magic yesterday."

"To show you how the victim's mind can trick him into anything."

"Do you think my mind can trick me into thinking I'm choking?"

This choking sensation was Abigail's latest symptom. It dated from one afternoon when Judith had described rather vividly the sufferings of a woman she had once known who was dying of a malignant throat ailment.

"Certainly your mind can trick you. There's nothing wrong with your throat."

"I'm having the same symptoms that woman had."

"Of course you are. I tried that story out on you just to see how impressionable you were. This proves it's all in your mind. Because you never had those symptoms until I told you how that woman complained of a sensation like a string around her throat choking her to death."

Abigail's eyes grew cunning. "I'll bet if we could find that doll we'd find a string tied round its neck so tight it's choking me."

Judith said, "That's just another symptom of hysteria," and smiled almost complacently.

"You think I'm crazy," said Abigail, "but you'll see. Wait till she begins practicing her tricks on you."

When her listener refused to snap at this bait she went on:

"You're befriending her because you want to please Richard. But the time will come when you'll hate her—just as I do."

A sharp slash of the scissors punctuated every phrase. "Then you'll try to get rid of her—as I did. And she'll put a hex on you. You'll begin choking and dying, just as I'm choking and dying, because she won't let you breathe."

The failing voice was indescribably eerie. Judith said firmly, "I'm not going to read to you any more," and she talked persistently of cheerful things.

But at night, in her bed, she would remember the words of the dying woman and she would be acutely conscious of the little girl sleeping beside her. It was a huge bed; the feather mattress made billowy hills between the two sleepers, so that neither touched the other. Yet she found it increasingly difficult to sleep because of Thorne's presence in the bed.

This was due to her lifelong habit of sleeping alone, undoubtedly. It was in no wise the result of Abigail's direful croakings. But she began wishing some circumstance might arise to relieve her of her strange bedfellow.

It came one night unexpectedly.

The children were in the habit of undressing by the downstairs fire because the upper rooms were unheated. One night when the two little boys had already scampered upstairs with their grandmother, Richard came from the sickroom to find Thorne, in her flannel nightgown, huddled on the living-room hearth. When he told her she'd better get to bed before she caught cold she surprised him by asking if she could sleep downstairs in the trundle bed.

"Why do you want to sleep down here, Cricket?"

She had always complained that the trundle bed was too short for her.

But when urged to give a reason for changing, she said she'd rather sleep on the floor than spend another night with Miss Judith.

"Why, Thorne! Aren't you ashamed?" Richard was so astonished that he was rather short with her. "When Miss Judith has been so kind to you!"

"It's not me, Richard. It's her. She doesn't like sleeping with me."

"Did she say so?"

"No. But I can tell."

Richard sighed. He was very tired. "You're entirely too sensitive, Thorne. Miss Judith is the only friend you have in this house."

Thorne's eyes flashed through sudden tears. "She's not my friend. You are. I don't want any friend but you."

Richard, worn to a thin edge, spoke sharply. "If it hadn't been for Miss Judith you'd have been shipped out of here by now. Why should she take your part if she disliked you?"

Ann Tomlinson had come back downstairs. She had heard the colloquy by the fire. She heard her son's question and Thorne's retort, flung back with a childish sob:

"She's trying to get on the good side of you, stupid! That's why."

Richard tossed the whole matter aside with a weary gesture, but his mother said, "Let the child sleep in the trundle bed if she likes," and bustled away to get the bedding.

But once out of the room she stopped still, while a half-formed suspicion in her own mind took root. Thorne had recognized what she herself had feared but refused to acknowledge: that Judith was in love with Richard.

Ann Tomlinson was never a woman to flinch from the truth. But seldom had she faced so unpleasant a truth as the one confronting her now. Judith was encouraging Richard in a course which might very possibly result in his wife's death.

The schoolmistress was in the dining room when Miss Ann came through with an armful of blankets. She was sitting near the lamp with the family darning basket in her lap. No one could deny that she had been most helpful during these trying days.

"I wanted to tell you, Miss Judith, that I'm putting Thorne downstairs tonight in the trundle bed."

Judith looked relieved. "Perhaps that's better. I don't think she rests well with me."

Miss Ann did not comment. She was busy folding a large-size blanket to fit a small-size bed.

Judith went on: "You don't suppose there's any danger of Miss Abigail's finding out how near she is?"

"We'll have to risk it tonight. And after tonight it won't matter." Ann Tomlinson looked straight at the schoolteacher. "Because tomorrow I'm sending Thorne to Kentucky."

There was the strangest silence in the room.

Then Judith said, "Don't you think that's a question for Mr. Tomlinson to decide?"

The tiny gray-haired woman spoke with quiet authority.

"Miss Judith, sometimes we have a mistaken sense of loyalty. You are loyal to Richard because he helped you in the matter of the school. And Richard is loyal to a little girl because he thinks she has no other friend. But both of you overlook the fact that a woman in this house is dying. Abigail's mind may not be right. I don't know. But I do know she'll die if she doesn't get relief from this feeling she has about Thorne. And the only way to relieve her is to send the child away. So I'm sending Thorne to my daughter in Kentucky."

It was a long speech for Miss Ann. She picked up her blankets and went back to the front room.

Judith laid aside the darning basket and went softly upstairs.

Her bedroom was icy, but she felt no chill. Her body burned. She closed the door behind her and turned the key in the lock. Then she lighted a pair of candles on her dresser.

Softly she opened her dresser drawer and groped beneath a pile of underclothing. Her fingers closed upon the rag doll.

CHAPTER 10

She could not have told at the time why she had
concealed it. Why she had kept silent while everything in
the house was searched except the personal belongings of
the schoolmistress.

Now she knew.

*I'll bet if we could find that doll we'd find a string tied
round its neck so tight it's choking me.*

Fingers cold as ice took a velvet ribbon from the box on
the dresser and tied it round the doll's rag throat; tight,
tighter, tighter; until the cotton neck was no bigger than
a slate pencil and the stuffed head lolled foolishly to one
side like a chicken's with its neck wrung but not severed.
The fingers knotted the velvet in a hard double knot and left
two streamers dangling. They were Judith's fingers.

The heat in her body had cooled now. She was so cold
she had no feeling; about anything. She sat with the doll
in her hands and listened.

Footsteps moving up the stairs. Richard's mother coming
up to bed. She had talked with her son. She had told him
she was sending Thorne to Kentucky. He had finally yielded.
The very tap of the shoes upon the bare oak stairs made this
announcement. Ann Tomlinson had settled her household
before coming up to bed.

Judith waited until the footsteps died upon the carpet
of the room across the hall. Then she slipped Thorne's doll
into the pocket of her voluminous skirt and went back
down the stairs.

She found Richard in the dining room. It was exactly as
she had guessed. His mother had told him her decision and

he had made no further protest. He realized at last that his wife would die unless her mind was relieved.

He looked drawn and haggard, utterly without hope. Whether the misery in his eyes was for his wife's condition or for the loss of his little friend, Judith could not tell. But the time was past for encouraging him to hold firm.

"Perhaps I was wrong," she admitted, "in urging you to keep Thorne. But I honestly thought I was helping you."

"You were. You don't know what a help you've been." He looked at her gratefully from hollow, sleep-starved eyes. And then he looked away.

"I'm convinced my wife will die, Miss Judith, if Thorne remains in this house. I don't pretend to understand how such a thing can be. But I have come to believe in witchcraft; the witchcraft of one's own mind."

There was silence between them. Judith's hand clutched something tightly within the folds of her skirt.

She said, "Thorne can come back—afterward——"

"What do you mean—afterward?"

"After your wife has—recovered."

"You think my wife will recover?"

"When the child is gone your wife will begin to eat. When she begins eating she will regain her strength." Unconsciously Judith's voice hardened. "Of course she will always be an invalid. But invalids usually live to a ripe old age."

Perhaps her companion noted the implication in her words, for his denial came swiftly.

"I don't agree with you. I believe my wife's recovery will be complete, once her mind is set at rest." Twin spots of color burned upon his gaunt unshaven cheeks; his hollow eyes flashed fire. Never had he looked less comely; never had he been more desirable to the woman than he was at that moment. For she guessed that he was lying, to himself as well as her. He did not believe his wife would ever be anything but a hopeless burden. He was trying to deny his own protest which he was afraid she might see.

"You need sleep, Mr. Tomlinson. Why don't you go upstairs and get a good night's rest? Let me stay with your wife tonight."

He passed his hand across his eyes, sorely tempted, yet muttering:

"No, no. It's my job. I can't think of putting it on you."

But Judith urged, "Tomorrow's Saturday. I can sleep all day if need be."

After much pleading he yielded, on condition that she call him at midnight. They would divide the watch between them. Abigail had been given some sleeping drops, he said. She would probably sleep for the first part of the night.

Judith waited until his hushed footfall had faded upon the stairs. Then she went noiselessly down the passage to his wife's room. She opened the door without making a sound and closed it in silence behind her. She stood motionless beside the sickbed.

Abigail lay, as Judith had so often seen her, in the attitude of death. The hands folded on her bosom rose and fell with the rhythmic respiration of drugged sleep.

Judith drew the doll from her pocket and laid it on the pillow beside the sleeper.

Then she prepared to wait.

There was a coal fire in the grate and a shaded night lamp on a little table by the easy chair. She sat down in the chair and tucked her cold hands under her shawl to warm them.

There was no sound in the room, not even the comforting tick of a clock. Richard's big gold watch lay beside the medicine chart on the night table, but it told the moments silently. The room was so quiet she could hear Abigail breathe.

In—out. Inhale—exhale. In—out. Inhale—exhale.

Richard had said she might sleep soundly all night.

In—out. Inhale—exhale. In—out. Inhale—exhale.

Judith hugged her cold body closer.

The hands of Richard's watch moved slowly past the half-hour.

There was another sound in the stillness beside Abigail's breathing. It came from beyond the locked door leading to the front room. It was a muffled sound of childish sobbing. She recalled that Thorne was sleeping in the trundle bed.

Strangely, the sound held companionship. She was not alone with that measured breathing.

The hands of the watch moved past the three quarters—the hour—the quarter hour.

The sobbing beyond the door had ceased.

She was alone.

In—out. Inhale—exhale. In—out. Inhale——

She waited for the exhalation, but it did not come.

Abigail was awake.

Judith did not have to move from her chair to see what was happening. She had only to turn her head. The shade of the night lamp cast a shadow that obscured the chair.

But the coal fire shed a glow that illumined the bed.

Abigail had turned toward the fire and was facing the doll on her pillow.

She lay rigid, motionless, eyes fixed and glassy as death. For a moment it seemed as though she had died at a single shock.

Then very slowly she put out a hand and clutched the doll and found it real. A convulsive shudder ran through her body. She opened her mouth to scream. No sound came.

The doll was in her hand. She could not let it go. In fascinated horror she drew it closer, examining it in detail. Its head lolled ludicrously to one side.

And then she saw the velvet ribbon about its neck; tied so tight the rag throat was no bigger than a pencil.

She dropped the doll with a sound of speechless terror and clutched her own throat.

The doll fell noiselessly upon the carpeted floor.

Judith, in the shadow of the night lamp, slid from the high-backed chair onto her hands and knees. Creeping to the side of the tall bed, she stealthily retrieved the doll. Then, still on her hands and knees, she edged over to the closet door and opened it a crack. Her groping hand found a gap between wall and floorboard. She stuffed the doll down this convenient hole.

Abigail, gasping, strangling, choking, writhing upon the bed, could never have seen her.

"Miss Abigail! Miss Abigail! What's the matter?"

But Abigail could not speak. Whether the bulging eyes accused or implored the woman bending solicitously over her no longer mattered. For the sounds that rattled from her throat were unintelligible.

"Oh, my dear, forgive me for going to sleep in my chair. Are you in pain? Tell me, what's the matter? Can't you speak?"

Only inarticulate gurgles of fast-failing breath. Abigail could tell no one anything.

It was perfectly safe to call Richard.

The trundle bed was too short for Thorne. Perhaps that was why she could not go to sleep.

She lay on her back, eyes closed, while tears seeping from under her eyelids trickled into her mouth and ears. For the first time in her life she had gone to bed at odds with Richard. She loved him so completely, so utterly to the exclusion of all else, that the sharp note in his voice had almost broken her heart. He had never spoken like that to her before. And never before had she flared up in anger at him. Her tears were as much for her own anger as for his reproof. She had called him stupid! She had called Richard—darling, darling Richard—a stupid, when he was the only friend she had in the world.

But he was stupid not to see what Miss Judith was up to.

Her sobs came thick and fast. She turned on her face to smother them, shrinking from a fear as yet only half recognized. She cried until, from sheer exhaustion, she fell asleep.

She woke from her first short nap to hear voices somewhere. Lights bobbed fantastically in the hall, and hushed commotion filled the house. From the room beyond the alcove strange noises filtered. In terror Thorne started from her bed.

Chilled hands caught her and put her firmly back. She started to scream, but a cold palm closed over her mouth.

"Don't make any noise." It was Judith. Her voice was colder than her hands.

"What is it?" whispered Thorne fearfully.

"Abigail."

"Is she worse?"

"She's dying."

There was dim light from the hall. Thorne's eyes searched the schoolteacher's face, so strange was the tone of her voice.

"How do you know? Have you been in her room?"

"I sat with her. So Richard could get some sleep."

"Did she have another spell?"

"Yes."

Judith sat down on the side of the bed, her whole body tensed with listening.

There was the sound of hurrying feet, subdued voices that told nothing, strangling gasps from behind the connecting door, the ring of horses' hoofs on the frozen ground outside.

Judith whispered, "The doctor! Will went for Dr. Caxton."

Together they sat and listened to the heavy tread of the doctor's boots, to the one unhushed voice that now dominated everything. They caught fragments of talk beyond the door:

"Membranous croup . . . get kerosene . . . the woman's choking to death . . ."

They heard arguments over the dangers and merits of kerosene and goose grease, with Dr. Caxton shouting down Ann Tomlinson:

"I know it's inflammable, but goose grease won't cut phlegm. Bring me some coal oil, Richard."

They heard feet racing to the kitchen. They heard windows being raised to give the choking woman air. They knew when coal oil was administered. They knew when it failed.

Together they listened, the woman and the child, bound in this moment by some fearful community of interest.

Once Thorne said in sudden panic, "I don't want Miss Abigail to die," as though in strange foreknowledge of the potentialities of the event.

Judith said coldly, "They were going to send you to Kentucky," as though showing cause why some judgment had been pronounced.

The child trembled and involuntarily shrank away from the schoolmistress.

When certain sounds from the other room conveyed a dreadful message to the listening woman she rose and drew the girl swiftly from the trundle bed.

"Come upstairs to my room."

Unquestioning, Thorne obeyed.

It was nearly daylight when Ann Tomlinson came upstairs. She found Judith sitting by the bedside of Richard's sons. The candle had burned low, and its guttering flame threw a queer light on the face bent over the sleeping children. For a moment Miss Ann was stunned by the expression on the schoolteacher's face. Then the flame burned brighter and she saw only a look of compassion. Perhaps that exultant smile was a shadow cast by a smoking wick.

"I knew I couldn't be of any real help downstairs," said

Judith, "and I was afraid the little boys might wake and start looking for you."

Miss Ann nodded silently. She, too, bent over the sleeping children and tenderly touched little Rodgie's curls.

"I'm too old to bring up so young a child. Too old—and too tired."

It was the only time anyone ever heard Ann Tomlinson admit weariness.

Judith whispered, "Is it——" But the words stuck in her throat.

"It's all over," said Miss Ann quietly. "Their mother died at quarter to three."

CHAPTER 11

The funeral of Abigail Tomlinson was an event of widespread interest. Every family in the district was represented. School was closed for three days because Richard was a township trustee.

The services were conducted at the house, with the choir from the Woodridge church singing "Rock of Ages" and "Lead, Kindly Light." Mr. Jameson spoke briefly. Too briefly, in some people's opinion. There was talk afterward about how he "skimped" in his praise of the deceased.

"You'd have thought the woman was alive and well, the way he ignored her."

It was true that the minister had little to say about Abigail except that God had now released her from her sufferings. He spoke with sympathy of the bereaved husband and two small sons. But his real tribute was paid to the small gray-haired woman who sat between Richard and his children, as though gathering all three beneath her wing.

"You who know Mrs. Ann Tomlinson—and who that has had sickness or death or calamity in his house does not know her?—can rest assured that these children are not left without a mother, and this man is not left without as stout a heart as God ever put in a woman's breast to cheer him through his trouble."

There were moist eyes in weather-beaten faces at that. Everyone loved Miss Ann.

Abigail looked surprisingly young in death. The lines which illness had etched upon her face were magically erased. She looked fair and fragile as she lay in her pale gray casket.

This matter of the casket caused comment. It was the first time that anything except black for an adult had ever been seen in the county. Richard had sent to Indianapolis for it, and that in itself lent a kind of glamour to the woman who lay within it. It stood before the drawn curtains of the alcove, facing the clock which no longer told the hours. More than one person remarked afterward that the face of the dead woman was turned slightly toward the clock, as though listening for it to strike.

She was buried in the family burial ground on the hill. Young Will Tomlinson, Mr. Otis Huse, Lucius Goff, and John Barclay carried the casket to its final resting place. The plot already held the graves of Roger Tomlinson, four children who had died in infancy, and Millie's husband.

Abigail died between midnight and dawn of a Friday night. She was not buried until the following Wednesday. During the interim the body lay in the unheated front room and people went about on tiptoe. The house was hushed and its inhabitants lived withdrawn.

Judith found the interval of waiting almost unendurable. She spent most of her time with the children. There was the chance that by keeping close to Richard's sons she might see him more often. But whether purposely or unintentionally, he seemed to avoid her. She saw him only at mealtimes.

A restlessness possessed her. It made it almost impossible for her to stay in the house. It drove her to take long walks with the children. Once out of doors, she talked of anything, everything, except the somber circumstance that was throwing them so much together. She told them stories, even jokes of a subdued nature, and was altogether so pleasant a companion that the little boys clamored to be with her. They were awed but not saddened by their mother's death. Abigail had been merely a disquieting presence in their lives too long for them to feel any great sense of loss. So while they behaved with gloomy propriety within the house, once out of doors their walks with Judith became increasingly pleasant excursions.

Thus it was with Richard's sons. Not so with Thorne. Thorne, who of all people should have felt no loss in Abigail, was silent, grave, and thoughtful.

Judith became exasperated with her.

Finally she took her to task.

It was the day before the funeral and Judith, knowing the ordeal in store for them, was anxious to give the little boys a pleasant time. She had taken them for a tramp through the sugar orchard, where snow lay thick-crusted on the ground again after the February thaw. They had come out above the pond, and the boys had discovered good sound ice upon its surface and soon were making a slide. They shouted to Thorne, who stood on the bank, not joining in the sport.

"Come on, Thorne! Come on and slide."

"Yes, Thorne, why don't you play with them?" asked Judith.

Thorne did not answer. She stood with her back to the raw March wind, looking cold and pinched and unhappy.

Judith said impatiently, "What's the matter, Thorne?"

Thorne looked at the schoolmistress strangely. She could

not put into words her vague, foreboding fears regarding this woman. Neither could she explain the dread in her own heart, which she was yet too young to understand.

She whispered, "I think it would have been better if Miss Abigail hadn't died."

For a second Judith's determined cheerfulness froze.

Then she rallied. "Of course, Thorne. We all wish that Miss Abigail hadn't died. We feel very sad about her death. But we should not show our sadness to the children. It makes it harder for them."

"That's not what I meant." Thorne's candid brow puckered in a frown. "I'm not sad—about Miss Abigail. She made Richard very unhappy. On his account, I'm glad she's gone."

"That's a terrible thing to say," said Judith sternly.

"Yes, I know." Again that elfin look came into Thorne's eyes. "Do you suppose she knows?"

"Who knows?" said Judith sharply.

"Miss Abigail. I'd hate for her to know how we feel about her dying."

"What do you mean, how we feel?" Judith's voice rose shrilly. "Be careful how you include other people in your remarks."

"I'm sorry. I thought you felt the same way I did."

"Well, you thought wrong. I have nothing but the deepest regret for Mrs. Tomlinson's death."

The strange child nodded. "That's what I mean. Now that she's gone, I think maybe it would have been better if she hadn't died."

There was company for supper following the funeral: friends and relatives who had driven from afar to attend the services. As many as could be accommodated stayed overnight. The strange faces at the table, the added bustle in dining room and kitchen lent an air of somber conviviality to the house. Miss Ann and Millie had worked for three days preparing the feast which they knew would be expected and which really justified Cousin Lutie Simms's unfailing tribute on such occasions: "My, my! Regular harvest dinner." Judith found the change of atmosphere exhilarating after the oppressive silence of the last five days.

But if she had hoped for a re-establishment of her old subtle contact with Richard, she was disappointed. He sat at the head of his table, hospitably attentive to the needs of his guests, but dignified and remote. Except for exchanging a few words with Otis Huse, who sat on his right as nearest relative of the deceased, the newly made widower was silent throughout the meal.

This was approved by all present.

Privately, no one believed for a moment that Richard felt anything but relief for his wife's death, and speculation was already rife as to how soon he would marry again. But his behavior as a bereaved husband was beyond criticism.

Judith was seated midway of the long table, with Lucius Goff on her left and young Will Tomlinson on her right. Of the two, she found it easier to talk to Will. This was odd, for the eighteen-year-old lad had always been antagonistic and had openly charged her with encouraging his brother in the matter of Thorne. But Will was practical and rather hard-minded. His sister-in-law was dead and there was no use pretending that all concerned, herself included, weren't better off. Judith found him a comfortable neighbor.

On the other hand, Lucius Goff's smile was absurdly unnerving. It seemed to say, "Why are you mourning?" She flushed under it, though his remark was perfectly innocuous.

"Have you ever noticed how heartily people eat following a funeral?"

Perhaps he was only trying to be amusing. But there was a knowing twinkle in his black eyes. Judith looked the other way.

It was long after the usual bedtime when she came down-stairs with her book. Knowing that she was to share her bed with fat Cousin Lutie, who probably snored in her sleep, Judith was in no haste to retire. Taking a candle, she slipped down the covered passage to the kitchen. Just after prayers she had heard Richard say that he would smoke a pipe by the kitchen fire before going to bed.

She found him sitting alone before the open grate of the big cookstove.

There was no light in the smoke-blackened room except the red gleam of coals through the grating. It made sharp high lights of the man's features, changing the familiar out-lines of his handsome open countenance, giving a dark brooding look to his face.

"I beg your pardon. I didn't know there was anyone here."

At the sound of Judith's voice he started, almost guiltily, and rose to his feet.

"Please don't go. I just thought I'd read a bit before going to bed. There's no fire in my room." Judith set her candle on a convenient shelf and drew an old rocker close to the stove.

He sat down again without speaking. Judith settled herself with her book and pretended to read. The clock on the shelf ticked noisily. The man seemed oblivious of her presence.

When she had turned two pages she laid her book down and delicately stifled a yawn. Then she stole a glance at her silent neighbor. He was looking at her intently.

She felt that he had been watching her for some time.

Inadvertently she spoke. "What's the matter?"

He leaned toward her and said in a lowered tone, "Do you know anything about that doll?"

If he had struck her she could not have recoiled more sharply. Fortunately the recoil was mental and the light was poor.

"You mean—Thorne's doll?"

He nodded.

"Why do you ask?"

"My wife did not die of membranous croup."

"What did she die of?"

"Heart attack. Following sudden shock."

The kitchen clock ticked stridently above their heads. The book in Judith's lap was tightly clutched with sweating hands. She neither moved nor spoke.

"When you came to call me that night you said my wife had wakened from a sound sleep and seemed to be having trouble with her breathing. Remember?"

"I remember."

"Had there been anyone else in the room besides yourself during the night?"

"No one."

"Did you leave the room at any time?"

"Not until I went to call you." Judith seemed to be having trouble with her own breathing. "Why do you ask?"

"When I got down to Abigail's room I found her clutching her throat and gasping that she was being strangled. She couldn't breathe, she could scarcely speak, yet she tried to tell me something about the doll. She said she had waked to find it lying on the pillow with a velvet ribbon tied round its neck. The string was tied so tight it was choking her to death. She begged me to cut it so she could breathe. And all in gasping whispers while she clawed for air. Oh, my God, it was piti-ful!"

"What did you do?" asked Judith.

"There was nothing I could do," he answered. "The doll wasn't there."

The hands gripping the book relaxed. "Hallucination."

Richard muttered, "I wish I could believe it."

"What did the doctor say?"

"By the time the doctor got there Abigail was unconscious."

"Then you didn't tell him about the doll?"

He looked guilty. "It was too late to do anything. Dr. Caxton seemed to think it was membranous croup."

"It was membranous croup, wasn't it?"

He shook his head. "It was her heart. I'm sure of it. She always fainted easily. She died of fright."

"Then it was self-induced," said Judith. "Because you found no doll, did you?"

"I searched everywhere. On the bed, under the bed. There was no doll in the room."

"There! You see? Pure hallucination."

"But she described so accurately the ribbon about its neck. Do you think she would have mentioned a *velvet* ribbon if it had been hallucination?"

"She might," said Judith calmly. "Velvet ribbons are the fashion, you know. I wear them myself. She was already having trouble with her breathing when I went to call you. Her imagination started working. The doll was never out of her mind. She began thinking about it—and saw it with a velvet ribbon around its neck."

"And you think that's all she saw—just an image of her own excited fancy?"

"I do indeed."

"Then why did she say"—he seemed to force the words—"when I asked her what became of the doll, why did she say, 'She knows'?"

Cold sweat drenched Judith's body under her woolen undergarments.

"I know what you're thinking, Mr. Tomlinson," she said carefully. "You're thinking she meant Thorne."

"No, no!" The very fervor of his denial was confirmation.

"The doll belonged to Thorne, of course. And Miss Abigail always believed she had it hidden away somewhere."

Now that she knew his fear Judith's relief made her slightly giddy.

"I never thought of it before—but I suppose someone *could* have slipped into your wife's room while I was out—and laid the doll on her pillow—then taken it away before you came down."

A stifled groan was the only sign that he had heard her.

"I remember now that Thorne slept in the trundle bed that night, just beyond the door that connected with Miss Abigail's room."

He, too, remembered. The lines in his face, the pain in his eyes were proof of his tortured thinking.

"She could have seen me go upstairs," Judith went on, "and seized the opportunity while I was out of the room. And of course she *could* have tied a velvet ribbon around the doll's neck. After all, she's little more than a child; she'd naturally dress her dolly in the current fashion. But that doesn't prove your wife actually saw the doll on her pillow. I still think she was suffering from hallucination."

"Do you really believe that?" His eyes pleaded desperately for reassurance.

Judith weighed for a second one alternative of self-interest against another. Then she saw that by erasing this man's fear she could bind him heart and mind to herself.

"Yes, Mr. Tomlinson, I do. For when I came downstairs again that night I found Thorne in the trundle bed, fast asleep. She could hardly have left her bed in the meantime and fallen asleep so quickly."

"God bless you, Judith, for telling me that."

For the second time in their acquaintance he had called her Judith. And it had been, curiously, as on that other occasion, when she had relieved his anxiety about Thorne.

He was able to talk now without restraint.

"You don't know what thoughts I've had, God forgive me! But Abigail hated her so—made her life so miserable. You could hardly blame the child if she had held enmity in return. I was afraid—she might have been tempted—to work on Abigail's insane superstition. She's very bright, you know—— But now"— he looked at Judith with wet eyes—"this may sound strange coming from a man who has just buried his wife, but I think I love you, Judith, for your kindness to my poor little Thorne."

Judith sat very still, uncertain what kind of declaration of love this might be.

"I am very fond of Thorne, Mr. Tomlinson."

"I know you are. That's why it will be a personal loss to both of us not to have you teaching at Timberley next year."

So unprepared was Judith for this shock that she cried sharply, "Not teach at Timberley? What do you mean?"

"Al Carpenter has recovered. He wants the school back."

"And I'm to be turned out to accommodate him!" Just in time she remembered that she would gain nothing by a display of shrewish temper. She asked in a different tone, "Haven't I given satisfaction?"

"You have indeed. But Mr. Carpenter has many friends in the district. And a male teacher is always preferred. You understood the position was only temporary, didn't you?"

There was no argument on this point. But Judith had trusted to her gambler's luck that Al Carpenter might be permanently disabled.

"Then you've known for some time that I was going to be let out?" Frustrated anger rose in her throat, tears of disappointment in her eyes.

"I've known since Christmas," said Richard.

"Why didn't you tell me?"

He looked at her with such disarming kindness that her anger melted.

"I didn't want to give you bad news until I had something to offer you in its place."

Hope rose again. He had waited till after his wife's death— because he had something to offer. . . .

She whispered, "What do you mean?"

"I have found you a school near Staunton."

"Oh."

Staunton was in another county.

Judith studied her slim white hands. This was March. Rural school was out in April, so that the bigger boys could help with spring plowing. She would have to work fast or everything would have been done in vain.

"It is good of you, Mr. Tomlinson, to go to so much trouble on my account. I know I should be happy to have the promise of a school at Staunton. And I would be if it weren't for leaving Thorne. I'm afraid when I'm gone that your mother will send her to Kentucky."

"Mother! Send Thorne away? Oh no. Mother has no grudge against the child."

"I don't mean that," said Judith gently. "I stayed with the children the night—Miss Abigail died. Thorne was very nervous. I had to take her up to my room. Your boys never woke up. I was sitting with them when your mother came upstairs."

He seemed touched by that.

"I told Miss Ann about Thorne, and she said a strange thing, Mr. Tomlinson. She said, 'I'm too old to bring up so young a child. Too old—and too tired.'"

"But Thorne is much older than my boys." He looked puzzled.

"Thorne is a girl," explained Judith delicately. "Girls in their teens are sometimes difficult. That is what your mother meant."

He sat in troubled silence. The brooding look came back into his eyes.

"Your mother is no longer young, Mr. Tomlinson. Three children are no small job. Your boys are her grandsons and no trouble to her because she's had them from infancy and understands them. But Thorne has a peculiar background. Your mother can hardly be blamed for feeling she's unequal to the task of bringing her up."

"But she doesn't need bringing up. All she needs is love and a little patience."

"I agree with you." Judith's eyes were sparkling with moisture. "If you could have seen how she clung to me that night— like a child to her mother."

He said naïvely, "You're rather young to be Thorne's mother," and then flushed as he realized what he had said. But he looked at Judith with pleasure, as though discovering beauty where he had seen none before. Something that had stretched like a delicate cord between them from the beginning tightened like a bowstring. Was it mutual love for an orphan girl or was it something more personal? He was not a vain man, but it was impossible not to know that this charming young woman had practically offered to become his wife.

"Miss Judith, this is neither the time nor the place for me to speak of what should not even be in my mind at this moment. My wife's death—and before that, her long illness— has been too sad a thing for me ever again to give much thought to personal happiness. But with three children on my hands I realize that I must in time make other plans for the future."

He paused in his lengthy, stilted speech, and every pulse in Judith's body seemed suspended.

"I can't speak of those plans at the present. But someday, if you are kind enough to listen, I should like to talk to you about them."

Judith said, "How can you talk to me if I am at Staunton?"

He looked at her with a faint trace of his old mischief.

"Perhaps we shall meet again in Terre Haute next fall and see a Shakespeare play together."

CHAPTER 12

The summer following Abigail's death was the happiest Thorne had ever known. She woke each morning, expectantly, to the crow of a very young rooster. Always before she had protested the cockcrow and the enforced early rising of the farm. But now she sprang joyously from bed, as though the summer day were not long enough to hold all the delight it promised. Sometimes she was dressed and roaming the woods before Millie had her breakfast fire started. Berries were ripe now and nothing, to Richard's thinking, equaled a bowl of blackberries fresh with dew to begin the morning meal.

Never, since early childhood when parental love cushioned her against reality, had Thorne lived in such security. The hand-to-mouth existence of her carnival days, succeeded by the constant threats of Abigail, had so inured her to anxiety that for a time it was hard for her to realize that she no longer had anything to worry about. Not until after school was out and Judith had returned to the city and it was known for a fact that she would not be coming back was Thorne able to accept the permanency of her happiness. Even then, her first thought on waking was a swift, imploring prayer.

"Please, God, let it last. Don't take it away. Let it be like this always." Sometimes, remembering Abigail, she would add, "Don't let me be glad she's dead. But if I am, please forgive me."

Remembering Judith, she would not pray at all.

Sometimes there was the faintest shadow of a cloud on the clear blue of her horizon, like the morning Ricky knocked upon her door while she was braiding her hair. She had inherited the bird's-eye-maple room upon Judith's departure, and it gave her a wonderful feeling of grown-up importance to have a door upon which people must knock and to be able to say "Come in" to her former bedfellows. The little boys still called upon her to button them up before going down to breakfast.

"Oh, look what Miss Judith left behind," cried Rodgie, who had followed his brother into the room. He was exploring the mysteries of the bureau and had discovered a cut-glass bottle with a rubber ball attached. When squeezed, it filled the air with delicious scent.

Thorne, intent on connecting Ricky's panty waist with his drawers, looked up. "Where did you get that, Rodgie?"

"In the little cubby. Didn't you know it was there?"

She had not seen it until that moment. "Let me have it, please."

"No. It's not yours. It's mine. I found it." Rodgie clutched his treasure to his stomach.

"It's not yours," said Ricky with an air of superior judgment. "It belongs to Miss Judith, and you'd better put it back where you found it. She won't like it when she comes back, if she finds her scent bottle gone."

Thorne's face blanched. "She's not coming back," she said quickly.

Ricky said smugly, "Whatcha wanta bet?"

"What do you mean?" asked Thorne.

The young man, who still had trouble with buttons and buttonholes, looked wise with the newly acquired wisdom of seven years.

"Jesse Moffat bets she's comin' back. I heard him talkin' to Uncle Will. She never woulda left that bottle if she wasn't comin' back."

Thorne stared at the inoffensive bottle as though it had been a sharp instrument on which she had inadvertently cut herself.

There were other storm warnings from Millie. Perhaps it was only the black woman's superstition, perhaps it was the irritability of advancing age and rheumatism which made Thorne's suddenly released spirits the subject of gloomy foreboding. As she watched the girl who had once been afraid to lift her voice, who had slipped through the house like a shadow, now running in and out as she pleased, laughing, shouting, playing games, Millie's dark speculations took voice.

"Steppin' mighty free and easy now Miss Abby's daid, ain't yuh? Bettah watch out."

The words—still more, the tone of voice—cast a pall on Thorne's young gaiety.

"What do you mean, Millie?"

"Bad luck dancin' on a grave."

The two were alone in the big black kitchen. It was after supper and Thorne was helping with the dishes so that Miss Ann could sit on the porch under the June roses. The evening was lush with fragance, and by and by Richard was going down to the crossroads for the mail and Thorne was going with him. The world was right and good and brimming with promise until Millie spoke.

"I'm not dancing on a grave. Why do you say a thing like that?"

"Good luck don' las' that comes from somebody dyin'," warned the old woman grimly. "Bettah not act too happy. *She* won't like it."

"But she's gone, Millie. What I do can't bother her now."

The turbaned head nodded gloomily. "That's whut I mean. She's gone. An' we don' want her comin' back." The familiar black face was frightening in the murky shadows of the room.

But outdoors the sky was red with sunset, and from beyond the open windows Richard's whistle set the earth back on its axis. Thorne flung down her dish towel and ran out to join him, glad to escape from the dusky kitchen and Millie's baleful croakings.

As they crossed the side yard they heard buggy wheels and voices, topped by a high youthful giggle. Thorne recognized the giggle.

"It's the Turners. Nancy said they'd be over this evening. If she's seen me I'll have to go back."

Richard seized her hand and drew her behind a clump of lilacs. Together they waited, like two conspirators, while the Turner surrey passed along the lane and deposited Kate and Hugh Turner, their three children, and Hugh's fifteen-year-old sister Nancy on the Timberley lawn. When the visitors had disappeared around the corner of the front porch the truants ran swiftly down the slope toward the shelter of the woods.

"Remember, we didn't see them," cautioned Richard. "If they're still here when we come back we must be quite surprised to find we have company."

His mischievous wink belied the droll gravity of his tone, and Thorne laughed rapturously. Oh, it was fun to be running away from only Nancy Turner. To have no greater fear than the danger of being caught by that harmless giggler. It was good to be clasping Richard's hand, unafraid of watchful eyes peering from the window. In a flash of clarity Thorne realized that all the inexplicable joy of this summertime was born of the freedom to clasp Richard's hand.

It was dim and cool beneath the beech trees, like the aisles in an empty church. As they went on their pace slackened. The hushed privacy of the leafy world was conducive to intimate talk.

"I don't know what you see in Nancy Turner," Richard began. "You never used to play together, but now it seems everywhere I turn I hear that giggle or see that toothy smile. She's too old a chum for you, Cricket."

Nancy was a plump, overdeveloped girl for her age and so obviously boy-struck that her elders found her society slightly wearing.

"She likes to talk to me," Thorne explained.

"What about?"

"Oh, everything."

He frowned. Nancy was beginning to have beaux, a fact which he thoroughly disapproved.

"Half the fun of being in love," said Thorne sagely, "is having an interested listener."

He stopped short in the path. "What do you know about being in love?"

"Nothing. That's what Nancy says."

"And you're an interested listener, I suppose."

"Very."

He made an unintelligible sound that might have been a growl or a cough. He was suddenly very much out of temper. He didn't want that featherbrain sister of Hugh Turner's filling Thorne's head with her silly ideas. He wondered just what she had told Thorne. For that matter, he wondered just how much the little nitwit had to tell. She had been going about with the Henderson boy, and young Chet Henderson was known as a wild one. Richard couldn't imagine what Hugh and Kate were thinking of not to clamp the lid down on Miss Nancy. But that wasn't his concern. Thorne was his concern, and he wasn't going to have her spoiled. She was sweet and fresh and innocent and he was going to keep her that way. He did not want her changed, ever. He grew quite warm thinking about it and looked down at her half fearfully, as though expecting to find some change already occurred.

"When did you start putting your hair up?" he demanded, as though it were the first time he had seen the dark braids wound about her head.

"I've been wearing it this way all summer," said Thorne. "It's cooler."

"Isn't that the way Nancy wears hers?"

"Yes. Don't you like it?"

His answer was to extricate the two shell pins that held the braids and toss them away. "Hairpins!" he muttered. Then, with his fingers, he combed the thick loose plaits into their accustomed curly tangle.

"You shouldn't have thrown the pins away," said Thorne. "They belonged to Nancy." She looked at him anxiously. "Are you angry? I didn't know you'd mind."

In the twilight of the beeches her face was a dim pale shape. He took it between his hands as though to see it better. He could no more be angry with her than with his own hand or heart, but he was troubled. She was growing so fast and he had no knowledge of how to deal with a girl child who was growing up. He would have talked to his mother about her but that he recalled what Judith had told him about Miss Ann's belief that Thorne would do better in Kentucky with his older sister. If his mother held that opinion it would not do to betray his own uneasiness. Doubtless his other sisters agreed with her. He had no one to turn to in his perplexity, unless . . .

Inevitably his reasoning brought him to the point round which his thoughts had milled all summer: Judith.

Over and over he had relived their talk by the kitchen fire. He realized that he had practically committed himself to marry her—if he ever married anyone. But this summer of absolute freedom had been so to his liking that he had decided he did not want to marry again. He had persuaded himself that he could manage his household without any woman's help, when this troublesome business about Thorne obtruded and destroyed his peace of mind.

"I'm not angry with you, Cricket. I just don't like you shooting up so fast. You're growing like a spring colt."

"Am I?" she laughed happily.

He said jealously, "You sound as though you were glad."

"Of course I'm glad. Aren't you?"

He did not answer. He only stood stroking her hair, as

though his hand upon her head could postpone growth and some dimly foreseen heartache.

"I don't want to be a child all my life," said Thorne. "I'd like to grow up right now—this very summer."

"Another speech like that and I'll turn you across my knee." He gave her a little shake as he released her.

They went on in companionable silence through the deepening twilight of the woods. All about them the unseen life of feathered, furred, and creeping things grew vocal with the fall of evening. A squirrel barked just over their heads, from some hidden pool of rain water came the croupy plaint of a frog, a thrush cleared his throat in a thicket, and on all sides rose the pulsing croon of katydids. It was the time, of all others, Thorne loved to be in the woods. She was sorry when they came out of the grove and crossed the road to the store.

Timberley store was kept by an elderly bachelor named Witherspoon who lived on the premises with his family of cats and never closed up till bedtime. On mail days—Tuesdays and Fridays—he never went to bed until a late hour, because as sure as he did some tardy customer would bang on his door and demand that he open up and give him his paper. The mail consisted mostly of periodicals. Those who could afford it subscribed to at least one—sometimes two—weekly papers. Those who couldn't afford subscriptions borrowed from their neighbors. The Tomlinsons took both the Indianapolis and Terre Haute papers and after reading them passed them on to the Schooks.

As Richard and Thorne entered the store Henry Schook hailed them from his seat on the sugar barrel.

"Our papers've come, Richard. Here's the *Express*." He tossed over one of the newspapers as blandly as though it had been his own. "You can run through that while I see what's doin' in Indianapolis."

The room was filled with men, newspapers, tobacco smoke, and conversation. Richard was greeted from all sides. Thorne edged her way to the row of mailboxes at the back of the room, where Mr. Witherspoon was still sorting the contents of the two sacks labeled "U.S. Mail."

"A—B—C—D—E—F—G—Garcey—— Humph! Wonder what Widow Garcey's brother in Ohio's writin' her about—— Oh, hello, Thorne. How're you this evening?"

"Fine, thanks. Want me to put that in Mrs. Garcey's box?"

"Might as well." Mr. Witherspoon surrendered the envelope dubiously. "Always hate to see people get letters. So apt to have bad news in 'em."

"Why?" Thorne was interested. "Why should letters be apt to have bad news?"

His reason was cogent. "No point in writin' if things are goin' well."

Thorne had never considered it in this light before. The remark excited her imagination. Mr. Witherspoon's moroseness had always fascinated her. Now it was explained. At some time in his life he had undoubtedly received bad news in a letter. That was why he lived alone, like an embittered old maid, with his cat Sheba and her occasional offspring.

"Well, I'll be switched! Here's one for you, Thorne."

Thorne looked up blankly. The storekeeper was holding out a square white envelope gingerly, as though distrusting its contents. The superscription, plain as faultless penmanship could make it, was *Miss Thorne Tomlinson, Timberley Farm, Woodridge, Indiana.*

"Now who could be writin' letters to an innocent young thing like you?" wondered Mr. Witherspoon darkly.

Thorne knew only too well whose hand had penned her name with that beautifully shaded stroke. She had seen that writing on blackboards too often to mistake it. The sight of it now gave her a queer sick feeling in the pit of her stomach. The storekeeper, mistaking her change of color, said kindly, "There now, don't be scared 'count of what I said about bad news. Nobody could be writin' you bad news 'cause you ain't got any folks to have things happen to. Go ahead, take it. See who it's from."

"I know who it's from," said Thorne, and slipped the letter into her pocket.

"Aren't you going to read it?" asked Mr. Witherspoon. He was disappointed.

"I will—later," said Thorne, and went out on the side porch, where Sheba and her daughters were making their evening toilets. Here Richard found her some time later when he inquired of the storekeeper what had become of her.

"She went outdoors to read her letter."

"Did Thorne get a letter? Who from?"

"She didn't open it in here," was the somewhat injured reply.

But Thorne was not reading a letter when Richard joined her. She was sitting on the porch step, so motionless that Sheba's kittens had made a bed of her wide-flung skirt.

"Hello! Hear you got a letter." Richard dispossessed the sleeping cats and sat down beside her. Leaning forward, he peered into her face and sharp anxiety seized him. Had someone connected with her old life—that good-for-nothing prestidigitator, Pete McGraw, to be exact—communicated with the child after all this time?

"Who's it from, Cricket?"

"I haven't opened it yet."

In her eyes was a look he had not seen there since Abigail died. His own fears immediately became facts.

"Listen, Thorne. No matter what's in that letter, you've nothing to worry about. There's not a person in this world—now—who has the power to hurt you. So give me the letter. If someone's trying to annoy you I'll send him about his business."

But when he reached for the envelope her fingers tightened upon it. An oil lamp flared in the room behind them. He saw tears upon her cheek.

"Thorne! What's the matter?"

"Nothing. I'm going home." She sprang up suddenly, like a young wild thing, and began walking rapidly toward the road. He had to hurry to catch up with her.

"Wait, Thorne. You're crying."

"I'm not."

She crossed the road and started running. Wildly she fled toward the woods, hearing him gain upon her and seized with a foolish panic. When he caught her she screamed and struggled in his grasp, beating his chest with small ineffectual fists while her face contorted with tears. "Let me go!" she sobbed.

"Thorne! What's come over you? We're not going back through the woods. It's too dark. Here, take my handkerchief. Your face is a sight. You shouldn't rub your eyes with hands that have been petting dirty cats."

The mild scolding restored her wonderfully. She accepted the handkerchief, used it, and returned it with a casual "Thanks," as coolly as though her sudden tantrum had never occurred. But as they went on their way she proffered the letter with a gesture slightly apologetic.

"Here—you can read it if you want to."

The large elegant black script was perfectly clear in the fading light. At sight of it Richard was relieved.

"Well, no carnival tramp wrote that. It looks like a woman's hand. Who could it be from?"

Thorne gave him a sidelong glance. "Don't you know?"

"It's not my sister Annie's scribble." He looked extremely innocent. "I can't think of any other feminine correspondents with Timberley—unless——" He stopped as his eyes fell on the postmark. Thorne, watching him, saw color rise beneath his summer tan.

"It's from Terre Haute," he said, rather too carelessly. "Maybe it's from Miss Amory."

"I'm sure it is," said Thorne, and quickened her pace.

"Here, wait! Don't you want to read it?"

"It's too dark."

"Nonsense. It's quite light, now that we're clear of the trees."

"All right then, you read it," said Thorne, so shortly that he might have wondered at her tone had he not been so intent upon learning what had prompted Judith Amory to write to her former pupil.

It was an innocuous missive, quite brief. He read it in silence first, just in case it bore reference to any conversation the writer might have had with Mr. Richard Tomlinson.

"Dear Thorne,

"I've thought of you so often since leaving Timberley and always with the pleasantest memories of our companionship. How is the reading coming on? I can't chide you if you find little time for it these long summer days. There are shut-in hours next winter for Shakespeare and Dickens, and Timberley must be at its loveliest in June.

"I envy you, my dear. The city is so hot and the work I am doing —tutoring for fall examinations—so tiresome. I long for your cool green woods, but the next best thing would be a visit from you telling me about them. If any of the family should chance to be coming to the city do ask them to bring you to see me.

"With kindest regards to all, I remain

"Your friend,
"Judith Amory"

"Well, what a nice letter," was Richard's comment as he folded the sheet of note paper after reading it aloud. "A very thoughtful thing for a schoolteacher to keep in touch with her old pupils."

Thorne looked at him in eloquent silence. Her futile anger melted before the colossal stupidity of man. To her the purpose of the letter was so obvious it seemed that even Richard must see that the woman had used the device to recall her own image to his mind. That she had succeeded, a glance at his face would attest. Even in the gathering darkness a kindling glow was visible.

When they came in sight of Timberley, Thorne ran ahead of him up the slope to the house. Fireflies starred the dusk, and the young Tomlinsons and Turners were chasing them over the lawn. She shouted to the children and threw herself into the sport; threw herself back into childhood, from the precarious ledge of adult reasoning on which she had teetered. What if Judith had written her a letter? It meant nothing. Why shouldn't Richard be pleased? He was always pleased when someone showed her a kindness. He was her dear friend, and no one, nor anything, could make him less. *Neither death, nor life . . . nor height, nor depth, nor any other creature* should separate them.

She had an ear for the majestic phraseology of the Bible, independent of its connotation. In the fragment which had lingered from last night's prayers she had failed to note that it was the love of God from which she was promised no separation, not the love of friend.

CHAPTER 13

Far from being the unsuspecting dolt that Thorne would have had him, Richard was perfectly aware of the purpose in Judith's note. The little strategy by which he was reminded that he had a rendezvous, come autumn, amused him. In the security of his resolution he was flattered rather than alarmed. For he had quite made up his mind that he was not going to marry again.

But the letter, carrying a delicate whiff of the scent she always used, brought Judith sharply before him. The elegant handwriting, expressing concern and affection for his little friend, revived the old feeling of gratitude. Judith was very kind; much too kind to be hurt. He had intended simply forgetting any vague promise to see her again. Now he realized the frank and gentlemanly thing to do was to call upon her and in a kind and impersonal way make it clear that he had no intention of remarrying. Perhaps he would take the children with him so that she could not possibly misconstrue his visit. He would go to the city as soon as harvest was over.

Wheat harvest dominated the month of July. The Tomlinsons owned the only reaping and threshing machines in the district, and it was the custom of the neighboring farmers to lend their services at Timberley in return for the loan of the back-saving machinery for cutting their own crops. When the Tomlinson grain had been harvested the whole crew moved on to the next farm, and so on in rotation. Women accompanied their men to assist in preparation of the harvest dinners which were cooked in the farmhouse kitchens and carried out to hastily constructed tables under the trees. Children accompanied mothers, and the whole season was in the nature of a prolonged community picnic.

After the reaping came the threshing. The great horsepower threshing machine, driven round and round by twelve tough mules to the accompaniment of an infernal din, threshed out a crop in two days that would have taken a week's toil on the threshing floor. Many a man in his prime could recall riding horse at the threshing when the grain had been tramped out by hoofs on the floor of a barn.

By the first of August the crop was garnered and sacked, the portion reserved for the family's use stored in the barn, the portion to be marketed hauled to Woodridge or the mill on Big Raccoon. Young Will usually attended to the marketing of the Tomlinson wheat. It was a job for which Richard had no enthusiasm. The drama of the harvest, he loved. The mounting tension of the rush to outstrip the ever-present threat of rain thrilled and exhilarated him. But the business of selling the crop was anticlimactic. He was glad that his younger brother seemed to enjoy it.

The second week in August brought a lull which seemed an admirable opportunity for his trip to the city. He announced his intention one evening at supper, then waited for repercussions, for seldom did a farmer journey twenty miles from home in summer. But his mother only said, "I'm afraid you'll find it pretty warm this time of year." His brother gave him an oblique look which, oddly, Richard felt called upon to answer.

"I'm going for the purpose of giving the children an outing. I've always promised to take them to Terre Haute, and summer's the time to do it, when the roads are good. You won't mind the heat, will you, boys?"

Ricky and Rodgie were immediately incoherent with excitement.

Ann Tomlinson said warningly that Richard didn't know what he was letting himself in for. "Those two are a handful anywhere. They'll get themselves killed and you too. You'd better wait till one of your sisters can go with you."

"Thorne will go with me. She's all the help I need."

"Thorne's nothing but a child herself."

"But I'm used to cities," Thorne interrupted eagerly. "I've gone about on city streets since I was smaller than Rodgie. I'll keep tight hold of each boy, Miss Ann, so Richard will be free to attend to his business."

Richard said hastily that he had no business to attend to. Young Will and Jesse Moffat exchanged glances.

Nancy Turner happened to be present, and suddenly, to Richard's chagrin, she proposed that she go with them. There was nothing, under the circumstances, with which he could have more readily dispensed than Nancy's company, but he could not refuse in the face of his mother's approval.

"That's a splendid idea, Nancy," said Miss Ann. "You can

help with the children. I won't have a minute's peace if they're turned loose with Richard. They're sure to be run over by those fast horses in the city."

"You talk as though I weren't responsible, Mother."

"When you get your mind on something, Richard, you forget everything around you."

The idea seemed to persist that some errand was taking him to town.

They were up betimes next morning. Nancy spent the night with Thorne, and the two girls dressed in fluttering haste to be ready by the time the carriage and team were at the door. The little boys, so heavy with sleep that Thorne had to dress them, were stowed away on the roomy back seat, and Nancy, by right of seniority, appropriated the front seat beside Richard, to that gentleman's complete exhaustion. It was a five-hour drive to Terre Haute, and her tongue outran the horses all the way. On the back seat, Thorne and the children slept peacefully.

As soon as they reached the city the boys awoke and demanded to eat. They had been too excited for breakfast and now they were ravenous. As it was nearly noon, Richard put the horses in a livery stable and piloted his little crowd to a quiet family eating house on Wabash Avenue. Dinner at a restaurant was an unprecedented experience for at least three of his charges and would consume, he hoped, considerable time. It would be bad manners to call upon Miss Judith before two o'clock.

But long before the meal was over he felt as though the expedition had already lasted for weeks. The day was scorching. The children were restless, excited, noisy, thirsty, and embarrassingly tormented by the demands of nature. They discovered a water cooler with a fascinating little spigot which turned on and off, and they imbibed so much liquid that it seemed to their harassed young father that it went right through them. He made so many trips out of the room, with first one, then the other, that Nancy giggled insufferably and even Thorne teased him. They were all in a state of hilarity, but he was too weary by this time to smile. When he wiped Rodgie's nose and discovered too late that he had used a napkin instead of his handkerchief, he groaned. Six hours of caring for his own children had worn him threadbare. He wondered how his mother had put up with them all these years.

Upon their demand at the conclusion of the meal for further entertainment, he explained somewhat grimly that they were going to see a lady. Thorne had received a note from their friend Miss Judith—they remembered Miss Judith, didn't they?—inviting her to call. Of course Thorne couldn't go alone, so they were all going with her. Thorne's clear eyes widened rather blankly as she heard herself thus credited with the purely theoretical motive for the excursion. But loyally she made no comment.

They walked through the broiling heat to Mrs. Prewitt's boardinghouse and stood about in languid attitudes of boredom while Richard rang the bell. Calling on a schoolteacher was not their idea of making holiday. Watching their perspiring disappointment, he half wished he had not come. It was a fool's errand anyway. He had a mind even now to return to Timberley without seeing Judith. He was in no mental state for the delicate mission before him. He would likely make an ass of himself and be ordered from the house. He hoped fervently she was not in.

Thorne hoped so too.

But Judith was in and very glad indeed to see her friends from Timberley. One glance at Richard's face was sufficient to tell her why he had come, why he had fortified himself with four limp, bedraggled children. He had thought better of his rash commitment and had come to withdraw it. Like a forewarned general, she swiftly altered her own strategy to meet the attack.

Leading the little party around to the cooler side porch, she listened to Nancy's chatter and questioned the boys and Thorne about their summer's activities until her adult caller had time to cool off. Then she brightly suggested that the young people make a visit to the ice-cream parlor just a block away. They served delicious cream and ices and had cunning little tables and chairs at which to eat them. At the mere mention of ice cream the children revived astonishingly. Ice cream was an unheard-of treat. Before Richard could collect his scattered faculties and fumble for his wallet Judith had sped up to her room and back and pressed the money into Nancy's plump, moist palm.

They were gone, the four of them, with Richard's tardy dollar bill entrusted to Thorne, and Richard flushed with embarrassment, putting his wallet back into his pocket while Judith laughed at his discomfiture.

"Don't look so concerned, Mr. Tomlinson. I'm not too impoverished to treat the children to ice cream. Besides, this is a special occasion. When they've come so far to see me I should feel quite distressed if I had to let them go back without some little gesture of hospitality."

She looked so cool and neat in her crisp green chambray, she had been so gracious and clever in her handling of his dilemma, that he looked at her admiringly, wondering if he were making a mistake in letting this woman go.

"Miss Judith—I c-can't tell you——" he stammered boyishly, and fanned his hot face with his hat. He felt crumpled and untidy beside her immaculate daintiness. If he had known that his damp hair, curling moistly in the heat, gave him the artless charm of his son Ricky, he might have been even more dubious of his mission than he was.

He inquired naïvely if there was anyplace less public where they could talk. Judith led him into what was elegantly referred to as the garden but was literally Mrs. Prewitt's back yard. There was grass, however, and a pergola covered with

Virginia creeper. They took refuge here from the torrid sunshine, and he tried to summon the thoughts he had so carefully arranged the night before.

It was a hopeless endeavor. No sooner had they entered the privacy of the little summerhouse than he found Judith's cool fingers touching his and her face uptilted temptingly close to his lips.

"Richard!" she whispered. "You don't have to tell me why you have come. I know. Only I didn't expect you so soon."

And then—he never quite knew how it happened—she was in his arms and he was kissing her with a roughness that was a compound of embarrassment, August temperature, and long-pent-up desires. Not for years had he touched a woman. Never had he held one like this. He realized with a shock that he had wanted to kiss her ever since that night at the theater.

Somewhere in the giddy tumult of his mind, whence rational thought had retreated, a disquieting note sounded clear for a single second. It was the instinctive knowledge that this woman who yielded so eagerly to his embrace was not the artless lover that she seemed but a schemer, wily and ruthless. Then his own generous nature rose, indignant, at such heresy and drowned it in fresh ardor.

There were footsteps in the yard, and Judith hastily released herself, whispering, "Mrs. Prewitt! She saw us come in here and she's followed us. Quick! We must set her straight or she'll be telling all sorts of things."

Before he had time to envision what Mrs. Prewitt might tell more incriminating than the truth, he found himself drawn across the lawn and given a rather startling introduction to the redoubtable landlady.

"Mrs. Prewitt, I want you to meet my fiancé."

In his confusion he was conscious that Mrs. Prewitt was not the only recipient of the sensational announcement. Around the corner of the house came four disheveled children, replete with candy and ice cream. They had spent Richard's money as well as Judith's and now they were surfeited and ready to go home. They entered the yard in time to hear Judith add, "Mr. Tomlinson and I are going to be married in the fall."

They stood in silence while Mrs. Prewitt beamed and congratulated and crumpled an overdue board bill in her pocket. Then Nancy found voice and began gurgling, "Oh, Richard! Are you really going to marry Miss Judith? How thrilling!" and went off into a series of giggles which brought a furious frown to Richard's face and a brusque reply in confirmation. His small sons, not understanding the trend of events but not liking their father's scowl, set up a cry and blubbered piteously for Gran'ma. Altogether there was quite a commotion before the young Tomlinsons were quieted and made ready for departure. Richard had only a sketchy last moment with Judith, but she managed to make it conclusive.

"I'll send in my resignation to Staunton immediately. We'll be married in October. Tell your mother not to worry about a thing. I'll make all the plans."

He bade her good-by in a kaleidoscopic fog and looked about for Thorne, who had disappeared. It was some time before she was found behind the grape arbor, being very sick all by herself. Mrs. Prewitt said it was the ice cream; Judith said it was the heat. Richard said nothing.

He watched Thorne bathe her face at the pump and suggested that she wait on the porch with Miss Judith while he went to the livery stable for the carriage. But this proposal Thorne flatly rejected. She was perfectly able to walk; in proof of which statement, she immediately set forth. Nancy followed, and Richard, with only the briefest word of farewell, collected the little boys and hurried after. His newly betrothed watched him out of sight with a faint frown of annoyance which, fortunately, there was no one but Mrs. Prewitt to see.

CHAPTER 14

The news of Richard's forthcoming marriage was received with shocked relish everywhere but in his immediate family. The Tomlinsons maintained a discreet attitude, taking their cue from Miss Ann, whose only comment was, "You are old enough to know what you are doing, Richard. I hope you are happy."

But in Woodridge and throughout the countryside tongues wagged aplenty. For a widower of twenty-six to marry again was to be expected. But for him to wait a bare six months and then select as his bride a stranger who had lived under his roof during his first wife's lifetime cast an interesting suspicion over the whole affair. Too many eager widows and hopeful spinsters had fixed their hopes on Richard for this action to pass unassailed. Speculations were rife concerning the precipitancy of the arrangements. It was prophesied that Abigail would turn over in her grave.

Judith, in her hot back bedroom at Mrs. Prewitt's, busily sewing on her wedding garments, shrewdly divined what the local reaction would be and prepared to offset it. She was well aware that she could not cop the prize matrimonial plum of a small rural community without making enemies. For herself, she cared not a fig. But she was determined to make the second Mrs. Tomlinson a more popular figure than the first Mrs. Tomlinson had been. If she married Richard in Terre Haute and went back to Timberley as his wife she would be forever an outlander. But if she returned to Woodridge as plain Judith Amory and married him on his own ground she would have the sympathy and good will of all who attended her wedding. And it was her plan that everyone of importance should attend.

So the first week in September she packed up, paid off Mrs. Prewitt, and departed from her select boardinghouse forever. Twenty-four hours later she was installed in the Barclays' front parlor in Woodridge, penning a chaste note to her betrothed, notifying him of her change of address. And here she waited, surrounded by Barclays all busily stitching on Judith's trousseau, while she listened for Richard's step on the walk and the ring of the Barclay doorbell.

But when the Timberley surrey stopped at the gate one afternoon it was Ann Tomlinson and not her son who had called. After a momentary qualm Judith was pleased. This was as it should be. Whatever Ann Tomlinson's personal feelings might be regarding this marriage—and Judith had a lively suspicion of their nature—Richard's mother was prepared to do the correct thing.

"My son tells me that you plan to be married in Woodridge." Miss Ann went straight to the point as soon as greetings were disposed of. Judith had conveyed this information in her note.

Actually, she had no such plan in mind. The wedding she visualized could never be encompassed in the Barclays' tiny dwelling. But she intended letting Richard—or his mother— make the suggestion that would accomplish her purpose.

"I dislike the idea of being married in a boardinghouse," said Judith wistfully. It was an effective touch. Miss Ann softened.

"I'm sure Richard would never have let you be married from a boardinghouse, even in Terre Haute. Now that you're in Woodridge you must have a church wedding at our own church."

But Judith favored a home wedding. "It's so much more intimate, I think. Of course, I have no home, but Mrs. Barclay has kindly consented to let me be married from here. I hope it won't put her to too much trouble."

The Barclays, mother and daughters, interrupted in concert. It was no trouble at all. Their only fear was that they would never be able to get all the guests inside their tiny cottage.

"You plan to have guests, Judith?" asked Miss Ann dubiously. She had talked to her son and he had agreed with her that the quieter the wedding could be made, the better. Neither of them had spoken the thought aloud, but it was in the mind of each that festivities of any kind were in bad taste so soon after Abigail's death.

But Judith had no such scruples. "I want everyone at my wedding whom I hope to have for a friend, and that means practically everyone Richard knows. It's hard enough for a second wife to win a place for herself, without having hurt feelings on all sides to start with."

Ann Tomlinson could have explained that in this community it was harder to live down scandal than to cope with hurt feelings. But she held her tongue. And when the younger woman said, "You don't know how much it means to me to have Richard's friends like me. You see, I have none of my own," the prejudice which Miss Ann had felt since the night she discovered the schoolteacher's love for her son was forcibly put aside. Judith was not the daughter-in-law she would have chosen, but she was a young woman entering into her first marriage and entitled to the favors which are a bride's prerogative. If she wanted a home wedding, then a home wedding she should have. But it must not be at the Barclays'.

"If you plan to invite all Richard's friends you'd better be married at Timberley. It's the only house around here large enough to hold them."

Judith dropped her eyes before Ann Tomlinson caught their sparkle of triumph.

"Do you suppose it would be proper?" she demurred for the sake of appearances. "I mean, being married from the home of the bridegroom."

Quite as proper as being married six months after his first

wife's death, said the gleam in Miss Ann's eyes. But she answered kindly:

"It was your home last winter. It will be your home from now on. Under the circumstances I think you should return at once to Timberley and make all your arrangements from there."

This was what Judith had been angling for from the start. Now she need not be separated from Richard during this tiresome interval of waiting. But before she could express her pleasure at the invitation her future mother-in-law dashed her hopes.

"Fortunately an old college chum of Richard's has been wanting him to come to Greencastle and he can pay him a visit now as well as later."

Judith's face was a study in chagrin. "You mean Richard won't be at home?"

"Oh no. It would not do for the bride and groom to live under the same roof before their marriage," said Miss Ann calmly.

To Judith this attitude was sheer stupidity. Her first furious disappointment almost erupted in words. She had counted on this time with Richard to further bind him to her, for she was not yet sure of him. She had not seen him since that day in Mrs. Prewitt's garden, and their only intercourse had been a brief correspondence. She had no fear that he would try to jilt her, for he was a gentleman. But she was uneasily aware that she had taken him by surprise and that he might have regretted his capitulation. She had hoped for a chance to re-kindle him. Now all her wiles were useless. Silently she cursed the hidebound conventionality of this rural community which forbade him her lips before their marriage night.

But she kept her disappointment to herself and decided to make the most of her opportunities. At least she would have nothing to distract her from her immediate objective, which was to stage a wedding at Timberley which should be the talk of the county. Three days later she returned, laden with goods bought on credit, and took personal charge of arrangements.

The Tomlinson women, catching a certain fire from her enthusiasm, good-naturedly followed her leadership. Kate, Jane, Nancy Turner, and Cousin Lutie Simms practically moved into the house to assist in the preparations. They sewed, cooked, cleaned, and garnished until the house bloomed like an autumn garden. A little bower of late fall flowers was erected in front of the drawn curtains of the alcove, and here the wedding ceremony was to be performed.

It was not until the last moment that Judith had the inspiration about Thorne. She had planned from the first that Richard's little sons were to be ring bearers. Kate and Cousin Lutie had cut up an old velveteen skirt of Miss Ann's and under Judith's direction had fashioned clever little pageboy suits for Ricky and Rodgie. She was using the double-ring ceremony (to the secret confusion of the easygoing Methodist minister), and Thorne was making two tiny satin pillows for the rings to lie on.

It was while watching Thorne bent silently over her work that the idea came to Judith. For the first time since her return she found herself really looking at the child. Either Thorne had avoided her, or Judith had been too busy to notice anyone in whom she was not interested. She had not bothered to apologize, when she found she had dispossessed Thorne from the bird's-eye-maple room, but she had invited her to share it until the wedding. Thorne, already installed in her old berth with the children, preferred to remain where she was. It came to Judith now that Thorne's feelings were hurt because the boys had a part in the wedding and she hadn't.

To Judith, personally, nothing was less important than Thorne's feelings. But she forced herself to recall that Richard made no difference between this girl and his own children. She did not intend to snare her enterprise on the reef which had wrecked Abigail. Not at the outset, anyway. Richard must be pleased with every detail of the wedding, and Thorne moping in a corner was sure to catch his eye.

"How would you like to be in the wedding, Thorne?" she asked brightly, and watched with interest the startled uplift of the curly dark head.

"Judith, I think that's the smartest notion you've had yet," said Cousin Lutie, who was putting the finishing touches to the bridal veil. "If there's one thing that'd make Richard happy at his wedding it'd be to have Thorne standing beside him."

It was an unfortunate remark. Judith discounted it, as coming from a person of no consequence, and continued watching Thorne, who dropped her eyes to her work again.

"There's yards of that tulle left over, plenty to make you a dress. You can wear my satin sash and carry a basket of roses as flower girl. You're too young to be a maid of honor, but I really should have an attendant since Will is acting as Richard's best man. Would you like that, Thorne?"

"Do you think Richard would like it?" asked Thorne.

Annoyance flushed Judith's cheek. Any other girl of fourteen would have thrilled at the invitation. She had half a mind to retort that Nancy Turner was available if Thorne was not interested. Then she recalled her purpose in conciliating this strange child.

"As Cousin Lutie says, I'm sure Richard would be pleased to have *all* his children taking part in his wedding." Thus, having put Thorne in her place—back in the nursery—Judith gave orders that the tulle dress should be made up.

The wedding was set for the first Friday in October. Relatives from as far away as Bainbridge were expected, and from Monday morning till Thursday night the house buzzed with preparations for overnight guests. Judith came upon Miss Ann one morning emerging from the downstairs bedroom, her arms full of window curtains for the washtub.

"You're not cleaning that room?" she said blankly.

"Yes indeed. It's the first good cleaning it's had since——"
Miss Ann stopped just in time. "We passed this room up on
spring house cleaning, so it's due for a real turnout now. We're
clearing everything out of the closet so——"

"The closet! Why bother with closets at a time like this?"
The sharp tone brought a flush to the older woman's cheek,
and Judith realized her voice had risen unnecessarily.

"I mean, you've done so much already, Miss Ann. I'm afraid
you'll overdo. Guests who are only staying the night are not
likely to go poking into closets."

"This room is not for overnight guests," explained Ann
Tomlinson. "This room is the bridal chamber."

For a second Judith could neither move nor speak. Then
she shivered, as though a cold wind had passed over her. Why
had she not foreseen such an eventuality? She had taken for
granted that she and Richard would occupy the bird's-eye-
maple room. She had overlooked the fact that the downstairs
bedroom was and always had been his room, built for him as
a lad, with his own private entrance, long before his marriage
to Abigail. He would expect, naturally, to go on living in his
own quarters. And he would expect Judith to live there with
him, in the room in which she had watched a dying woman
fight for breath. . . .

A sudden paroxysm gripped her throat. She felt as though
she were choking. When she spoke her voice was so queer
that Ann Tomlinson noted with concern her strange pallor.
Like so many brides, Judith was wearing herself out before
her wedding.

"Miss Ann, I don't want to seem difficult—but I'd much
prefer staying—for the present—in my old room upstairs. I
believe Richard will understand—when I explain to him."

Ann Tomlinson understood. She had hinted to her son that
his second wife might find unpleasant associations in the room
where his first wife died, but he had scoffed at the idea. Judith
was too level-headed to mind a thing like that. Besides, the

bird's-eye-maple room had been given to Thorne, and as soon as the wedding was over she was going to move back into it. He had considered the matter settled when he departed for Greencastle.

He did not return until the day before the wedding. It was his mother, not Judith, who informed him of the changed arrangements.

"Now don't say anything you'll be sorry for, Richard" (as he started to explode). "It's a natural feeling for a new wife to have. Judith may be above the average in brains, but she's a woman like the rest of us. No woman wants to start her married life in the bed where her predecessor died." It was a double-barreled word for Miss Ann, but she brought it forth roundly, clinching her argument. Richard, somewhat grudgingly, gave in.

"It's only for one night, though, I warn you. As soon as the company's gone Thorne's moving back into her own room."

Judith did not see him until they met in the dining room on Thursday evening. The minister, Mr. Jameson, Lucius Goff, and John Barclay were already gathered there in view of the wedding rehearsal which was to take place after supper. As Judith came in she wondered anxiously how Richard would greet her before his family and friends. She hoped for something a trifle warmer than a handshake. But she was not prepared for the charming gallantry with which he lifted the hand she gave him to his lips.

"Where did you learn that pretty gesture?" She smiled to hide her delight in him.

"It was Lucius's idea." He and Lucius had come out from town together. "Lucius holds that ladies of the—er—intellectual type prefer a kiss on the hand to a kiss on the lips." He looked down at her with a meaning twinkle. "I did not undeceive him."

If there was impudent reminder in his smile, there was also promise. Her last uncertainty vanished. She was thrillingly happy.

The rehearsal was the prolonged, nerve-racking ordeal such occasions usually are. The children were boisterous, young Will swore audibly at the confusion of the two rings, and John Barclay got lost in a medley of both wedding marches. The bewildered minister perspired freely and wished Lucius Goff had license to officiate since he seemed the only person present, except the bride, who knew what was going on. Lucius, who had covered many fashionable weddings for his paper, was in his element. Under his guidance the rehearsal was finally got through. But it was a late hour when the womenfolk retired, leaving the downstairs rooms to the bridegroom and his friends, whose traditional privilege it was to make merry till all hours.

Judith had hoped for a moment alone with Richard, but it was not to be. The house was full of men and others were arriving. To have remained among them would have offended rural propriety. So she made her good nights general and withdrew.

Thorne also slipped away, but not before Richard spied her. He caught her at the foot of the stairs and swung her clear off the floor in a hearty hug, demanding to know where she had been hiding all evening.

"I've been away, young lady, or hadn't you noticed? And not so much as a welcome home from you. Look up here," he commanded. "Give me a kiss."

She lifted her face obediently and they kissed. Two arms went round his neck and he held her close. There was a moment of poignant awareness that this was the end of something precious; the beginning of some loss. Then she drew quickly away from him and said:

"It's you who haven't noticed anything all evening. I was at supper and I was in the rehearsal, but you didn't see me. You were in a fog."

And laughing at the blankness of his face, she ran swiftly up the stairs.

CHAPTER 15

It was the prettiest wedding ever seen in Woods County (so the Woodridge *Sentinel* reported), and the prettiest thing in the wedding was Thorne (which the *Sentinel* did not report). From the moment Judith saw her in the tulle dress she realized it had been a mistake to dress Thorne up. With her curls caught in a band of pink ribbon and a little flower basket on her arm, she looked like one of her own roses. No doubt it was her old training in stagecraft that taught her to walk with that slow poised grace. But as she moved down the stairs ahead of the bride, the eyes of the guests fastened on the flower girl and went no farther. Judith was in an ill frame of mind by the time she reached the altar.

Then she saw Richard, looking handsomer than ever in a new black broadcloth suit, and her annoyance was forgotten in the thrill of her achievement.

The ritual, so tediously rehearsed, proceeded without a hitch. The children behaved impeccably. The rings were not dropped. The minister coughed only twice. The solemn hush that filled the rooms lingered even after the final words were spoken.

Then it was shattered startlingly by the shrill high voice of old age.

"They're standing right on the spot where Abigail was laid out."

The speaker was old Judge Shane, a local patriarch, stone deaf and embarrassingly given to thinking out loud. For a shocked second the incident put a slight damper on the newly made marriage.

Then John Barclay's hands upon the piano plunged into the Mendelssohn march, and suddenly it was the merriest gathering imaginable. Perhaps it was because Lucius Goff took hold, and he was slightly exhilarated. Perhaps the old judge's soliloquizing had made everyone a bit hysterical. Perhaps, as Ellen Barclay said afterward, it was a relief to find you could laugh and cut up again at Tomlinson's after all those years of having to mind your P's and Q's on account of Abigail. Whatever the cause, there had never been seen so much backslapping and handshaking and kissing of girls—old and young.

Ann Tomlinson, looking sedately festive in gray poplin, stood in the dining room with Dr. Caxton and watched the loaded table swept clean again and again by the onslaughts made upon it. Baked hams, fried chickens, cakes, pies, and jellies disappeared as though a swarm of locusts had passed over. As fast as they vanished replenishments came through the covered passage from Millie's inexhaustible kitchen, borne by Cousin Lutie and Henry Schook's wife, who was "helping out." The preacher was heard to sigh, "It's discouraging to see so many good things before you, when you've already had more than you should eat." Mr. Jameson's popularity with the ladies put him in a fair way to rival Jesse Moffat as a trencherman.

Ann's eyes met the doctor's and they both smiled. These two understood each other. They belonged to the same generation. He had been her husband's friend. She was not afraid to let him see, behind her smile, her mind's unease regarding this marriage.

"You've set a new goal for local society tonight, Ann."

"I'm afraid that was not what I was aiming at, Doctor."

"You don't feel right about this wedding, do you?"

"I wish Richard had waited longer."

"I shouldn't worry on that score. Considering the life Abigail led him, I think six months' mourning was too damn good for her."

"I don't mean—on Abigail's account. Though considering Otis Huse's sharp tongue, I think it would have been wiser. But it's Richard I'm thinking of. He's never had a chance to be a bachelor. We married him off so soon. Every young man needs a little time of freedom. And now—just six months after his release from——" She looked at him with eyes suddenly moist. "You know how it was."

He said fervently, "God knows I do," and then they both were silent.

"It won't be like that this time," he went on. "Richard's getting a healthy wife; one who, if I'm any judge, has plenty to offer a husband. You must remember he's human, Ann." He added bluntly, "He needs a woman."

"He needs love," said Richard's mother.

"Bah! There's no such thing," scoffed the old cynic.

There was dancing in the front room. From somewhere John Barclay's violin had appeared and Lucius Goff had organized a Virginia reel. Hearing the rhythm of tapping feet and stringed music, Ann Tomlinson glanced anxiously at the minister. But Mr. Jameson was still surrounded by attentive ladies bent on giving him indigestion and apparently oblivious of the turn the festivities had taken.

"I suppose I should go in and stop them," Ann murmured dubiously.

"You'll do no such thing," growled the doctor.

Nevertheless, she hurried down the hall, still doubtful of the propriety of Terpsichore and Theology consorting. The doctor followed, snorting, at her heels.

The dance was in full swing. Every man young enough to twirl and sashay had captured a partner and was cutting as lively a figure as Sunday breeches and tight shoes would permit. The voluminous skirts of the ladies dipped and swirled. It was a pretty sight. Eyes sparkled and cheeks glowed with the rollicking exercise. The doctor muttered in his companion's ear, "Now if you can see anything wrong in that I'll eat Jameson's coattails, swallow by swallow."

Ann looked about for Richard. He was not dancing. He was standing apart, watching his bride dance with Lucius Goff.

Judith danced well, if somewhat stiffly, in a far more ladylike fashion than the others, who were growing more boisterous with each round. Richard's eyes followed her, smiling, as though he approved the way she danced. She caught his eye, and as the next turn of the reel deposited her near him Miss Ann heard her say, "Please, Richard, come on. I'd much rather dance with you."

"I think I'd better wait till Mr. Jameson leaves."

"If you feel that way, I shouldn't be dancing either."

"But I want you to dance. I've no objection personally. It's just that—on Mother's account—— There! It's your turn. Hurry, or you'll miss Lucius."

As she swung back into line to meet her partner Dr. Caxton muttered to Ann Tomlinson:

"See what you've done with your bluestocking notions? Made a wallflower of the best dancer in the room. I know," he replied in answer to her surprised look. "I saw him dance a schottische one night at Henderson's. If you don't go tell him to get in that reel *I'll* go and push him in."

But before she could take action the two were cut off from Richard by a swarm of children who had been playing blindman's buff out of doors. They flung themselves upon Richard, clamoring that they wanted to dance too. A junior reel was organized, composed of the Turner boys and Nancy, the younger Barclay girls, Richard's two youngsters, and Thorne. In the scramble to pair off, Thorne was left without a partner. She seized Richard's hands and pulled him into the dance. He seemed to need no urging.

It was a sight worth watching, the way those two danced together. Like many tall men, Richard was surprisingly light on his feet, and Thorne was like blown thistledown. Before long everyone else had stopped dancing to watch them.

Judith stopped dancing and stood quite still. She had taken Richard's refusal to dance with her as a subterfuge to hide his deficiency in the graceful art. She had not dreamed he could dance like that. Ann Tomlinson, catching a glimpse of her new daughter-in-law's face, recalled sharply the taste of a green persimmon.

As Thorne came tripping down the line, hands outstretched that Richard might twirl her, Judith made a movement swift as a darting hawk. She seized the hands before Richard could reach them and pulled Thorne out of the dance.

"You've stayed up long enough, Thorne. It's past your bedtime. You'd better go upstairs."

The cold, harsh command was astounding. Fortunately only a few people heard, for the room was crowded. But those few looked blank with consternation. Richard's own boys—six and seven—were staying up as late as their elders. Thorne, fourteen, was being sent to bed like a naughty child.

Ann Tomlinson looked at her son. Richard's face was a stony mask.

The doctor said softly, "She shouldn't have done that."

Ann whispered, "What do you think he'll do?"

"What can he do?" growled the doctor. "Just married. He can't start arguing with the woman before he's even bedded her."

Ann turned to look for Thorne. She had vanished. Judith was explaining sweetly, graciously, to a roomful of curious people that she was asking them all to stop dancing in deference to Mr. Jameson.

"I know Miss Ann doesn't think we're showing proper respect to the minister."

Dr. Caxton mumbled in his beard, "Something tells me Abigail was a housebroken angel compared to this filly."

Fortunately no one heard him.

Richard's foot was as light on the stairs as it had been in the dance. No one heard him go up. He paused outside the door of his mother's room and listened to a sound of muffled sobbing within. He tried the door. It was locked.

He called softly, but the sobs seemed to come from beneath a pillow. He dared not lift his voice. He would be heard downstairs before he was heard within the smothering feathers of his mother's bed.

His heart ached for the unseen weeper. He blamed himself for the whole stupid business. He had committed an unpardonable error in dancing, even with the children, after refusing his bride. He tried generously to excuse Judith. She had reason to be hurt by his behavior.

But she had no right to vent her feelings upon Thorne. His first shocked anger at Judith flamed again, frightening him by its vehemence. This was no way to feel toward the wife he had just wedded. But she had no cause to reprimand the child in that shameful fashion before a roomful of people. She had behaved exactly like—Abigail.

His thoughts retreated in panic haste from that comparison.

He put his ear to the door. Mingled now with the sobbing was an audible refrain, repeated over and over.

"I wish I was dead. Oh, I wish I was dead."

Strangely, the forlorn little wail reassured rather than alarmed him. It was the moan of childhood, wishing itself dead because of some injury, real or fancied. He smiled and drew his hand caressingly across the hard-oak door. Then he turned and went back downstairs.

He had not been missed. Judith was preparing to toss her bridal bouquet, and it was well that he came down when he did or they would have passed on the stairs. He stood in the hall below and watched her lean from the rail of the landing and throw the flowers straight into the hands of the oldest Barclay girl, and he knew she had done it to please him. John Barclay was his friend, and it was fitting that one of his five daughters should receive the hopeful token. Judith was very tactful. But Richard, watching the giggling maidens, could think only of Thorne, who should have had a part in this pretty scene, sobbing her heart out upstairs.

He went out onto the side porch, where some of the more convivial spirits had been withdrawing at intervals all evening. It was as he suspected. Something more potent than his mother's raspberry shrub was circulating. One of the Henderson boys had brought it from town. When he was invited to sample the fiery nectar he did not refuse. He had to get rid of this feeling he had toward Judith. If he did not go to her tonight a little drunk he might not go to her at all.

Judith sat before the mirror in the bird's-eye-maple room, alone at last. It was the custom of the community, so she had learned, for all the marriageable women to gather in the bridal chamber and help the bride disrobe. She had meekly submitted to this barbarous rite, but first she had locked the bureau drawer which hid her wedding nightgown. It was not the virginal garment which the ladies of Woods County would be expecting. Now, rid of her unwelcome attendants, she quickly unbuttoned the thick muslin gown in which they had sheathed her.

It was a handsome gown, hand-tucked and embroidered, a gift from Richard's sister in Kentucky. The sleeves came down to her wrists; the yoke was finished with a ruffle at the throat. She unfastened a dozen fine pearl buttons before the heavy nightdress fell to her feet.

Unlocking the bureau drawer, she took out another gown and slipped it over her head. It was not quite transparent, but it might as well have been. She had made this gown herself, in secret. No one, not even Cousin Lutie, had seen it. It fell about her body like trailing mist.

She was trembling now, weak with apprehension. She had watched Richard's face, following that little scene with Thorne. What had come over her to make her behave like that? All along her every conscious effort had been to conciliate and win Thorne's friendship. And suddenly she had pounced on the child and ordered her off to bed as though something had taken possession of her; some malevolent imp, bent on causing her to do the one thing that would alienate Richard on her bridal night. It almost seemed as if some power outside herself had driven her to wreck her own happiness by behaving like—Abigail.

She gazed into the mirror fearfully as she whispered the name.

It was the first time she had let herself think of Abigail since the day she met Miss Ann coming out of the downstairs bedroom. Now, curiously, the thought of the dead woman brought no reminder of anything that had happened in that room, only a vivid recollection of Abigail's jealous hatred of Thorne. That hatred had puzzled Judith once. It alarmed her now. Because now she had felt it too. She had taken it unto herself this very night, as she had taken Abigail's husband. And it had caused her to behave as Abigail would have behaved. The thought was sinister; it was frightening.

Of course she would never let it happen again. She would watch herself. She would explain to Richard that she had been momentarily ill—or disturbed about the minister—or something—if it was not too late. . . .

The house was quiet now. All the overnight guests had retired. Doors along the hall were closed. Voices and footsteps were silent. Still he had not come to her.

Was he too angry to come? If he did come, would he desire her? Judith's eyes grew haggard with waiting as the little clock on her dresser ticked away the minutes of her marriage night.

A wind was rising. The branches of the locust trees lashed against her window like frantic arms beseeching entrance. The tall house moaned and sighed. A creaking sound moved up the stairs, and for a moment she knew a thrill of pure terror. Then she recognized it as a footstep moving slowly—reluctantly?—toward her door. When the light tap sounded discreetly she had no voice to answer the summons. A stricture, like a band, tightened about her throat.

He came in softly and closed the door. They looked at each other in silence. She feared that the flush on his face was anger and that he had come to have it out with her. Then she saw that he had been drinking. He must have been exceedingly wroth with her, for he was not a drinking man; but if the drink had dulled his anger she did not care.

He came slowly across the room to her and stood looking down at the misty nightgown. Its charm was not wasted. Whatever had been on his mind when he entered was not there now. She smiled, half giddy with relief, and felt herself lifted in his arms.

But even as she was borne to the marriage bed she had a strange conviction that he had not come to her like a bridegroom. He had come, as his look betrayed, like a guilty lover keeping a rendezvous.

The big house groaned and creaked throughout the night. The wind whined at the windows and rapped at the doors; it stole in through the cracks and went sighing through the halls and passages. It was an increasingly chill and bitter wind, as though its mission was to blow summer and soft pleasure away. The household slept but fitfully. There were numerous calls for more bedcovers. Miss Ann, going downstairs in the small hours to fetch a drink for the wakeful children, encountered Cousin Lutie getting a snack from the kitchen in the hope that it might induce sleep. She hadn't closed her eyes all night, she declared. Miss Ann said that Thorne seemed the only one in her room able to sleep. "And she's sleeping so heavily, it frightened me. I thought when I lit my candle that she had stopped breathing."

"The witches are sure riding tonight," said Cousin Lutie as they trudged back upstairs together. Miss Ann thought it would either rain or snow before morning.

But toward morning the fierce gale subsided. Suddenly, ominously, there was hushed stillness in the starless hour before dawn. Weary bed tossers turned on their sides and sank into heavy slumber. Miss Ann looked at Thorne and saw that color had crept back into her pale cheeks, the deathlike stillness of her body had relaxed. She was warm and moist and breathing naturally. With a sigh of relief Miss Ann lay down beside her and fell into restful slumber.

In the bridal chamber Judith, sleeping in her lover's arms, had a strange, disquieting dream.

She thought she was standing before her old pupils in Timberley schoolhouse. In the midst of hearing a class she suddenly discovered that she had no clothes on. Her pupils were staring at her with horrible relish, and she saw that they were not the children of Timberley district, they were the silly women who had undressed her for her bridal bed. They had stolen her clothes and left her nothing, not even the misty nightgown. She demanded indignantly, "Who did this?" And they all giggled, pointing to a rear desk where someone hid behind a big Atlas. "She did it!" they chorused. "It's one of her tricks." It was Thorne's desk to which they pointed.

Judith seized a riding whip and went down the aisle between the seats and cried in a choking voice, "Come out from behind that Atlas. You can't play tricks on me. Tell me what you did with my clothes or I'll flog you." But when she jerked the Atlas away from the culprit, it was not Thorne who looked back at her. It was Abigail. She was dead and they all knew she was dead. Yet she moved among them as though she were living.

Judith awoke from this dream in shuddering terror and clung to Richard. He did not waken, but his arms about her tightened automatically. Gradually reality asserted itself. She had been the victim of nightmare. But the macabre quality of the dream had been so peculiarly vivid that it was a long while before she slept.

The sun rose clear and cold on a world of extreme untidiness. The lawn of Timberley looked as though it had been the playground of imps and demons. Trees and shrubs were stripped of leaves, and their naked limbs were decked with debris from all over the neighborhood. Or was it debris . . .

Jesse Moffat was late getting down that morning, owing to difficulty in finding his socks. He finally put his bare feet in his boots and came down to the kitchen to start the fire for the lavish breakfast which must be prepared for the houseful of guests. When he ignited his fresh-laid fire, smoke belched into his face. He examined the drafts in the stove. There appeared to be some obstruction in the pipe. Smoke rapidly filled the low-ceilinged room.

Millie, in her room over the kitchen, smelled smoke and yelled, "Fiah!" As she came clattering down the back stairs Jesse hushed her sternly.

"Do you want to scare everybody in the house? Nothing's on fire. The pipe's stopped up. Here, give me a hand and we'll see what's blocking it."

They took down a section of the stovepipe and found it stuffed with what appeared at first to be rags.

"Rags, nothin'!" snorted Millie. "Them's somebody's clo'es."

And clothes they were. Wearing apparel of divers sorts stuffed the stovepipe far into the chimney. When Jesse pulled the last article out he found to his amazement a handsome pair of new whipcord breeches.

"If those aren't the pants Lucius Goff was wearing last night, I'll eat my hat!"

"Who do you s'pose played a low-down dirty trick like that?" said Millie. "Stuffin' folkses' best clothes in that ole chimney. Looky there! Nice white shirts covered with soot, coats and pants that'll nevah come clean."

Jesse said, "I looked for 'em to play pranks at this wedding, but spoiling good clothes is going too far."

"Wait'll Miss Ann sees this," said Millie. "Somebody'll get a blistered behine."

"Maybe the fellow that did this is too old to blister," grinned Jesse.

When Miss Ann appeared she demanded sternly, "Where are everyone's clothes? Someone sneaked through all the rooms last night and stole the clothing of our guests. Are you the culprit, Jesse Moffat?"

The hired man's denial was emphatic. "Look what I found in the chimney." He pointed to the sooty clothes upon the floor.

Ann Tomlinson was angrier than either of the two had ever seen her.

"A charivari is one thing. A stupid joke like this is a disgrace to Tomlinson hospitality. If I find that any member of this household had a hand in it, he shall certainly hear from me."

There was commotion now through all the house. Doors were slamming, excited voices clamoring. Feminine squeals and masculine growls were mingled in a rising chorus of indignation. Will Tomlinson charged down the back stairs in his nightshirt, demanding, "Who hung my drawers at the top of the big locust tree?" The little group in the kitchen stared at him blankly.

"At the top of the tree!" said his mother.

"At the very tip of the topmost branch. If you don't believe me, go look. I saw them from my bedroom window. It's disgraceful."

They all hurried outdoors. A weird spectacle greeted them. The trees and shrubs of Timberley bore strange foliage. It was as though the wind, which had stripped them of their autumn glory, had swept through the house collecting what it could to clothe their nakedness. Neckties, socks, and handkerchiefs fluttered from airy twigs; waistcoats, pantaloons, and petticoats dangled grotesquely from boughs. Nor were they hung on lower limbs where they could be easily picked off. They were suspended from the highest and most inaccessible branches.

"No man—or woman either—could possibly have crawled up there," said a voice behind Miss Ann. It was Lucius Goff, in night clothes and greatcoat, shivering with excitement.

They were all coming down, guests and relatives; a fantastic little company of half-clad people wrapped in shawls and cloaks, for the morning air was crisp. Good nature predominated, though some were inquiring rather pointedly if anything of the Tomlinsons had been touched.

The Tomlinsons, fortunately, had suffered as much as anyone. Miss Ann's stays decorated the pasture fence. Jesse Moffat's socks hung from the top of the windmill. Even the bride had not escaped. The bridal underclothing—which the women had neatly folded the night before—was draped over the tops of the two tall poplars that guarded the family burial ground.

Only one Tomlinson had been passed over by this angel (or demon) of mischief. Nothing belonging to Richard had been touched.

"Where's Thorne?" someone asked suddenly.

It was Judith. She had come down with Richard when the murmuring excitement spreading through the house had reached their room. She had not yet discovered her own loss when Richard, wrapped in a dressing gown, had stepped out into the hall to see what was happening. When he reported that someone had been playing jokes and everyone's clothes were missing Judith had laughed. It all seemed part of the delirium of the night and the luxurious detachment of the morning. And then she glanced toward the chair where her own garments were laid and—she saw that the chair was empty.

Springing from bed in queer panic, she searched frantically all over the room. Her clothes were gone. Richard laughed at her consternation.

"You don't think they'd pass up the bridal chamber," he teased.

"Nothing of yours is gone," said Judith. Her face was pale. She remembered her dream.

But she followed Richard downstairs and listened to the talk of the others. The two cousins from Bridgeport—small, wiry lads and notorious practical jokers—were the favorite suspects. They in turn affirmed their belief that Richard was the culprit, since nothing of his had been touched. Lucius Goff retorted that Richard had something better to do last night than play pranks on his guests, and then blushed at his own ribaldry when he saw Judith appear with her husband.

"Granted someone was agile enough to climb up there," he said hastily, "granted he was able to collect clothes from every room without waking anyone, I still don't see how he had time to hang so many small articles in so many outlandish places."

"Working by himself, he couldn't," said young Will, "but if he was twins he might," and he cast a dark look at the cousins from Bridgeport.

One of them said quickly, "Nothing but a cat could have crawled that high."

"Or a child," amended his brother.

At this implication Miss Ann said emphatically, "The children slept in my room. I was up and down with them all night. Not one of them could have left his bed without my knowing it."

"Thorne too?" asked Judith.

Richard gave her a look which she pretended not to see. But other voices took up the question. Where was Thorne? All who had seen her dance the night before suddenly recalled that her body had seemed as light as thistledown. Would those branches bear her weight?

Ann Tomlinson put an end to all conjecture. "Thorne didn't stir all night. I know, because she slept with me. And she slept like the dead."

Judith shivered. It was just a wedding prank, but it was so queerly, so damnably, like her dream.

It took the better part of the day to dislodge all the pilfered clothing. Ladders were requisitioned; boys with fishing poles were sent up into the trees. When the last piece of wearing apparel had been extricated from a willow down on the creek the owner was heard to declare, "By golly! There must have been a witch in that house last night." And that was what everyone was saying by the time the tale reached Woodridge.

CHAPTER 16

Seasons were reversed in the country. Winter, the period of greatest activity in town, was the farmer's time of relaxation. Judith had been well aware of this fact when she insisted upon a fall wedding.

She had plans for the winter. It would have shocked the entire family had it been known how long these plans had been incubating. From the moment she first set foot in the house, not quite one year ago, she had mentally tabulated certain changes she would like to make at Timberley.

But she was not long discovering that living among the Tomlinsons as a daughter-in-law was quite another thing to living among them as a boarder. The winter before she had found them completely charming. They were quite as charming now. But she had never been so aware of their formidable unity until she became one of the family. She began to feel that she had married, not a man, but a tribal community in which married daughters, sons-in-law, and grandchildren had an equal vote with herself. She never had a moment alone with Richard except at bedtime.

Of all the family she preferred young Will, because he was silent and sullen and usually took himself off after supper, either to his own room or into town to see some girl. He had no steady sweetheart, and his trips into Woodridge were matters of anxiety to his mother. After talking to him subtly once or twice, Judith decided that there was basis for Miss Ann's fears. The lad was lonely and in fair danger to get into bad company. He should have had a nice girl whom he could eventually marry. She tucked this knowledge away for future reference and dismissed young Will from her immediate calculations.

She wished she could dismiss the rest of the family as easily. She had, by Thanksgiving, done nothing toward furthering her plans for making Timberley the center of a charming little group of intellectual society and gradually shedding the burden of constantly entertaining relatives and family friends. Richard's education and talents fitted him for leadership in such a society. All he had ever lacked had been a charming cultured wife for hostess.

Early in November she proposed to Richard that they give a small party; just a few congenial spirits interested in discussing something besides neighborhood affairs. He grasped her idea immediately and was enthusiastic. They began to discuss the chosen few—and struck a snag. He insisted that any such gathering at Timberley should include Doc Baird. She had difficulty in making him understand that the local blacksmith was not her idea of gentility. She decided to postpone the whole thing until after the holidays and concentrate on small innovations.

These could be lumped under two heads: domestic and religious. Under the first came house furnishings and service at meals. Under the second, family worship. Her idea on this point was iconoclastic. The family altar had no place in the picture she was creating of modern life in a postwar Timberley. But she was too wise to suggest this to Richard just yet.

She began with lesser changes. "You know, dear, I think we should get rid of that old clock."

They had been married six weeks and still occupied the bird's-eye-maple room. Richard had hinted more than once that it was time they moved downstairs and let Thorne have the smaller chamber. Judith had dealt with this problem by having Jesse Moffat install a heating stove in the room, making it so cozy that Richard had been wooed to its warmth and luxury and finally agreed that the downstairs room be kept for a guest chamber.

He lay now in bed, drowsily comfortable, watching the movement of Judith's bare arms as she brushed her hair for the night. She kept the room at a temperature that made a wrapper unnecessary. Bedtime, she had discovered, was the ideal time for securing his endorsement of controversial issues.

"Did you hear what I said, Richard?" She was watching him in the mirror.

He murmured, "Um ummmmm," his eyes on her breasts as they rose and fell with each upward movement of the arm holding the brush.

"Well—what do you think?"

"I think"—he smiled—"that's it's fun being married to a hussy."

"Richard!" She laid down the brush and reached for a night robe. "I was talking about the clock downstairs."

"What about it?"

"It doesn't run."

"Naturally." He yawned. "It has no mainspring."

"And a new one can't be got, I understand."

"I'm afraid not. It's a very old clock—made in Switzerland. I don't believe parts for it can be bought in this country."

"Then let's get rid of it."

He opened his eyes wide, as though he had been asked to shoot one of the family.

"Get rid of Grandfather Tomlinson's clock? Why, it's over forty years old. Father brought it all the way out here from Virginia."

"But it doesn't keep time. A timepiece that doesn't run and

can't be fixed is as useless as a chronic invalid who won't die."

The words had scarcely left her lips before she wondered, in consternation, what had induced her to make such a remark.

He carefully avoided her eyes in the mirror, but he answered casually enough:

"We'll see if it's possible to get a new spring. Mother said the clock had a beautiful tone. I'm sure she'd be glad to hear it striking again."

Judith did not want the clock repaired; she wanted it removed. It was the gloomiest piece of furniture she had ever seen. But when the jeweler in Woodridge reported that only a Swiss clock mender could repair the clock, the family voted unanimously that the defunct timepiece should remain where it was. That was when she learned about the corporate unity of the Tomlinsons.

She was more successful with her mother-in-law.

"Miss Ann, dear, do you mind if we serve the soup first? And then remove the plates before bringing in the meat and vegetables? Let's not put the pie on the table until we have finished with the rest of the meal. It's really no more trouble and it makes more room than putting everything on at once."

Ann Tomlinson had not made up her mind what she thought of this new daughter-in-law and her advanced ideas. She did not consider that it mattered what she thought. She had advanced ideas herself regarding the limitations of parenthood. Richard was no longer the inexperienced lad for whom a bride had been selected willy-nilly. He was a mature man who had made his own choice. He must be allowed to manage this second marriage his own way. She had held her tongue and refrained from saying one word against it when there was still time. Now that the time was past, her only interest was in co-operation. She had discerned that small things were important to Judith. A pleased wife made a happy husband. Richard's mother could help, at least that much.

"It takes more time, Judith, to serve the meal the way you

suggest. The men are always in a hurry at noon. How would you like to try it out at the evening meal?"

Judith was elated with her easy victory until she thought it over later, and then she was not sure whether she or her mother-in-law had scored.

But the more formal service of the evening meal was installed, with Millie grumbling audibly at the extra steps entailed until it was discovered that the table was cleared—or nearly so—by the time the meal was over and the business of dishwashing really expedited. The Tomlinson daughters, on their first visit, were charmed with the arrangement, and Kate announced that she was going to try it in the Turner household. The Tomlinson males—with the exception of Richard—were bored with the whole procedure. Richard declared that he liked it.

It was that way in everything. During the first weeks of their marriage he approved every suggestion Judith made. Many were so impracticable as to impede seriously the work of the busy farm household, but Richard merely advised getting more help if it were needed. Sometimes his brother Will looked at him in exasperation and once scornfully asked if he were losing his wits. Richard's infatuation seemed complete.

But Judith could have told her brother-in-law that actually her influence over her husband went no deeper than the play of sunlight on the face of a cliff. He agreed with her when it was a matter which concerned him little, such as the laying of a supper table. On a question which touched him personally he was impervious as granite.

This was brought home to her very soon after their marriage.

They attended a lecture in Woodridge one evening. It was their first appearance in public since their wedding, and after the speaking they held quite a little reception among their friends. The talk turned on the wedding and the joke that had been played on the overnight guests. Richard was asked if he had ever discovered the identity of the mischief-maker and he answered promptly that he had. His two cousins from Bridge-port had been the culprits.

On the way home in the phaeton Judith said to him, "You really shouldn't have told a falsehood, darling, about our wedding charivari."

"I told no falsehood."

"Of course, dear, I realize you were trying to protect Thorne."

She felt him stiffen at her side.

He said, "The Cary boys played the prank, and when they saw how people's clothes were ruined they were ashamed to own up to it."

"Did they confess their guilt to you?"

"They did. I saw them in town the other day and frankly charged them with the mischief."

After a moment's silence Judith said, "I don't believe it was the Cary boys."

"You mean you think I'm lying?"

"No. I mean I don't believe it could have been an adult. Everyone agreed that only a child or small animal could have crawled to the tops of those trees. An animal is out of the question, so it must have been a child. Your boys are much too young. There was only one other child in the house."

He said, "A ladder and a fishing pole were used to bring the clothes down from the trees. The same implements could have been used to put them up there."

"And who," murmured Judith, "is more adept at using theatrical props than Thorne?"

He gave his attention to the horse, who had fallen into a jog.

"Have you ever questioned Thorne about this?" asked Judith.

"No." His voice was the voice of a stranger.

"Then how do you know whether it was her work or not?"

"Because I'm satisfied it was the work of the Cary boys."

But still Judith seemed unable to let the matter drop.

"You must remember, Richard, that Thorne went to bed that night very angry at me." This was the first time Judith had alluded to the incident, and she now proceeded to eat humble pie in cathartic doses. She pleaded nerves, headache, all the timeworn feminine alibis for bad temper, concluding meekly, "I take the whole blame. Thorne was perfectly justified in feeling a desire to get even with me for sending her to bed."

"I agree with you," said Richard much too promptly. "But because she was justified, it does not follow that she was capable of harboring a feeling of petty revenge. That prank was horseplay of a very low order; a performance of which Thorne would have been incapable."

"But she's just a child, Richard, with a child's love of mischief. You're making the thing entirely too serious."

"It's you who are making the thing serious, Judith. Even when I tell you that Bob Cary admitted to me that he and his brother planned it in advance, you seem inclined to doubt my word."

Judith said suddenly, "Will you let me do one thing, Richard? Will you let me tell Thorne what you have just told me —and watch her reaction?"

"I intend to tell the whole family. You may watch the reaction of anyone you choose."

He made the disclosure the next morning at breakfast. It was greeted with mingled amusement and indignation. Miss Ann said she had suspected the Bridgeport cousins from the first. Will said he had felt all along it was the work of more than one person. Jesse Moffat was relieved to learn it wasn't witches. Thorne was frankly overjoyed at this proof of her innocence.

"I was afraid people would think I had done it. It was so much like my magic tricks."

"You couldn't have done it, Cricket, with all your cleverness," said Richard. "Not unless you were twins."

Judith did not join in the laughter that greeted her husband's sally. She felt as though she had lost the first skirmish in a battle which had barely begun.

Yet she was very happy those first months of her marriage. He was all that she had anticipated. If he was a little more than she had bargained for, that was only an added stimulus. He was ardent, yet aloof. He delighted and at the same time provoked her. Sometimes she wondered if she ever would know what went on inside his mind. He was a passionate lover but strangely absent-minded. She could not recall that he had ever told her that he loved her.

But he was the man she had desired above all others, and the satisfaction of having him for a husband was worth all it had cost her. She had been obliged to perform a number of unpleasant chores in order to bring the present felicity to pass. She regretted nothing, but she did think it rather too bad that she had to be reminded of Abigail at every turn.

For instance, there was an album on the table in the front room filled with pictures of Abigail and Abigail's relatives. Judith saw no reason why that album couldn't be put away with the dead woman's other things, instead of being left out where she must look at it. She had a queer compulsion which moved her, every time she was near the album, to open it and look at Abigail's picture. It was most unpleasant.

She took the matter up with Richard in a roundabout way.

"There don't seem to be any Tomlinsons in the album."

He answered, "Not in that one. That's the Huse family album. Abigail had it before we were married."

"Don't you think, dear—I mean—really, it's not good taste to keep family pictures in the front room, is it?"

"I don't know." He glanced at the fireplace, above which hung portraits of his Tomlinson grandparents. "Most people around here keep family photographs—if they're fortunate enough to have any—where they can be seen."

"But these are photographs of strangers."

"They are my children's maternal grandparents, uncles, aunts, and cousins," said Richard quietly. "And the only likenesses we have of their mother."

"Oh, I didn't mean——" Judith blushed at her own *faux pas.* "Of course the pictures will be priceless to Ricky and Rodgie when they're older. That's the reason they should be put somewhere for safekeeping."

"Where would you suggest?" he seemed amenable. "Maybe we'd better take them upstairs to our room."

Judith repressed a slight shudder. "I don't think they should be kept out at all. They should be preserved, like the treasured heirlooms they are. Didn't"—finding it impossible to speak Abigail's name, she was at a loss what to call her—"didn't the boys' mother have a chest in her room in which she kept her most cherished belongings?"

"Yes."

"Then why not put the album of photographs in there?" Judith looked up from her work to find him regarding her with a curious smile.

"All right," he said, "if it bothers you having them around."

She flushed. "It doesn't bother me. It doesn't matter to me one way or the other. I merely——"

"I think it does," he interrupted, still smiling. "I think you find it unpleasant to open the album and see Abigail staring back at you. Of course you don't have to open it every time you pass the table——"

"We'll say no more about it, Richard." She bent over her fancywork with flaming cheeks.

"Oh, come now. I was only teasing. It's nothing to be ashamed of, Judith. I believe second wives are supposed to feel that way about things belonging to the first. And I think I'm supposed to feel flattered."

She hated the whole conversation. She resented the mischievous twinkle which usually she adored. She loathed being reminded that she was a second wife.

"Please, Richard, don't say any more."

But he picked up the album and left the room. When he returned he tossed a small key into her lap.

"The album is now in the chest, along with her quilts and silver. The chest is locked, and there is the key."

"Keep it yourself," muttered Judith, and tossed it back to him. He caught it, laughing, took a bunch of keys from his pocket, and slipped it on the ring.

"Abigail was a great one to hoard silver," he went on. "Would you believe it, her purse was filled with quarters and dimes, besides four silver dollars and a fifty-cent piece."

"What did you do with them?" asked Judith idly.

"Oh, I put them back for the boys. They're quite a rarity these days. She must have had them before we were married, because this house hasn't seen any silver since before the war."

As he put his key ring back in his pocket he drew forth a roll of paper money: two-dollar bills, one-dollar bills, and small currency as low as ten cents in value. "Shinplasters," he chuckled. "How Abigail detested shinplasters. And brass and wooden tokens for nickels and pennies."

"Is it absolutely necessary that we discuss Abigail?" asked Judith sharply.

He glanced at her in mild astonishment. "Why, no, I wasn't aware that I was discussing her. I was talking about postwar currency." He returned the money to his pocket, but he continued to look curiously at his wife.

"You know, Judith, I believe you're afraid of Abigail."

Her face went so white that had he not been intent on his own thought he might have been alarmed.

"What do you mean—afraid?"

"I think you're afraid I have tender memories. Well, you needn't be. I never loved Abigail. She wouldn't let me."

Relief made Judith suddenly bold. She asked the question she had never dared ask before.

"Do you love me, Richard?"

His answer was appallingly frank. "I don't know."

She wished sickeningly that she had remained in ignorance. "Don't know!" she spoke lightly. "Surely you know how you feel."

"I feel slightly drunk most of the time." He smiled. "And so far I've no desire to sober up."

He put his hands on the arms of her chair, and she raised her face to his. His mouth on hers was a lover's mouth. And with that she had to be content.

She watched him that night with the children. The fireside reading, which had been such a delightful feature of the previous winter, had been replaced by home tutoring in schoolwork. Judith herself, to her own chagrin, had brought this change to pass.

"I don't think, dear, that Thorne should be permitted to sit with us in the evenings until she has prepared her lessons for next day." It was during one of their bedtime chats, following an evening when Thorne had embarrassed the reading circle by asking for a definition of the word "platonic." "She should be studying her schoolbooks," said Judith, "instead of listening to you read aloud."

"I didn't know she had to study at home." Richard looked concerned. Judith pursued her advantage—a little too far.

"Arithmetic is difficult for her. I know; I taught her last year. I had to stretch a point to give her a passing grade. If she doesn't study at home this winter she'll never get through partial payments. You wouldn't like to see her fail, would you?"

Richard was alarmed. He questioned Thorne, who frankly admitted that partial payments were too much for her. Mr. Carpenter gave such long assignments that only the smartest boys in class could cope with them. She had given up trying to keep abreast of the others.

Richard promptly announced that the evening reading would be postponed until Thorne's problems were disposed of.

"That's unfair to the other children," Judith pointed out. "Ricky and Rodgie have to go to bed early. Let Thorne take her work into the dining room. There's a fire in there. She can study as late as need be and no one will disturb her."

But Richard had a better plan. "I'll help her with the problems. Then we'll get through in time for all of us to enjoy the reading together."

They worked every evening after that, Richard and Thorne at the dining-room table. The little boys, not to be left out of anything, brought primers and slates and joined the class in home instruction. And because Richard had that rare quality of inciting general interest in whatever he was doing, the lessons in the dining room soon became the focus of family attention. They usually ended in a hilarious romp about the time Jesse Moffat appeared with the bedtime basket of apples.

On the evening in question Thorne had been particularly cloudy on the subject of decimals. Stupid, Judith would have called her. But Richard's patience seemed inexhaustible. Over and over he explained, but every time the troublesome point came up in the wrong place. Thorne's face grew pale with weariness and strain and finally she burst into tears.

"Oh, Richard, I just can't learn arithmetic. You're wasting your time. Let me stay home from school and help Millie."

If there was one thing calculated to arouse him, it was the mere suggestion of Thorne occupying the position of a servant.

"Cricket! How can you say such a thing? You don't want to quit school like that silly Nancy Turner. What's come over you tonight?"

She could have told him that Judith's critical presence in the room was no stabilizer. But she answered nothing;

only sat silent, while her tears sponged the errors from her slate.

Richard put his arm around her comfortingly. "You're tired, dear. You should be in bed. I'll tell you what we'll do. We'll let the lessons go tonight, and tomorrow morning you and I will get up an hour early and tackle them while we're fresh. How's that?"

"Oh, for goodness sake, Richard, stop babying her." Judith's annoyance burst from her at last. Thorne slipped quickly from under his arm and went upstairs.

In the morning she arose before daylight and went doggedly at her books again, but Richard did not join her. Judith saw to it that he overslept.

He was full of apologies at breakfast. Thorne did not reproach him. She had surprisingly got through the bothersome problem by her own effort. And as she walked to school that morning with Ricky and Rodgie she took herself sternly to task. Where had she got the idea that she had a right to be happy all her life? She had had last summer, hadn't she? That was more than some people ever had.

"Who're you talking to, Thorne?" asked Ricky.

Rodgie said, "You're not mad at me, are you?"

She laughed at their startled young faces and offered to race them to the horse steps.

CHAPTER 17

Thorne was at last reconciled to the passing of summer. Not by anything that had happened, but by the simple change of season that told her it was gone. There had been frost on the ground for a month now, and one or two light snows had fallen. The corn was gathered, the hogs were butchered, the potatoes were dug. In the kitchen houseflies dropped dead from the ceiling and ice crusted the basins in the early mornings. The children had put on their long underwear, and shoes and stockings once more appeared in Timberley schoolhouse. The spicy sweetness of baking pumpkin was in the air, and the big turkey that had strutted so arrogantly all fall was meekly roasting in Millie's huge oven.

Then without warning, the day before Thanksgiving, she wakened in a sweat under a pile of blankets and dashed to the window to find the sky a warm summer blue. Cows trotted friskily down the lane as though it were spring, bells tintinnabulating. The creak of a pump handle, the brisk clucking argument of hens, the neigh of a mule in the pasture were again the sounds of summer. For a moment time flowed backward. She was racing to get dressed and out to the woods to gather berries for Richard's breakfast. Nothing that was had ever been. She had dreamed the last three months.

Then recollection stabbed her. This was only Indian summer, that sly deceiver that came every year to taunt you with false promises of spring long after spring was dead.

But the poignant joy of her awakening was with her all day. Nothing seemed quite real. She moved in a dream as unsubstantial as the smoky haze that softened the bare bleakness of fields and woods so that the loss of their verdure was forgotten. But underneath this ecstasy of unreality was a strange sense of foreboding.

The entire Tomlinson clan gathered at Timberley for Thanksgiving. Because of the extra company, Thorne slept downstairs in the trundle bed. She did not rest very well because Cousin Lutie, in the alcove, snored all night. Throughout the wakeful hours Thorne heard strange noises all over the house. In the room adjoining, the sound of someone moving about was so disturbing that once she cried out.

"Who slept in the south bedroom?" she asked at breakfast. "I heard somebody moving around in there in the middle of the night."

The visiting Tomlinsons exchanged shocked glances with the members of the household. It seemed that no one had slept in the downstairs bedroom. There had, in fact, been a slight argument over the matter, with both Turners and Mitchells declining to occupy the room in which their sister-in-law had died.

"You must have been dreaming, child," said Miss Ann, and there the whole thing would have dropped had not Judith interposed. She felt that Thorne should be made to retract her false statement.

Richard immediately took exception to his wife's remark.

"Thorne is not well. She's a bundle of nerves, and no wonder. She has no regular place to sleep. Whenever there's company and somebody has to be inconvenienced, it's Thorne who's made to sleep downstairs in a bed that's too short for her."

This was a direct thrust at Judith for her refusal to vacate the bird's-eye-maple room. No more was said. Richard opened the Bible for morning prayers.

He began reading at the fifteenth chapter of Luke, the eighth verse:

" 'Either what woman having ten pieces of silver, if she lose one piece, doth not light a candle, and sweep the house, and seek diligently till she find it?' "

Something dropped from the big limp book in Richard's hands and rolled briskly across the table. Everyone heard the metallic clink as it struck the butter dish and caught the gleam of silver. Every eye saw it lying bright and shining on the tablecloth. It was a fifty-cent piece.

For a breathless moment there was not a sound. Then there came a surprised gasp from little Rodgie: "Oh! that's one of Mama's silver pieces that she kept in her purse."

Millie, always present at morning prayers, groaned, "Oh Lawdy! That's what she was lookin' for last night," and rolled her eyes fearfully.

There was general commotion then. Children cried and adults talked excitedly. Even Richard changed color, and his wife was seized with a fit of choking—or was it laughter? It was some time before order was restored to the breakfast table.

Richard put the money in his pocket and told the children to finish their meal.

"This money didn't come from your mother's purse," he explained to his sons. "The chest is locked and I have the key in my pocket." And that was the end of the incident for the time being.

But the following day Miss Ann decided to take advantage of the warm spell and ordered the chicken house cleaned. The oldest Schook boy was hired to help Jesse Moffat. It being Saturday, the children all trooped out to watch them work. The Turner boys, who were finishing the holiday week at Grandmother's, organized a game of Indian, with the log hen house for a fort. It was while scaling this bastion that Jimmie Turner made a discovery.

"Look what I found!" he cried. A pile of photographs had been tossed on top of the hen house. They were pictures of Ricky's and Rodgie's dead mother.

While they were exclaiming over their find, Peter Schook, within the house, called to Jesse Moffat. "Look here, will you? See what I found under these nests."

The children ran into the chicken house to join the two hired hands in as weird a treasure hunt as could be imagined. Photographs were found in all sorts of places: hidden under piles of straw, flung far back of the roosts, as though someone had been hastily bent on putting them out of sight. Tintypes, daguerreotypes, and some of a later school of photography mounted on cardboard, all were likenesses of Abigail and Abigail's relatives. All had reposed, until a few weeks ago, in the album on the front-room table.

"Ooooh! Wait till Father finds who did this!" said Ricky. Someone was going to catch it. Youthful faces paled with pleasurable excitement.

All but Thorne's. Thorne, who had been sitting on the fence with Nancy Turner, watching the game of Indian, had a premonition that she was going to be charged with this mischief.

As the dinner bell was ringing by this time, Jesse Moffat and the Schook boy dropped their work and went up to the house, the children at their heels like excited terriers.

"Look what we found in the hen house," said Jesse, and laid the photographs in front of Richard.

"Who did this?" he demanded sternly.

"We don't know," the children chorused loudly.

Judith came into the room at this moment. "What is it?" she asked.

"Here are the pictures I put away in the chest," said Richard. "Jesse found them out in the hen house."

Judith regarded the photographs without comment.

"Are you sure you locked the chest?" asked Miss Ann.

They went immediately to the south room and examined the chest. It was locked. On being opened, its contents appeared to be intact. But the album was empty. And the half dollar was missing from the purse.

Ann Tomlinson said, "Someone stole your key, Richard, and put it back later."

"How could they? The ring is never out of my pocket."

Judith said, very innocently, "Spiriting a key from your pocket, darling, would require a sleight-of-hand performance."

Richard's face flushed ominously. "Whom are you accusing, Judith?"

"No one, dear. I was merely making a joke."

Thorne sat down on a stool in the corner. They were back

in the dining room now. It seemed to her that she had lived all this before. She had only to close her eyes and see, not Judith's firm ripe contours, but an emaciated figure in a challis wrapper screaming, "Now do you believe she's a witch!"

Judith was not screaming. She was smiling sweetly, but she had caused every eye to turn suspiciously on Thorne.

"Why not put a direct question to everyone?" she suggested to her husband.

Ann Tomlinson promptly added, "Now is the time to do it, son, while we're all gathered for dinner."

Richard, thus coerced, deliberately began with his own children.

"Ricky, what do you know about this?"

"Nothing, Father, except finding the pictures."

"Rodgie, have you been playing games with these photographs?"

"No, sir."

To Nancy, Jimmie, and Frank Turner, he put the same question and received the same answer. Even his brother Will was not passed by.

"Do you know anything about this, Will?"

Will said, "I didn't even know the pictures had been put in the chest," and gave his brother a sly grin, as though he guessed the reason for their removal.

"Jesse, you're usually the cutup around here. Is this your idea of a joke?"

On and on went the questioning. It sounded a little absurd now to everyone. It sounded absurd to Thorne, sitting wretchedly alone on her hassock, because of course no one believed these people guilty.

But Richard doggedly pursued his inquiry. "Peter, how about you?"

"As God is my judge, Mr. Richard, I never saw them pictures before."

"Mother, do you think Millie could have had anything to do with this?"

The idea was ludicrous, but Miss Ann went out to the kitchen to question her old servant.

"Judith"—Richard turned to his wife, and their glances met combatively—"you said every member of the household should be examined. Have you any light to throw upon this business?"

Judith said, still sweetly, "Nothing, except to remind you that you've overlooked Thorne."

"I haven't come to her yet."

"You've come to her now."

He looked across the room, where Thorne sat motionless on the stool. Her face was pale, but no paler than his.

"Cricket, do you know anything about this?"

"I didn't do it," said Thorne.

"Then that's all that matters," said Richard.

But Judith was not satisfied.

"You know, Thorne, you're quite clever enough to remove a key from a man's pocket without him being aware of your action."

Thorne said in a curious tone, "Yes, I know that. Other people know it too."

Judith said sharply, "What do you mean by that statement?"

Richard interrupted, "She's said she didn't do it, Judith. Why can't her word be accepted as well as the others?"

"Because she is insinuating something."

"You're not insinuating anything, are you, Cricket?"

Thorne's face was so pale now that she looked almost ill. It was very hard trying to explain with all of them staring at her. She said, "I've had a feeling something like this was going to happen."

"Make her tell what she means, Richard, by those veiled hints."

179 ह

How could Thorne put into words what was so clear to her own sensitive perception? That sense of foreboding which had underlain her strange ecstasy had meaning now. This was what had been moving toward her, this incriminating circumstance. Judith would convince Richard of Thorne's guilt. And to lose Richard's trust and friendship would be a blow which should satisfy Thorne's bitterest enemy.

She said, "I've been too happy lately. I was afraid something would happen."

"That's superstition," said Judith.

"Yes, I know." Thorne wrinkled her smooth young brow with the effort to make her meaning clear. "I think whoever played this trick was hoping it would be laid at my door."

Judith's face flushed with anger. "Be careful how you make accusations, young lady."

"I'm not accusing anyone," said Thorne. She looked about the little group, noting the suspicion in the farm hands' faces, even in the wide clear eyes of the children. "But you can see how well it succeeded. You all believe I did this."

"We believe nothing of the sort," said Richard.

No one else spoke.

Miss Ann came back from the kitchen to report that Millie was ready to swear to her own innocence. Richard informed his mother of Thorne's belief that someone was trying to incriminate her.

"And I for one think it's the explanation for this mischief," he said, "and the stolen coin as well."

Miss Ann asked Thorne, "Who do you think has this spite against you, child?"

Thorne shook her head. It was not clear whether she refused to answer or did not know. But Judith suddenly decided to terminate the discussion.

"We're not interested in theories, we're interested in

facts. Thorne, by her own admission, is the only person who could have stolen your key, Richard."

"And Thorne, by her own admission, did not steal my key, Judith. So that's the final word upon the subject."

But it was not the final word. There was one thing more, which Judith seemed impelled to say.

She waited until bedtime, when Richard was comfortably ensconced with his book, a candle at his elbow. It was not flattering that he had reverted so soon to his old habit of reading in bed. The ritual of hairbrushing no longer engrossed him.

"Of course it's quite plain what Thorne was hinting at this morning," Judith began.

He looked up from the page he was reading. "What did you say about Thorne?"

"Why, it was quite evident," said Judith, "Thorne would have had you believe *I* played that silly prank in order to incriminate her."

Richard looked not at all shocked, only interested.

"Yes, of course. You are the one person who has the perfect opportunity for taking my key and replacing it—while I'm asleep."

Judith dropped the brush she was wielding. She did not speak until she had retrieved it.

"My dear Richard, are you accusing me?"

He smiled innocuously. "You are quite as likely a suspect as Thorne. You had the opportunity and the motive."

"What motive?"

"Those pictures of Abigail were a source of irritation to you. You might have decided that you would feel happier if they were out of the house altogether. So you stole down in the dead of night; and Thorne, sleeping in the trundle bed, heard you and cried out and gave you a frightful scare. I don't believe you meant to incriminate Thorne—at first.

Your thought was to punish her for the shock she had given you. Abigail's purse was at hand. You filched a coin from it and slipped it into the family Bible, where you knew I would find it. Later your own fear of discovery prompted an accusation of Thorne, which I believe—or hope—you're ashamed of." His voice was pleasant throughout.

Judith turned back to the mirror. The hand that held the brush was trembling.

"Of course you don't believe a word you're saying."

"Whether I do or not, my dear, we'll say no more about it. Thorne knows that I'm convinced of her innocence. It's not necessary for her to know any more."

"I suppose she put that idea about me into your head."

"Oh no," said Richard quickly. "I'm sure Thorne never thought of you. Poor child, she was afraid of Abigail."

"Abigail!" said Judith sharply. And then she laughed. "Do you mean the silly thing is afraid of a dead woman?"

"When you consider how she was persecuted by Abigail, it's small wonder she should imagine the woman's spirit was hounding her, playing pranks from beyond the grave to incriminate her."

Judith said, "Her purpose in advancing that theory is to frighten me."

"Now you're being ridiculous." Richard slumped back on his pillow. "Why should Thorne try to frighten you?"

"You may not have noticed, Richard, but Thorne has never liked me. As far back as a year ago, when she shared this room with me, I was conscious of her reluctance to sleep with me."

"That's interesting," said Richard, and picked up his book. "Because Thorne had the same idea about you. She felt that you didn't like sleeping with her."

"There!" said Judith triumphantly. "You see how she lies?"

He slammed down the book with a force which, unfortunately, did not register on the soft feather bed.

"Thorne does not lie. She has too much sense."

"She has no sense at all, as you ought to know; you've been coaching her in arithmetic. She's only precocious—emotionally."

It was out at last, the word that held significance. With its utterance two spots of color burned in Judith's cheeks.

Richard said, curiously, "What do you mean?"

"I mean I'm beginning to understand why Abigail didn't like her. Abigail wasn't as crazy as people thought. In some ways she was smart." Suddenly Judith realized she was talking to the man who had been Abigail's husband.

She went on more lightly, "I suppose it's growing pains with Thorne. She'll stop behaving like a spoiled child eventually and turn into a respectable member of adult society—at least we hope so. In the meantime, it's rather uncomfortable for the people who have to live with her."

Richard laid his book on the night table and blew out his candle. When Judith came to bed there was no response from the other occupant of the big four-poster. She wondered if he really suspected her guilt in the matter of the photographs. Doubtless his startling accusation had been a random shot, more or less facetious. If he knew how accurate had been his aim he would probably never speak to her again. She had skated on very thin ice for a moment.

How stupid she had been! How childishly stupid, to risk her happiness on such a paltry issue. Abigail herself could have behaved no more senselessly. She seemed to have been driven, as on her wedding night, to act as Abigail would have acted; to do the thing which, if discovered, would utterly alienate her husband, as if she were bent on wrecking her marriage.

Heaven helping her, she would never be such a fool again. She would overcome the silly feeling she had about Thorne, this stranger feeling she had about Abigail. She would do nothing henceforth to jeopardize her marriage.

183 𝄡

CHAPTER 18

The new year was well into February before Judith
achieved her purpose of giving a party at Timberley which
should be something other than a family reunion. Twice she
had postponed her date; first during the holiday season, when
an annoying irritation of her throat had prompted Dr. Caxton
to prescribe a few days in bed.

"But I'm not sick, Doctor. I feel quite well except for this
choking sensation. It catches me suddenly without the slightest warning."

"A nervous paroxysm," pronounced the doctor. "You probably talk too much." From his quizzical expression a facetious
dig was indicated. "Public speakers frequently suffer that
way."

"But I'm not a public speaker."

He blandly included schoolteachers in this occupational
liability.

"I'm not teaching any more. I only use my voice in conversation."

"Try letting it rest for a day or so," was the crusty advice.
"Go to bed—give your entire body a rest. Don't talk except
when necessary. And keep yourself isolated from the children
until we see what this is."

"You think it might be something contagious?"

"There's diphtheria over by Mullen's Mill," he told her
bluntly. "I knew there'd be an epidemic of some sort. Some
hogs died of cholera there last fall and were allowed to rot
unburied during that warm spell. Someday we'll have laws
about things like that, but I shan't live long enough to see
it."

Judith went to bed for a week and had a wonderful time: reading, resting, and devising little services for Richard to perform. He was so sweet-tempered about waiting on her that she toyed with the temptation of prolonging her convalescence in order to enjoy his attentions. But on the doctor's next visit she was told to get out of bed and put on her clothes.

"We don't want any more invalids around here for Richard to coddle. There's nothing the matter with you."

Relieved, if somewhat indignant, Judith plunged into preparations for her party, which she now set forward to January, only to find a religious revival usurping the calendar for that month. Nothing daunted, she set her date for the first week in February and laid her plans before Richard, as a subtle means of persuading him that they were his own ideas.

Unfortunately he was inclined to be difficult. He had agreed heartily enough that they should give a party, but he failed to grasp its significance. It was not a family affair, she delicately pointed out. Neither the Turners nor the Mitchells were to be included. It was a little gathering of congenial spirits, and the only entertainment, besides a light refreshment, was to be the free flow of intellectual conversation. Richard seemed more interested in the fact that the party gave him an excuse to buy Thorne a new dress.

With remarkable patience and self-restraint Judith explained that Thorne would not need a new dress because she was not going to appear.

They argued this point exhaustively.

"This is an adult party. None of the children will be in evidence."

"That's all right for Ricky and Rodgie, but you said yourself that Thorne was growing up."

"I said she was suffering from growing pains. There's a difference."

Richard growled, "She's read a damn sight more than young Will."

By Judith's express invitation Will Tomlinson was to be among those present.

Miss Ann put an end to the argument by agreeing with Judith that Thorne was too young for a party of this sort. She would take all the children up to her room on the evening in question. Richard yielded, on one condition: that Thorne should be given a birthday party in May.

"Is her birthday in May?" inquired Judith.

He didn't know if it was or not, but May was a beautiful month for a party. His mother acquiesced, and Judith said it was a charming idea. They would give a party for all the children in May.

After that things went more smoothly. Invitations were so choice and few that they were accepted enthusiastically. An author of national repute chanced to be visiting old friends in Woodridge, and Judith captured him as the lion of the hour. In addition, there was the editor of the *Sentinel*, an oldish bachelor with a university degree and a spinster sister; there were the Barclays (Ellen included on her husband's account), Lucius Goff and a lady friend from Terre Haute, Albert Carpenter (present incumbent at Timberley school), and a few more of the intelligentsia.

Doc Baird was not invited, but Richard did not learn of this until it was too late to do anything about it.

The party was doomed from the outset. As an initial embarrassment everyone inquired for the absent Tomlinsons and seemed unable to grasp the idea that neither illness nor calamity was responsible for their non-appearance. Judith realized that she had committed an error in excluding the family.

But the major disaster was beyond her control, She had stated in her invitations that the gathering was complimentary to the visiting man of letters, Mr. Fairchild, and had indicated that literature was to be the subject of the evening's discussion. But unfortunately the six weeks' revival had just closed in a blaze of excitement, with the flaming oratory of the evangelist focused on the burning issue, "Is there a personal devil?" And those who had heard him were still smoking. Literature paled beside the incendiary topic of devils, both personal and general. Opinions ranged from the avowed skepticism of the *Sentinel* editor—who believed nothing he could not feel, taste, or smell—to the unshakable conviction of Mrs. Barclay, who declared the devil a part of her religion and accepted him complete with horns, hoofs, and tail. Discussion was livelier than anything Judith had dared hope for, but alas! on the wrong subject. Even Richard astonished her by affirming his belief in an incarnate spirit of evil.

"How else can you explain the brutality of war," he demanded, "or the lust for power, or selfishness, greed, or murder? Either there's a devil in the world or there's one in every human breast."

Once before she had heard him talk like this. It was on the occasion of their first meeting, when he had argued so earnestly over the use of the supernatural in *Macbeth*.

From devils it was a simple and natural progression to ghosts. In vain did Judith bring forth a copy of Mr. Fairchild's latest book as a hint that literary talk was to have been the order of the evening. The author himself waved her aside as though the book had been written by someone else. He had, he confessed, a keen interest in things metaphysical. Lucius Goff, emboldened by sympathy, promptly declared his belief in spirit communication. The editor jeered at him; Mrs. Barclay warned him that though the devil was orthodox, ghosts and spirit rappings were not. The argument grew so heated that even the elderberry wine which Richard brought in failed to cool it. In fact, the refreshment gave rise to fresh discussion, for Mr. Fairchild, as though reminded of something by the homemade beverage, asserted that since his sojourn in this community he had come into possession of some interesting data on the subject of poltergeists.

187 ᘒᕽ

Mrs. Barclay demanded to know what polter—whatyoumay-call'ems might be.

The author explained that poltergeists were spirits of the dead returned to earth to wreak mischief. He had heard about a case in this very county, he said.

The *Sentinel* editor came down upon him with hallucinations, spectral illusions, and acute inebriation. But the writer stood his ground.

"I have it on the best authority. There was a wedding a short while back at which the wearing apparel of the guests disappeared and was later found scattered at impossible heights in the surrounding trees."

He went on describing in detail the Tomlinson charivari, obviously unaware that he was talking to the people involved.

"I understand that the bridegroom has given out that two distant cousins were playing a practical joke." The author smiled significantly. "Naturally he would prefer to believe that, since his first wife had been dead but six months."

The silence was acutely uncomfortable. But the speaker took it for rapt attention on the part of his listeners and went innocently on:

"Other queer things have happened in this house. Some photographs of the dead wife, which were locked in a strong chest within the house, were found in a shed some distance from the dwelling. Silver coins, also locked in the chest, were found between the pages of books."

Again his hearers suffered extreme embarrassment. The story of the photographs and the coin had reached Woodridge by way of Jesse Moffat, and a number of those present had assisted in its circulation.

The only person who seemed unembarrassed was Richard. "Who told you these stories, Mr. Fairchild?"

"I've heard them from any number of people."

"Did you learn the name of the family?"

"If I did it's slipped my mind. I've a wretched memory for names. But I've talked with creditable witnesses."

"And it's the general belief that these pranks are cases of supernatural phenomena?" Richard was smiling now.

"That's one theory. I prefer it to the other advanced by local gossips."

"What is that?"

"Some people have gone so far as to accuse a young girl in this household of witchcraft."

Richard's smile vanished. "I can assure you the wedding prank was a practical joke, to which the jokers have confessed. As for the displaced photographs and silver—I think your theory of the poltergeist is rather interesting."

John Barclay felt sorry for Judith. He guessed that the evening had not gone the way she had planned. She sat with her back to the light, resting her cheek on her hand, looking almost ill with fatigue and wretchedly pale. He sat down at the piano and launched into a medley of popular songs to dispel the embarrassment and gloom of the unfortunate discussion. He could not understand why Richard continued to pursue the unhappy theme with Mr. Fairchild. Every time the music diminuendoed their voices could be heard in animated debate.

Judith listened to John Barclay's music and wished he would play louder and drown the voices of the men. Her face was rigid with the effort of smiling. She was so stunned by the turn her party had taken that she was not even indignant. Tomorrow, after a night's sleep—if she was able to sleep—she would remember this talk and be able to weigh it; perhaps dismiss it. But just now she could feel nothing but fear. All this talk about ghosts was not as purposeless as it seemed. Richard was deliberately fostering it. He did not really believe that his dead wife's spirit was among them. Yet he was announcing to all present that he preferred that theory to even the slightest suspicion of Thorne. Could this be a subtle reminder to Judith that he knew of her guilt in the matter of the photographs; that she must either confess or admit the possibility of Abigail's unquiet ghost?

When at last she looked at Richard she found his eyes fixed upon her with a curious expression which she could not fathom.

When the party broke up she went swiftly to her room as to a refuge. She was in bed when he came upstairs, the covers drawn over her eyes to shut out the light. It was he who undressed leisurely this night. He did not disturb her with talk, but he seemed in unusually good spirits, whistling softly as he moved about the room. When he had extinguished the light and climbed into bed, he unexpectedly gathered her into his arms. He was softly laughing.

"Richard!" She was thankful for the darkness as she clung to him.

She wanted to ask why he was so exuberant; whence came this strange buoyancy which had restored him to her arms; and then she preferred not to know. When he was like this nothing else mattered. She even forgot her nagging fear.

But she remembered it in the morning, when, waking tardily, she found him still lightsome and inclined to conversation.

"I'm glad you gave that party, Judith. It was quite a success. We must have that fellow Fairchild out again."

Heartened by daylight, she took the situation firmly in hand.

"People like that are amusing, but you should be careful, Richard, how you endorse his fantastic ideas. Mr. Fairchild is a writer, and writers are expected to be a little eccentric. But you are a solid citizen, a man of some importance in your community. You don't want to be quoted as saying you believe the ghost of your dead wife is playing pranks in this house."

"But I do." He was smiling, inscrutably innocent. "Hiding those photographs out in the shed—her own photographs, mind you—is exactly the sort of perverted jest Abigail would delight in."

It was seconds before Judith could speak.

"You don't believe any such thing, and it's too early in the morning to be funny."

"I'm not being funny. You know we agreed at the time that only two people could have accomplished it by natural means: you and Thorne. Of course it was neither of you, so it must have been accomplished by supernatural means." He had taken his stand. Apparently nothing could shake him from it.

"I'd advise you not to let your mother hear you voice such an opinion," said Judith, and sprang quickly out of bed before he could discover her trembling.

This was the beginning of a subtle change in their relationship. It was also the beginning of a change in the house at Timberley which in time was felt by all its inmates. At first it was felt by none but Judith, who queerly shrank from giving utterance to her forebodings. But when the talk at her party was reported—as it inevitably was, by young Will—Judith was astonished to discover that Richard's stand did not shock anyone, not even his mother. In this sternly orthodox household she sensed a feeling which she could not have defined but with which she was to grow more and more familiar. It spread from Millie's kitchen to the big room upstairs which the children shared with Miss Ann. That this feeling was unacknowledged, tacitly ignored, made it the more manifest.

Spring came early that year. By the first of April the lilacs were a green mist. Redbirds whistled from the cedar trees; catbirds called from the woods. Coming home from school, the children found violets and snowdrops blooming along their path. On the banks of Little Raccoon the redbud floated like a pillar of fire.

The young Tomlinsons, loitering one evening, saw a covered wagon cross the bridge and whooped joyously, for this was a sure sign of approaching summer. When they reached home they found, as anticipated, that the wagon had turned in at Timberley and its occupants—two brothers from Ohio named Cochran—were spending the night. This meant there would be tales of adventure and misadventure around the evening fire. Thorne, setting the table for supper, sang, "Oh! Susanna, don't you cry for me!" The sight of a covered wagon wakened nostalgic yearnings sometimes for the vagabond existence of the wayfarers.

It was during a lull in her crooning that she became aware of voices in the hall outside the dining-room door.

"I suggest, Richard, that we dispense with prayers tonight, since there are strangers among us."

"Why should we? We're not dispensing with supper."

"Don't be facetious, dear."

"I didn't mean to be. Hospitality is offering your home to your guest, isn't it? Timberley, without family prayers, is not the home of the Tomlinsons."

"For all you know, these Cochrans may not be Protestants."

"They are no less welcome to join us if they care to. If they don't, they can retire."

"All of which is most embarrassing."

"No more than a preference for white meat instead of dark."

His imperturbable calm seemed to irritate his companion, for her voice rose impatiently.

"Family worship is an outmoded custom. It belongs to the days of Puritanism. I'm trying to make of Timberley a cultured home, and this nightly exhibition of religion makes it seem like a backwoods farmhouse."

"What is it except a farmhouse?"

"It's not a backwoods cabin, at any rate. Though it might be, from some of its customs."

"Are you suggesting that prayers be discontinued—permanently?"

"Not immediately, of course, on your mother's account. But I do favor a gradual tapering off. That's why I suggest that you omit them this evening—when you've a very good excuse—then later drop to once or twice a week—and eventually stop altogether. How does that strike you?"

"It strikes me as curious that you never objected to prayers before we were married."

"I was a boarder in the house then; I had no voice in its management. But now I'm its mistress. I think my wishes should be respected."

There was no reply. The dining-room door was flung open, and Judith came in with high color and a look of exasperation. She demanded of Thorne, "What are you doing here?" and without waiting for the obvious answer took the silver from her hands and told her to go to the kitchen and help Millie. With only a swift glance at Richard, who had followed his wife into the room, Thorne obeyed. She could not tell from his remote expression whether Judith had won her point or not, but the possibility depressed her. Her knowledge of God (once confined to Pete McGraw's profanity) was now all mixed up with her feeling for her friend. That he could yield a principle to please his wife troubled her.

When bedtime came two people waited with sharp anxiety for Richard's decision in the matter. When he picked up the Bible as usual, inviting his transient guests to join in the family ritual if they so desired, excusing them if they did not (the Cochran brothers chose to remain), Judith caught a look from Thorne which, to her incensed imagination, seemed to sparkle with triumph.

Judith's face turned livid with anger. Her humiliation was twofold because Thorne had witnessed her defeat. She returned the girl's bright glance with a fixed hard stare that caused Thorne to retire to a remote corner and sit down in the shadow of the big clock.

As Judith watched Richard turning the leaves of the Bible,

looking for some favorite passage, she heard the clock begin to strike.

It was the strangest thing to Judith that no one seemed to react to the stroke of the clock. Richard looked up, as did everyone, but they looked at Judith, who had given a queer gasp. She muttered, "The clock!" and Richard glanced at the clock on the mantel which pointed to twenty minutes of nine. The hands of the big clock stood at half-past one. He nodded, "Yes, we're late," and went on turning the pages of the Bible. The clock struck again. The tone of the gong was deep and ominous. It fell chillingly on the ear like some dread warning.

It was not until the third stroke that startled looks began to appear in the fireside circle as faces turned toward Judith, who had made a strangling sound and put her hand to her throat. Ann Tomlinson hushed a whimpering child. But Richard seemed quite unmoved.

He began to read, choosing the first line his eye fell upon, surely, or he never would have read that particular passage.

" 'Then Saul said unto his servants, Seek me a woman that hath a familiar spirit, that I may go to her, and enquire of her. And his servants said to him, Behold, there is a woman that hath a familiar spirit at Endor.' "

He paused, frowning, as though that was not what he had intended to read. But when he started to change his selection Judith's voice arrested him:

"Go on, Richard. This is an appropriate time to read the story of a witch."

He looked about the room as though in search of someone. The candlelight did not penetrate the corner where Thorne sat in the shadow of the clock. Richard resumed his reading. He read the whole story of Saul consulting the witch of Endor and bringing the ghost of Samuel up from the grave to answer his questions. As long as the reading continued Judith counted the strokes of the clock.

Verse after verse Richard read: from the forecast of Saul's death at the hands of his enemies, to the panic of the poor frightened witch woman, who had killed her fatted calf for the king when she learned with whom she had been trafficking. To the end of the chapter Richard read, apparently oblivious of the striking clock. When his voice ceased, the clock stopped. Judith had counted one hundred and forty-four strokes.

There was a moment of silence before the summons to prayer. A leaping flame in the fireplace threw a rosy shadow across the face of the clock, and Judith saw that the hands, which had been fixed at half-past one, now pointed to a quarter of three.

Abigail had died at a quarter of three.

When the others knelt in the nightly petition Judith did not join them. Her eyes searched the room for Thorne. As the concerted murmur of "Our Father which art in heaven" rose about her, she strained her ear for a clear young voice she would have recognized in any choral chant. She did not hear it. Her pale face was glowing with elation when the others rose from their knees.

"This is a trick I had nothing to do with," she thought. "This time we've caught Thorne red-handed."

There was no comment on the clock's behavior as long as the strangers were present. But when they had been shown to a room upstairs Judith demanded that Richard examine the erratic timepiece. He inquired mildly why he should examine a clock at this time of night.

"To see who's inside it," said Judith.

Amid a pregnant silence, with the entire household looking at her most strangely, she repeated her demand that Richard explore the interior of the clock.

"There's no one inside it," said Richard. "There couldn't be."

Judith pointed to a little door in the side of the cabinet

large enough to permit a very small person (or child) to conceal himself in the clock.

"Where were the children during the Bible reading?" she asked.

Miss Ann answered for her grandsons. They had sat throughout the evening, where they were at this moment, on the hearthrug.

People were looking at Judith very curiously now.

"Where was Thorne?" she asked sharply.

A husky voice answered, "Here," and Thorne rose up from a cushion in the corner, so nearly invisible in her gray dress that she seemed a part of the shadows.

"You were inside the clock, weren't you, Thorne?" said Judith.

Thorne said, "No," and looked surprised.

Richard said, "Of course she wasn't in the clock," as though the idea were absurd. "She never left that stool. I saw her there all evening."

He couldn't have seen her; Judith knew he couldn't have seen Thorne from where he was sitting. Something tightened in her throat: anger for her husband's partisanship and a desperate need to prove Thorne guilty. She felt that she could not bear it if the girl were cleared of this mischief. The mere thought filled her with uncontrollable nervous excitement. She was conscious of intense cold; the temperature of the room seemed to have dropped several degrees. Shadows closed round her like a smothering fog. She had the strangest difficulty in breathing. . . .

When she looked about the room she found that she and Richard were alone. He was standing beside her, a glass of water in his hand, and she was tugging at the band of ribbon around her throat. She asked where everyone was. He told her his mother had taken the children upstairs; the others had retired. She thought, "Here! I can't have anything like this happening. What made me faint?"

He asked, "Feel all right now?"

She answered, "Certainly," as though the question were irrelevant. But she noted that she was sitting on the couch. She had been standing when that queerness seized her.

"There's a reasonable explanation for all this, Richard." She resumed the argument as though there had been no interruption. "The sound we heard did not come from this room. Somewhere else in the house a clock was striking."

"I don't know what you're talking about, Judith. There's not a clock in this house that strikes."

"I know that. That's why I say someone was hiding in the cabinet, making the clock strike."

"You mean that clock?" Richard turned to look at the tall clock in the shadowy corner. "That clock couldn't be made to strike. Half its works are missing. It has no bell."

"But it did strike," said Judith. "It struck one hundred and forty-four times. I counted. And the hands moved from half-past one to quarter of three."

He picked up a candle and went over to the clock and held the taper so that the light fell across its face. The hands rested, where they had rested for years, at half-past one.

He said quietly, "The clock didn't strike, Judith. It couldn't have struck without my hearing it."

Judith gasped, "You—didn't hear it?"

He shook his head.

"But you must have heard it. Everyone else did."

"No." His eyes rested on her, half curiously, half solicitously. "No one heard anything. When you fainted, Mother asked what there was about the clock to alarm you."

"He's lying," thought Judith, and pushed back the creeping horror that assailed her. They were all lying to protect that girl. She must believe this, even though it was the last step in the progress of her defeat. She was more conscious at the moment of defeat than of fear, because she saw with terrible prescience that there would be no end to eerie mischief in this house. And Richard would defend Thorne to the extent of denying what his ears had heard and his eyes had seen. That the alternative to Thorne's guilt was one which filled his wife with horror apparently had no weight with him. The calm finality of his allegiance was devastating.

She heard his voice remotely. "Come upstairs, Judith. You'll feel all right after a good night's sleep."

CHAPTER 19

It was the hottest summer in years: the greatest corn weather, the most bountiful harvest since the war. It seemed to Judith that she never saw her husband any more. He was out of doors from daybreak till dark and at night he was asleep, from sheer healthy exhaustion, as soon as he touched the bed. She grew to hate the summer before it was over.

The children, too, were out of doors all day. Sometimes when Judith appeared belatedly for breakfast and inquired for them, she was told, "They went with Richard over to the south forty this morning." This tract of Timberley land lay beyond Little Raccoon. When the men worked there they seldom came home at noon. They took a substantial lunch with them.

"Did Thorne go too?"

"Yes. The men wanted coffee for dinner, so Richard took Thorne along to make it."

All day Judith's mind held the picture of a picnic shared by congenial spirits on the bank of a shady creek.

Day after day it was like that. Thorne never seemed to be in the house when Richard was out of it. Judith took to watching from windows when it was time for his return. If the two came in together she was wretched. If he came in alone her unleashed imagination ran rampant.

She suggested to her mother-in-law that Thorne be given more duties about the house. Indoors, as well as outdoors, the work of the farm was doubled during the summer months. Endless preserving of the abundant fruit, drying of beans and peas for winter, cooking for the additional labor employed. The Tomlinson daughters frequently lent a hand, but there was still work enough to keep Miss Ann busy from morning till night.

"Thorne should be taking some of this drudgery off you," said Judith, ignoring her own remissness. But the older woman did not agree.

"Thorne does enough for her age. Let her play while she can."

Ann Tomlinson felt, as she grew older, an increasing yearning toward the young. She had not felt it so much with her own children because she had been still young herself. But now that she was old and seasoned with living, she could understand the pain of growing up. She could not look at Thorne these days without a strange compassion. So she said to Judith, "Let her alone. This is the last summer she will be a child."

May had come and gone, likewise June and July, but there had been no party for the children. Perhaps Richard had forgotten; perhaps he had been too busy. Since only Judith remembered his plan, there was no one to remind him—or be disappointed.

In August the trees hung motionless, heavy with foliage; the air was murmurous with the drone of insects. Judith would go up to her room at night to find it swarming with mosquitoes, gnats, and millers. She would drive out as many as possible with a paper fly brush, then pull down the windows, strip off her clothes, and fling herself upon the sun-baked bed. She might as well have flung herself upon a hot griddle. In a matter of seconds she was off the bed, divesting it of sheets and pillows, in the delusion that the bare mattress was cooler. When Richard came in he would gasp, "Whew! Why don't you raise the windows?" and immediately fling them wide open. In would troop the old enemy with reinforcements, and the battle with the insects would begin again. There was mosquito netting over the beds, but wire screens were an innovation which had not yet reached Woods County. Judith wondered how she had ever fancied the country would be more pleasant in summer than the town.

"You don't have to sleep up here," Richard reminded her. "There's a bedroom downstairs with an eastern exposure, and it's comfortable on the hottest nights. There's no point in punishing yourself by sleeping up under the roof."

He refrained from mentioning the obvious fact that she was punishing him too. He was still very polite in all their intimate relations. If she preferred to swelter upstairs, he would not leave her to swelter alone. But he delicately hinted that he considered it a piece of foolishness.

"This is the hottest room in the house because it's only a half story. Last summer when Thorne had it, she used to sleep outdoors in the hammock because she couldn't stand it up here."

Judith asked idly, "Wasn't she afraid?"

"What of? The hammock was swung between two trees just outside my window. She couldn't have moved without my hearing her."

"I see. You slept downstairs last summer."

"I did. And there wasn't a night that I couldn't stand a sheet over me."

She scarcely heard him. Her mind was filled with a picture of Thorne asleep in a swaying hammock beside an open window; and on the other side of the window Richard, alert even in slumber for every movement in the hammock.

"I wish you'd try it downstairs just one night, Judith. If

you don't have the best sleep you've had in weeks I'll never mention the subject again."

Her own discomfort finally drove her to accept his suggestion. Her reluctance in the first place had come more from morbid distaste than superstitious fear. Now, on investigation, she found that the room in summer dress did not reek so strongly of Abigail as she had expected. The bed was gay with cool fresh chintz, the fireplace banked with honeysuckle, and the tree-shaded south windows were covered with cotton netting. It was possible to keep both cool and unbitten down here. The candlelit bogies of a winter fireside vanished in the bright white heat of an August day.

She slept one night in Abigail's room.

She was fully prepared to lie awake in nervous insomnia or be troubled with fitful dreams. Instead, she slept so soundly that not even Richard's rising at daylight wakened her. He dressed quickly, quietly, and left her sleeping. But as he opened the outer door and stepped immediately into the morning coolness of dew-drenched shrubs and bluegrass, the comfort and convenience of his old room struck him as never before. He hoped fervently that Judith slept till she was rested. He wanted her to be so charmed with this room that she would never wish to sleep upstairs again.

The children came round the corner of the house, barefoot and scantily clothed. Ricky and Rodgie wore nothing but panties and Thorne the briefest of pinafores. They hailed Richard with the announcement that they were bound for the creek and invited him to join them in a swim. He hushed them softly, vehemently, and led them away from Judith's window. Ten minutes later, stripped to his underclothes, he was splashing in the deepest pool in Little Raccoon, teaching the boys to float. When he offered to teach Thorne she paddled away from him and climbed out on the bank. He shouted to her, but she called back that she was going to look for berries and ran dripping toward the woods. He decided the boys had had enough swimming and ordered them out of the water, but by the time he had dressed there was no sight of Thorne. She had disappeared.

Judith slept until the sun rose high enough to pierce the east window. There was no net over this window because Abigail had had it nailed down against the winter snows. But there was a window blind, and Judith wished drowsily that Richard would lower it. Then she realized that Richard was up and abroad and she had overslept.

She did not rise immediately. The outer door was open, and she lay luxuriating in the fresh breeze coming from the south. How silly she had been to hold out against this delightful room. Coming down here was like moving to a different climate.

At the first peal of the breakfast bell she sprang up and dressed briskly. She was so rested, so full of energy, that she could think of any number of pleasant things to do this morning. She paused for a last glance in the mirror of the big walnut dresser, which stood in the corner between the east window and the south door. She heard a pane of glass shatter in the window and something hurtle behind her to fall with a thud near the door.

She screamed, wheeling in alarm to stare at the object that had narrowly missed her head. It was a half brick, heavy enough to have killed her had it struck her.

A murmur of voices came down the hall. There were hurried footsteps in the passage and Richard's voice outside the door. "Are you all right, Judith?"

She said, "Come in."

"I thought I heard you scream," he said as he entered. "What happened?"

Judith said, "A brick came through that window. It was thrown."

"Where is it now?" asked Richard.

Judith pointed to the spot where the brick had landed. It was gone.

Richard said, "There's nothing there."

She stared at the spot, dumfounded. "It came through the east window. I heard the crash of glass."

"That window is open," said Richard. "I got up in the night and pried the nails loose and raised it." He went over to the window and pushed back the muslin curtain. Neither glass nor netting prevented the breeze from blowing through the room. "I guess you heard Millie break something in the kitchen," he said lightly.

Judith drew her hand across her eyes. It was possible that a crash in the kitchen had come simultaneously with the hurling of the brick. . . .

"But I saw the brick. I felt a *whisssssh!* of air as it passed my head. Someone threw a brick through that window, then ran around the corner of the house, reached through the door, and recovered it while my back was turned."

Richard stepped to the open door and searched the premises with a keen glance. Suddenly his hand came up with a gesture as involuntary as breathing.

Judith said, "It's too late to warn her, Richard. I've seen her."

Thorne was approaching the house, her apron filled with berries.

She was still wet from her swim in the creek. Her dark hair dripped liquid gold where the sun touched it; the childish pinafore clung damply to her small body. The two in the doorway watched her approach; the man's eyes fixed upon the dripping curls and berry-stained face, the woman's upon the budding curves revealed by the clinging apron.

Judith said, "Did you throw that brick, Thorne?"

Thorne said, "What brick?"

"Judith thought she saw someone throw a brick," said Richard.

"Where would I get a brick?" said Thorne.

"Exactly," said Richard. "Where would she get a brick? There's none on this farm." He was beginning to speak impatiently. "Furthermore, there's no brick in the room. Are you right sure, Judith, you didn't imagine the whole thing?"

Judith chilled, though the August morning was already hot. She felt as if there were someone close beside her—not Richard, closer than that—close enough to touch her. She moved farther back into the room, and when something brushed her thigh she almost swooned. She had backed into the bed.

"I'm moving upstairs again," she announced. "I never liked sleeping on the ground floor. I tried it to please you, Richard, but I much prefer the bird's-eye-maple room."

He made no comment. He told Thorne to go wash her face and hands for breakfast, and when they went into the dining room he explained to the others that some hoodlum had thrown a brick through the bedroom window. "He must have got frightened when he heard Judith scream and retrieved his missile, because the brick's disappeared."

That was the first brick. It was not the last. Judith heard and saw them intermittently for several weeks. Always half bricks; always through the same window, the one Abigail had nailed down. In what ever part of the house Judith might be at the time, she could distinctly hear the heavy thud as the brick hit the floor. She would rush immediately to the south room and find the missile lying where she had seen the first. But when she had hastened to bring some other member of the family to verify what she had seen, the brick would be gone.

Because of the heat the window was still open. Judith no longer heard a crash of glass when the brick fell. Miss Ann suggested closing the window.

"Then we'll know whether the brick comes through there or not. A shattered windowpane is substantial evidence."

"You think I'm lying?" said Judith.

"No, no, my dear." No one doubted Judith's testimony regarding the bricks. She was too intelligent to be suspected of hallucination, as Abigail had been, and her reaction to the disturbance was too sincere to permit a doubt of her veracity. "But it's just possible the sound you hear is something outside the house," said Miss Ann, "because no one else ever hears anything."

The brick thrower seemed to confine his activities to periods when only Judith was in the vicinity of the south room.

"But I saw the brick. Time and again I've seen a brick on the floor."

"And you always run to fetch someone, which gives the culprit time to make off with it. Next time pick the brick up before you leave the room."

But Judith could not bring herself to touch the bricks. Neither would she allow Miss Ann to close the window. She had a horrible fear of hearing the crash of glass again and finding the brick as usual, and of finding the windowpane unbroken. Better to cling to the alternative made possible by the open window and the convenient door.

The Tomlinsons searched the countryside for the tramp or urchin who might be responsible for the mischief, but no such person was found. News of the disturbance spread throughout the neighborhood, and self-elected guards posted themselves at outlying points of vantage to watch for the culprit. But the brick thrower was never seen.

Judith insisted that Thorne was guilty. For a time she was able to persuade others to this opinion, particularly young Will. The bricks always seemed to come when Thorne was out of the house. In vain did Richard caution her to stay within-indoors until the nuisance could be tracked to its source. When Thorne remained in the house nothing happened.

As the suspicions of the others deepened against her, Richard grew more frantic. He had words with his entire family. He had violent arguments with his wife. Their disputes were the more bitter because Judith's insistence upon Thorne's guilt was based on a fear which Richard, in his desperation, continually fostered. He had said once, lightly, that he thought it possible the spirit of his dead wife might be plaguing them. He stated now, unequivocably, that only Abigail could devise so cunning a persecution as this incrimination of an innocent girl. His words shocked his family, but he did not care. He would fight both the living and the dead in Thorne's defense.

As for Thorne, she had nothing to say beyond her repeated assertion that she had no knowledge of this thing. But she grew thin and pale with nervous anxiety. She stayed indoors when Richard so ordered, effacing herself from Judith's eye by industriously helping Miss Ann. But when the strain of her position grew more than she could bear she would escape to the woods and the solitude which now provided her only respite. Invariably, when she returned to the house, she would find that Judith had heard and seen another brick.

One evening Thorne was returning after a full day's absence. She had fled early in the morning from Judith's tongue, and so hopeless had seemed her plight that she had seriously considered running away and never coming back. But toward sundown she remembered that Richard would be coming from the fields before long, so she turned her steps toward home.

Dusk had fallen by the time she came within sight of the house. The log kitchen glowed with lighted windows, and red sparks flew from its chimney. Appetizing odors reminded her that she had had nothing to eat since breakfast. As she started up the slope from the springhouse she saw a familiar figure cross the barn lot and her heart swelled like a homing pigeon's. "Richard's home," she thought happily, and started running.

Judith, watching from the kitchen window, also saw Richard coming from the barn. She likewise caught sight of Thorne running to meet him. She slipped outside, determined to forestall the meeting. As she stood watching Thorne's flying figure she saw the girl pitch suddenly, violently, forward and then lie very still.

Judith ran swiftly down the slope to be at the spot before Richard. She would spare him the necessity of drying Thorne's tears.

But Thorne was not weeping. She was lying still as death, with a great bleeding cut on her head. On the ground close by, Judith saw a half brick.

Her first thought was that Richard must not see that brick. He would take it as concrete proof of Thorne's innocence. Because Thorne could not possibly have struck herself with the brick at which Judith was now staring.

She could hear her husband's pounding footsteps. He was running from the barn. She must dispose of the brick before he reached them. . . .

She could not bring herself to pick it up.

Richard knelt in the path, lifting Thorne in his arms, cursing softly in his rage and anxiety. "My poor Cricket! What happened?" he asked Judith.

Judith said, "Put her down. She'll come out of her faint quicker."

He laid Thorne gently on the grass. Then he wet his handkerchief in the overflow from the spring and bathed her face. Judith wondered how much longer it would be before he saw the brick.

"There must be a rock in this path that tripped her," he said.

"Do you see anything?" asked Judith.

"No." His eyes scanned the darkening hillside. "Whatever it was must be close by." He searched the grass. The brick lay near the spot where he had put Thorne. His eyes moved over it as though it were not there.

Suddenly panic gripped Judith. It became more important for Richard to see the brick than for herself to preserve the fiction of Thorne's guilt.

She cried, "There, stupid! There on the ground beside her is the thing that felled her."

His gaze followed her pointing finger. He said, "I don't see anything."

"Look where I'm pointing," cried Judith—and then stopped. The brick was gone.

"That's nothing but a clump of grass," said Richard. "Here's what probably did the mischief." With the toe of his boot he scraped the hard-packed earth from an embedded rock in the path.

Thorne was beginning to regain consciousness. Richard lifted her in his arms and carried her up to the house. Judith followed, like a woman in a dream.

They found Miss Ann in the kitchen with Millie.

"Get ointment and bandages, Mother. Thorne's had an accident."

Ann Tomlinson gasped at sight of the girl's bloody head. Millie groaned, "Oh Lawdy!" and set down a tray of dishes with a clatter.

"What happened to her?" asked Miss Ann.

"She was running up the hill and took a nasty fall."

"What tripped you, child?"

Thorne murmured, "I don't know." She was feeling faint again. "I don't know what happened."

Richard said, "Luckily I saw the whole thing. So did Judith." He then described the incident. Young Will and Jesse Moffat came in while he was talking and listened with interest.

"There was a rock embedded in the path which must have tripped her," finished Richard. "At least it was the only thing we could find. And we both looked, didn't we, Judith?"

Judith said coldly, "Thorne didn't trip over anything."

"What do you mean?" said Richard sharply.

Judith said to Thorne, "What did you do with that brick?"

"What brick?" said Thorne blankly.

Richard said, "What are you talking about, Judith?"

"When I reached Thorne there was a brick on the ground beside her." Judith's face was pale, but there was no hysteria in her voice. "I pointed it out to you, Richard. But you pretended not to see it until Thorne had time to conceal it beneath her skirt."

"Judith! Do you accuse Thorne of giving herself a blow that knocked her unconscious?"

"No. I accuse her of taking a stage fall, first dropping a brick beside the path to make it look as though she had been struck down by our brick thrower."

But the idea of Thorne's having a heavy brickbat concealed on her person was too preposterous to be credited. Besides, the girl's injuries were serious enough to preclude malingering. There was outspoken, indignant rejection of Judith's theory.

Jesse Moffat, however, was inclined to agree that Thorne might have been struck by a brick. "If Judith says she seen one, I reckon she seen it. Somebody might have made off with it before Richard got there, but it couldn't have been Thorne, with her knocked unconscious."

Richard said, "If Judith did see a brick, then this clears Thorne of throwing them." Will's eyes rested on the girl as though he were ashamed of the stand he had previously taken.

Judith made one last effort. "It's been your contention, Richard, that these bricks have been thrown for the purpose of incriminating Thorne. In that case, why would her enemy exonerate her by striking her down?"

He had an answer, even for that. "The malice that failed to drive her from home might have decided to kill her and have done with it."

Without another word Judith left the kitchen and went up to her room. She felt as though she had reached the limit of her endurance. All during these terrible weeks she had clung to her conviction of Thorne's guilt as a drowning man clings to a spar. Now it had been wrested from her by a wave which threatened to engulf her. For if Thorne was not guilty of this mischief—*whence came those bricks and whither did they go?*

She had seen them again and again; yet when she brought others to view them they were never there. Who, besides herself, would go to any lengths to prove they had been thrown by human hands?

Her desperation furnished the answer. Lighting a candle, she sat down at her desk, took a fresh quill pen, and rapidly covered a sheet of note paper with her clear, impersonal handwriting. When she had finished she locked the letter in her desk, pending an opportunity to mail it.

There was a cessation of her torment after that. For weeks the letter lay in her desk, not forgotten, but postponed, like a desperate remedy to be used only in extremity. Then when the harvest was in and Richard made his usual trip to the city, Judith was ill and unable to accompany him. Instead of deferring the excursion, he went off by himself, returning late the same day, pockets bulging with gifts for everyone, and bearing a large dressmaker's box which Judith was sure contained the new faille silk she had been wanting. But when the box was opened it was found that the object of his trip had been to buy Thorne the long-promised new dress.

It was then that Judith decided to post the letter she had written to Otis Huse.

CHAPTER 20

The square in Woodridge was a sea of mud. Wagons and buggies, mired to the hub, crept sluggishly. Horses and mules, flat-eared and streaming, stood resignedly at hitching posts. The hot spell had broken with an equinoctial storm. It had rained for a week.

Two men sat in the bar of the hotel, morosely regarding the weather.

"If this keeps up much longer there'll be another flood."

The speaker was a drummer from Indianapolis. He carried a line of household supplies: toilet goods, patent medicines, thread, needles, pins, et cetera. Crossroads stores were his clientele, the weather his concern.

"Little Raccoon is over its banks. Sure plays whaly with my business."

The other man merely looked bored.

"I'm in the commercial line," explained the drummer. "What's yours?"

"People," said the other shortly, and stood up, stretching his legs. He was a tall man, dressed genteelly but rather funereally in black. His saturnine expression and cryptic reply led the drummer to wonder if he might be the local undertaker.

He inquired respectfully, "Live around here?"

The gentleman said, "Yes," and rubbed a clear spot on the steaming windowpane, as though looking for someone down the muggy street. "I'm a lawyer," he added curtly.

The drummer looked properly impressed, but before he could frame a suitable comment the hotel manager, who was also clerk and occasional bartender, came in to light the lamps and announce that supper was being served in the dining room. The lawyer inquired if the hack had come up yet from the station.

"No, Mr. Huse." The tone was deferential. "I've been keeping watch. If you care to go in to supper I'll call you the minute the hack reaches the square."

Otis Huse nodded his acceptance of this courtesy and went into the dining room. The drummer, to whom any companionship was manna from heaven, promptly followed.

There was a sprinkling of local patronage in the hotel dining room on account of the rain, which prevented country people from getting home. As Otis Huse looked about him he was glad he had the drummer in tow, for the garrulous fellow would insure him against the danger of being joined by some acquaintance. He was in no mood tonight to give more than a nod to people he knew.

So when their supper of spareribs, boiled cabbage, fried potatoes, and apple pie had been put before them, Huse thawed sufficiently to listen to the salesman's chatter. He suddenly realized the talkative stranger might be able to give him information.

"You've been out through the county this month?"

"From Bridgeport to Mullen's Mill. Never missed a cross-road."

"Did you stop at a place called Timberley?"

"Sure. The store just beyond the second tollgate."

"There's a farm by that name too."

"I know. But I don't call at private houses. Peddlers do that. I'm strictly wholesale." The drummer drew himself up a bit as he reached for the salt shaker. "I know the farm though. Belongs to a man named Tomlinson. From what I hear, he's somebody in these parts."

"What do you mean—by what you hear?"

The drummer looked cagey. "Oh, nothing. Only Wither-spoon—he's the Timberley storekeeper—warned me Tomlinson was not the sort of gent you carry tales about."

"Tales?" The lawyer's pale eyes kindled with interest. "You mean there is gossip about the Tomlinsons?"

The drummer glanced about the room, discreetly noting the diners. They were farmers mostly, as was evidenced by their weathered faces and the gusto with which they attacked the rather frugal fare provided by the house. At a near-by table a gaunt, loose-jointed fellow in a coonskin cap was stolidly eating his way through a double portion of everything on the bill of fare. Recognizing him, the drummer pointed him out, saying, "There's the party who was doing the most talking."

Otis Huse cast an oblique glance as directed and identified Henry Schook.

"What sort of talk was he spreading?"

"The damnedest cock-and-bull story you ever heard." The drummer dropped his voice. "It seems Tomlinson's wife claims that somebody has been throwing bricks through a certain window of their house, trying to frighten her."

So it was true, thought the lawyer. The letter had not exaggerated. Could Henry Schook have written it? Hardly.

He said aloud, "Some youngster with a grudge against the lady. She used to teach the Timberley school, you know."

"I said it was a young one too," agreed the drummer. "But down at the store they're saying no one is throwing the bricks. They've watched, it seems. Tomlinson's wife has reported bricks falling inside the house when there was never a soul in sight to throw 'em."

"Do they question the woman's sanity?" asked Huse dryly.

"Oh no. She's considered the most intelligent female in the district. But about this window—it's a bedroom window, downstairs"—the drummer leaned across the table impressively—"and they say it's the room in which Tomlinson's first wife died."

The lawyer moistened his lips. This was what he had been waiting for. Now he knew for a fact that the letter was worth investigating.

"Are they trying to make something of that?"

"Are they! Listen. You know George Tunney—has a workshop here in Woodridge—buggies, light spring wagons, coffins, and pumps?"

The lawyer's nod duly accredited this witness.

"Tunney's just installed a new pump in the kitchen at Timberley. And he had a lot to tell. He went so far as to say there'd been something funny about the first Mrs. Tomlinson's death.

But I think he's just sore because Tomlinson sent to Indianapolis for her casket instead of giving him the job." The drummer grinned at this professional pique on the part of local industry.

"But there are others," he went on, "farm hands, boys around the livery stable, plenty of people talking about the queer doings out at Timberley. Haven't you heard any of it?"

"I would be the last person to hear such things," said Otis Huse. Then he added carelessly, "Was there any talk about a girl out there who's said to be a witch?"

"Sa-a-a-ay! How do you know about that?" The drummer looked startled. "I never told you. That's the thing Witherspoon warned me to keep under my hat. He said Tomlinson would stop at nothing short of violence to keep down talk about that little girl."

The lawyer looked bitter. "And what does Tomlinson say to this superstitious talk about his dead wife?"

"Nothing. He pays no attention to it."

The hotel manager appeared. "The hack is in, Mr. Huse. Lucius Goff just went into the academy."

Otis Huse pushed back his chair without another word and hurried away. Before a waiter could clear the vacant place Henry Schook stalked across the room, combing his mustache with thumb and finger, and slid into the chair opposite the drummer.

"Howdy, Mr. Jenkins, remember me? Schook's my name. Heard you telling Otis Huse about the queer pranks out at Tomlinson's. You didn't know, did you, that you were talking to the first Mrs. Tomlinson's only surviving relative?" And with a gratified feeling of having punished the outlander for poaching on his preserves, the local news dispenser fell to upon the lawyer's untasted supper.

Behind the drawn blinds of the academy Otis Huse faced Richard Tomlinson's three friends with much the same sense of gratification. It was Lucius Goff whom he had wanted to see, but he considered it a stroke of luck to find John Barclay and Doc Baird with him. He came immediately, almost insolently, to the point.

"Which one of you sent me an anonymous letter?"

There were three prompt, matter-of-course denials.

"Why should you think one of us sent it?" frowned Lucius. He was dripping like a wet hound in front of the stove and inclined to be truculent.

"Because the subject of the letter was Richard Tomlinson."

The three friends were instantly alert. John Barclay said, "An anonymous letter is usually written by a coward. Since the writer hadn't the nerve to sign his name, I take it the letter was not friendly to Richard. It couldn't have been written by one of us."

"On the contrary," said Huse, "the letter was written by a friend of Tomlinson who waxed almost maudlin in his attempt to save a fool from his folly."

"What folly?" demanded the blacksmith.

"The folly of circulating lies about ghosts in order to conceal the mischief of that wicked girl."

Three glances encountered uneasily.

"Ghosts!"

"Who said anything about ghosts?"

"What mischief are you talking about?"

The lawyer's keen eyes darted from face to face. "That is something you should know better than I. You visit at Timberley. I do not. You doubtless have heard about Tomlinson's wife and the bricks she claims are being thrown at her."

Yes, they had heard about Judith's bricks.

"You must also have heard what Tomlinson is saying about the origin of those bricks."

No, this they had not heard.

"He is saying that the spirit of Abigail Tomlinson—my cousin—is tormenting his second wife."

215 &

At this statement, even the friends of Richard looked aghast.

"I don't believe it," said Doc Baird.

John Barclay said, "Richard would never say such a thing."

Lucius Goff asked, "Is that what the anonymous letter contained?"

"It is."

"And you thought one of us wrote it?"

"Frankly, Lucius, I suspected you. You've always been interested in that devilish cult of spirit rapping. I thought perhaps you had gone too far and got frightened by Tomlinson's gullibility. But now I'm convinced that the writer of this letter is more sincere than any of you; I mean, sincere with me. I'm going out to Timberley and get the truth of this matter."

The schoolmaster rose from his desk, almost in panic. "Mr. Huse, I beg of you, discount this whole business as the idle gossip of a country neighborhood." But even as he was wondering how he might get word to Richard, Lucius leaped blithely into the breach.

"You say you are going out to Timberley?"

"I am," said Otis Huse.

"May I ask when?"

"Tomorrow, if the weather permits."

"Then if you've no objection, I'll ride out with you. I've a birthday gift to take to Miss Ann."

The rain had stopped, but the streets were a churning mass of thick clay mud when the two men set out from Woodridge the next afternoon. Otis Huse kept good horses, and they were soon on the gravel road, where the buggy wheels gradually shed the mire of the town. But travel was slow and the day far spent by the time they turned down the lane between the poplars. An overcast sky warned that the storm was not over. Huse remarked carelessly that they might have to stay the night.

The house looked dignified as ever. Lucius scanned the

premises, searching for signs of disorder. There were none to be seen. Even the heavy rains had not disturbed the tranquil tidiness of the place.

"There's the window the bricks went through, purportedly." Huse pointed with a flick of his whip to an east window in the south wing. It had been closed against the rain. The glass pane was intact. There had been no bricks, evidently, since the rain started.

"The downstairs bedroom," murmured Lucius thoughtfully.

"The room in which my cousin died," said Huse darkly, "from causes that were never satisfactorily determined."

"She died of membranous croup, didn't she?"

"That's what Caxton put on the death certificate, but he told me himself he found no phlegm in her throat." It was all too plain that the lawyer was seeking to inject a sinister note into the circumstances of Abigail Tomlinson's death.

They rang the bell on the front porch. After an interval the door was opened by Richard's wife.

"Good afternoon, gentlemen. Won't you come in?" The greeting was as cordial as though they had been expected. Otis Huse, who had long since made up his mind he did not like the woman who had succeeded his cousin, found himself grudgingly changing his opinion.

Lucius glibly explained that they were calling to bring felicitations to Miss Ann on her birthday, and Judith, after showing them into the front room, went to call her mother-in-law.

"Oh, Miss Ann! Come in, dear. You have company."

When Ann Tomlinson appeared, wearing her black alpaca and cameo brooch, it was apparent that some sort of festivity was afoot. If she was surprised to see Otis Huse, she did not betray it. She greeted both callers hospitably and invited them to remain for her birthday supper. All the floods ever brewed by the Wabash, she said with a twinkle, could not keep the Tomlinson clan from celebrating her birthday.

Even while she chattered with her visitors, married daughters, sons-in-law, and grandchildren began arriving, bearing gifts of homemade delicacies; and while the men joined the group in the front room, the women repaired to the kitchen and took over the business of preparing the feast. Before long odors seeped through the covered passage that set the men at the front of the house sniffing hungrily. Lucius glanced slyly at Otis Huse. The lawyer looked somewhat disgruntled. He had not come to Timberley to make merry, but he could hardly pick a quarrel with Richard while others were doing so. Lucius began to hope that he might be got back to Woodridge without mentioning the object of his call.

When Richard appeared his hope seemed assured. Otis Huse might be the last person in the world whom Richard would have thought of inviting to Timberley, but when he came unheralded he was treated as a chosen guest. In the face of such hospitality Huse could do no less than respond in kind. Lucius began to relax and enjoy himself.

It was Miss Ann's party. She sat in the seat of honor, her busy hands folded in her lap as placidly as though every nerve were not twitching to know what was going on in her kitchen. It was a time of utter relaxation for Millie, who retired to the chimney corner with her snuffbox and let the young folks do as they pleased. But not for worlds would Miss Ann have betrayed to her children that she might have preferred an orderly kitchen tomorrow to playing the fine lady tonight. It was the family tradition that she must have nothing to do with the preparation of her own birthday supper, so she sat in the front room, pretending to listen to the men's talk, while she tried to figure where she would put all these people to sleep.

Cousin Lutie Simms had arrived, which meant that she would have to occupy the big four-poster in the alcove. Thorne could sleep in the trundle, which would release one of the beds in Miss Ann's room. If the weather turned bad so that Lucius and Otis Huse had to stay, they could have the downstairs bedroom. It was silly to shut that room up simply because

Judith had seen a few bricks come through the window. She would speak to Richard about it when she got the chance.

But she did not get the chance because his duties as host kept Richard busy. His wife had disappeared somewhere, leaving him to ease the constraint of the lawyer's presence and to see that young Will did not get into arguments with his brothers-in-law. Will was at the age when controversial discourse was the only sort in which he was proficient.

But Richard did not need any woman, thought his mother, to make people feel at ease beneath his roof. Her eyes followed him as he moved about the room. He was easily the handsomest man present and he wore his broadcloth suit and linen collar with a careless grace which even Lucius Goff might envy. Alec Mitchell and Hugh Turner, good men both, always managed to look uncomfortable in their Sunday clothes. But no one would ever take Richard for a farmer. When he smiled at her from time to time her heart swelled with pride and ultimate fulfillment.

Another pair of eyes watched Richard as he moved among his guests. Thorne had slipped in so unobtrusively that only one person had seen her. She sat on a hassock, quietly, saying not a word, because she did not want to be sent out to help in the kitchen or mind the younger children. Only her large eyes moved as they followed Richard about the room, and only Otis Huse took note of her.

Lucius, a time-honored visitor on this occasion, had brought Miss Ann a box of sweets from a Terre Haute confectioner's. The ribbons and lace paper, the delicate hues of bonbons and candied fruit delighted and somewhat awed the recipient. "My, my, it looks too pretty to eat," she murmured, candidly adding, "We won't pass it around till after supper or it'll spoil people's appetites." So the ornate box was set with other gifts on the shiny new sewing machine which was the gift of the entire family.

It was at this moment that Otis Huse chose to make a facetious remark. "Aren't you afraid to leave that lying around? The Timberley witch might get it."

The merry chatter was instantly stilled. Richard's face flushed ominously.

"There's no witch at Timberley."

"I've heard testimony to the contrary."

Lucius Goff's black eyes flashed the lawyer a warning threat, but it was blandly ignored.

Richard said, "If you're referring to the practical joke played at our wedding, I can assure you that has been satisfactorily explained."

"I'm referring to a letter I received," said Huse, "advising me to investigate more recent mischief in this house and clear my dead cousin's memory by putting the blame where it belongs." He had not intended saying this much; but, once started, he seemed unable to stop.

Richard's flush paled to the cold white of implacable anger. But before he could trust himself to speak his younger brother had leaped to his feet.

"You two-faced son of a b——" Remembering his mother's presence, Will choked back the word. "You wolf in sheep's clothing! Coming here like a member of the family, on Mother's birthday, pretending friendship in order to spy on us. You never did like us. Now you see a chance to make trouble for us. I've a mind to throw you out of——"

"Will!" Richard found his voice, temporarily lost in astonishment at his brother's tirade. Heretofore Will had been one of Thorne's accusers. Now he was furiously attacking her enemy.

"You are forgetting, Will, that Mr. Huse is our guest."

"He's no better than a spy."

"He is a guest and a relative of my children. You will please remember your manners."

The lad subsided sulkily, and Otis Huse was left feeling uncomfortably embarrassed. He muttered something about taking his leave, but rain had set in again and at this moment it came down in torrents, so that departure was out of the question.

He said to Richard, "I'm not trying to make trouble for anyone. But as your children's sole maternal relative, I think I've a right to firsthand information about the queer things happening around here." He glanced significantly at Thorne sitting tense and watchful on the hassock.

Involuntarily Richard's hand went out to her protectingly, though he did not touch her.

"I assure you nothing has happened worth investigating."

"You call bricks hurtling through a window, disappearing almost as soon as they fall, *nothing?* The memory of your children's dead mother insulted, blasphemous talk of her unquiet spirit—all this is nothing, I suppose. To me it indicates a mischief-maker who will not rest in the attempt to dishonor the dead."

In the uneasy silence which followed the door opened and Judith came into the room.

That she had been listening outside, Huse was certain. Her glance went first to him, as though in warning, before it turned upon Richard. And suddenly, intuitively, he knew who had sent him the anonymous letter. He watched with interest as she greeted her husband.

"I didn't know you had come in, dear." She lifted her face for an expected kiss, and as Richard bent to her lips other members of the family averted their eyes. Tomlinson husbands did not kiss their wives before a roomful of people.

Judith murmured audibly, "You still kiss like a bridegroom, darling," and brought a rush of color to his face.

There was a slight movement near the fireplace, the swish of a door closing, and the hassock was vacant. No one noted Thorne's departure except Otis Huse—and Judith.

"What's that on your arm?" Richard was asking, to cover the general embarrassment. A crocheted afghan, Judith explained, which she had made for Miss Ann. She spread it across her mother-in-law's knees, and while Ann Tomlinson examined the gift with genuine pleasure Judith went gaily to the piano.

"We must have music when Miss Ann goes out to supper. Will some gentleman be kind enough to give me a little assistance?"

There was an immediate rush of volunteers to raise the heavy lid of the piano. Miss Ann, looking on with amusement, wondered why it was that Hugh and Alec could watch their own wives struggle with a piano top and never lift a finger, yet they fairly stumbled over each other to wait on Richard's wife. Men were funny. They were this way or that, according to the woman who had hold of them. Her eyes searched for Richard, to share this joke with him, but he had left the room.

Judith took her place at the piano, surrounded by attentive males, and turned a sparkling face to her mother-in-law.

"What shall it be? Tonight is your night, Miss Ann. You must choose the song," and then before the older woman could reply, "Why—where is Richard?"

"He went out," Miss Ann explained, "to look for Thorne, probably." And then she added, "Let's sing 'Praise God from Whom All Blessings Flow.'"

Judith's hand struck a chord, not harshly, which was well. For it was a discordant clash of notes, like teeth grinding against each other.

Richard's first remark, as he raised his head from saying grace, was addressed to his own small sons.

"This is your cousin Otis, boys. You've grown so tall since he saw you last that perhaps you'd better be introduced. Otis, the young man with the freckles is Richard; the one with the snub nose is Roger." He performed the introductions with a seriocomic twinkle that removed the last trace of embarrassment from the lawyer's presence among them.

Thorne had changed her dress. Instead of the drab gray homespun in which she had appeared before supper, she was decked out in a soft bright cherry-colored merino, with cherry-colored ribbons in her hair.

Judith noted the change with disapproval. "Thorne, who gave you permission to put on that dress? Go upstairs and take it off."

Richard said, "I told her to change, Judith. All the other young folks are dressed for a party."

This was true. From sixteen-year-old Nancy Turner to Jane's baby, the young people were "dressed up" for Miss Ann's birthday.

"She needn't have put on that dress, Richard."

"Why not? You say it's too frivolous for church and it's much too nice for school. So it should be just about right for a party, don't you think?"

Across the long table husband smiled at wife and invisible rapiers clashed between them.

"By all means, dear. If you insist upon her wearing the dress, let it be in the bosom of the family." Smiling, Judith appealed to her sisters-in-law. "No man knows how to select clothes for girls, does he?"

"Did Richard buy that dress?" Kate's eyes rested on Thorne dubiously, as though questioning her brother's taste.

Thorne said quickly, "He brought it to me from Terre Haute, and I like it better than any dress I ever had." She flung a loyal look toward the man at the head of the table and he smiled back at her.

"Thorne shares my fondness for colors. The others think we have bad taste."

We—WE—WE!

Otis Huse watched Judith writhe behind her fixed, determined smile.

There was a birthday cake so huge that Miss Ann had to stand to cut it. There was floating island, which the children loved because it was so pretty. There were nuts and ladyfingers and fortunes told in coffee grounds and then, crowning excitement, there were charades in the front room.

This latest amusement had just reached the Timberley neighborhood and was extremely popular with old and young. Judith and Lucius Goff were elected captains, sides were chosen, and the fun began. Judith chose Otis Huse, Hugh Turner, Jane, Cousin Lutie, Nancy, and Ricky. On Lucius's side were Richard, Kate, Alec Mitchell, Jesse Moffat, Thorne, Will, and Jimmie Turner. The younger children and Miss Ann were audience.

Judith's side led, with a simple noun so obviously enacted that it was guessed immediately. Cousin Lutie, in a rocking chair, held Ricky on her lap, while he indulged in an extremely artificial paroxysm of coughing, which ceased when Jane appeared with bottle and spoon and liberally dosed him—presumably with cough syrup. In the second scene Otis Huse sat behind a table, looking bored but professional, and advised Hugh Turner about the legality of a business transaction. When Hugh had agreed to follow his attorney's advice he inquired how much he owed him. Mr. Huse replied that his fee was two dollars. A chorus of voices shouted, "Cof-fee!"

When Lucius's troupe took the stage it appeared that something more ambitious was to be offered. Furniture was rearranged, more candles were lighted, and a fair semblance of a hotel lobby was achieved. All the company were on stage, sitting, standing, talking together, while Jesse Moffat wandered among them droning in his best hogcaller's voice, "Call for Mr. Jones! Call for Mr. Jones!" in comical imitation of a bellboy.

In the midst of this activity Thorne came in and asked if some lady would lend her a handkerchief. Kate produced a lace-trimmed bit of linen with the admonition to take care of it. Thorne assured her that the borrowed article would not be damaged.

Lucius then entered, very dapper with walking stick and hat, and struck a match to light his cigar. He was about to throw the match away when Thorne stopped him. "Don't throw it on the floor. You'll burn the carpet."

Frowning dramatically, he looked about for a place to toss the burning match. Thorne said, "Let me have it," and taking the match from Lucius, she dropped it, blazing, into Kate's dainty handkerchief and squeezed it up in her hand. Kate cried that her handkerchief was ruined, but Thorne only laughed and shook it out prettily by one corner. The match had disappeared. There was no burn or smudge on the handkerchief.

Lucius and Kate cried, "It's *magic!*" Jesse Moffat shouted, "*Call* for Mr. Jones!" The word was "magical," but no one bothered to guess. No one was interested in charades any more. They were interested only in Thorne's magic tricks.

She went through her entire little repertoire because no one disapproved and Richard smiled encouragement. Perhaps he had a purpose in it, for Otis Huse could not fail to see how innocent her little sleight-of-hand performance really was. She plucked cards from the lapels of men's coats and made paper flowers bloom in women's hair. She caused Alec's and Will's wallets to change places in each other's pockets and pulled a tiny red ball out of Jane's snood. Each trick brought heartier applause and increased astonishment, until she glowed like a rose with her pretty triumphs. Never before had she been allowed to display her talents; never had she looked so captivating as while mystifying her audience with the old act of Thorndyke the Magician.

Otis Huse, standing near Judith, admitted without prejudice that the child was exceedingly clever. "She ought to be on the stage," he said.

Judith agreed. "She belongs in a theater, not in a private home."

The acid in the words was not lost upon the lawyer. He

shrewdly guessed that this second wife of Richard Tomlinson hated the pretty child as violently as had his cousin, and the knowledge gave him curious satisfaction. It also, oddly, lessened his suspicions of Thorne. Jealousy, he decided, had prompted the writing of that anonymous letter.

"It was you who sent me the letter, wasn't it?" His cold light eyes bored deep into Judith's.

"Yes," she admitted, and felt a chill creep down her back as she realized what she had revealed. Now this man knew her weakness. This kinsman of Abigail's knew that she was no stronger, no happier, than the woman she had supplanted.

You'll know what I mean someday. You don't believe me now. You think I'm crazy. But you'll find out.

She turned her head as though someone had spoken, and when she saw no one behind her she shivered uncontrollably. Someone put a shawl about her shoulders. It was Otis Huse. He was still beside her. The magic act was over. The men were besieging Thorne, begging for an explanation of her tricks, but she escaped them all and fled to Richard, who laughingly barricaded her with his arms and announced that the show was over.

Judith said to the man at her side, "You have seen how clever she is. Do you need any further explanation of our witch?"

CHAPTER 21

Prayers were over. The fire was low, the backlog covered with ashes for the night. Candles brought from the kitchen waited in a row upon the table to light the way to bedrooms. In the corner near the alcove a feminine caucus was being held.

"You and the children can come into my room, Kate," Miss Ann was saying, "and Hugh can double up with Will. We'll put Alec with Jesse Moffat, and Jane and the baby can share Thorne's bed with Nancy Turner. That leaves the big bed down here for Cousin Lutie."

"There's still Lucius Goff and Otis Huse," said Kate.

"We'll put them in the downstairs bedroom."

A look passed between the Tomlinson daughters.

"Do you think they'll mind?" wondered Jane.

"If they do they'll have to sleep on a pallet in the kitchen," said her mother.

"That doesn't take care of Thorne," said Kate.

"She can sleep on the trundle, as she always does when there's company."

"She won't like it."

Jane murmured, "I feel guilty, taking her bed."

A voice came unexpectedly from across the room. "Thorne will sleep where she's told to sleep, whether she likes it or not."

The Tomlinson women turned with a start. They had not realized their talk could be overheard.

Judith was standing near the table, about to pick up her night candle. She had taken no part in the domestic discussion for the simple reason that she was not interested. But she turned now and sharply addressed Thorne.

"You will sleep in the trundle bed as Miss Ann says, and no acting the crybaby about it. Do you understand?"

Since Thorne had not complained, the reprimand seemed uncalled for.

Richard said, "There's no need to speak to her in that tone, Judith." He turned to his mother. "The trundle bed is too short for Thorne. Why can't one of the younger children take it?"

Miss Ann explained that the younger children were doubling up as it was.

Judith said, "Thorne will sleep in the trundle bed and we'll hear no more about it." She turned to Alec Mitchell. "Will you draw the bed out, please?" She seemed to have taken charge of operations.

But Miss Ann was still, to her sons-in-law, the head of the house. Alec cast an inquiring glance in her direction and received a nod of assent.

A queer tension gripped Judith as she watched Alec draw the trundle from under the bed in the alcove and pull it out into the center of the room.

As she remembered it afterward, they were all standing in an irregular circle about the bed: Hugh Turner, Otis Huse, and Lucius at the right of the fireplace; Richard a few feet away near the piano; herself by the table where stood the night candles. Jesse Moffat, who had already picked up his candle, was near the hall door. Miss Ann and her daughters, with the children, formed a group near the alcove.

Judith saw Thorne, who had been standing near the hearth, move closer to Richard. Anger rose within her, followed by a queer nausea. She felt—as she had felt that other time when she heard the clock strike—as though the temperature of the room had suddenly dropped. A strange premonition of impending mischief gripped her. She told herself that this was imagination and looked about to see if others felt it too. Then suddenly, while she was looking at it, she saw Jesse Moffat's candle go out. One by one she watched the candles all over the room go out. The smell of smoking tallow was acrid in her nostrils.

All the people in the room were in shadow now. She could not see their faces, only indistinct shapes. The only light was the glow from the fireplace, which fell upon the trundle bed. This was the bed on which she had sat with Thorne while she listened to Abigail's dying gasps. She stared at it now as though it were a sentient thing that could remember and accuse.

While she watched with fearful fascination the bed began to move. It trembled convulsively in all its joints, like a palsied old man. Its agitation increased until it rattled like a wooden cart rolling over a corduroy road.

A voice rose thinly: *"She's* doing it, Richard! Make her stop!" Tone, cadence, pitch were like a reproduction of another voice, heard long ago when a cucumber cow was milked. Judith, listening, chilled. And then she realized it was her own voice she had heard. At the realization she sickened and closed her eyes. When she opened them the bed had stopped shaking. But she no longer saw a trundle bed. She saw a replica, in miniature, of the bed in the south room.

Richard started toward his wife, alarmed at the ghastly pallor of her face. The skirts of his coat almost brushed the bed. Judith cried, "Don't touch it! Stay where you are."

The bed shuddered and began shaking as before. Judith closed her eyes against the motion, which made her seasick. When she opened them the bed was still. It was again the trundle bed.

In the silence that followed there was no sound except her own heavy, half-strangled breathing.

She turned on Thorne, screaming in that voice which did not seem to be her own, "You did this, you little witch! This is another of your magic tricks. Light the candles, Richard. We'll see if she gets her way by frightening people out of their wits."

Richard said, "The candles were lighted some time ago."

Judith looked about the room. Incredibly, flame flared from every taper, including Jesse Moffat's. The shadows had receded; faces were again visible. And every face was turned toward her in curious wonder. She looked to her husband. He was regarding her anxiously.

"Are you ill, Judith?"

She could feel every eye upon her, particularly Otis Huse's. She was conscious of the fascinated interest of the farm hand. But she saw only Thorne's white face, with dark eyes wide and watchful. She noted that from where the girl was standing she could not have touched the trundle bed.

Richard repeated his question: "Are you all right, Judith?"

"Quite all right, thank you."

There was a concerted sigh of relief from the onlookers. Miss Ann began collecting the children, marshaling them to bed.

Thorne asked, "Am I to sleep down here in the trundle bed?"

"No," said Richard. "Anyone can see the bed is too short for you. There's a couch in our room which will do for me. You can sleep with Judith."

His mother agreed. "Put the trundle back in the alcove, Alec."

Before Alec could obey, Judith astonished them all by countermanding Miss Ann's order.

"Leave the bed where it is. We might as well have a showdown now as later, Richard."

He said, "I don't know what you mean by showdown."

"Thorne's cleverness tonight has gone to her head. She doesn't want to sleep in the trundle, so she performs a sleight-of-hand trick, making the bed appear to—dance." Judith passed her hand across her eyes. She shrank from mentioning the weird metamorphosis she had seen. Now that it was past, she told herself it had been a trick of her own eyesight, caused by the movement of the bed. She appealed to the others for support. "You all saw the magic Thorne worked tonight. A dancing bed is no more remarkable than a burning match that disappears within a cloth without leaving a trace."

Curious, half-fearful glances passed among the people in

the room. Half-audible murmurs and whispers circulated among them.

Richard said to Thorne, "Cricket, did you do anything to the bed?"

Thorne said, "No. I wasn't near it."

"That's true." Richard turned to Judith. "Thorne was at least six feet from the bed when you screamed. I know, because you frightened her so, she grabbed hold of me."

"Then who played that trick with the bed?" demanded Judith.

"There's been no trick played with the bed. What are you talking about?"

Suddenly she knew sickeningly that he was going to deny having seen the thing which had frightened her.

"If you didn't see it, Richard, it was because you were looking elsewhere. It was perfectly visible, even if the candles did gutter down. The rest of you saw it, didn't you?" She looked about the room; sharply, at first, then frantically, as she saw blank denial in every face. "You know you saw it! You, Will—you, Jesse Moffat—Lucius—why do you all just stare at me, pretending you didn't see Thorne's trick of legerdemain? You were kinder to Abigail. You were quick to assure her that you had seen milk come from a cucumber cow."

No one answered her appeal. The men addressed returned her frantic gaze in silence that became so oppressive it was like shutting off the air to her lungs. She loosened the ribbon at her throat and looked about for a window to open, wondering why it was so hard to breathe. Her eyes bulged as though she were choking, and she breathed openmouthed like a fish, gasping for air.

Richard's voice seemed to come from a vast distance. "No use having hysterics, Judith. I'm putting the trundle bed away."

His brother Will came forward to assist him. Judith saw

them whispering together as they pushed the trundle back under the bed in the alcove. She told herself that they were agreeing on some course of action to protect Thorne.

After that there was a slight rearrangement of sleeping accommodations. For when Richard said, "There! That puts the trundle out of sight," a wail arose from an unexpected quarter.

"If you think I'm going to sleep in the alcove with a piece of furniture Judith saw cuttin' up, you're crazy!"

Three hundred pounds of quavering terror faced him belligerently. Cousin Lutie, her mouth still full of the coconut cake for which she had made a surreptitious trip to the kitchen, looked so ludicrous that Richard began to laugh, and his laughter eased the tension.

"The furniture has not been cutting up, Cousin Lutie."

"Judith said it did. Personally, I'd take a schoolma'am's word against a farmer's any day."

"All right, if you're afraid to sleep down here, you can have our room. And Thorne can sleep with you. Judith and I will sleep in the alcove. Unless Judith is afraid."

Judith had recovered from her hysteria. Kate had brought smelling salts and made her lie down upon the couch. She sat up now, protesting that she was not afraid and never had been. She was merely annoyed at having tricks played on her. If Richard slept in the alcove, of course she would sleep there too. Whereupon the rest of the family took their candles and departed for rooms above, still laughing at Cousin Lutie. The fat woman's round face, smeared with fright and coconut icing, had restored to the Tomlinsons their forgotten sense of humor.

Richard showed Lucius and Otis Huse into the downstairs bedroom. As he set his candle on the mantelpiece he said casually, "Judith has not been well lately. I'm afraid her eyes are bothering her." And that was the only apology offered for his wife's unusual behavior.

Lucius was chagrined to find himself quartered with the lawyer. He had hoped for a chance to talk privately with Richard, and the presence of Huse made this impossible. But when he was alone with his uncongenial roommate he decided it might be as interesting to get the attorney's reaction to Judith's strange conduct as Richard's.

"Well, what did you make of it?" he asked chattily as he began taking off his boots.

Huse was looking about him with interest. This was the first time he had been in the room in which his cousin had died. He noted the outer door in the south wall, the window in the east—the window through which the alleged bricks had come. He examined this window with interest. It was closed, its pane intact.

Lucius, watching him, repeated his question: "What do you think Judith Tomlinson saw tonight?"

The lawyer frowned thoughtfully. "I'm more interested in what she sees when she claims bricks are thrown through that window, only to disappear."

"What do you mean?" asked Lucius.

Huse indicated the angle at which the window set to the outer door. "Bricks thrown through the window could pass straight through the door if it was standing open."

"Oh no." On this point Lucius was positive. "The bricks always land on the floor. They make a loud thud when they fall."

"Has anyone ever heard them fall except Judith Tomlinson?"

"Not that I know of."

The lawyer shrugged. "And no one else has seen them," he said dryly.

His attitude nettled Lucius. "Why should you doubt the

woman's word? Do you think she's making this up out of whole cloth?"

"Do you consider her a creditable witness," countered Huse, "after the way she behaved tonight?"

"I think her behavior tonight proves that something is frightening her to death," said Lucius stoutly.

"Are you suggesting," said Huse coldly, "that she saw something which was not visible to anyone else?"

"Did you see anything?" retorted Lucius.

They undressed in chill silence, literally, for the fireless room was cold. Huse snuffed the candle; and Lucius, already submerged beneath the bedcovers, was surprised to find a misty light coming from the east window. The skies had cleared. There was a late-rising moon.

He mumbled, "Pull the shade, will you? Bad luck sleeping in the moonlight."

With a disdainful sniff for the other man's superstition, Huse drew the blind to its full length, then climbed into bed. Within a matter of seconds both men were asleep.

They awakened simultaneously, with a crashing sound in their ears and a streaming light in their eyes.

"Did you hear——"

"What the devil——"

Both men were sitting erect, rigid with cold and some nameless alarm. It was like waking from nightmare: still gripped with fear, but unable to recall its origin.

Huse muttered, "What was it?"

"Sssh!" whispered Lucius. "There's something in this room."

They waited, listening, their eyes strained to pierce the black shadows that lay on either side of the bed. The moon focused a spotlight on the counterpane.

"I don't see anything," said Huse.

"Did you hear that noise?"

"Yes. That's what woke me."

"Damn that moonlight! It blinds me."

"Look! The window blind. That's what made the noise."

The dark green blind, which Huse had so carefully lowered, had fallen. Moonlight streamed through the unshaded window.

With a snort of absurd relief Huse climbed out of bed and found the fallen window blind on the floor. It had rolled itself neatly back upon its roller as it fell.

"Here's what made the noise," he explained. "The spring in the roller suddenly released, and the blind flew up with such force that it jerked the roller off the hook. Simple, eh? I suppose you thought it was a ghost."

Lucius withheld comment. He pulled the covers over his head again, while Huse replaced the roller on its fixtures, lowered the shade to exclude the moonlight, and crawled back into bed.

"One of the hooks was bent. I straightened it. It won't happen again, I'll warrant." And turning on his side, the lawyer was soon asleep.

But Lucius could not sleep. One of those wakeful spells that sometimes beset the healthiest sleeper descended upon him. He turned on his left side, he turned on his right; he sprawled on his stomach, he flopped on his back; but he could not regain the sound slumber he had lost.

He threw off one of the many quilts because he was too warm. Then he felt a chill and pulled it back. He seemed to be smothering. He began to fear he was having a heart attack. Perhaps if he turned over—Dr. Caxton had said that if the left arm pressed against the heart . . .

He lay on his back, gasping for air, trying to summon courage to get up and raise a window. The room was suddenly stifling. But he was afraid to leave his bed. And he was loath to call Huse, who had already been up once.

The smothering sensation was in his throat now. Something was too tight about his neck. He tore frantically at the collar of his borrowed nightshirt.

The collar was not even buttoned. It was open at the throat.

He tried desperately to call his companion. He could make no sound. He was strangling—choking to death—unable to cry for help.

When the crash came the second time it did not even startle him. He was almost gone. But he knew, in his semi-conscious state, that the window blind had fallen again and that somehow it had brought relief. Moonlight streamed through the pane once more, and though the window was closed fresh air seemed to blow through the room. Lucius took great gulps of it into his bursting lungs and found that he was able to breathe again. The room seemed full of sweet fresh air.

Otis Huse sat up in bed, muttering, "This is getting to be a habit." But he got up and restored the fallen blind. Half asleep, he crawled back under the covers and was immediately dead to the world. He had replaced the rolled shade on its fixtures, but he had neglected to pull it down.

The moon shone straight into Lucius's eyes. He was ashamed to ask Huse to get out of bed for the third time and, to his disgust, he lacked the nerve to do it himself. So he lay staring at the moonlit window, his body icy with sweat.

He tried to remember afterward whether he closed his eyes or took them from the window, but he was never sure. He could not have told how it came or when; but suddenly it was there: a hand pressed against the windowpane.

There was nothing dim or misty in its shape. It was as vividly outlined against the glass as though the moon were a powerful spotlight. It was a woman's hand, slender, long-fingered, and so white that its texture seemed luminous.

There was curious pathos in the way the hand was pressed against the pane, slightly cupped, as though shading a pair of eyes that were trying to peer into the room. Yet Lucius saw no face, no arm, no body; nothing beyond the window but inky shadow, except for the spot of moonlight illuminating the hand.

While he looked at it he felt a strange compassion for someone, or something, that almost made him weep. As long as this pity gripped him, he was not afraid. As long as he knew no fear, he kept his eyes upon the hand. How long this lasted, he did not know.

Then realization came, and with it fear. Suddenly he told himself that he was looking at a hand that had no arm, and terror swept him so that he cried out hoarsely.

Otis Huse sat up in bed.

Lucius pointed to the window. The hand was gone.

He did not tell Huse what he had seen. He could not. He was still in the grip of a nightmare that tied his tongue. He told himself that in the morning he would tell the lawyer of his experience and let him question it if he dared. But he could not speak of it tonight.

So when Huse climbed out of bed for the third time and drew the blind, shutting out the disturbing moonlight, Lucius turned on his side and went quickly, soundly, to sleep, like a man drugged. He did not waken until voices and footsteps beyond the hall door warned that it was morning and the rest of the household was astir.

Huse was already out of bed. The two men dressed in curious silence. Perhaps it was only the natural glumness of early morning. But for some reason Lucius's resolve to relate his nocturnal experience began to dissipate with daylight. He was certain the lawyer would not believe him; Huse would discredit the whole episode as a nightmare. The thing should have been told at the moment, before any doubts—even his own—had time to germinate. Already Lucius was beginning to wonder if he had been the victim of an exceedingly realistic dream.

And then an odd thing happened. Huse, in dressing, dropped a collar button. It rolled through a crack under the closet door. The walls of this closet were unfinished, and rough two-by-fours left a space of several inches where floor and wall failed to meet. Huse cursed lustily when he saw where the button had gone.

"Damn the luck! It's rolled down that hole. Lend a hand, will you? Your fist is smaller than mine."

Lucius's long slim hand slipped easily under the floor boards and retrieved the missing button; likewise a bundle of rags stuffed between the sleeper and the floor.

"Lucky those rags were there. They kept your button from dropping through to the cellar."

Huse did not answer. He was regarding with queer interest the handful of rags, which were not rags at all, but a home-made doll with a velvet ribbon tied round its neck so tight that its head lolled foolishly to one side.

When Lucius saw the doll his face paled.

"Have you ever seen this before?" asked the lawyer.

Lucius nodded. He had an uncomfortable sensation of being on the witness stand.

"This is the doll my cousin feared, isn't it?"

There was no doubt it was the same doll. Lucius remembered it only too well. He reluctantly admitted as much.

"I wonder how it got under the floor of that closet," said Huse.

"Maybe it fell down there by accident."

"It couldn't have *fallen* through a crack that narrow." The implication was obvious. The doll had been hidden under the floor.

Sharply Lucius recalled his weird experience of the night. He debated whether or not to tell the lawyer. Desire to prove a point overrode prudence. Briefly he told of the hand he had seen at the window and the peculiar suggestion it carried of eyes peering into the room. Both men glanced at the window from which the blind had fallen three times. It was on a direct line with the spot where the doll was found.

For once Huse had no ready argument to sustain his own skepticism. He recalled what the doctor had told him about his cousin's death: that she had choked to death from no apparent cause. All that he had seen in this house, all that he had heard of it suddenly assumed a sinister significance.

"Suppose, for the sake of conjecture—mind, I don't claim to believe any such thing—but suppose your experience last night was something more than nightmare; do you think it was in any way connected with the secret of this doll's hiding place?"

"I do," said Lucius.

"That means you believe this doll was responsible for my cousin's death," said the lawyer.

But Lucius was not prepared to go that far. "Oh no. How could it be?"

"Knowing poor Abigail's fear of this thing," said Huse harshly, "and her nervous state at the time, I should say the sight of this doll with a strangling cord around its neck would have been sufficient to frighten her to death."

Lucius, now thoroughly alarmed, said hastily that he did not think anything of the kind and suggested that they put the doll back where they had found it. But this Huse refused to do.

"In that case, then, we'll show it to Richard," said Lucius, and on this point they finally compromised.

They talked to Richard after breakfast, behind closed doors in the bedchamber, for Lucius made it clear that what they had to tell was for his ears alone. Richard listened calmly to the account of the falling window blind; even Lucius's nocturnal experience failed to move him. But when Huse took up the narrative and told of the rolling collar button and what was found beneath the closet floor, every trace of color drained from Richard's face. There was no question of the shock he received when Thorne's doll was laid before him.

He regarded it for a long moment in silence. Then he said, "Thank you, gentlemen, for coming with this to me. I should have destroyed it long ago. I'd forgotten it was there."

"You mean—you knew about it?" The lawyer's sharp query betrayed collapse of a rapidly building case.

Richard said coolly, "I put it there myself."

For a second the two lifelong antagonists faced each other in open hostility. Lucius, the onlooker, thought, "Richard is lying and Huse knows it."

"My late wife had a morbid fear of this doll," Richard explained. "So I hid it where she could not possibly find it."

"In her own room?" said Huse skeptically.

"Where no one could find it," said Richard. "There are children in this house. The doll was their plaything. The one place they were never allowed to play was in their mother's room." He said *children*. Both men noted that he pointedly referred to his own small boys, ignoring the girl who had made the doll.

"As for your experience last night, Lucius, I ask you please not to spread that tale around the country. There is nothing extraordinary about a falling window shade. And your dream of suffocation is not remarkable, considering that from boyhood you've suffered from nightmare. I've slept with you too often to be fooled by that." Richard smiled at his friend good-humoredly, but a spot of color burned now in each cheek.

The lawyer said, "Do you consider that choking string around the doll's neck part of your friend's nightmare?"

Richard's eyes blazed. At last he made no effort to hide his feeling toward this uninvited guest.

"I've tried to treat you courteously, Otis Huse, because

of your relationship to my children. I don't know what you came here to find, and I'm neither interested nor alarmed. But I do ask you to leave my house because I don't like your libelous insinuations."

Perhaps it was the unlooked-for explosion, perhaps it was the word "libel," which brought the lawyer to realization that he had nothing but dreams and toys on which to found his vague suspicions. He was much too astute to risk a suit for damages, so he took his departure forthwith, leaving his luckless companion to get back to town the best way he could.

"Don't worry, Richard. Otis won't do anything. He's no fool, even if he is mean as gar broth." Lucius tried to reassure his friend when the other man had gone. "Suppose he did find Thorne's doll with a string choking it. No court in the world would call it——" And then at sight of Richard's face he stopped, appalled at his own words.

"I mean—the doll had nothing to do with Abigail's——" He floundered helplessly and gave up. Muttering something about business in Woodridge, he asked if he might have the loan of a horse.

CHAPTER 22

From an upstairs window Judith watched Otis Huse drive away and knew that her hope in that quarter had failed. He had spent a night at Timberley; he had witnessed her discomfiture, but he had not come to her support. If this shrewd, not disinterested attorney had failed to see anything on which to base an accusation of Thorne, there was nothing left to Judith but her fear.

She wondered what the three men had talked about behind

the closed door of the room downstairs. All night long she had tormented herself with the fear of what might be discovered by the two who were sleeping there. Once, unable to close her eyes, she had stolen from the bed in the alcove and slipped outdoors, in wrapper and nightgown, to peer through the window of the adjacent room. With her hand pressed to the moonlit pane, shielding her eyes from the eerie radiance, she had been able to satisfy herself that both men were abed and the closet door fast shut. She had crept back into the house and her own bed without waking her husband and fallen at last into slumber.

But now the caucus following breakfast had revived last night's fear. With the men gone she was free to question Richard, but she was afraid she might betray herself. She could no longer trust her tongue to speak her mind's intention.

The feeling of someone close beside her was with her constantly now, prompting her every utterance, possessing her very soul. It was not of her own volition that she quarreled with Richard. She had listened, helpless, last night to her own tirade as it poured from her mouth upon Thorne, knowing that with every word she was driving her lover from her. He had slept by her side in the alcove, in a bed that was strange and comfortless, and not once had he touched or spoken to her. Did he really believe she was lying about the thing she had seen? Or did he think she was losing her mind?

This was the beginning of a significant change in Judith. As winter came on she spent more and more time in her room. She made it bright and cheerful, and there was always a fire to attract visitors, so that gradually it became a family habit to sit in Judith's room instead of the room downstairs. Ann said one day to her daughter Kate, "We sit with Judith now almost as much as we used to sit with Abigail," and then, as the words sank in, mother and daughter exchanged a troubled look.

Judith's most frequent visitor was, surprisingly, young Will. The lad was obliged to pass her door in order to reach his own room, and she always called some pleasant greeting to him. At first he responded sulkily and went on by; then he took to lingering in the doorway; finally he came in and sat down.

He never had much to say, but he seemed flattered that Judith should enjoy talking to him. The talk always turned subtly upon himself. What was he doing these winter days when there was so little work upon the farm? Whom did he see when he went to Woodridge? Why hadn't he attended the housewarming at Tatum's the other night? Because he had no girl to take? Fie! There must be dozens of girls in the neighborhood to choose from.

Little by little the taciturn youth revealed himself to this clever sister-in-law as he had never revealed himself to mother or sisters. And Judith discovered a curious thing about young Will. He was jealous of his older brother. That he was unconscious of this jealousy was as evident as that it existed. But it had been the mainspring of his industry on the farm, just as it had been the stimulus for his adolescent wild oats. Because Richard had been born with that charm which pleases without effort, it had been necessary for young Will to prove himself the better farmer and to boast of his prowess with women.

"You're old enough to be looking for a wife, Will." After a few confidential chats Judith could talk to him as though she had his welfare at heart. "Those girls in Woodridge have served their purpose, but you don't want to be playing around all your life."

He grew very red and muttered something unintelligible, but she saw that the idea was not unpleasing to him.

"I think you should go to the next party, and if you don't like going alone why don't you ask Miss Ann to let you take Thorne?" Judith threw in this suggestion carelessly, expecting to meet with reluctance, if not actual rejection. To her surprise the idea was accepted with a promptness that startled her. Will said he would speak to his mother.

Ann Tomlinson, when approached, was likewise surprisingly co-operative. She seemed quite willing for Thorne to attend the neighborhood taffy pulls and sleigh rides with her younger son. And when Thorne, pleased and excited at the prospect of wearing her pretty dress wondered if Richard would approve, she was told to say nothing to Richard about it. Judith laughed to herself at the way the three of them, unwittingly and with conflicting purposes, conspired with her to keep Richard in ignorance of what was going on.

Her health began to improve after that. Before long she was going out again with her husband. They were seen together at church on Sundays. They attended the midwinter lecture course in Woodridge. From time to time there were guests at Timberley, and no one was merrier than Judith. It would have seemed that the simple circumstance of young Will taking Thorne to a neighborhood party now and then was all that had been needed to restore her health and tranquillity. For Richard, when he learned of the parties, did not disapprove. He seemed only glad that Thorne was having fun like other young folks.

It was this outward semblance of peace, sanity, and good spirits which made the more shocking Judith's collapse when it came.

Since the night Otis Huse slept in the downstairs bedroom her mind had been teased with uncertainty as to whether he had made any discovery. During the autumn it was this desire to know if the doll was still under the floor of the closet and her lack of nerve to investigate which had made her ill. Now, fortified by her new feeling of security about Thorne, she determined to find out once and for all if the doll had been found.

She waited till an afternoon when Miss Ann had gone over to her daughter Jane's and Richard was in Woodridge. Will and Jesse Moffat were busy in the sugar orchard, and the children were at school. Judith was alone in the house except for Millie, whose presence in the kitchen was attested by the lusty strains of "O! Susanna" coming through the covered passage.

Judith went boldly to the downstairs bedroom and opened the door. Her nerves were as calm as though this were not the room in which she had seen bricks come through a window, only to disappear when they hit the floor.

The room was dusky with drawn blinds and cold with the chill of the fireless grate. She did not linger to look about her. She went straight to the closet door. As she passed the tall canopied bed she heard a sound like something whizzing through the air and the next moment felt a coil about her neck. She screamed, but her scream was strangled as the noose—or whatever it was—tightened, choking her until she lost consciousness. . . .

Cold air blowing across her face restored her. The outer door was open, and Richard was standing there. But the person bending over Judith, sponging her face with a wet towel, was Thorne. And on the floor beside Thorne was a jumping rope. She had been coming from school, she said, when she heard the scream and ran into the house through the dining room a few seconds before Richard entered by the outside door. He had heard his wife's scream as he rode up the lane.

Judith sat up, and as her strength returned words poured from her mouth, ugly venomous words, accusing Thorne of trying to kill her with a piece of rope. Richard paid no heed to her raving. He carried her upstairs to her room and dispatched Thorne for his mother. And when Will came in shortly after he was sent to Woodridge for the doctor.

Dr. Caxton was just sitting down to supper when Will rode up to his house. To the disgust of his elderly housekeeper, the doctor left his meal untasted (there would be a better one for him at Timberley) and went out to the stable where his horse stood, still saddled from the day's rounds. He wondered what in damnation was the matter with Richard's wife now. If it wasn't one pain it was another, and not a thing the matter with her (as he'd been telling Richard for years) that a baby wouldn't take care of. If you wanted to keep a woman healthy, keep her pregnant.

And then the doctor's aging memory clicked into place. He hadn't been telling Richard anything about this wife for years. It was Judith—not Abigail—whom he was going to see.

Yet the feeling that he was repeating a timeworn procedure was still with him when he reached the house. As he puffed upstairs after Richard he said irritably, "Why'd you move her up here?" And when the answer came, "Judith's room has always been up here," he felt all kinds of a fool. But when he sat down at the bedside he had a strange sense of having lived the scene before. The woman with the haggard eyes and restless hands plucking at the collar of her nightgown might have been Abigail, so familiar were the words which greeted him.

"I don't want a doctor. There's nothing the matter with me that a doctor can cure. Go away! I don't want anyone near me but Richard."

He asked, "How long has she been like this?"

"I found her in this state when I came home this afternoon."

"Had anything happened to upset her?"

"I'll tell you later."

He administered a dose of laudanum. Being unused to sedatives, the patient succumbed quickly to its soothing effect. Her mutterings ceased, her nervous twitchings quieted, her eyelids drooped. In a few minutes she was asleep.

Ann Tomlinson had come into the room. She offered to sit with her daughter-in-law while the two men went down and had their supper. How many times had Richard's mother performed this same service, when the woman in the bed had been Abigail instead of Judith.

Dr. Caxton determined to have a straight talk with Richard as soon as they were alone. But Will was likewise in the dining room, and Thorne was putting supper on the table for the three of them, so there was no opportunity to ask Richard what had happened to throw his wife into hysterics.

Thorne had eaten earlier, but at Richard's suggestion she slipped into Judith's chair and presided over the teapot with a quaint little air of importance, as though she felt her responsibilities as temporary mistress of the house. Richard, from the moment he sat down, relaxed noticeably. He did not speak of his wife's illness beyond asking the doctor if a good night's sleep wasn't the best medicine she could have. Being assured that it was, he accepted the steaming cup which Thorne handed him and began to talk of other things.

He talked about neighborhood matters, news of the town, books they had been reading, politics; he talked with a quiet zest, like a man who was at ease and feeling good. It occurred to the doctor that this was a strange way for a man to feel whose wife lay ill upstairs. It was as though he had been carrying a heavy load up a hill and had put it down for a moment to rest.

It came as a slight shock to Dr. Caxton, a little later, that Richard's curious relaxation stemmed from Thorne's presence behind the teapot. He could not have told how or why the idea presented itself, for Richard took no notice of her except to glance her way now and then, and Thorne did not join in the conversation, which was mostly man-talk. She busied herself with supplying the wants of three hungry males, and this she did as efficiently as Ann Tomlinson herself might have done. She refilled empty cups and replenished empty plates with a cheerful largess suggestive of a good housewife who likes to see her menfolk eat. If Thorne's hospitality lacked the polish which Judith had brought to the Tomlinson table, it was somehow more in keeping with the farm atmosphere. Perhaps it was this absence of formality which put Richard at his ease. Perhaps it was the knowledge that everything he did was correct in the eyes of the lady behind the teapot. If he violated all rules of etiquette by demanding maple syrup on his pie, Thorne not only refrained from censure but co-operated by supplying the syrup.

Suddenly the doctor was struck by a truth so simple it amazed him. All these years, when people had wondered at Richard's fondness for this child, they had missed entirely its significance. Thorne was probably the only person in the world with whom he was completely himself. A doctor might sit down to eat with these two every day for the next forty years and never once hear the word "nerves." For where a man and his wife know completion in each other there is no friction. Only Thorne, of course, was not Richard's wife. For a moment Dr. Caxton forgot her youth and thought irritably that she should have been.

The longer he watched them, the more he was struck with his unique discovery. Why hadn't Ann Tomlinson seen what to him was perfectly obvious: that this waif from a carnival was the only woman in the world who would ever be able to cope with the dreams, the inconsistencies, the lovable vagaries which were the sum and substance of her son Richard? Thorne would never require him to toe the mark of Abigail's dogmatism, nor fit into the mold of Judith's sophistication. Thorne would simply love him and let him alone.

Why hadn't Richard been able to see this and hold his patience for a little while? To an old man nearing seventy, two years was such a little while. If Richard hadn't made that damn-fool second marriage . . .

So engrossed did the doctor become in his own speculations that it came as a second shock when young Will said to him, "Have you noticed how Thorne is growing up, Doc? I had the belle of the ball on my hands at Jennie Barclay's the other night." Great Scott! Will Tomlinson beauing the child? This would never do.

"How old are you, Thorne?" asked the doctor.

"Fourteen," said Richard promptly.

"Fifteen," corrected Thorne.

"You were ten when I saw you at the Bridgeton fair. Thorndyke's posters said so. That was four years ago."

"I had been ten on those posters for a long time."

"You think you are more than fourteen?" asked Dr. Caxton.

"Yes, sir. I'm sure I was at least twelve when I came here."

"That means you'll be sixteen this summer," said Will with a wink.

Richard's hand came down on the table with a force that rattled the dishes.

"She'll not be sixteen for another year, and I'll thank you, Will, not to be putting ideas into her head. And you, Cricket, no fibbing about your age or I'll forbid you going to any more parties."

Gone was the cozy peace of the supper table. Will pushed back his chair with maddening insouciance and had the impertinence to make deaf-and-dumb talk to Thorne as he left the room. Richard, black as a thundercloud, took his pipe to the chimney corner where he sulked in silence. Thorne alone seemed unperturbed by the brisk sortie. She pushed a chair to the hearth for the doctor, cleared the table, then took her place on a stool near Richard's feet. He looked down at her without speaking. Anger still rendered him inarticulate, but his brow cleared and he smoked in deep abstraction.

A tardy sense of professional duty reminded the doctor that he had a patient in the house.

"You were going to tell me about Judith," he said. "What happened to bring on this spell?"

Richard said to Thorne, "Isn't it time you were in bed?"

She looked at him with grave amusement. "Isn't it time you stopped treating me like a child?" To the doctor she explained, "Richard doesn't want to talk in front of me for fear of hurting my feelings. You see, Judith thinks I tried to strangle her."

The doctor said, "Great heavens!" and looked to Richard for confirmation.

"Judith had a bad scare this afternoon," said Richard. He related how they had found her and the strange tale Judith had told when she regained consciousness.

Thorne added, "I was the first person she saw when she opened her eyes. On the floor beside me was a jumping rope."

The doctor had listened in silence to this point. Now he leaned forward, his rugged beak silhouetted against the fire-light like a vigilant hawk's.

"Thorne, you're in a bad spot."

"I know it, Dr. Caxton." She was serious but calm. There was a womanly dignity in her tonight that was a far cry from the high-strung child whom Abigail had bullied. "Richard has only my word for it that I wasn't in the house when Judith screamed."

"Your word is all I need," said Richard, but the doctor waved him aside without taking his gaze from the child who this night, before his very eyes, had ceased to be a child.

"Judith hasn't complained of any disturbances around here for some time, has she, Thorne?"

"Not since the night she had that funny scare about the trundle bed."

Richard, listening, felt a stab of relief that was near pain. She did not mention the ghostly hand which Lucius had seen at the window. That meant she had known nothing of it. That meant, to Richard, that she had not known of the doll hidden under the floor of the closet. She was innocent of everything, and he was freed from a dread that had gripped him ever since he learned of Otis Huse's discovery.

The doctor was saying to Thorne, "It might look to some people as though the witch that's been plaguing Judith had been quiet long enough. That she had to make Judith notice her again or be forgotten. Witches have to keep in the limelight, don't they, Thorne?"

"I don't know anything about witches. I don't believe in them."

"Then who do you think is frightening Richard's wife?"

"I don't know."

"You deny having anything to do with it yourself?"

"Yes, sir."

"Will you swear to that on the Bible?"

Richard started angrily to protest. The doctor hushed him with a look and reached for a Testament on a near-by table.

Thorne laid her hand on the book and said, "I swear that I'm telling the truth. I've had nothing to do with any of the strange things which Judith has seen." She withdrew her hand and added childishly, "Except the magic tricks on Miss Ann's birthday."

"And we believe you," said Richard. "No one accuses you."

"Except Judith," said Thorne.

"Judith is ill. When she's well again she'll be your friend, just as she's always been."

She looked at him strangely, as though seeking to learn whether he believed his own words. He flushed and said hurriedly that she'd better be getting to bed. But his eyes followed her as she left the room. And he was no more aware of what he had revealed to Dr. Caxton than he was of the depth of devotion which she aroused in him.

He said, as though dismissing the whole matter, "Judith suffers from too much imagination. She's been bothered with her old throat trouble lately—I think she had another of those paroxysms—and, being already keyed up, fainted from sheer fright."

The doctor said, "Has it struck you, Richard, that she's having the same symptoms that Abigail had? When I saw her tonight I got a shock, she looked so damned much like your first wife."

Richard nodded gloomily. He, too, had noted the queer similarity.

"It's a plain case of hysteria," the doctor went on. "She probably feels guilty about marrying you so soon after Abigail's death. I'd say the best treatment she could have would be—ahem!—a little more affection on your part."

When Richard went into his wife's room shortly before noon the next day he found her sitting in front of the dresser combing her hair. She greeted him normally.

"Why didn't you wake me sooner, dear?"

He tried to conceal his surprise. "You were sleeping so soundly, I thought you needed the rest." He looked at her anxiously. She was wearing a most becoming boudoir wrapper. "You look better this morning."

"Better? You talk as though I had been ill."

"Don't you remember Dr. Caxton coming last night?"

"Why, Richard, what are you talking about? I never felt better in my life."

He had the strangest feeling that she was dissembling; that she remembered the doctor's visit but preferred to ignore it.

"Well, you look fine this morning, Judith. I guess all you needed was a good night's rest." His eyes met hers in the mirror, and there was relief in his smile. The specter of another ordeal by invalidism had been removed.

"Richard, what has become of that friend of yours who used to come out from Woodridge—such an unusual person— a blacksmith, wasn't he?"

"You mean Doc Baird?"

"That's the one. He was so interesting. Why don't we have him out to supper sometime?"

Richard's astonishment was so great he could scarcely conceal it. Of all his acquaintances, the blacksmith was the one on whom Judith had most definitely turned thumbs down.

"I thought you didn't care for Doc Baird."

"Why, dear, whatever gave you such an idea? I like all your friends." She turned from the mirror brightly as she rose. "If you can get word to Mr. Baird, why not have him out tonight?"

"You really mean that?"

"Of course I mean it."

He was boyishly pleased. "I'm going in to Woodridge today. I'll bring Doc back with me."

"Good." She kissed him, her delicately scented hands framing his face. Her kisses always reduced him to helpless confusion. Last night he had faced stark fear for her sanity. A moment ago he had faced, almost as disturbingly, suspicion that she was not dealing honestly with him. But when she kissed him his mind was washed blank.

He muttered, "I have work to do," and tried to break away. But she held him, with her arms and her lips.

"The work can wait. Stay with me," she coaxed.

"There's the trip to town——"

"You'll have time for that—afterward——"

He put his hand behind him and closed the door.

"The trouble is," said Judith, "we've never been able to discuss these things because Richard always loses his temper." And she smiled indulgently at her husband, as at a retarded child.

They were sitting in the front room after supper, Judith and Richard and Doc Baird. Judith had some dainty needlework in her white hands. Richard, watching her, tried bewilderedly to identify the gracious lady who had just spoken with the hagridden woman of the night before or the beguiling hussy who had lured him, a busy farmer, to bed in midmorning.

"I thought, Mr. Baird, you might be able to explain to Richard how that trundle bed had been made to dance by the same principle by which you used to make tables move."

How the subject of the trundle bed had come up, Richard could not have said. It was weeks since the incident had been mentioned, and Judith's revival of the topic puzzled and disturbed him.

Doc Baird explained to her: "In table tipping, the hands must rest upon the table. Was anyone touching the bed when you saw it dance?"

"I couldn't tell," said Judith. "A draft had blown out the candles."

Richard looked at his friend significantly. "The candles were burning all the while. No one but Judith saw the bed do anything."

"That's because you were all watching me," said Judith. She explained to the blacksmith, "I screamed, very foolishly, and distracted everyone's attention from the trick that was being performed."

"No trick was being performed," said Richard.

"Tricks were being performed all evening."

"But not with the trundle bed."

Voices of husband and wife were rising.

Doc Baird interrupted, "You're sure no one was touching the bed?"

"Thorne wasn't." Richard brought the name forth boldly, looking straight at Judith.

She asked, "How do you know whether or not she was touching it?"

"I had hold of her hands."

A bright flush drenched Judith's face. She bent low over her work.

Doc Baird said, "If no one was touching the bed, it couldn't have been animal magnetism. There has to be physical contact to establish the current." He spread his huge hands with justifiable pride. On this subject he was something of an authority.

"What I object to," said Richard, "is not a frank discussion of these disturbing experiences of Judith's, but the implication that Thorne is lying when she says she has nothing to do with them."

The suggestion that Judith longed to make and dared not was unexpectedly offered by Doc Baird.

"Of course, there's one way to clear Thorne."

"What's that?"

"If she were sent away for a while and Judith continued to be frightened in her absence, Thorne's innocence would be proved beyond doubt."

"And suppose Judith were not frightened in her absence," said Richard coldly, "should that be taken as proof of her guilt?"

Doc Baird did not remain long after that. When he rose to take his departure he was not asked to stay the night. He was offered, instead, the loan of a horse to ride back to town.

But his visit had far-reaching consequences.

"What do you think of Doc's suggestion?" Judith asked her husband as they were preparing for bed.

"What suggestion?" Richard was sitting in a low chair, taking off his boots.

"About sending Thorne away."

He sat up in shocked alertness. She went quickly on before he could speak:

"She could go to Kentucky and stay with your sister Annie. She's not doing well in school here. Perhaps she'd do better there."

He said, "You're talking like Abigail," and bent once more to his boots, so that he failed to see the fear that leaped to Judith's eyes. For a second she looked as she had the night before.

Then she continued: "I'm making a reasonable suggestion.

As Doc Baird said, with Thorne away we can determine whether or not it is she who is trying to frighten me. These annoyances are no longer trivial, Richard. My experience yesterday might have been fatal. I think I've a right to know who made that attempt on my life."

At last he saw through her strategy. The evening's talk had been a base from which to launch a criminal charge against Thorne. Not in hysteria, but in cool-considered reason, Judith was accusing the girl of murderous assault.

Shocked, horrified, and angry as Judith had never seen him, he told her in unmistakable language that Thorne was not going anywhere. Timberley was her home. "And I warn you right now, if she leaves this house, I leave it!"

His unexpected violence so alarmed Judith that had he stopped with those words he would have left her in a state of apprehension which might have insured peace for all time. But because his anger held the fury of the disciplined man driven beyond control, he had to go on, shouting in his rage:

"No attempt was made on your life. You had a fit of hysterics; the doctor said so. But if there's any more talk of Thorne's guilt in this matter I'll give people cause to have hysterics. And that goes for every last mother's son of you!"

As there was no one else present but Judith—and she was certainly no mother's son—the absurdity of this last threat struck her as humorous and restored her equanimity.

"You shouldn't make speeches in your underdrawers, darling. They distract the attention of your audience."

Without another word he picked up his boots and his breeches and marched downstairs to sleep in the alcove. Judith blew out her candle and climbed into bed. She was not troubled by his temper. It was more reassuring than his silence.

She would let him sweat a little as a matter of discipline. It would be all the better when he came back. It always was, after a quarrel.

What she never dreamed was that this time he would not come back.

CHAPTER 23

It was several days later that Richard came upon Thorne dragging a small hair trunk out of the back hall closet. He had been out in the fields all day and his boots were mired with spring mud, so that he entered the house through the kitchen and went straight to the back closet for dry shoes. There he found Thorne shoving and pushing at the trunk.

"What on earth are you doing, Cricket?"

"I thought it would be easier to pack this if I pushed it out into the hall."

"Who's packing it?"

"I am."

"Who for?"

"Myself. I'm going to boarding school."

Richard put an end to the trunk moving by sitting down on the trunk.

"Who said you were going to boarding school?"

"I said it." Thorne blew the dust off her hands with remarkable coolness, but she avoided Richard's eyes. "I've thought it over and I've decided that's what I want to do."

"Oh! You've thought it over, have you? And who helped you think it over?"

There was no reply to this. Thorne had stooped to examine a pile of old copybooks that lay upon the floor.

"What put the idea of going to boarding school in your head?"

"Well, you know I never have liked Timberley school. I've no head for numbers."

"And what do you expect to find at boarding school that you'll like better?"

"Judith says I can study music and elocution and maybe Shakespeare."

"Oh, she does!"

"And you know yourself, Richard, I wasn't so stupid when you used to read us Shakespeare." She was sitting on the floor now, her lap piled full of copybooks.

"Look at me, Thorne."

She was too busy searching for a clean book among the castoffs to lift her eyes. "I thought I might keep a diary," she explained.

"Don't change the subject! Do you really want to go away? Do you think you'd be happier at boarding school than at home?"

She looked at him then seriously. "Do you think anyone in this house has been very happy lately?"

He said, "You're going away because you've got a silly notion it's the way to prove your innocence about these things that have been frightening Judith. I think I know who gave you the idea."

Thorne said carefully, as though striving for perfect fairness, "Judith has always been a friend to me, Richard. We must remember that." Unconsciously she allied herself and Richard against the woman of whom they were speaking.

"Listen, Cricket. Your running away won't prove anything. It is quite conceivable that with you away nothing would happen to disturb her. Have you forgotten how she never saw the bricks when you could account for your whereabouts? Whoever or whatever is doing this—I still believe the motive is to drive you from home."

"You mean—Abigail?"

"I don't know—I honestly don't know. But there are people —living people—who have never liked you, Thorne. Take Otis Huse. He's always been unfair to you because he doesn't like me. You see, he expected to marry his cousin Abigail before I came along. He'd stop at nothing to hurt me, even the persecution of an innocent——" Remembering his last talk with the hostile attorney, Richard's voice failed.

"I don't see how Mr. Huse could have played these tricks," said Thorne. "He hasn't even been around here, except that one time."

"I don't mean that I think he's the culprit." Richard frowned. He dared not put into words his fear regarding Otis Huse. "I'm just trying to show you that running away will be taken as an admission of guilt by those who would like to prove you guilty."

They argued this point pro and con. Thorne said finally, "Maybe you're right. I hadn't looked at it that way before."

"Certainly I'm right. So let's hear no more about going off to school. I can teach you college English here at home."

Satisfied that he had settled the question, Richard changed to dry shoes and went in search of his wife. He was thoroughly out of temper with what he considered female duplicity in going behind his back to engineer a course upon which he had emphatically set his veto less than a week ago.

He found the women in the dining room, Judith and his mother and Henry Schook's wife, who had come on an errand. They were trying out the new sewing machine, which Martha Schook had not yet seen.

"How much thread do you suppose it'll use in a year, Miss Ann?"

"If you don't do any sewing it won't use any thread," said Ann Tomlinson dryly. Then seeing her son glowering from the doorway, she asked quickly, "What's wanted, Richard?"

He said bluntly, "I'd like to speak to you and Judith alone, Mother."

This curt speech, so lacking in his usual courtesy, was the signal for Mrs. Schook's precipitate departure and subsequent report to her husband that Richard Tomlinson was a changed man and no doubt the Timberley witch was at him again. Which gossip was in general circulation within forty-eight hours.

Richard began, "Judith, why did you put Thorne in the notion of going away to boarding school?" and without waiting for a reply, "Mother, did you know of these plans?"

"Why, yes, Richard. We've been working for three days getting her ready to go. I thought you knew."

"How could I know? No one told me. How do I know what you women are doing when I'm out of the house?" He looked sternly at his wife.

Judith met his gaze steadily. "I've seen very little of you, Richard, since you moved downstairs."

"You've seen me at mealtimes."

"There are always so many things under discussion then, trivial matters slip my mind."

"Do you call Thorne's leaving home a trivial matter?"

She dropped her eyes to the petticoat she was hemming. He turned again to his mother.

"Surely you, Mother, could have found an opportunity to tell me what was going on."

"Well, son, you were in Woodridge the day we talked it over."

"Who talked it over?"

"Judith and I—and Will."

"Will!" Richard reddened angrily. "What business is it of Will's?"

Miss Ann took off her spectacles, which she wore on the end of her nose so that she could see over them. What she was about to say troubled her; not for its import, but for the effect it would have upon her son. She knew that it would make him very angry, and that was what troubled her. For it was news which Richard should welcome if he had only Thorne's welfare at heart.

"Your brother Will," she said, and looked at Richard as though the two of them were alone, "is going to be Thorne's husband one of these days."

If a charge of powder had exploded at his feet he could not

have been more stunned. He looked at his mother like a man out of whom all sense had been knocked.

Then he muttered, "What are you talking about? She's not old enough to——"

"Not now. But Will is satisfied to wait. He's also willing for her to have a year at boarding school. It's what she needs to help her finish growing up. It will give her a polish—like Judith's."

Something within him cried, "I don't want her to have a polish like Judith's!" But he could not speak. He was stricken dumb.

His mother went on: "Thorne's age has always been uncertain. She says she will be sixteen her next birthday. But it doesn't matter. In her position, the earlier she marries, the better. My mother married at fifteen and was very happy." Miss Ann put her glasses back on her nose and picked up her work with a sigh of relief for having put a dreaded chore behind her.

Richard still stood like a man turned to stone. All this had been discussed and decided behind his back. They had done this to Thorne—his Cricket—as though it were something which did not concern him.

"But she's mine—she's always been mine—nobody else ever cared anything about her except me——" He was stammering like a schoolboy in his pain.

"She's a woman, my son. She's not a stray kitten you brought home in your pocket from the fair. She has a woman's life to live."

That was the charge of powder that had exploded in his brain. Thorne—with a woman's life to live—and his brother Will . . .

"I'm the head of this house. Why didn't Will come to me about this business?"

"Because," said Ann Tomlinson, "I'm Will's mother and the nearest thing to a mother that Thorne possesses. Neither of them are of age."

"And you gave your consent, Mother, to anything as pre-posterous as her betrothal to young Will?"

"I see nothing preposterous," said Ann with dignity, "in any girl's betrothing herself to a Tomlinson. I was proud to do it. And both your wives, Richard, seemed glad of the op-portunity."

Judith lifted her eyes from her work and smiled agreement with her mother-in-law. "If there's anything preposterous in this match, it is that a Tomlinson should be willing to take a wife who has no name except the one he will give her."

"Nay"—Miss Ann spoke quickly, before the gathering storm in Richard's eyes—"that makes no difference to Will. He loves Thorne for herself. And I've no doubt she'll make him a good wife—when she grows up a little."

"And what about her?" said Richard. "Has anyone con-sidered her happiness?"

"Will is a hard-working boy. A much better farmer than you, my son. He'll always provide for her."

As if happiness were compounded of those ingredients!

"I mean, has Thorne been consulted about this?"

"Oh yes. That's why she was willing to go away to school."

A great light broke upon Richard. Here was the explanation of Thorne's desire to leave home. It had nothing to do with witch pranks. It was the urge to separate herself from young Will.

A tremendous lightening of his heart was followed by a surge of wrath against his brother for forcing his attentions on a lonely child. Now he understood the purpose behind Will's kindness in taking Thorne to all the candy pulls and neighborhood frolics this winter. He, Richard, in his dumb complacency, had never given it a thought. But who could tell what had gone on in the snug, close warmth of straw-filled sleighs and Thorne, poor child, afraid to say anything about it? In his rage Richard longed to lay hands upon his brother.

He heard his mother say, "There's been a lot of unkind talk

about Thorne. But it will all stop, once she's the wife of a Tomlinson. That's what you've always wanted, isn't it, Richard?"

Oh God, yes! But not this way. . . .

He said aloud, thickly, "She's not going to boarding school. I just talked to her. She's changed her mind."

"That's what Will was hoping she'd do," said his mother.

He went into the south bedroom to wash. Since the night of Doc Baird's visit he had slept in the alcove and used the adjoining room for dressing. He was not afraid to sleep in the bed he had once shared with Abigail, but he preferred the one over the trundle. He could not have told why.

The water in the porcelain pitcher was cold, but he never felt the chill. He was stripped to the waist and vigorously scrubbing when Judith knocked at the door. She had brought him a kettle of warm water from the kitchen.

He paused in his ablutions and waited silently while she tempered the icy water in the bowl, then plunged his hands into the grateful warmth of the heated suds without even a word of thanks. He hoped she would leave the room.

But it seemed she had something to say.

"Don't you think, Richard, that you owe your mother an apology?"

There were times when the schoolteacher in Judith was still evident.

He waited to dry his face on the towel she handed him. Then he replied: "I said nothing disrespectful to Mother. I said what I thought about members of this family who have gone behind my back to make arrangements which they knew I would not approve."

"I suppose that includes me."

His silence indicated that if the shoe were the right size she was privileged to try it on.

"There was no reason," said Judith, "why anyone should consider your approval necessary."

"Except that I had already stated my objections to Thorne's going away to school."

"Oh no. You had stated your objections to her going to Kentucky."

Richard looked at his wife in helpless exasperation. The Machiavellian quality of her mind was almost frightening.

"Kentucky—boarding school—what's the difference? I made it plain I didn't want her leaving home."

"That's what I told your mother."

"When?"

"When I talked to her about this marriage to Will."

"Oh! It was you who broached the subject to Mother."

"Yes."

"No doubt you also broached it to my brother."

"No. He came to me about it. He asked me to speak to Miss Ann."

"And why should he have picked you as a go-between?"

"Because he knew I would be sympathetic. He was afraid he might have trouble with you—and your mother. He knew I would help him."

"Since when have you and Will been such friends?"

"We're not. It's just that our interests coincide. I've known for some time that Will was getting ideas about Thorne. And he knows nothing would please me better than to see her married."

"But why?" Richard's anger found vent in the violent friction of the rough towel against his chest. "Why all this rush to marry off a child who has hardly outgrown her dolls. Thorne doesn't love Will. She doesn't love anyone but——" He stopped short in his furious toweling with a startled look.

"But you, Richard. That's what you were going to say, wasn't it?" Judith's voice was deadly cold. "Thorne doesn't love anyone but you, does she?"

He laid the towel on the washstand slowly and carefully, as though it were something which might break. He reached for his shirt and began putting it on, all without speaking a word.

"And you don't love anyone but Thorne, do you, Richard?"

"No." It seemed the most amazing circumstance of his life that he had never realized this simple truth before.

He buttoned his shirt and completed his toilet. Judith watched in silence as he combed his wet curly hair. There was nothing for either of them to say. The thing which had been between them all along, unacknowledged by the woman, unsuspected by the man, lay out in the open at last.

It was Richard who began to speak finally, as though striving to clarify for Judith something which only this moment had become clear to himself.

"I don't want you to misunderstand what I said just now. About Thorne, I mean." There was touching earnestness in his voice, almost humble appeal. His anger had quite gone. "There's not a wicked thought or feeling in her heart, Judith. She's good and sweet. Her love for me is as pure as mine for my mother."

"And is your feeling for her on the same high spiritual plane?" asked Judith bitterly.

Yesterday he would have answered without hesitation that it was. Now—since this business about his brother Will—he could answer nothing.

"How long have you felt this way about Thorne?"

How could he say? Always. Since that first day he saw her—at the fair. . . .

"Then Abigail was right when she said Thorne was the cause of her ill-health."

"Judith—please——" He looked at her imploringly, but Judith went ruthlessly on:

"It was really Thorne, then, who killed your first wife. If not by witchcraft, then by breaking her heart. It was Thorne, after all, who killed Abigail." She kept repeating this, as though there were some unction for herself in the thought.

"Why did you marry me, Richard? Why didn't you wait

awhile and give your little peach time to mature? You needn't have waited long. She would have dropped in your hands at the first touch."

"Judith—don't talk like that! I tell you, I never thought of her that way. She was a child—whom I loved as innocently as——"

"As you loved your mother. I know. By the way, does she know?"

"Who—my mother?"

"No, stupid! The girl. Have you told her how you feel about her?"

He looked shocked and said, "No!" But almost instantly a curious look came into his eyes. Judith thought, "He doesn't have to tell her. She knows."

"Judith, you won't let this make any difference, will you?"

"Between you and me?"

He wasn't even thinking of that. That was all over anyway.

"In your attitude toward Thorne. She's innocent, Judith. She hasn't a thought that isn't a child's thought."

"I've seen her looking at you."

Suddenly Judith began to laugh softly, her whole body shaking with almost silent mirth.

"What are you laughing at, Judith?"

"At myself. What a fool I've been! It was for this that I planned and schemed and groveled and lied." There was something frightening in her strange, unseemly laughter. It mounted hysterically. "It was for this that I spent hour after hour in this sickening room with a whining invalid. It was for this that I——"

She stopped as short as though a band had tightened about her throat, cutting off her breath. Her hands went to her neck, plucking at the velvet ribbon, but her body still shook with soundless mirth.

"Judith, stop it!"

Richard took her by the shoulders and set her down in the

low rocking chair. He did not like the look in her eyes. She had had that look a week ago, when it had been necessary to summon the doctor.

"Sit still while I get your smelling salts."

She looked at him mockingly. "I'm not fainting, Richard. Not this time."

But he hurried away, alarmed and remorseful for what he had done.

Judith sat very still in the rocking chair. It was the same chair in which she had once sat by Abigail's bedside. She could almost see the emaciated figure propped up in bed, cutting out quilt pieces with a pair of sharp shears.

You don't believe me. You think I'm crazy. But you'll see. Someday.

The eerie voice was only a memory, but she could almost hear the clean sharp sound of the scissors as they cut through the pieces of silk.

She did hear it!

She sat up, tense, alert, listening.

The sound of scissors cutting briskly through fabric was quite distinct.

Cold seeped upward over Judith's body like the rising waters of an icy flood. This was the room in which she had seen the bricks fall. This was the room in which, only the week before, she herself had been seized in a weird attack.

She started to rise and leave the room.

She found she could not move from her chair.

Cold sweat poured from her body. The sound of scissors was very sharp and brisk now.

A voice called, "Miss Ann! Are you in there?" And Thorne appeared in the open hall door.

"Oh! I thought Miss Ann was in here." She seemed disconcerted at sight of Judith.

Judith looked at her in silence.

"What's the matter, Judith? Are you ill?"

"Stop it!" The words burst from Judith's stiff lips.

"Stop what?"

"The scissors."

"What scissors?"

"You know what scissors." Judith gripped the arms of her chair as though trying to rise. "Make them stop that noise."

Thorne stood very still, listening. "I don't hear anything."

To Judith, the sound of the scissors seemed amplified. She could hear them cut rapidly through a whole length of cloth. Then pause. Then start again. There was no one in sight but herself and Thorne. There were no scissors in sight at all.

She cried, "You're doing this. It's another of your tricks. But you can't frighten me to death as Abigail was frightened. Stop that noise before I scream for Richard."

"But I'm not doing anything," said Thorne.

"You're making that sound. I suppose ventriloquism is among your charlatan's talents. But you can't deceive me. You're dealing with an intelligent woman now, not a crazy fool."

Richard came back into the room with Judith's smelling bottle. He looked from one pale face to the other and asked, "What's the matter?"

Judith pointed to Thorne and said, "She's at it again, Richard."

Thorne said, "She says she hears scissors going. Do you hear anything?"

Richard listened, then shook his head. "Mother may be sewing in the next room."

"Your mother," said Judith, "is in the dining room."

Richard opened the door connecting with the front room and looked inside. There was no one in sight.

"I don't hear a thing," he said.

Judith's voice rose shrilly, accusing Thorne. Richard handed her the smelling bottle, but she thrust it aside. She continued to hear the scissors very clearly. She was beginning to locate the sound now. Fear lifted her from her chair. She went over to the oaken chest and put her ear to the keyhole.

"It's coming from in here," she cried.

Richard drew his keys from his pocket, selecting, with maddening deliberation, the key to the chest. Judith snatched them impatiently from his hand. She unlocked the chest and raised the lid. Then she stood staring in fascinated horror at what her eyes beheld.

She saw Abigail's quilts neatly folded, one on top of the other, as they had been the last time she looked at them. But the beautiful coverlets, which had been the pride of the dead woman's heart, were now cut through every fold as though sharp shears had slashed them.

CHAPTER 24

Judith's screams brought Richard's mother hurrying down the hall.

"She did it, Richard! It's another of her witch tricks. She cut the quilts to pieces to frighten me, just as she made the doll to frighten Abigail. *She* made the doll that murdered your first wife, Richard. Remember that!"

Ann Tomlinson entered the room to find her son trying to quiet his distraught wife while she hurled invectives at Thorne.

"Look in the chest, Miss Ann! See what she's done to Abigail's quilts. And she made a sound like scissors to make me think I was going crazy."

Miss Ann went to the chest and bent over the quilts, examining them fold by fold. Richard said, "There's nothing wrong with the quilts, Mother. I've looked."

His mother gave him a significant look. Then, putting her

arm around Judith, she said kindly, "You'd better come upstairs." Together they led her from the room.

When Judith was quiet, in drugged sleep upon her bed, Richard and his mother went back to the south bedroom and made a second and more thorough examination of the quilts. To the bottom of the pile they were found to be undamaged.

Richard said, "Judith worked herself into a state of hysteria over some fancied noise. Of course, when she looked at the quilts, she imagined she saw them cut." He told about the sound of scissors which Judith claimed to have heard before the chest was open.

His mother looked at him seriously. "Who made the sound of scissors?"

He flushed defensively. "If you mean Thorne, she's no ventriloquist."

"There's no denying, Richard, someone is trying to frighten your wife."

"Mother! Surely you are not turning against me."

"Against you, my son?"

"If you can believe this of Thorne, then you must believe that I am capable of shielding someone guilty of criminal mischief. What do you think of me, Mother?"

She looked into the troubled eyes of this best loved of all her children and said gravely, "I think I blame myself, Richard, for not warning you."

"About what?"

"About the haste of your second marriage. There is good reason, besides propriety, for not being in too great a hurry sometimes."

There was no mention of Thorne's name, but because there was understanding between them Richard said to his mother, "You don't take seriously what Judith said about Abigail's death, do you?"

"No. I'm sure Thorne made that doll innocently, to amuse the children. But I think you should talk to her about what happened this afternoon. After all, she used to be with a carnival show. No doubt she learned strange tricks with her voice as well as her hands."

It was late that night before he found a chance to talk with Thorne. There was another visit from the doctor, and Richard spent most of the evening by his wife's bedside. Dr. Caxton pronounced Judith's condition critical. It was his belief there was something preying upon her mind. Unless she got relief, she was heading for a mental collapse. Only the old doctor put it more bluntly.

"You know she could be going bugs, Richard."

But Richard had his own theory, as yet unacknowledged, regarding Judith's state.

When he finally came downstairs he found Thorne sitting by the kitchen fire, her head between her hands, like a weary little old woman. Much of the work had devolved upon her this evening.

"How's Judith?" She looked up quickly.

He told her what the doctor had said.

"Does she still blame me?"

He sat down heavily in the nearest chair and spread his hands to the fire. "I don't think she knows what she's saying."

"What does she mean by saying the doll murdered Abigail?"

"Abigail had a weak heart. And a superstitious fear of the doll. I suppose, if she had suddenly seen it, the shock might have been fatal."

"But she didn't see it. It was never found. Was it?"

He was silent, considering which course to take. And then he decided to be frank with her.

"The night Abigail died she claimed to have found the doll on her pillow with a tight string tied round its neck."

"I see. And everyone thinks I put it there."

"Certainly not. No one knows about it except Judith and me."

"Judith thinks I put it there."

"What Judith thinks is beside the point."

"What do you think?"

"I think Abigail imagined the whole thing. At least, that's what I thought at the time——"

"And what do you think now?"

"It's possible that one of the children had it in his mother's room—or something——" He sounded vague.

"What made you change your mind?"

"The doll was found the night Lucius and Otis Huse slept in the south room."

He told her everything then, and he watched her keenly while he talked. If there was any unacknowledged doubt of her innocence in his mind, it was expelled once and forever. It was impossible to believe that she had guilty knowledge of what he was telling her.

When he had finished she said, "I swear to you, Richard, I don't know how the doll got there. But if Abigail saw it, she probably died believing that I murdered her." They were both silent as this thought, in all its significance, gripped them. Then she asked, "Did Lucius think it was her hand he saw at the window?"

Richard said, "Lucius has always inclined to a belief in such things."

"What do you think?"

"I think Lucius had a nightmare. But if Abigail's spirit *is* roaming this house, I don't intend to let her intimidate me."

There was a sound in the covered passage. For a moment both Richard and Thorne felt a thrill of terror. Then they realized that one of Millie's traps must have caught a rat.

Thorne said, "It's not you she's trying to intimidate, it's me. She's still trying to drive me **away,** just as she did while living. And that's what seems so strange——"

"What's strange?"

"That Abigail should mind about me, when it was Judith you married."

"But she knows it is you I love."

"Yes, I suppose she does."

They both spoke so matter-of-factly that they experienced a shock when they realized what they had said. Their eyes met gravely in silence while that clear statement of truth sank in.

Then Thorne asked curiously, "What do you mean by saying that you love me, Richard?"

"You know very well what I mean. You're dearer to me than anything else in life." He spoke gruffly, almost angrily, as though in protest that he could use nothing but words to tell her. "Abigail knew it before I did. That's why she was jealous. But you weren't to blame. I never loved Abigail."

She asked, in that same puzzled tone, "Why did you marry Judith?"

He colored violently, as though surprised in transgression.

"It was one of those things—that happen sometimes. But it wasn't love. I've never loved anyone but you."

She sighed, and her sigh was weighted with sadness, as though she were years older than he.

A lump swelled in his throat. He spoke thickly. "Thorne—you—what I heard this afternoon—about you and Will—it isn't true, is it?"

"It's true that he's asked Miss Ann for me."

"But you haven't——"

"I'll do whatever Miss Ann thinks best."

"Good heavens! You can't——"

"I'll have to marry someone, Richard, if I stay here."

"Not for years and years yet."

"Not so many years."

"Thorne, has he"—his voice was a tortured whisper—"has he ever touched you? Answer me! Those sleigh rides—has he ever——"

She turned grave eyes upon him. "Is it any business of yours,

273 &

Richard, if he has?" And then, because she could see the wound she had given him, she added quickly, "He hasn't though. He's been very nice."

"Thorne, do you actually mean you could love my brother? Tell me the truth. If you think you could, then I'll never say another word upon the subject. But please be honest with me."

She was lost in thought for a moment. And then she spoke quietly, as though telling a thing long past.

"When your wife died, Richard, I was sorry. I couldn't understand why. But now I know it was because I was afraid you would marry Judith."

He started to speak, but she went on: "And then Judith went away and all that long summer I had you to myself. I decided my fears were imaginary. That summer was the first time I dreamed about what it would be like to love a man— the way Nancy talked about. And of course the man was you. I couldn't imagine loving anyone else. I'm afraid I never shall."

The thickness in his throat would not let him speak.

"And then that day we went to Terre Haute—and you told us Judith was going to be your wife——" She paused, as though reliving the darkest hour of her short life.

"I wanted to die. But I couldn't. I wanted to run away. But there was no place to go. And then your mother was so kind. I believe she understood. Will's not bad either. Only sulky, sometimes. I was surprised—and rather flattered—when he asked me to marry him. I thought, 'If I marry Will I'll always have a home close to Richard.' So I said yes."

A sound like a sob came from the man beside her. There was nothing now for Richard to say.

But there was more for Thorne to say. "That was before I knew you loved me. Before I had told you how I felt about you. Now that we have told each other it wouldn't be right for me to marry Will."

"It would be monstrous," muttered Richard.

She agreed. "It wouldn't be right for me to marry anyone around here. That's why I think I should go away."

To her surprise he said, "Yes. I think you should. And I'll go with you."

She looked at him incredulously. "You mean—you would?"

"I mean I *will*." He was suddenly alive with energy and purpose. "There's nothing to hold me here. The children have belonged to Mother since they were born. Will has always been the best farmer in the family. I'll never be missed."

Thorne said, "There's Judith."

He reddened. "We're nothing to each other any more."

She sat looking at him, lost in wonder and heartache unbearably sweet. She would have this for a memory always.

"But of course I can't let you do it," she said.

"What do you mean, you can't let me?"

"I won't let you ruin your life. That's what you'd do if you ran off from your wife and family with a girl who most people think is a witch. You'd be eternally damned by your neighbors, if not by God."

They argued heatedly. He pleaded with all the eloquence he possessed, but in vain. Thorne proved to have unsuspected rigidity of principle, on one subject at least. She was opposed to any course which would bring disgrace upon Richard.

In the end they compromised. She would remain at Timberley for the present, if for no other reason than to keep Richard from leaving his family. As for the pledge she had made to Will, time could take care of that.

CHAPTER 25

The torment of the bricks began again next day.

Judith was seated at her dressing table in nightgown and wrapper, when she heard the unmistakable thud in the room below. She had slept late that morning. The rest of the family were already at breakfast. She hurried downstairs to investigate, and as she passed the open dining-room door she called excitedly, "It's begun again," and sped down the hall to the south bedroom to view the brick.

She saw it near the door, where the other bricks had fallen. The door was open, the windows raised; the fresh morning breeze swept through the room. She noted it was a half brick, as usual.

There was a general exodus from the dining room. Judith could hear the footsteps coming down the hall. She turned eagerly as young Will, the first to reach her, demanded, "Where's the brick?"

"There!" Judith pointed triumphantly. This time she had not left the spot until she had witnesses to corroborate what she had seen.

"Where?" said Will. "I don't see anything."

"There, by the door——" Her voice broke with a gasp. In the split second in which she had removed her eyes from the brick to look at Will the thing was gone.

She was not frightened; she was furiously, frantically angry.

"It was there a moment ago! Look outside and you'll catch the imp who snatched it away from under my very nose."

Will, Jesse, and Richard's boys swarmed outdoors to search the premises, but neither the brick nor the brick thrower was in sight.

Judith said, "Where's Thorne?"

Richard said quickly, "She went over to Jane's before breakfast."

His mother explained, "I sent her on an errand."

The rest of the family went back to their half-eaten breakfast.

Richard closed and locked the outer door of the bedroom and lowered all the windows.

"We'll settle this business," he said. "If a brick is thrown through that window *now*, it will have to smash the glass. And if it is sneaked out the door, it will have to go through the key-hole."

Judith shivered as with a chill. She went back upstairs in silence.

The others returned to their regular duties. The men went back to the work from which the breakfast bell had summoned them; the women, to their household tasks. Cousin Lutie Simms arrived to spend the day, but no one mentioned that Judith had seen another brick.

About an hour later they heard her scream.

Miss Ann and Cousin Lutie were in the kitchen with Millie. The black woman groaned, "Oh Lawdy, she's seein' things again!" Miss Ann hurried to the south room, Cousin Lutie at her heels.

They found Judith standing in the doorway. She still wore nothing but nightgown and wrapper; her long braids hung over her shoulders. She was staring at a spot on the floor.

"Judith, you shouldn't have got out of bed," said Miss Ann.

"I heard a whizzing sound—and then a thump." Judith's voice sank to a whisper as she looked at the closed window. "I knew what had happened—but I was afraid to come down —until it was too late."

"You didn't see a brick?" said Cousin Lutie in the tone of one who has been cheated.

Judith shook her head. "It was gone. But I heard the sound —a kind of *whissht!* like something rushing through the air."

Almost as she spoke Judith heard the sound she was trying to describe, then the familiar thud on the floor. She turned sharply—and saw a brick lying in the spot where the others had fallen.

There had been no crash of glass.

She pointed weakly to the brick. "There it is. Don't you see it?"

Cousin Lutie's face turned the color of cream. "I'm gettin' out."

Judith's cry was like the mew of a cat. She clung to her mother-in-law as she felt herself swooning. When she opened her eyes the brick was gone.

Miss Ann opened both windows and door that she might have air.

"Call Richard!" gasped Judith.

"He's already gone to the field."

"Ring the bell!"

"That will call all the men from their work." Miss Ann spoke practically to still the younger woman's rising hysteria.

"You think I'm going crazy."

"I think some noise outdoors sounds to you like falling bricks. And your imagination is doing the rest."

Judith seized on this eagerly. "Then now is the time to catch the person who is making that noise. Ring the bell!"

To quiet Judith, the bell was rung.

The ringing of the Timberley bell in the middle of the morning was a signal of such ominous import that not only did it bring the Tomlinson men to the house, but all the neighbors within hearing began gathering in expectation of fire, accident, or some other natural catastrophe. When it was learned that Tomlinson's wife had again reported bricks flying, the news spread like a prairie blaze. By noon half the countryside had assembled on the southeast lawn to watch for bricks.

"All I've got to say is, if Miss Judith seen bricks go through that window, then bricks have gone through it. A schoolteacher's too smart to be fooled," was the consensus of opinion, though one hardy individualist muttered, "If you ask me, the woman's gone daft," and at the chorus of protest added darkly, "There's others that think the same thing."

There was speculation as to the point from which the bricks were being thrown. No tree offered a vantage point from which that window could be bombarded. Yet all who claimed to hear bricks pass through the air (and it was remarkable how many people made this boast) insisted that they came from some point higher than the window, hurtling downward toward the house. Those who claimed to have heard the *whisshing* sound said it seemed to be above their heads. Henry Schook said, "If there was a windmill about fifty yards southeast, I'd say a feller on top if it might hit that window."

But there was no windmill southeast (as someone pointed out) nearer than Mr. Schook's own.

Another interesting circumstance was that people standing close to the house began claiming to hear the thud of falling bricks in the south room. Mitch Rucker—of Appomattox fame —had the temerity to venture so close to the window that he insisted he came very near being struck; in the head, this time. Those who were bold enough to approach the open door reported that no bricks were to be seen inside the room, but this only gave rise to the fiction that the Tomlinsons were disposing of them as soon as they fell.

No one went so far as to claim, actually, to have seen a brick. But from time to time rumors circulated that Judith Tomlinson had seen another one. These little flurries of excitement came with maddening irregularity. There might be an interval of quiet. People would decide that nothing was happening and they might as well go home, when a woman's thin scream within the house would cause the mass hysteria without to mount wildly. People would again fancy they heard the *whissht!* And no doubt they did, for half the crowd were now making the sound with their lips. It went on like that all day. Very little work was done in Timberley district that long bright spring day.

The excitement reached the crossroads store, and storekeeper and customers decamped and hurried off to the big white house on the knoll. The drummer, Jenkins, happened to be in the store at the time. He carried the news to Woodridge. By midafternoon half the idle citizenry of the town (and some not so idle) had joined the crowd about the house at Timberley. A covered wagon bearing the slogan CALIFORNIA OR BUST turned in from the toll road on the mistaken assumption that the buggies, horses, and people milling around denoted a camping site for overland travelers.

It was remarkable how calmly the Tomlinson family seemed to take the annoyance of having half the countryside camped on their lawn. The work within the house went on as though this were a normal day. Some busybody coming up to the well for a drink called to Miss Ann in the dining room and asked what she did with the bricks that fell inside the house. Her retort was quoted far and wide.

"No bricks have fallen in the house. If they had, I'd have used them to disperse this crowd."

Both the Tomlinson daughters and their husbands came over in answer to the bell summons. They remained to help their mother, for Millie was too demoralized and Cousin Lutie too excited to be of any use. Judith, soon after her husband's arrival, retired to her room. There were sharp words between Richard and his wife over the ringing of the bell.

"Why didn't you send one of the children for me, Judith? Then we wouldn't have had the whole neighborhood swarming over here."

"I'm glad they've come. Now maybe we'll catch the person who's torturing me."

"No one's doing anything to you. Mother said the last time you saw a brick the window was closed. Why wasn't the glass pane smashed by the brick you *heard* pass through it?"

"I don't know. I'm not an expert in sleight of hand."

"So that's why you rang the bell. So that people would be here to see Thorne as she comes from Jane's. I believe you'd do anything, Judith, to incriminate Thorne. I believe these fits of hysteria have been staged for that purpose, just as Abigail's were. You're getting more like Abigail every day."

"Don't say that!" cried Judith, and clutched her throat.

"Then why do you hate Thorne, who's never done you an injury?"

"You can ask that, after what you told me yesterday?"

"She's not to blame. The fault—if there is a fault—is mine. She's innocent, Judith. She doesn't deserve to be hounded for something she had nothing to do with. She's good. You don't know how good she is."

Judith said meaningly, "Perhaps I do."

Suddenly he was enlightened. "It was you we heard in the passage last night. You were supposed to be in bed and you were listening. Have you no shame, Judith?"

"Under the circumstances, I had a right to listen. It is you, Richard, who should feel shame. Offering to run away with that little baggage. Don't think I couldn't see through her sly pretense of virtue. Of course she put you off. She knew I was hearing what she said."

"She didn't know. Neither of us guessed you'd stoop to eavesdropping."

"A wife must stoop to scotch the snake that has crawled into her bed."

"JUDITH!"

She could feel the impact of his shocked anger. But she had said the thing that had been beating in her brain since the night he left her room.

"You didn't think I knew, did you, Richard? How clever of you to pick a quarrel with me so you could move downstairs to the room *she* would have us believe is haunted. The room no one ever enters any more. You've been quite safe there, the two of you, haven't you, Richard?"

So great was his horror at this charge that he did not even think to deny that he had been sleeping in the isolated chamber.

"Judith! Do you know what you're saying, or are you really losing your mind?"

"You may as well admit the truth, Richard. I shall find means to prove it."

He tried to control himself. He tried to remember that this woman was his wife, whom he had vowed to cherish and protect. For otherwise he surely would have struck her in his rage.

"You are mad, Judith. Mad with jealousy, just as Abigail was. Only you are more vicious. Because you are smart. I shouldn't care to have your brains, Judith. Anyone capable of harboring such foul suspicions of an innocent girl would be capable of planning something equally monstrous."

"What do you mean?" Judith's face was suddenly ashen. There was no comeliness left in her at all. He wondered how he ever could have desired her.

He said softly, "Have you really seen bricks, Judith?"

"Don't try to change the subject! Say what you mean, Richard. Don't stand there accusing me of unspeakable things."

"I'm not accusing you, Judith."

"You are. I can see it in your eyes. And it's false, do you hear? Lies! Lies! All lies! You can prove nothing against me."

He said quietly, "Go back to your bed, Judith. You and I have talked long enough."

Richard went out into the yard where his neighbors were fast gathering. He stood gazing toward the southeast, as was everyone else. But it was not the unseen thrower of bricks for whom he was looking. He was watching for Thorne.

She did not return to the house until midafternoon. Jane had asked her to mind the baby till she came back, and it was well after the noonday meal before Jane was free to leave Timberley and return to her own house.

"I wouldn't go home through the fields," she said as Thorne set forth. Kindhearted Jane had noted her brother's anxiety and guessed its source. So she advised Thorne to go round by the turnpike and the lane through the grove so that she would not be seen coming from the southeast.

The covered wagon was camped in a little clearing in the grove. The family from Pennsylvania were making their supper. They had got permission, they explained when Thorne stopped to speak to them, from the people at the house. Camping privileges were never refused at Timberley.

Thorne laughed at the banner CALIFORNIA OR BUST. The wayfarers were an amusing family, curiously unlike the country jakes they appeared to be. There was something gay and dashing about them all, from father and mother down to the youngest child. A debonair, happy-go-lucky bohemianism that touched a nostalgic chord. When Thorne inquired what they expected to raise in California, the father—a dapper, youngish fellow in spite of blue jeans and graying hair—winked at his wife and said, "Vegetables," and the whole family laughed as though he had cracked some sort of joke.

Suddenly Thorne cried, "You're show people!"

"How'd you guess?"

"I used to be with a show myself."

After that they were no longer strangers.

"The best show I've seen in many a day is going on right now up at that house yonder," said the man. "They tell me some fellow with an aim like a knife thrower is hurling bricks through a window no bigger'n that"—he spread his hands to indicate—"and they say he's so far off he can't even be seen. That fellow's wasting his talent on a farm. He ought to join up with us. Out in California performers get gold nuggets big as walnuts tossed on the stage when their act makes a hit. And anything goes, even second-rate stuff. That brick thrower would panic 'em."

"Did you see any bricks go through the window?" asked Thorne.

"No. There's such a crowd you can't see anything. But I got close to a fellow that claimed he heard one go over his head. Said it might' near hit him. But they tell me nobody's been struck yet."

"And no one has seen the brick thrower?" Thorne repeated.

"No, little lady, seems they haven't. I stuck around awhile, trying to find out. Then I got hungry and came back to the wagon. If you know who's doing it, I wish you'd tell him to get in touch with me. I believe I could make him a proposition that'd interest him."

Thorne said, "No one's doing it. There aren't any bricks."

When she had gone the mother of the migrant troupe said to her husband, "She was a pretty little thing, wasn't she?"

The man said with a knowing look, "I didn't tell all I heard up there. Brick throwin' ain't the only funny business, according to the talk."

"What kind of talk?"

"Witches, ghosts, goblins, all sorts of queerness. And ugly tales about a half-grown girl who used to make flowers bloom in mid-air and pull rabbits out of hats."

The woman's mouth dropped open. "Do you suppose——"

"She said she had been with a show."

"Poor child!" The kindly woman sighed and shook her head. "She'd better get back with show people, then, before these crazy farmers burn her for a witch."

The man said wistfully, "I sure could use her in the act."

Judith sat by the window in her room, her knitting in her hands. She saw Thorne enter the house and went to the top of the stairs and called to her.

"Come up here, Thorne. I want to talk to you."

"In a minute. Soon as I get something to eat." Thorne had been too busy with Jane's baby to make herself any dinner.

When she appeared in Judith's doorway she had a slice of bread and butter in one hand and an apple, rosy as her cheeks, in the other. Her hair was flying, her dress was soiled, and there was a rent in her stocking where she had climbed a fence. Never had she looked more like a heedless gypsy.

"Did you want something, Judith?" Her mouth was so full she could barely articulate.

To an onlooker it would have seemed the height of absurdity that the little hoyden could possibly be an object of jealousy to the carefully groomed woman plying the knitting needles. Yet the hatred in Judith's heart was so vehement that it gave her strength such as she had not felt since her ill-health began. No emotion she had ever experienced, not even her passion for Richard, was so exhilarating as was this violent anger against Thorne. It seemed to justify everything she had done, everything she purposed to do. It even made her forget for the moment the pain which now almost ceaselessly clutched at her throat.

"Are you feeling ill again, Judith?"

"I'm feeling quite well, thank you."

"If there's anything I can do for you——"

"There's something you can do for all of us, Thorne. That's what I want to talk to you about." Judith's voice was gentle, holding no threat of what was coming.

"What do you mean?" asked Thorne.

"I should think it might have occurred to you without my suggestion. After last night."

"What do you know about last night?"

"I know all about last night. Richard has told me. As of course you would have known he'd do had you been a little older. Men always tell their wives, Thorne. That's what girls of a certain type never seem to understand."

"But——" Thorne was bewildered. It was Richard's privilege, perhaps his duty, to repeat to his wife the conversation he had had with Thorne by the kitchen fire. Though in Thorne's code of ethics such behavior was not only unnecessary but extremely silly. Still, if Richard had confessed to Judith that he had asked Thorne to go away with him, then he must also have told her that Thorne had refused.

"Did he tell you everything, Judith?"

"Everything."

"On both sides?"

"On both sides."

Thorne considered this a moment. "Well, maybe it's better that he did. At least you know why I'm staying on here. I had decided to run away. Until I found that Richard planned to go with me."

Judith lifted her eyes from the sock she was knitting.

"Don't lie, please. I'll grant it's revolting to think of a girl so young trying to entice a married man from his wife and children under his own mother's roof—though with your background such morals are to be expected—but please don't lie. It's quite useless."

Thorne's astonishment at hearing herself thus branded as a home wrecker was so great that she stood speechless, staring at the woman who was damning her so very genteelly.

"I've expected something like this for a long while," Judith went on. "I've watched you throwing yourself at Richard in a way that—well, if you hadn't been so very young I should have ordered you out of the house. But I knew how friendless you were and how kind my husband is, even to dumb animals. We've talked it over many times. He always said that turning you out was like abandoning a homeless dog. But after last night he realized you were not a fit person to live in the same house with his wife and mother. So he asked me to tell you that you must leave."

Judith's eyes dropped to the work in her hands. Thorne's

remained fixed upon the woman who had just uttered this outrageous falsehood. That it was a falsehood, Thorne never doubted for a second. Her faith in Richard was unshakable.

Yet Judith was Richard's wife, just as Abigail had been his wife. And Judith had succeeded to Abigail's jealousy as she had succeeded to her husband. Richard was bound until death to this woman, for there was no tolerance for divorce in the strict creed of the Tomlinsons. So long as Thorne remained at Timberley, Judith would make Richard's life a torment, as Abigail had done.

"I'll go, Judith. But not for the reason you ask. I don't know what Richard said to you. You must have misunderstood him. For he would never have lied about me. And it would have been a shameful lie if he had told you I asked him to go away with me. I love him far too much to let him do a thing that would bring disgrace on himself."

"Oh! You admit that you love him."

"Of course I do. I've never pretended anything else. I've always loved him; I always shall. But it's not true that I tried to take him from you. It was to keep him from leaving Timberley that I promised to stay here and go on as we had before."

"What do you mean—go on as you had before?"

"Nothing—I meant nothing, Judith—— Don't, please!"

Thorne backed away in sudden fear, for Judith had risen, the long steel knitting needle clutched like a dagger in her hand, and was coming closer and closer as Thorne retreated toward the door.

"Tell me what you promised to go on doing that you had done before!" The terrible gasping voice hissed the words in Thorne's face while the point of the needle pressed her breast.

But Thorne was too frightened to speak. All her old fear of Abigail came upon her, only now it was fear of Judith and ten times more potent. For Abigail, at her worst, had threatened only banishment. But Judith, Thorne suddenly realized, would be capable of doing an adversary to death.

With a smothered scream she broke from Judith's clutch and fled in terror from the room, from the house, and down the long slope to the grove.

Judith, watching from her window, saw her disappear beneath the canvas top of a covered wagon.

As Richard came up to the house at dusk he had to stop in the lane to let a wagon pass. He smiled at the ludicrous banner announcing its destination and waved farewell to the driver, the only occupant in sight. The rest of the migrant family was under cover, and as the lumbering vehicle pulled out on the turnpike, the popular ditty of the road—slightly revised—floated back on the evening breeze:

> *"I come from Pennsylvania, my banjo on my knee,*
> *I'm goin' to California, my true love for to see:*
> *O! Susanna, oh don't you cry for me . . ."*

CHAPTER 26

There was a first and second supper table at Timberley that evening, for among the people who had come out from Woodridge were a number to whom the Tomlinson hospitality was a matter of course. John Barclay, Dr. Caxton, Doc Baird, and that loquacious war veteran, Mitch Rucker, were among those who put their legs under the long table that night. Mitch declared he had not seen anything since Bull Run to equal the day's excitement.

"I've a standing offer of five hundred dollars to anybody

who'll explain the bricks your wife saw, Richard. Or produce the ones we heard whiz through the air. I don't expect to be taken up." Which was just as well, since Mitch hadn't five hundred dollars to his name.

They were halfway through the meal before Richard noticed Thorne's absence. The children were being served in the kitchen, and he supposed she was with them.

But when the company adjourned to the front room after supper and Thorne still did not put in an appearance, Richard drew his mother aside and asked her to send Thorne in.

"I don't want her hidden away, Mother. It looks as though we thought her guilty of something."

"No one's hiding her away, son. She's not here."

"Where is she?"

"She hasn't come back from Jane's yet."

"Then I'll go for her. It's too late for her to come home alone."

"You have company, Richard. Your place is here. Jane won't send the child home alone. They'll probably keep her all night."

The company stayed late. There was much talk. Because there was not a person present who hadn't some anecdote or theory to add to the rapidly growing legend of the brick throwing.

Dr. Caxton said, "If I hadn't seen it with my own eyes I wouldn't have believed an entire community could so hypnotize itself as to credit what did not exist. Half the people who were here today will tell their grandchildren, years hence, about seeing bricks from nowhere crash through the Tomlinsons' window."

Miss Ann glanced uneasily at her daughter-in-law. Judith had appeared at the supper table, looking much as usual and apparently in better spirits than she had been all day. Ann Tomlinson hoped this talk would not disturb her.

"Otis Huse was out there this afternoon," she said, to change the subject. "I expected him to come up to the house for supper. But he drove away."

This turned the talk on Huse and his long-standing grudge against Richard. It was agreed that Huse would stop at nothing to embarrass the man of whom he had always been jealous. But here, even the lawyer's disparagers stopped and went no farther. No one who had mingled with the excited mob that afternoon could accuse Otis Huse of having assembled it.

The strangest experience of the day was reported by John Barclay and Doc Baird.

"Doc and I went close to the house once," said the schoolmaster. "Doc stood in front of the window. I stood not far from the door. We determined to stand there until somebody fancied he heard another brick coming."

Richard grinned. He seemed determined to treat the whole thing lightly. "Weren't you afraid you might be struck?"

The blacksmith said gravely, "I wish I had been."

"Why?"

"That would have proved that bricks were being thrown," said Doc, and glanced significantly at Judith.

An uncomfortable silence fell upon the group.

"Well," said Richard after a pause, "I suppose when no brick came——"

A voice said coldly, "A brick did come." It was the first time Judith had spoken. She looked straight at the schoolmaster. "Tell them, Mr. Barclay."

Barclay, visibly embarrassed, took up the tale. "Somebody in the crowd called out that he heard a brick coming. Someone else cried that he heard it fall. A few minutes later we heard a muffled scream within the house. Doc and I rushed inside and found Miss Judith. She was staring at—a spot on the floor."

Judith said in the same cold voice, "Of course either of you could have removed the brick."

"We could have," said John Barclay, "but we didn't."

"Because," said Doc, "there was no brick to remove."

Judith's hands gripped the arms of her chair to still their trembling. "You accuse me of lying?"

"We know you're not lying," said the blacksmith solemnly. "You saw something on the floor that frightened you speechless. We saw nothing at all. That's why I said I wished I had been struck by a brick."

Richard said matter-of-factly, "What Judith saw on the floor was a spot of sunshine," and put an end to ghostly speculation.

But the pallor of Judith's face caused Dr. Caxton to look at her sharply. She laughed to show how little the talk affected her. But there was a shrillness in her laughter that the doctor did not like. He lingered a moment when the other men had departed.

"You don't look so good tonight, Miss Judith. Maybe I'd better leave you a dose of calomel. Spring of the year makes people bilious."

"If you leave me anything, Doctor, let it be some more of that sedative."

"Still having trouble sleeping?"

"Now and then."

"Well, go light on this." He handed her a bottle from the black bag without which he never traveled. "You can't take this like you took that other stuff. Enough of this will put you to sleep permanently."

Judith smiled. "You can trust me to use it in the right proportions."

When the doctor had gone Judith said to her husband, "Your friends tried their best to make me believe I've been seeing supernatural manifestations. It's what might be expected from that ignorant blacksmith. But I'm surprised at a man of John Barclay's intelligence."

Richard's reply was smothered in a yawn. He had decided in his own mind that Judith was malingering and he was no longer concerned with what she saw or claimed to see. He was troubled and uneasy because Thorne had stayed at Jane's. He was afraid something had been said to hurt her feelings, but he did not like to start another argument with his wife. So he banked the fire and mumbled good night and waited for Judith to go upstairs so that he could go to bed in the alcove. The rest of the family had retired.

But Judith had something on her mind. She was burning to know if he had missed Thorne.

"By the way," she said casually, "where was Thorne this evening?"

"She's spending the night at Jane's."

"Oh. I see." She stood turning the bottle of sedative in her hands.

"Don't take too much of that stuff, Judith."

"Why?"

"I heard what Dr. Caxton told you."

"Would you care, Richard, if I took too much?"

He looked at her sharply; alarmed, at first, then exasperated.

"I think you'd better give it to me."

He reached for the bottle. She surrendered it obediently, like a child. She was in a queer mood tonight.

He said, "I'll bring this up to you if you need it. But try to sleep without it tonight." He yawned elaborately. "Better get to bed now. We're both tired and sleepy."

But she still lingered. "Richard——"

"Yes?"

"Surely you're not sleeping down here tonight."

"Why not? I'm not afraid of your bricks."

"I don't mean that."

She came close to him; her perfumed hands touched his face.

"Darling, haven't you sulked long enough? Come back upstairs to our room and stop behaving like a bad little boy."

The exquisite scent which had once stirred his senses no

longer moved him. There was nothing left of their relationship except a strange feeling of guilt. Why this should be, when she was his wife, he did not try to understand. But he knew now that always there had been between them the dark thrill of something illicit.

"I'll sleep down here, Judith."

The gentleness of his tone misled her.

"I'll stay with you then," she whispered.

"No." He spoke with harsh finality, so that she drew away from him. "There is too much that is wrong between us, Judith."

"You mean——" she began, then stopped. She would not bring Thorne's name into this. All that was gone now.

"I don't quite know what I mean, Judith. There's something dark and shameful between us that I don't understand. Sometimes I think it's because we married too soon after Abigail died. And again I think it came from that terrible feeling of relief I had when she was gone. But—whatever the cause—I've always had a feeling of guilt with you."

"That's your Puritan conscience convicting you of sin for finding pleasure in love."

"No, you're wrong. I don't hold love a sin, except when sinners indulge in it."

"And you call us sinners, with our double-ring marriage ceremony?"

"I don't mean that——" He made a futile gesture. It was something he could not explain.

"I have to think things out, Judith. If you don't mind, I'll say good night."

She took her candle and went up the stairs alone.

It was past midnight when Richard awoke from a sound sleep. For a moment he thought he was still dreaming, for he seemed to be in a theater watching Charlotte Cushman come down the stairs in the sleepwalking scene from *Macbeth*.

293 &

She wore a trailing robe and held a candle high above her head, and her hair fell in long braids on either side of her breasts. She looked pale and distraught, and in his half-slumbering state Richard acknowledged that she was a marvelous actress. She did not *look* haunted. She *was* haunted.

Then he started into complete wakefulness and realized that he was looking through his own open door and that the woman with the taper, descending the stairs, was Judith.

He sat up and reached for a night robe, but he did not go to her. If she were walking in her sleep it was dangerous to waken her. He waited till she reached the foot of the stairs and started down the hall. Then he followed her.

She went straight to the south bedroom. Carefully she set her candle on the table. Then she opened the closet door and dropped to her knees. He saw her thrust her hand into the hole under the floor. When she drew it forth, full of nothing but cobwebs, her eyes were wide with terror. But they were alert and conscious. She was not asleep.

"If you're looking for the doll, Judith, it's not there."

She turned in the direction of his voice, and he saw that she was utterly undone.

"Otis Huse found the doll the night he slept here."

She rose to her feet, swaying dizzily, and began brushing the dust from her hands. She offered no explanation for what she had been doing.

Richard went on: "Huse guessed that the doll had been used to kill Abigail. I had to tell him that it was I who hid it here—in order to protect Thorne."

She seemed not to be listening. She seemed only intent on getting the cobwebs off her hands.

"But now I know that it was you, Judith, who hid the doll. You tied the string round its neck and put it on Abigail's bed, hoping it would frighten her to death. You planned it, step by step, how she might die from fear. And you seized on a child's harmless toy to feed her superstitious terror. When you read her those books about witchcraft you had the doll even then and knew how you were going to use it. Didn't you, Judith?" His low, relentless voice was like a prodding hand, pushing her to the very brink.

"And when you had frightened her into a heart attack you hid the doll where you thought no one would ever find it. Because there was no one to see you, except the woman who was dying. You forgot about her, didn't you?"

She left off brushing her hands and began plucking at her throat.

"Maybe you have seen phantom bricks, Judith, and heard phantom clocks. Maybe that is why you were looking for the doll tonight. Because you suddenly recalled that only Abigail knew where you had put it."

She no longer heard him. She had crumpled in a senseless heap. He lifted her in his arms and carried her up to her room.

It was noon the next day before it was discovered that Thorne was not at Mitchell's. Alec came over to see how Judith was, and when Miss Ann inquired about Thorne he said that she had not been at their house since the day before.

The dinner bell had already rung, and the Tomlinson men could be seen approaching the house. Miss Ann said, "Don't say anything about this to Richard. Not till we've located Thorne."

But at first sight of his brother-in-law Richard demanded, "How much longer are you and Jane going to keep Thorne?" Then, catching a glance between his mother and Alec, "She *is* at your house, isn't she?"

"Why—no, Richard. She's not."

"Didn't she stay there last night?"

"No."

"And you waited till noon today to tell us?"

"Well, great Scott! I didn't know she was lost."

The word was like an alarm bell. Richard's face drained of color.

Miss Ann said quickly, "She's not lost."

"Mother! You told me——"

"Now keep cool, Richard. I took for granted when she didn't come home that she was spending the night with Jane. But I suppose she stayed with Nancy Turner instead. Will, get your horse and ride over to your sister Kate's and bring Thorne home." Ann spoke with as much certainty as though Thorne's presence at Turner's was an established fact.

"I'll go myself," said Richard, and before his younger brother could marshal his slower faculties he was out of the house and on his way to the barn. A few minutes later he could be seen galloping across the open field. The Turner farm was less than a mile as the crow flies. It was three miles by the road.

Judith stood by the window and watched her husband ride away. Young Will, looking unusually glum, sat down and began eating his dinner. Perhaps he resented his brother's usurpation of his own rights of primary concern for Thorne's safety. No one—not even their mother—had given a thought to Will's feelings. They had taken for granted that Richard was the one on whom the blow had fallen.

"Sit down, Alec, and eat with us," said Miss Ann. "Come, Judith. No use waiting for Richard. He won't be back till he finds Thorne."

Alarm leaped to Judith's eyes, as though this were a turn she had not foreseen. Miss Ann, misinterpreting, added quickly, "She's around the neighborhood somewhere."

The meal was eaten in almost unbroken silence. A rare occurrence at the Tomlinson board. A strange foreboding stilled the usually lively tongues. Even the children were quiet. Everyone seemed waiting for Richard's return.

He rode up on a sweating horse just as they rose from the table. One look at his face and they guessed his news.

"Wasn't she there?" asked Will quickly.

"Hasn't been there," said Richard. "Hasn't been seen by any of the Turners."

Dark color rose in Will's cheeks, as though something in his brother's look angered him.

He said shortly, "I'll go over to Cousin Lutie's."

Jesse Moffat volunteered to go over to Henry Schook's.

Alec Mitchell said, "The thing for us to do is to take different directions. There are four of us. And at each house we come to there'll be others to join us. We can comb the whole district before dark."

For the first time the gravity of the situation was put into words. Thorne might not be at anyone's house. She might be lying behind some hedgerow, or in some dark thicket of the woods. There had been a motley crowd at Timberley the day before. It had been afternoon when the young girl had set out to walk home alone from Jane's.

Alec's plan was put into action. Richard rode off again, not waiting for food, taking the dirt road to the south. As soon as horses could be saddled the other three men rode north and east and west, following by-lanes and fence rows as well as beaten paths, missing not a house. And at each house there was someone ready to join the search. By nightfall Timberley district had been combed as with a fine-toothed comb.

But no trace of Thorne was found.

No one could even remember seeing her after she left Jane's house, though nearly every person in the countryside had been to Tomlinson's the day before.

"No, sir, never saw Thorne while I was there," was the report on all sides. Frequently followed by, "I remarked about it. 'Cause there had been talk a while back that all the funny stuff Miss Judith had been seein' was nothin' but Thorne's magic tricks. But I says to myself, 'I reckon this clears the girl of witch doin's. Richard's wife is seein' things *this* time and Thorne ain't even here.' "

No, Thorne had not been seen by anyone the day before.

Only when it became too dark to see did the men return to the house. And then there were only three.

Miss Ann asked sharply, "Where's Richard?"

The men replied that they had not seen him. He would be in soon, no doubt.

But Richard did not come.

Ann Tomlinson, no longer gallantly pretending, prayed silently:

"O God, bring him home. O dear God, don't let him be hurt too much." And she remembered a time long ago when his dog had been lost and he had stayed out half the night—a little seven-year-old lad—searching the dark woods for his pet, until she and his father had had to search for him.

To his mother he was still that little boy searching for something he had lost.

Will Tomlinson, eating his supper, listening for his brother's step, wondered jealously why Richard should search later than *he*. And the anger he had felt at noon rose again within him. Then, remembering the look he had seen in his brother's eyes, he knew that he would never be able to grieve for Thorne as Richard would grieve. It would have been a terrible mistake for him to have married her when Richard loved her so. It was better, perhaps, that this thing had happened.

Judith's thoughts, too, were on that lonely rider searching the woods. How long would he look for the girl before relinquishing hope? And afterward—what then? Would he turn to his wife for consolation? Last night's discovery she could easily turn to her own account, as proof of her overwhelming desire for him. But would Thorne, absent, prove an even sharper barrier than Thorne, present, had been?

Supper was put by. Chores were done. Bedtime came, but no one went upstairs. At eleven o'clock Ann Tomlinson said to her younger son, "I think you should go look for your brother."

Will promptly rose, as though the thought were already in his mind.

Jesse Moffat said, "I'd better go with you."

Fresh fear struck Judith, sharper than any she had known. "Why should you look for Richard? Isn't he old enough to come home by himself?"

Will said, "There's no telling what he might do—if he found what he feared to find."

A scream rose in Judith's throat, but her clutching hand held it back. The thought of Richard . . .

"It is you who should jump in the millpond." She laughed to cover the scream. "Thorne is your loss, not Richard's."

"Thorne belongs to Richard," said young Will. And no one contradicted him.

They did not search for Richard after all. Before the men got started he came in, looking so tired and spent and utterly hopeless that those who sprang up eagerly at his step stopped in consternation at sight of his face.

"Richard! Where have you been?" cried his mother.

It was as they had feared. He had been dragging the millpond. He and Ralph Tatum had worked by the light of lanterns when it got too dark to see. They had found nothing.

But he had come home. The thing they dreaded had not happened.

He sat in his chair, his head between his hands, refusing the food his mother set before him. He did not seem to hear when the other men tried to paint as hopeful a picture as possible.

"No news is good news, Richard. Thorne has come to no harm or we should have found her. Remember, there were people here yesterday from as far away as Bridgeton. She must have gone home with someone."

The words held false comfort. Thorne never went anywhere without permission.

When Alec had gone home Will said, "There's nothing more we can do tonight. I'm going to bed." He took his candle and started for the stairs.

Richard's voice halted him.

"Don't you care?"

Will stopped with his foot on the step. "You mean about finding Thorne?"

"What else matters?"

"Why—a number of things," said Will. "The plowing of the south field matters. There's corn to be planted. If we don't get to bed pretty soon we won't want to get up in the morning." He went on up the stairs.

Judith had said nothing. She had sat in silence, watching her husband sunk in grief—and something worse than grief —the torture of the unknown. She wondered how far she dared go in putting an end to his uncertainty. He could not go on like this. He would be ill.

So when the others had retired she said to him, "Has it occurred to you that Thorne might have gone away of her own volition?"

"You mean run off? Never!"

"Not run off. Just decide to leave. She's often talked of it."

"She'd never go without letting me know. She promised."

"Not if she were suddenly offered a chance?"

Richard looked at his wife suspiciously. "What do you know?"

"Nothing," said Judith smoothly, "except what everyone knows: that Thorne left Jane's house yesterday and started for home. And what was going on here? An excited mob was milling about the house. I daresay there was plenty of talk circulating about Thorne. Suppose—this is just conjecture—someone on the outskirts of the crowd offered her a chance to escape from what was becoming an intolerable situation?"

"And who," said Richard skeptically, "could have offered such a chance?"

"Did you notice a covered wagon in the grove yesterday?"

For a moment every pulse in his body seemed to stop. He recalled the wagon which had passed him at dusk in the lane. Could Thorne have been beneath that canvas top—and his heart not have told him?

He said, "She would never go off with a Pennsylvania farmer."

"He wasn't a farmer," said Judith. "He was a traveling show-man."

"How do you know?"

"He came up to the house for water. I talked to him."

"Why? You're not usually so interested in vagrants."

The sarcasm was ignored.

"When Thorne came from Jane's," said Judith, "she must have passed this wagon."

"Not if she came across the fields."

"She didn't come across the fields. She came by the turn-pike and through the grove."

"How do you know?"

Judith's hand went to her throat. She had talked too much.

"You seem to be pretty well informed about Thorne's movements," said Richard. "Why haven't you told this be-fore?"

"Because it's only a suspicion. I don't know anything."

"You know she came through the grove, don't you?"

"Yes. I know that much. But that's all."

"I don't believe you, Judith. If you'd withhold that knowl-edge, when everyone else was searching, you'd withhold more. What else do you know?"

"Nothing. I saw Thorne from my window yesterday when she came home. She came through the grove—to avoid the crowd, I suppose—and ran into the house. I called to her. She said she was getting something to eat. A little later she ran out again and I saw her racing toward that wagon. That's the last time I saw her. And that's the truth, Richard. I swear it."

He looked at her with implacable coldness.

"Why have you waited twenty-four hours to tell this?"

"I never thought of it at first. Then it seemed such a bare possibility that I kept still rather than delay your search. After all, the most important thing was to make sure she had not suffered foul play in the woods. But now that you have failed to find any trace of her, I really believe she left of her own accord with those people in the wagon. They were her kind of people, Richard. That banner—CALIFORNIA OR BUST—would have caught her eye." Judith smiled as though the whole thing were working out in the happiest possible manner.

"I've always felt, Richard, that if Thorne were left to her own devices she would do the right thing. And of course the right thing was for her to go back to her own environment. So instead of wearing ourselves out with searching for the child, let's say our prayers tonight with special gratitude for the way God has worked things out for the good of all concerned."

Richard rose to his feet, and the impact of his words seemed the greater coming from that tall, stern height.

"Don't blame God, Judith, for your own conniving."

"You mean you don't believe me?"

"I believe what you've told is true. Only you haven't told it all. What happened between the time you called to Thorne and she left the house? What did you say to her, Judith? Don't answer! It would only be to lie. After what I learned about you last night, I know that you would stop at nothing to gain your purpose. You said something to Thorne that made her feel it was necessary for her to leave Timberley. Didn't you, Judith?"

Her face was white with the knowledge of defeat. She had lost everything now. She had nothing more to lose—or so she thought.

"And what if I did? Was I to stand silently by and see my home wrecked without lifting a finger?"

"Thank you for telling me, Judith." He almost smiled.

"Telling you what?"

"All I wanted to know. Now that I know *why* Thorne left, I believe the rest of your story is true. Those people were headed West, weren't they? And they pulled out yesterday evening. They're only a day's journey from here. A good fast horse could overtake them by tomorrow night."

"You mean you'd follow them?"

Fool, fool that she'd been to have spoken so soon! She should have waited a week at least.

"It will do you no good, Richard. It will only make you a laughingstock. After what I said to Thorne she'll never come back."

"In that case there'll be one more traveler bound for California."

"You're mad!"

"I was never so sane in my life."

"You'd leave your wife—your mother—your children—for that——"

"Don't say it, Judith! I warn you."

"Can you imagine what people will say?"

"It doesn't concern me."

"You're crazy—drunk!—you don't know what you're doing."

"For the first time in my life I *do* know what I'm doing." There was a glow in his face, a profound assurance that none who knew him had ever seen before in the eyes of Richard Tomlinson.

"God will punish you, Richard!"

"Do you know, Judith—this is a strange thing to say under the circumstances—but I feel right with God for the first time since I married you."

There was a spring in his step as he went up the stairs.

CHAPTER 27

Judith thought, "He must be stopped. Else he'll leave tonight."

She ran swiftly up the back stairs and burst into Miss Ann's room without knocking.

"Come quick! Richard's planning to follow Thorne to California."

Ann Tomlinson was reading her Bible. There had been no family prayers this night. She closed the book and laid it aside.

"Where is Richard?"

"In Will's room, I think."

Miss Ann went down the hall and tapped at a door that muffled a sound of voices. The voices ceased.

"Who is it?" called Will.

"Your mother."

The door opened to admit Miss Ann. Judith remained outside.

There was a rise and fall of voices for minutes—hours, it seemed—before Ann Tomlinson came out. Judith could not hide the trembling of her lips as she put the question: "Well?"

"I'm afraid there's nothing we can do, Judith. He seems to have made up his mind."

"You mean—you're just going to stand by and let him go?"

"He is a grown man. He has a right to make his own decisions."

This quiet acceptance of so cataclysmic an event was incredible. That the Tomlinsons, with their strict code, should not move heaven and earth to prevent it was beyond belief.

Yet when Judith spoke to Will she met the same strange neutrality.

"It's Richard's business. Not mine."

"The girl might be considered your business," retorted Judith.

"Thorne never bound herself to me," was Will's reply.

"Well, Richard bound himself to me, and I don't intend to let him make a fool of himself."

Richard, meantime, was making hurried preparations for departure. He put together a few personal necessities—no more than would go in his saddlebags—and filled a money belt with all the currency the house yielded. Brother and mother not only watched but actually aided in these preparations. The only deterring word spoken was Will's suggestion that Richard wait till morning to give the horses a rest. They had been run pretty hard that day.

But Richard would not brook even this delay. He would ride his own horse as far as Turner's and get a fresh mount there. His brother-in-law was always good for a horse trade.

When Judith appealed again to Richard's mother Miss Ann said, "If he's going, the sooner he starts, the better. He'll lose the trail if that wagon gets too far ahead."

"Then you're going to let him go and do nothing about it?"

Tears filled Ann Tomlinson's eyes. There was nothing she could say.

"So! The Tomlinson religion is only skin-deep after all," sneered Judith. "The household saint, the devout Methodist, who believes the Bible from cover to cover, can stand by and see her son desert his wife without lifting a finger to stop him."

"What can I do?"

"You could at least talk to him."

The small gray-haired mother shook her head. "The time for me to have talked to him, Judith, was before he married you."

But if Richard's mother and brother accepted the inevitable, his wife did not. Judith caught her husband as he was starting

305 ॐ

out to the barn to saddle his horse. She drew him into the kitchen and closed the door.

"I've something to say to you, Richard, before you go."

"Nothing you can say will alter my intention."

"You may change your mind when you have heard me."

He waited with restive patience for whatever new threat or entreaty her desperation had evolved.

"If you go to that girl, I swear, as God is my witness, that I'll charge you with the murder of your first wife."

He stood for seconds, speechless. Then he laughed mirthlessly.

"You're forgetting what I saw last night, aren't you, Judith?"

"You saw me hunting on the floor of a closet for a pair of old bedroom slippers. I told you nothing. I admitted nothing. But you talked at great length about a doll which you claimed was put on Abigail's bed for the purpose of frightening her to death. How did you know about the doll, Richard, if you didn't put it on the pillow yourself? You were the last person with Abigail before the doctor came. It was you who reported her ravings about a string tied round a doll's neck. You admitted last night that you told Otis Huse it was you who hid the doll under the closet floor, where he and Lucius Goff found it. I think it would be easy to convince Mr. Huse that you also put the doll on your wife's bed with murderous intent. And Otis Huse is a clever lawyer."

He looked at her in silence so long that her hand began moving toward her throat, where the nervous pain was gathering.

He said softly, "Your name should have been Jezebel." Then he drew a deep breath of release.

"Do your worst, Judith. Go to anyone you please. What you do can't hurt me now."

"Richard! I didn't mean it. I was only trying to frighten you. I love you, Richard. Everything I've done has been for love of you. Don't leave me, Richard—come back—come back——"

Her cry fell upon empty air. He was gone.

She lifted her eyes to the kitchen shelf above her head. A neat row of canisters held a motley assortment of condiments and household remedies. She reached for one plainly marked with skull and crossbones.

She had not yet played her final card.

Richard was saddling his horse by the light of a lantern when Jesse Moffat came running out to the barn in his night clothes.

"Come quick! Judith's dying."

Richard said, "Oh no, she's not. She's staging another scene."

"Not this time. She's took bad. Miss Ann's sent young Will for the doctor. She says you're not to go till we see what's happened."

"What do you mean?"

"She thinks Judith's taken something."

As they hurried to the house they passed Will on his way to the barn.

"What's happened?" cried Richard.

Will shouted, "Judith's taken poison," and went on running toward the barn. A moment later he dashed out of the yard on Richard's saddled horse.

Still Richard did not believe it. This was another ruse of Judith's to keep him from leaving.

But when he found her laid on the bed in the alcove, moaning and writhing in pain, he was not so sure. Her face was contorted, wet with sweat, and she seemed to be in agony.

"Tell me just what happened," he said to his mother.

"I found her like this. Lying on the bed here, groaning. And I found this on the floor beside her." Miss Ann handed him a water tumbler. There was a small amount of cloudy liquid in the bottom and white powder adhered to the moist rim.

"Is there anything in the house that she could have taken?"

"There's cockroach powder on the shelf in the kitchen."

He and Judith had been talking in the kitchen. The glass and powder had been close at hand.

"If she took something in the kitchen—by mistake, of course —why should she bring the glass in here?"

"If she did not take it by mistake," said Miss Ann significantly, "she might have wanted to be near the bed when she drank it."

Still Richard refused to believe that Judith would go so far as to commit suicide. He sat down beside her and felt her pulse. There was acceleration, but nervous excitement could have caused that. He wiped her face with his own handkerchief. The handkerchief was wet.

He was sitting by her when the doctor came. Old Dr. Caxton, roused from sleep and none too alert, made a hasty examination of the contents of the water tumbler.

"Roach powder. Full of arsenic. A good strong emetic as fast as we can get it into her."

They worked with Judith for over an hour. When the emetic had done its utmost she lay weak and exhausted but no longer writhing. She was actually too sick now to move.

"Go to bed, Miss Ann. You too, Will. Richard and I will sit with her the rest of the night."

Dr. Caxton issued orders, took off his coat, and prepared to make himself comfortable by the living-room fire. There was nothing for Richard to do but follow his example. He could not explain to the family physician that he was on the point of leaving his wife, when that wife lay possibly dying. For the doctor made it quite clear that the solution in the glass was strong enough to kill ten women.

"I can't figure out how she happened to take the stuff," he said over and over.

"She thought she was taking salts," Richard said in sudden inspiration.

"Humph! That's what comes of keeping physics in a kitchen cupboard. It's a wonder to me . . ."

The doctor's voice droned on and on in comfortable monotony. Judith, lying behind the curtains of the alcove, smiled to herself. She was sick enough now—the emetic had been pure torture—but it was small price to pay for what she had accomplished. Vomiting never killed anyone, and it had convinced Richard that she was not malingering. It would be days, according to the doctor, before she could be pronounced out of danger. And Richard would not have the face to leave while Dr. Caxton was in attendance. When that time of grace had expired she would think of something else.

Meanwhile, a covered wagon, moving steadily westward, would soon be beyond hope of tracing.

Nothing could defeat her. She was too smart. It had been sheer genius to sprinkle that roach powder into a wet water tumbler and set it by her bed.

She fell asleep, well pleased with herself. She would outwit them all yet. She would keep Richard from Thorne, just as she had taken him from Abigail: by the use of her remarkable intelligence.

She awoke suddenly with a pain in her throat. She had no idea how late it was, but she felt as though she had slept a long while. It was the pain which had wakened her: the same old pain which Dr. Caxton had assured her was nothing but a nervous paroxysm of the larynx. She had half a mind to call to the doctor, whose voice beyond the alcove, mingled with Richard's, indicated that the two were still awake and talking.

But as she listened to the indistinct murmur she grew drowsy again and the pain began to subside. She drifted into a delicious state of semiconsciousness that was neither sleeping nor waking, but rather a dreamlike contemplation of all the delights that would be hers now that her path was cleared.

Like an overtone to this ecstasy was the rise and fall of Richard's voice beyond the bed curtains.

Then gradually this sweet delirium merged into a deep uneasiness. She could not have told when the change began; she had no prescience of its coming until suddenly it was there: that old horror which she had had so long and lost for a time, the consciousness of *Something* beside her. It was only an awareness, at first, of an inimical presence. But strive as she would, she could not shake off the thought or the image of her fear. She recognized it at last for what it was: *Abigail.*

She had always known that someday she must have it out with Abigail. But for her to come now, when victory was within sight. To creep into her very bed and lie like this beside her, pretending that they two were sisters in defeat; that they had striven for the same prize and lost to the same opponent; that henceforth they must sleep forever side by side, the wives whom Richard Tomlinson had not loved. It was monstrous! Had the woman no sense, no shame, no delicacy, to be commiserating thus with a triumphant rival? Could she not see that Judith had won; that she had secured for herself everything which had escaped her predecessor? Then why must she pretend this loathsome sympathy and twine her emaciated arms round Judith's neck in suffocating compassion—closer, closer, tighter the embrace—until——

God in heaven! It was no embrace—it was murder; the thin clutch about her throat was not a skinny arm—it was a band of velvet—twisting, tighter, tighter, tighter——

"Richard!" she shrieked, and knew to her horror that she made no sound.

But the voices still came from beyond the curtains. She rose on her pillow to listen. She was not alone. They would not let her die like this. She would be able to scream when she had torn this band from her throat. Richard would come in a moment and waken her from this nightmare. . . .

And then she fell back on the pillows again as—incredible!

—the band about her throat tightened, squeezing out her last breath.

In the chill dark hour before dawn the doctor roused from fitful slumber in his chair and went to his patient's bedside to see how she was resting. He found, to his shocked amazement, that she was dead. Death was due, apparently, to strangulation. The collar of her nightgown was ripped apart. Her throat was scratched as though nails had clawed it. Her face was the face of a sleeper in the grip of a terrible dream. But she was cold and still and lifeless.

He summoned Richard and Ann Tomlinson, but there was nothing to be done.

"I can't understand it." He repeated the words, bewilderedly, over and over. "We sat here all night long. We never heard a sound. I supposed she was sleeping, so I never disturbed her——"

Miss Ann said, "Were you awake all night?"

Both men admitted to dozing off shortly before daylight. They had talked for most of the night, Richard explained. They had talked to keep from going to sleep. If Judith had called or made the slightest sound, he was sure they would have heard her.

The troubled old doctor said, "It must have been that the throat ailment she complained of was more serious than I realized—though damned if I could find anything organic. Maybe I'm getting too old to practice medicine. . . ."

What Richard's thoughts were, none present could have guessed. But a silent pressure of his hand exonerated his old friend from all blame.

They buried Judith one week from the day the big crowd gathered at Timberley. She was laid to rest beside Abigail, in the family burial ground between the poplars. People talked of it discreetly as they turned their faces homeward from attending the funeral. For the second time in two years Richard Tomlinson had stood by the newly made grave of a wife.

"Poor man! He's had enough to break him. No wonder he's leaving Timberley."

"Is he really going to California?"

"Starts tomorrow morning, I understand."

"Well, he always was a restless fellow. Never settled like his brother Will. Can't blame him, though, for wanting to get away. Hard on a man, burying two wives so close together."

FINALE

As the first pale promise of sunrise touched the waters of Little Raccoon, Richard rode his black horse down the lane and out through the grove to the turnpike. When he reached the rise of land he paused and looked back at the house where he was born. He could not see the faces of those whom he was leaving, but he knew that his mother's hair would be grayer, his children taller, ere he saw them again. He lifted his hat and waved—and said a prayer.

Then he turned his horse's head due west. Before him stretched a good rock road. Beyond that, miles of wilderness. And far ahead, by eight days' journey, a covered wagon. He did not know the route it had taken. He did not know the name of its occupants. He only knew that somewhere, some-day, he would find Thorne, though he had nothing to follow except a ludicrous banner and a foolish song, slightly revised:

> "O! Susanna, oh, don't you cry for me,
> I'm goin' to California, my true love for to see. . . ."